Praise for *Painter of the Damned*

"In this soulful sequel, hop into a Venetian gondola for the ride of your past life. Death stalks the shadows of every arched footbridge. Expect only the unexpected."

—**Avanti Centrae, eight-time award-winning author of the international bestselling VanOps thriller series**

"Samborn's *Painter of the Damned* manages that rare feat: weaving strands of the other world, history, art, and an ancient, secret order into an entrancing tale you just cannot put down. Fans of Dan Brown and Umberto Eco would love this lyrical, cinematic, yet fast-paced thriller that captures present-day and Renaissance Venice with equal ease. Having followed this wonderful cast of characters steeped in longing and desperation, I find myself wanting to visit Venice once again. An absolutely worthy follow-up to *The Prisoner of Paradise*."

—**Damyanti Biswas, author of *The Blue Bar* and *You Beneath Your Skin***

"The edge of your seat action continues for Nick and Julia O'Connor as they fight to expose a secret sect that imprisons souls in Tintoretto's masterpiece *Paradise*. Caught between the present and the past, Nick fights the shadowy figures of the Venetian underworld to release his long lost love. Full of detail and the idiosyncrasies of medieval Venice, Samborn's skill with prose and the fantastical world his characters inhabits shines in this thrilling sequel."

—**Laura Kemp, award-winning author of the Lantern Creek Series**

"Cleverly using time itself as a central theme, *Painter of the Damned* is an uncommonly intelligent, shrewd and deftly paced thriller, crafted with such lush language and provocative narrative that it kept me turning pages throughout the long nights."

—**Gary McAvoy, Bestselling author of The Magdalene Chronicles**

"Medieval and modern Venice collide in ways you simply wouldn't expect. I'll never view a Tintoretto in quite the same way again!"

—**KM Kelly, author of *The Sleepers***

"Deftly interweaving art history and fantasy into story that bridges time, Rob Samborn takes the reader into a Venice filled with mysteries from both the past and the present. With its complex plot, vivid characters, and adventuresome twists, *Painter of the Damned* is a page turner from start to finish."

—**Carolyn Korsmeyer, author of *Charlotte's Story* and *Little Follies***

"An incredibly imaginative, page-turning tale bursting with twists and turns like the alleys and canals of its setting of Venice, *Painter of the Damned* keeps you on your toes and shows how love never dies."
—**C. D'Angelo, author of** *The Difference* **and** *The Visitor*

"Picks up the pace from *The Prisoner of Paradise* and accelerates into a dynamic story that bridges time and geography, with a plot that never stops twisting. Samborn's narrative shifts seamlessly between past and present, with a cast of realistic characters that either attract or repel as in real life. Nick and Julia are the perfect duo for this sweeping drama that has the reader turning the last page to look for more."
—**Mike Krentz, author of** *Dead Already* **and** *Angels Falling*

"Rob Samborn has done it again! With cinematic action and exquisite writing, *Painter of the Damned* is a sweeping sequel that exceeded all my expectations. Combining classical art, rich Venetian history, compelling characters, and a centuries-old conspiracy, Samborn weaves an intelligent, intricate story with nonstop momentum that will leave you breathless. Engrossing, mysterious, romantic, and altogether original, *Painter of the Damned* is a literary triumph that cleared the extremely high bar set by its predecessor. I can't wait to see what tricks Samborn has up his sleeve for the next installment of the Painted Souls Series."
—**Shanessa Gluhm, author of** *Enemies of Doves* **and** *A River of Crows*

**Select praise for *The Prisoner of Paradise*,
book 1 in the Painted Souls series**

". . . vivid narrative, world-building and edgy suspense is brilliantly showcased in this immersive, time-traveling thriller infused with Gothic horror, supernatural danger and twisty suspense."
—**Jayne Ann Krentz,** *New York Times* **best-selling author**

". . . this book is brilliant! The plot is fantastic . . . unlike anything I've previously read. A fast-paced story, full of action, intrigue, religion, art and a secret order, you name it, this book has it!"
—**Amy McElroy, Book Blogger**

"The city of Venice soaks into your bones in Rob Samborn's *The Prisoner of Paradise*. As the painting comes alive, so does every word from the page in this gripping and transportive read."
—**EJ Mellow, bestselling author of** *Song of the Forever Rains*

"Wow! I picked this book because of the reviews, but even they didn't prepare me for the grandeur of the novel. . . . an epic well worth reading."
—**NetGalley Review**

"Riveting. Period. *The Prisoner of Paradise* is absolutely fantastic. A masterpiece."
—**Goodreads Review**

"A truly evocative and finely-woven tale reminiscent of Dan Brown and Gwendolyn Womack. Rob Samborn's *The Prisoner of Paradise* slips effortlessly between present day and 16th century Venice with intriguing characters, clever plotting, and deft pacing that makes this book difficult to put down. Filled with stunning writing, the Venetian art world, and well-researched and vivid historical detail, this thrilling story captivates until the very last page."
—**Charissa Weaks, author of *The Witch Collector***

"Combining romance, historical, metaphysical, and conspiracy elements into a thriller that supersedes several of today's best-selling authors is no easy task. However, Samborn's writing style indicates a writer whose skill shines through its smooth flow, akin to that of the great names in thriller fiction from Poe to Ludlum, Koontz, Child and, yes, Dan Brown."
—**Reader's Favorite Review**

"*The Da Vinci Code* meets *The Time Traveler's Wife*. In this imaginative thrill ride, Samborn transports the reader between modern day and Renaissance Venice unraveling conspiracy in the pursuit of destiny. I was dazzled from beginning to end. This ambitious debut does not disappoint."
—**Robert Gwaltney, author of *The Cicada Tree***

PAINTER
OF THE
DAMNED

PAINTED SOULS
BOOK II

ROB SAMBORN

Relax. Read. Repeat.

PAINTER OF THE DAMNED (Painted Souls, Book 2)
By Rob Samborn
Published by TouchPoint Press
Brookland, AR 72417
www.touchpointpress.com

Copyright © 2022 Rob Samborn
All rights reserved.

Softcover ISBN: 978-1-956851-29-8

This book is a work of fiction. References to real people, events, establishments, organizations, brands, or locales are intended only to provide a sense of authenticity and are used fictitiously. All other characters, and all incidents and dialogue, are drawn from the author's imagination and are not to be construed as real.

Except for review purposes, the reproduction of this book, in whole or part, electronically or mechanically, constitutes a copyright violation. Address permissions and review inquiries to media@touchpointpress.com.

Editor: Kimberly Coghlan
Cover Design: David Ter-Avanesyan @ter33design
Cover Image: Marti Bug Catcher (Shutterstock)

Connect with the author online at www.robsamborn.com

First Edition

Printed in the United States of America.

Books by Rob Samborn

The Prisoner of Paradise
The Swordsman of Venice

CONTENT WARNING

PAINTER OF THE DAMNED is a work of fiction about realistic characters in realistic settings. The content is written to evoke maximum visceral emotion within an entertaining and informative context. The story includes elements that might not be suitable for some readers, including graphic violence, adult language, sexual situations, abortion, and graphic medical descriptions. Readers who are sensitive to these elements should please take note.

For Tiffani and Sienna. No matter the distance,
be it spatial or temporal, I would find you.

*Of time
I have wondered.
When the sands fall
without a sound,
how do the blind know
when time is done?*

—Isabella Scalfini, one week before her trial, 1589

I paint because the spirits whisper madly inside my head.

—El Greco, c. 1595

To allow evil to walk the Earth sets evil onto oneself.

—decree no. 3, Ancient Order of the Seventh Sun

1589 A.D.
REPUBLIC OF VENICE

THE BLADE GRAZED ANGELO MASCARI'S CHEEK, missed only by the turn of his head, followed by a lunge to the chest. The Whip Snake lashed a lightning-fast double-tap. Angelo parried at the last second. His opponent pranced back on the platform and stared him down *en garde*, the tip of his sword trained on Angelo's throat.

Swiping the face was forbidden in this demonstration, but neither the judge nor Angelo's Master Fabris called it out. Despite the friendly nature of the bout, death seemed but moments away.

The crowd clamored for more.

Never had Angelo dueled before such an audience. Spectators filled Piazza San Marco to the edges of the Palazzo Ducale, the basilica, and the arcades. He raised his rapier in defense. Exhalations skated across the polished steel in heated cloud bursts.

The Whip Snake's epithet suited him not only for his speed but also for his physique. Lithe and reed-thin, taller and skinnier than Angelo, Rocco Bonetti—the name his mother surely preferred—grinned, knowing the potentially lethal move was illegal. Angelo had thought the moniker pompous before the bout, but now found it accurate. Deadly accurate.

Spectators shouted for Angelo's defeat—an outcome that seemed more inevitable with every passing second. Ten minutes prior, he was supremely confident; it was by luck or defensive maneuvers that it hadn't ended already.

He felt his tanned complexion reddening beneath the late-spring Mediterranean sun. Beads of sweat rolled from his wavy, dark locks, threatening to land in his eyes, but averting his focus for even a half-second to wipe his brow would lead to an embarrassing loss, if not the end of his career. Or worse.

The snake shuffled his feet and tapped the platform with his rapier.

Angelo jumped back, poised to protect himself.

Laugher erupted from the piazza. The Whip Snake's body vacillated in a hypnotic rhythm, his face breaking into a sharp smirk. At twenty-one, a single year older than Angelo, his opponent knew how to milk his moment, giving the audience the entertainment they desired. That he toyed with Angelo in front of the most eminent people in Venice, including the doge, the leader of the Republic, fueled white heat within. He'd have words with this so-called reptile—assuming the man didn't perform another prohibited move and kill him.

It seemed all of Venice watched. As a rising fencing star, he'd been selected to participate in an exhibition with the Whip Snake, who hailed from a rival academy. Angelo was flattered he'd been chosen as the top bill from Master Fabris's school. A victory could lead to a sponsorship from Renzo Scalfini, which was crucial to lighten Angelo's burdens. He owed too many debts to too many people, all of whom watched the contest from the jubilant crowd.

Yet despite the promise of laurels and coin, Angelo only cared about impressing one spectator: Isabella Scalfini—*Renzo's wife*. He would not disappoint her.

True to his name, the Whip Snake swayed side to side in his trademark stance. He swiped the air with his rapier, as if severing the head of an invisible foe kneeling before him. Angelo stood stock still, following Master Fabris's instruction. 'Patience for the right moment is a thing of beauty,' he'd say.

Beauty. *Isabella*.

Though Angelo couldn't see her, he felt her eyes removing his doublet, shirt, and pantaloons, as she'd done less than twenty-four hours prior. The warmth from her lips remained on his inner thigh. The taste of her body lingered on his tongue. He craved more.

The Whip Snake struck, as if sensing his opponent's internal distraction.

Angelo parried and stumbled backward, nearly slipping off the platform.

Spectators exploded with cheers. Even in a friendly bout with no purse, they hungered for blood.

Recovering his footing, Angelo shook his head and forced his brain to concentrate. How to beat a snake, particularly such a quick one? A child of an island city, he had little experience with the creatures. A friend once captured a serpent on the mainland. When the boy removed it from the box, he'd held it by the neck. But going for the Whip Snake's neck was an illegal move. Then again, the judge said nothing upon his opponent's cheek strike. Surprise made a snake more lethal, but snakes could be trampled— *especially* if surprised.

Without another thought, Angelo charged. He hacked relentlessly, startling the Whip Snake. Metal struck metal, clanging as Angelo's opponent parried and retreated down the platform. And then Angelo took a risk—he aimed for Bonetti's neck, but without intent to strike.

As anticipated, Bonetti postured for defense.

Switching to a more elegant form, Angelo flicked his wrist and struck Bonetti's breastplate.

The Whip Snake's jaw popped open, stunned.

Angelo, too, was momentarily dazed by his victory. When realization set in, he launched his fists into the air with a triumphant grunt and paraded the length of the platform to face the spectators on both sides. Though not one to gloat, he reveled in the adoration from a crowd that longed for his death moments earlier.

The whole of the festival applauded as he stepped off the platform.

The prettiest girls in Venice rushed over, congratulating him and clasping his muscles. Maidens batted their eyelashes and shielded their blushes with folding fans. He enjoyed the attention but scanned for his beloved in the massive crowd.

Every Venetian agreed this year's Festa della Sensa had been the most glorious in memory. In the symbolic ceremony of Venice's marriage to the sea, Doge Cicogna had lobbed a golden ring into the Venetian Lagoon as a thousand boats donned with flags of La Serenissima's coat of arms entered the Grand Canal. A parade of red and yellow flags bearing St. Mark's winged lion cemented The Serene Republic's position as the greatest naval power in the world. Partly a celebration of the successful conversion of the Rialto Bridge from wood to stone, each vessel passed beneath the structure to cheers.

Festivities had continued that afternoon in a feast for the senses, as the duke graced his citizens with the commencement of a week-long jubilee in Piazza San Marco, showcasing song, dance, and theater, as well as feats of strength, dexterity, and gallantry on the horse. The celebration culminated with the main event—prowess of the blade.

A slap to the back of his head cut Angelo's search short. He turned to find Master Fabris staring down at him, his crimson-and-gold flat cap angled to the side. The fencing legend, with his curly gray hair and long mustache, was half a head taller than Angelo; his perfect posture made him seem like Mars himself—and as eternally angry.

"I didn't teach you to hack away like a Turkish street rat," Fabris said.

"Apologies, Master Fabris, but—"

"You embarrassed me in plain view of the entire city. They'll think I instruct my students to cower in fear then flail wildly without a strategy or plan."

"But Master, that *was* my strategy."

Fabris narrowed one eye and raised the brow over his other.

"Snakes can only be defeated at the neck. Or crushed altogether."

Fabris relaxed his face and offered the slightest of smiles. "Rocco Bonetti is not a real snake."

"No, but the move brought a victory to your illustrious school."

If Master Fabris meant to offer his agreement or compliment, Angelo would never know, for Fabris received a pat on the back.

"Well done, Fabris," said the short, blond man with a long goatee. "You performed with purpose." He shook hands with Fabris, who nodded his thanks.

Angelo assumed the stranger was Nicoletto Giganti, master of the rival school, for beside him, with his head hung low, stood Angelo's recently deposed opponent. Giganti's fitted turquoise velvet waistcoat matched his beret adorned with an ostrich plume, which Angelo had thought fell out of fashion some years prior.

"We had wondered what strategy you'd use to best the best. It was the Whip Snake's first defeat." Giganti extended his hand. "Well played, indeed, Mascari."

"Gràssie, siòr," Angelo replied, giving the man a vigorous handshake.

Fabris tipped his head to Giganti, before Giganti nudged Rocco. "Don't stand there like you're still in the falcon's talons. Lose honorably."

"You did well, Mascari," the Whip Snake said. "This time. I look forward to our next bout." With a sullen bow, he turned on his heel and headed into the crowd.

"Forgive me," Giganti said. "I haven't had to train the cur to lose with grace. Now Angelo, I understand you seek a sponsor. I could introduce you to—"

Fabris held up his hand. "I shall ask favor of sponsors when he's ready."

The men exchanged words, but Angelo scarcely heard.

Despite the conversation about his future, he resumed scanning the pedestrians meandering amongst street performers and food vendors. He searched for her in eager anticipation, like a young boy expecting a panettone on Christmas morn. It wasn't long before he spotted his true love: Isabella Scalfini, the young wife of Renzo Scalfini, controlling partner of the largest timber collegantia in the Republic.

She stood beneath the Column of San Todaro, fanning herself, laughing with a friend. Isabella wore an intimately familiar sky-blue dress that accentuated her auburn hair and dark eyes. What her blonde friend wore, he noticed not.

"I believe I have found my sponsor," Angelo said. "Please excuse me, siòri."

After a bow to both men, Angelo continued his mission. A costumed marching band interrupted his path. Their drumming matched the excited beat of his heart. He allowed them to pass; then in rhythm to the music, he strolled over to Isabella.

"My ladies," he said to the women, taking a rare opportunity to converse with the eighteen-year-old beauty in flagrant view for all to see. "A most delightful afternoon for the grandest festa to be held in our most serene city."

Unable to look away, Angelo locked his gaze with Isabella's. Her almond-shaped eyes smiled upon seeing him. Her presence entranced—no, *ensnared*—him. And he savored every moment of it.

"Congratulations on your victory."

"Siòr Mascari, is it not?" she asked, her olive skin brightening.

The sweetness of her voice always sparked memories of delicacies Angelo's mother baked. Combined with the floral and cinnamon aroma emanating from Isabella's embroidered white leather gloves, his mouth watered.

"Gràssie, siòra," he replied. "We met at Siòr Balbi's Christmas Ball. Do you not remember?"

"Clearly I do. Otherwise, I wouldn't have remembered your name. Perhaps you are the one who has forgotten."

"I could never forget you, Siòra Scalfini."

"I meant you have forgotten your manners. Or are you generally in the custom of approaching noble ladies without our husbands present or without so much as a gentleman by your side?" Isabella widened her eyes as they landed on Angelo's neck.

His hand instinctively went to the target of her gaze—the silver crucifix she'd given him some weeks prior. He hadn't removed it since. It must've slipped out during the duel. He tucked it back into his shirt.

Her friend arched her eyebrows and snickered with disdain, oblivious to his silent conversation with Isabella.

"Siòra, I—" Angelo started.

"Go easy on the rascal, Siòra Scalfini," a voice said from behind them.

The three turned to find two men approaching.

Angelo was already acquainted with *i Fratelli Uccello*—the Bird Brothers. With every meeting, more and more, he wished their paths had never crossed. Though, had they not, he never would have met Isabella. The flaxen-haired Vito Uccello strode up to them. His sharp, eagle-like features and broad posture always posed a threatening presence. His smaller brother Ivan followed a step behind. With raven hair and a tight face, the man scowled at everything he saw. Beady eyes darted over Angelo, as if stalking a mouse. Without a word, he knew what the Bird Brothers wanted—the black book they'd tasked Angelo to retrieve from Renzo and Isabella's bedroom. After six months, he was no closer. Well, he *was* closer but hadn't the desire to complete the task.

"I'm sure Angelo has a strong reason for approaching unaccompanied ladies, and we can vouch for him," Vito continued.

"Indeed," Angelo said. "I was, in fact, looking for Siòra Scalfini's husband."

"I believe he's speaking with the Minister of Finance," Isabella replied.

"Ah, see," Ivan said to Isabella's friend. "No cause for concern."

Angelo stole a look at Isabella. She observed him a second longer than appropriate. That she was putting on a show prompted an audible sigh of relief. Scenes of the previous day's activities reflected in her eyes, causing a hardness in his pantaloons he needed to quell with less arousing thoughts.

Vito took a long gulp from his wooden mug and burped. A rank cloud of regurgitated anchovies, garlic, and red wine wafted through the air. The two wavered from inebriation, as Ivan took a swig from a bottle, then refilled his brother's mug.

The brothers cured his potential embarrassment.

"On such a day," Vito said, "there is cause for celebration and, and—"

"And gaiety," Ivan offered. He brushed a lock of hair off the shoulder of Isabella's friend.

"Guard yourself, sir," she said, shooing his hand away.

Ivan scowled, his tightened eyes seeming to bore into her skull. She sidestepped closer to Isabella.

"Come now, ladies," Vito said. "It's a beautiful day—and a day for beauty and love. Community and sharing. Perhaps a day for . . . sharing love." Vito massaged Isabella's shoulder. She tensed and looked at Angelo.

Fury sizzled within him. Vito surely meant to provoke a reaction; Angelo would be a fool to counter.

"Perhaps you can both join us at the masquerade tonight." Vito's hand slithered down Isabella's arm to her waist.

Angelo gripped the hilt of his rapier with such hatred that his knuckles turned ashen white.

"Remove your hand from Lady Scalfini," he said, "lest you wish to lose it."

"Mind your place, Mascari!" Vito kept his palm on Isabella.

"Mind yours, sir," Isabella said, squirming out of his hold.

"What did you say, woman?"

"Ah, there's my husband," she said, pointing to a man in his early forties with a pock-marked face and a frame twice the size of Angelo's. He limped toward them, tucking a large, thick envelope into his jerkin. "He's your friend, is he not?"

"Indeed," Vito said. He and Ivan stepped back from the ladies.

Vito's words were the last of the conversation Angelo heard. The thought of yet another man attempting to possess Isabella churned his stomach. He would abandon his career—he'd abandon *everything*—if it meant he and his love could live in peace. As the group turned toward Isabella's advancing husband, Angelo stole off into the crowd, nearly barreling over a boy wearing a red gondolier's hat with a white feather.

I

PRESENT DAY

NICK O'CONNOR BUMPED INTO A YOUNG boy in a red hat with a white feather as Julia dragged him through a throng of people. On either side of the corridor stood rows of marble columns, each topped with a crystal orb. A faceless, naked old man used a paintbrush to splatter a column. It wasn't the man's decrepit body, but the claret-colored streaks he made on the marble that caused Nick to shudder.

A rhythmic drumming pounded his ears.

"... Nick! Come on. Not again—not now!" His wife flicked her gaze back to him, her emerald eyes imploring him with exasperated desperation. She plowed forward, weaving through the people, hauling him along, her honey-blonde ponytail bobbing with their steps.

Nick glanced at the boy to make sure he was okay. The kid was fine. And his feathered hat was gone, replaced with a red baseball cap.

As Nick turned forward, the columns disintegrated into space. A busy train terminal, similar to a modern airport, appeared. He recalled where they were—Milan's Central Station. And where they were headed—the U.S. Consulate. But he couldn't figure out why they were walking at such a brisk clip, nor why Julia was leading him like they were seconds from missing their train. Though the regression to Angelo had receded and his memory was fuzzy, he was certain they just got *off* a train. It was a five-minute cab ride to the consulate, but it wasn't a life-threatening emergency. Or was it? Events of the previous days felt more nightmarish than nearly being killed by the Whip Snake. Fragments of images lurked in his mind: The Palazzo Ducale, Carlo, della Porta, Tintoretto, *Paradise* . . . Isabella.

The pounding intensified in volume and tempo, like a drummer on an ancient galley, gearing up for ramming speed.

Again, Nick checked behind him. A college kid also in a rush had a pair of headphones on; a thumping techno remix of *I Am the Walrus* emanated from them.

Relieved the intrusion came from modern technology, Nick unwound in the comfort that he and Julia were finally going home. Less than a day, and they'd be in their own bed. *No turning back now.* He wouldn't forget Venice anytime soon, or ever, but then he noticed the real reason why his wife was in such a hurry.

Fifteen feet behind the college kid, two uniformed cops matched their pace. One locked eyes with him. The other spoke into his radio.

"Please, Nick! Snap out of it," Julia yelled. "We gotta move."

A tidal wave of sickening emotions he couldn't begin to sort washed over him; memories stampeded his brain. After escaping Venice under cover of darkness, they had spent the night in an inn on the mainland. They woke early and caught a train to Milan. Their goalpost was the consulate, where they'd apply for emergency passports, if not protection, before flying home.

He assumed the cops were following them because Detective Fanella in Venice put an APB out. Rage boiled in his gut; the O'Connors were so close to their destination. Nick had enough of all the damn obstacles. He squeezed Julia's hand and matched her speed so she wasn't yanking on him anymore. She met his gaze and understood in a blink: her husband was back. He let her lead, grateful she had taken charge. The exit sign came into focus, his newfound fluency in Italian helping out.

Twenty feet to the door, then a cab. They could sprint to the consulate and request amnesty.

Julia skidded to a stop, holding him back. Two more policemen appeared at the exit, blocking their path. He pivoted around. The cops to their rear were nearly on them. A fifth officer approached from the side.

Sprinting back to the platform and crossing the tracks was an option, but he didn't want to put Julia in any more danger.

In their hesitation, the police were on them like a pack of dogs.

"THIS IS TAKING FOREVER," Julia said, sitting in the plastic chair next to him.

They sat on one side of a steel table in a small interrogation room in Caserma Garibaldi, the State Police's main station in Milan. Though the building must've been a few hundred years old, the interior appeared to have been modernized recently; the tiny, bare room felt fresh. His movie-and-TV-loving brain hoped for a one-way mirror on the wall, but security cameras in each ceiling corner did the job.

"You sure you're okay?"

"Yeah," he lied. He scratched the back of his sweaty neck. "It was just a quick one. I told you, the farther we get from Venice, the more I'm my old self."

"I wish you were saying that in the American consulate."

She had no idea how much he agreed.

He'd never forgive himself for the ordeal he put her through. Even after the hardships, she was still his rock and his heart. Typically, her presence was a panacea, but not now. Bile bubbled in his throat and coated his tongue, leaving an acidic taste he couldn't lose.

They showered that morning and bought new clothes before catching their train. Julia had swapped her dress and broken sandals for jeans, a tank top, and canvas sneakers. Nick had done the same, replacing his smelly, canal-soaked garb for jeans and a black t-shirt. Even with a shower and fresh fabric, Nick couldn't get comfortable. Bruises carpeted his body, and he needed to shift every thirty seconds. He couldn't seem to wash Venice—*or Isabella*—away.

He had glimpsed himself in the reflection of the squad car window as they were transported to the police station. Lines wove their way through his forehead beneath his brown hair, and his dark eyes were a maze of red highways. A week of stubble taunted him with a reminder of a vacation that spiraled into a life-threatening nightmare. Through it all, Julia managed to retain her beauty. Everyone had always said he and Julia made a good-looking couple, especially when her fair skin contrasted with his darker features. But Nick felt like a feral dog next to her. Or, more accurately, a wounded elephant. At 6'0" and 195 pounds, he wasn't a huge man, but sitting in that chair was no easy task.

Nick turned his mind back to their present situation, unsure why their looks—something he typically never cared about—popped into his head. It'd been what, three days since he was in a police station in Venice? Considering he'd previously only been in a police station once in his life—as a teenager he'd gotten caught smoking weed with his friends in the back of an unlocked van—three times in a week felt like a very bad omen.

"Wow, déjà vu," Nick said, settling into present-day reality. Fortunately, the driver of the van in Boston didn't press charges. Though the Milan police hadn't officially arrested him, he wasn't sure he'd be so lucky this time. Apparently, a French detective was on his way to question them.

Julia slugged his already bruised shoulder.

"Ow, what was that for?" He rubbed his arm.

"I hope that hurt. 'What was that for?' Are you serious? This better not be déjà vu, you a-hole. Gonna tell me what the hell you did to get Interpol involved, or what?"

Nick fidgeted with his tungsten wedding band and adjusted in the narrow chair. Each position exacerbated his bruises. Finding it impossible to sit without pain, he resigned himself to physical discomfort and set out to analyze their situation. He'd been pondering Julia's question for the last half hour.

Though the events in Venice weren't exactly guidebook-friendly, Interpol seemed over the top. He recounted the experience in his head. After hearing Isabella Scalfini's voice coming from Tintoretto's *Paradise* in the Palazzo Ducale, Nick had a past-life regression to Angelo Mascari, a 16th-century swordsman who had an affair with Isabella. Along the way, he discovered the Ancient Order of the Seventh Sun, a wealthy group of religious zealots who tapped a lost power from the Tangut Kingdom in Mongolia. The Order discovered that every person has a single soul which travels through seven consecutive lives. They also learned how to extract souls they deem evil and have sentenced thousands to *Paradise* as a type of purgatory. Isabella was caught and imprisoned, but Angelo got away, which is why Nick existed in the flesh, six lives later. Sure, Nick tried to bring down the Order. Who wouldn't? *They* were the criminals. But Interpol? It's not like he was a spy. He couldn't figure out how the Milano police even found them since they didn't have their passports, paid cash for everything, and never used their real names.

He still yearned to free Isabella, but given that they had narrowly escaped with their lives, it no longer seemed possible. Making it home with Julia was now his singular concern. They had five things to do to reach that elusive goal: go to the consulate; get emergency passports; book tickets home to Boston; go to the airport; and step onto a damn plane.

And now here they were—locked in an interrogation room.

Despite Nick's ability to converse with the arresting officers in their native tongue, he insisted on an English-speaking officer for Julia's benefit. His wife was in the middle of this mess; she deserved to understand the discussion. The officer's response was astonishing as she led them to the small room: "Everyone in Interpol speaks English." Nick wasn't surprised Interpol employees were required to speak English. He was amazed the International Police Organization was involved at all, let alone a detective.

Nick wracked his brain. He suspected della Porta had his hand in their detainment, but the last time he saw the head of the Order, the man was on the run himself, until Detective Fanella and the others caught up with him. No doubt della Porta convinced the cops to turn the tables on Nick.

"Babe, you know everything that happened," he said, turning to Julia. "You were right there with me."

"I can't tell if you're joking, if you have present-day selective memory, or if your supposed regressions are rotting your brain. You abandoned me for two days!"

Nick sunk into himself at her words and scratched the back of his neck. In his zeal to free Isabella and the thousands of other souls—and destroy the Order in the process—he got caught up in the moment. Della Porta sought an ancient journal that Nick's past life was blackmailed into stealing. Isabella's husband had possession of the book, but when the affair turned to true love, Angelo stopped searching for it. That didn't stop della Porta from kidnapping Julia to use her as leverage. Nick didn't want Julia involved at all, and it killed him that della Porta's goons brought them both to a torture room in the Palazzo. It was only because Isabella told him della Porta committed murder that they were able to escape. Along with Carlo's help, of course. Their Venetian artist friend may have been the Order's new Painter—the man responsible for the souls in *Paradise*—but they wouldn't have been alive without him.

"I meant you heard what della Porta said. The dude's a liar, but he told the truth about what happened to me. The regressions to Angelo are *real*." Nick didn't bother lowering his volume. The cops probably knew everything anyway, since the Order had its tentacles everywhere. He figured they left him and Julia in the same room to get some intel or confession out of him. That was their mistake; Nick *hoped* they were recording this.

"First off," Julia said, also raising her volume, "half the conversation in a damn torture room wasn't in English, so no, I didn't hear everything either of you said. Second, none of that explains why we're in a police station *now*."

It hit Nick. He snapped his fingers. "The countess."

"What countess?"

"That's who this is about. It's gotta be, Jules. I met her for like five minutes. She's Tintoretto's descendant. She wanted to free the souls, too, and della Porta friggin' killed her. And now he's trying to pin her murder on me."

"How are you saying that so calmly?" She threw a side gander at the cameras. "And loudly?"

"Because I didn't kill her."

Julia picked at her fingernails. She studied Nick's eyes before speaking in a hushed tone. "Did you kill *anyone*?"

"No." Nick clinched his jaw. He'd yet to tell her about Tintoretto. There was so much to unpack. *Yes*, he killed a man—but a man who should've died in 1594.

Julia's eyebrow raised, scrutinizing him. Though it was barely a lie, he needed to keep the truth hidden.

Nick covered his mouth and spoke in as low a whisper as he could. "I wish you let me toss the Palazzo blueprint in the water. They could use it as evidence against me."

"How?"

"Della Porta killed the countess there. He bludgeoned her to death."

His wife gasped and matched his volume. "You witnessed a murder?"

"No. Isabella told me."

Julia's eyes darkened at the name.

"It's not like I had an affair with her." Physically, it was the truth, of course, but he couldn't deny the pang of guilt that shot through him.

His wife swallowed and stared at the table. He took her hand, intertwining her fingers in his, thankful she let him. Warm shivers fluttered through him.

She released a forced chuckle and spoke in her normal voice. "Don't worry. I'm not jealous of a two-dimensional, four-hundred-something woman in a painting. Pissed at the whole situation, yes. Weirded out that you can speak Italian—"

"Venetian. Well, both."

"Even weirder. But jealous? No."

Nick shifted. His lower back begged him to lie down, even on the concrete floor. Though he was glad Julia wasn't jealous, it also bugged him that she questioned the reality of what he'd experienced. "After all you've seen..."

"Honey, paintings don't speak—"

"Yeah, except when they do." Nick shook his head and looked away.

Julia pressed her other hand over their intertwined clasp. "Like I said, I agree some unexplainable things happened, but... you say 'all you've seen.' What did I see?"

Nick turned back. Now it was his turn to be pissed. "Carlo saw me speaking with her. He saw the whole damn painting come to life. Ask *him*, if you don't believe me."

"A Venetian artist is your best friend now?"

"No, but I'll admit when I'm wrong about a guy. So, yeah, I do trust him. And you know him better than I do. You guys got pretty chummy."

"Don't even," Julia said, freeing her hands. "Carlo was the *only* person I could turn to. The only person I *knew*. And he saved us."

"Yeah, because he knows exactly what happened."

Julia chewed her bottom lip. "It's not that I don't believe *you*. It's . . . it's just that it's so hard for me to accept. Like you said, Carlo saw it. *You* saw it. *I* didn't. But I believe you and trust you. More than Carlo, for the record. A lifetime more."

Nick crumpled his brow. How could she not accept what he'd been through? One day, he'd convince her. But that time wasn't now. "I just wish you'd left the you-know-what in the water."

She patted her jeans on her thigh and winked. After they had frisked her, Nick allowed himself to breathe when they didn't find it.

"And if you get caught with it," he whispered, "it's a blueprint for *your* arrest, too."

"Wow, not funny. Anyway, they haven't arrested you, either."

"Yet."

"We don't even know if this is about the countess."

"I didn't kill her, Jules."

Julia squeezed his hand. "I know. We need a lawyer."

"They want me arrested because they want me gone."

"Why?"

"I think you know. You just haven't accepted it yet."

The doorknob turned.

A mid-forties man, at least 6'2" with a round face, light-brown complexion, and prematurely graying wavy hair entered the room and closed the door. Despite his physique, he moved with an effortless glide. Clearly mixed race, Nick had no clue what the man's background was. He sat in the opposite chair without a sound, his light-gray suit and pastel blue tie camouflaging him into the walls. He set a file on the table and steepled his fingers before speaking English with a nasally French, yet remarkably soothing, accent.

"I am Richard Lacasse, a detective with Interpol." He tapped the file. "You are Nick and Julia O'Connor, both twenty-eight, from Massachusetts. Monsieur O'Connor, you are a software architect at Fidelity Invest—"

"You have my file," Nick said, not hiding his impatience. "Gonna ask me what color my shirt is?" Knowing he and Julia had been so close to freedom felt like an unseen hand clenching the back of his neck.

Lacasse remained emotionless. "Inside this file is overwhelming evidence against you, monsieur."

"I didn't kill her," Nick blurted out.

The detective perked an eyebrow over his sanguine, carob-colored eyes. "Didn't kill who?"

"Countess Tintoretto. I don't even know her name."

"Nick," Julia said, squeezing his knee. "Let's hear him out. What evidence are you referring to, Detective Lacasse? My husband didn't commit any crimes."

Lacasse whistled through his teeth. "We shall get to that in a moment. I'd like to discuss the countess first. I presume you're referring to Faustina Baldesseri—a countess in title only, of course."

"Yeah. I. Did. Not. Kill. Her. And there's not a shred of evidence I did."

"And why would I think you killed her? Or anyone, for that matter?"

Nick jerked back in his seat. He wanted to kick himself. How could he have made such a dumb, rookie move? Always let them speak first. Don't give them anything they don't ask for.

"You tell me," Nick said.

Lacasse resumed his tranquil confidence and authority. "You're on vacation, oui?"

"We *were*."

"Have you contacted your friends or family in the last few days?"

"What does that have to do with anything?" Julia asked.

"If people haven't heard from you, they do not think you've been murdered, oui?"

Nick rubbed his temples. This guy was winning, and it felt like the game hadn't even started.

"Such is the case with the countess," Lacasse continued. "I heard about her because of you and your actions, Monsieur O'Connor. Now, let's get to those actions."

"We'd like a lawyer," Julia said. "And we want to speak to someone at the U.S. embassy."

"You're not under arrest," Lacasse replied.

"So we can go?" Nick asked.

Without answering, Lacasse opened the file and spread out a series of photographs on the table.

II

"LOOK AT ME WHEN I TALK TO YOU, you sniveling worm," he shouted over the roar of the machines.

He drove the dirty shoe into the man's face with such force, the tattered leather shattered his nose, spraying blood on both men, which caused his head to whip back, cracking against the iron printing press.

CARLO ZUCCARO'S EYES snapped open. The dream was bizarre. Dreams never made sense to him, but a fight in a 1920s printing house? He chalked it up to a long-forgotten movie he'd seen at some point in his life. Though the visuals faded, the drone of the machines persisted in his head, much like the anguished cries from the souls in *Paradiso*. He hadn't been able to shake them. A thousand voices, screaming at him simultaneously; the shrill buzz hammered a part of his brain he'd never used.

"Hello?"

Carlo rolled his head to his left. The naked Asian girl next to him bulged her chestnut brown eyes as if she'd been waiting for a response for a year.

"And here I thought those light hazel beauts were attentive," she asked with a pronounced Australian accent.

"Scusami, Julia."

The girl's eyes widened even more. "Um, who the fuck is Julia?"

Realizing his trespass, Carlo shimmied his thin frame onto to his side to face her. "Jordan. Sorry, Jordan." He tucked her hair behind her ear, exposing a bit of acne on her cheek. Stockier than Julia, with shorter hair, Jordan wasn't his type physically, but he couldn't deny their chemistry, especially in bed. He also found her fascinating—an Asian Australian of Chinese descent who didn't know a word of Chinese. Compared to his own heritage of Venice ad infinitum, people from less homogeneous places offered him a transient opportunity to see the world through different lenses. Perhaps that's why tourists and exchange students attracted him.

"I had a strange dream," he said.

"You're always strange, but that's what I like about you. Stranger than usual last night." She ran a finger down his chest, which was as smooth as his stubble-free face. "But in a good way. With a different energy." Her finger continued its journey. "How does an artist get abs like these?"

Her touch sent warm shivers through his body, but he wasn't in the mood for physical intimacy. He grabbed a pack of cigarettes from the nightstand and shook one out.

"Don't even think about lighting that disgusting thing in here," she said, removing her hand.

"It's my flat."

"It's my lungs."

Carlo lit the cigarette and slid off the bed to open a window. Sunlight streamed in, glistening off the chandelier above his bed. The hum of a lazy motor drifted by in the canal that abutted the rear of his loft.

It was the first time in three days he'd slept more than an hour. He rubbed his tatted forearms. Between Jordan, becoming the Order's Painter, and his day job as a normal artist, his brain had been on overdrive. His schedule was also catching up with him—five paintings due for an upcoming group show weren't going to paint themselves. He glanced around the room for his mobile, then remembered it was charging in the kitchen.

"What time is it?"

Jordan checked her Apple Watch. "Almost noon. I've been trying to get you up for a while."

"I need to work." He hadn't touched a paintbrush since he was last in the Great Council Room and suddenly felt motivated to start a new piece. A vision flashed in his head: a classical siren, layered on top of an abstracted mechanical boiler room, painted on metallic glass. Was the inspiration sparked by the dream? Could Jordan be his muse? It didn't matter; his acrylics beckoned him.

Grabbing his wrist, she stopped him from going. "That's not why I was trying to wake you."

"Then why?"

She grinned. "Because I'm naked in your bed, drongo."

"Drongo? Is that supposed to be Italian?"

"It's Aussie slang. And it means dummy, you drongo. Focus on the naked bit."

"I need to paint something *now*."

"I have a ten-pager about Veronese due tomorrow, but you don't see me racing out of your flat to the uni, do you?"

"Because I promised to help you." Carlo took a drag, then sat on the edge of his bed.

"There's more than one way people can help each other, mate." She traced a long, French manicured fingernail around the compass tattoo on his left forearm, giving it goosebumps. Maybe physical intimacy wasn't such a bad idea after all.

The corners of Carlo's mouth involuntarily tilted upward. She was right, of course. Plus, a little more inspiration couldn't hurt. "You're not mad about the name?"

Laughing, she stole the cigarette from his fingers, took a puff, and quashed it in the ashtray on the nightstand. She threw the sheets off before pushing him down and climbing on top of him. "If you root me like you rooted me last night, call me Hugh Michael Jackman, for all I care." Their lips met as she pressed her body into his.

Though Carlo had only met Julia recently and was a big player in her and Nick's ordeal, that adventure seemed to magnify time. Was a week a month? A year? For how long did he know her intelligence, her morality, her passion? Were they truly first-life souls? Would they meet again in another life? A grim reminder hit Carlo. As the Order's Painter, he had *one* life—not seven lives like everyone else. The present mattered more than anything. He buried his tongue into her neck. Her soft skin tasted of salt and lilacs. She arched her back with a moan and tangled her fingers in his thick, dark hair.

He rolled over on top of her.

"Julia. . ."

The girl beneath him—the exchange student from Sydney—jutted her head back. "Seriously?"

Carlo mentally cursed himself. Why couldn't he get Julia out of his head? "Jordan," he said firmly. "Sorry. Julia . . . is, uh, an old artist I'm studying. Like dead, old. She's dead."

Jordan giggled. "To call you a rank liar is an insult to rank liars. If Julia's such a cherry, give her a call, have her join us."

Carlo cocked his head. Jordan seemed serious. He gave it a brief thought but realized it was yet another fantasy—as much a fantasy as giving Julia a single kiss on the lips. It was bad enough Julia was married to his friend. Plus, she and Nick were back in the States, and he'd never see them again.

Compartmentalizing his swirling thoughts, Carlo gave Julia—*Jordan*—what she wanted.

He enjoyed it, of course. She was a dynamo like always and a much-needed release for his pent-up stress. He verbally—and mentally—called her Jordan, and as they explored each other's bodies, an increasingly familiar energy surged through him. Each sense felt heightened, hyper-real. Colors were vivid; Jordan's floral bouquet caressed his nose. His strength swelled, too. Of all the times he'd been with a woman, including Jordan, he'd never considered himself the dominant one. But now, he was in complete control. He steered their sex like an assertive dancer directing his partner. More than that, he had newly found potency to do whatever he pleased. If he wanted to dominate her physically, he could—and she wouldn't have a chance to resist. Of course, he'd never do such a thing, so he nuzzled her neck in an apology.

Thoughts of the Great Council Room zipped back to Carlo's mind, when the Sun Crystal's lifeforce imbued his body with Tintoretto's power.

At the time, he described it as an excess of life. As he melded with Jordan's body, he realized he was right.

He just needed to figure out if he liked the sensation—and what he'd do with it.

III

A DOZEN CELL PHONE SHOTS OF NICK'S fight with Bernardo and Dante in the Palazzo Ducale, all from different angles: Nick hitting Dante's ear, with the Protector crying out; Nick elbowing Bernardo; Nick breaking Dante's nose, blood splattering the man's close-cropped beard. Security camera footage of Nick sprinting from the Palazzo grounds. Other shots of Nick escaping the police station. For good measure, Lacasse pulled out an iPad and showed amateur videos, not only of the fight, but also of Nick climbing the chairs to touch *Paradise*.

"So much for cameras not being allowed in the Great Council Room," Nick mumbled under his breath. Examining the photos spread across the table, he had to admit, it didn't look good. At least he wasn't wanted for murder. All things considered, it could've been way worse.

"One good thing about all the tourists in Venice," Lacasse said, "is there's an image of everyone and everything, every second of the day."

Nick scoffed. "At least one thing is good for both of us."

"What's that, monsieur?"

"Those cameras have selective memory." Nick wasn't surprised not one photo was taken during the Convocation, when he'd rained chaos down, started a fire, and fought multiple men. Of course, all that would've also shown Tintoretto and the Order's ceremony. The lack of photos didn't prove Lacasse was with the Order, but it *did* strengthen the suspicion in Nick's gut.

Leaning forward, Julia pored over the photos, shuffling them around. "How is a skirmish and inappropriate behavior some massive international crime that gets Interpol involved?" she asked.

"Yeah," Nick said, smiling at his wife. Julia's innate sense of justice never failed to inject a rational common-sense approach into any conflict. "Can't I just pay a fine or something?"

Lacasse leaned back in his chair and intertwined his fingers on the table, as if resting his case. "The Doge's Palace is not merely a museum." His French accent and soothing diction were the inverse of della Porta's abrasiveness. "It is an Italian landmark and a UNESCO World Heritage Site. Had you cooperated in Venice, this would have been a minor affair. But you fought in the building, fought the police, and attempted to flee the European Union. *That* is why I am here."

"The police attacked me," Nick said, forcing himself to not pound the table. "The guards at the Palazzo tried to kill me. I have the ridiculous sword wound to prove it." He rolled up his sleeve and showed Lacasse the ugly, scabbing five-inch cut.

Lacasse cocked his head a bit and raised an eyebrow. "Why would you fight the police when reporting a crime?"

"Because—" Nick clammed up, realizing he had no proof. Julia was right. He needed a lawyer.

"Because they're corrupt assholes," Julia said, her face reddening, her eyes pinched into a tight scowl. "They fucking kidnapped me! When are we gonna get a lawyer?"

Now definitely concerned, Lacasse appeared unsettled by this information. "What do you mean they kidnapped you?"

Julia folded her arms and spoke in measured tones. "They told me they had information about Nick and then brought me to della Porta in a dungeon and tied me up. *That's* what I mean."

"I presume you're referring to Salvatore della Porta, the museum director?"

"There better not be another," she said.

Lacasse spoke to Nick. "You accused him of killing Madame Baldesseri."

"Yeah," Nick said. "*He's* the guy you should be interrogating."

A slow, uneasy breath exited Lacasse's nose. "I am not saying I don't believe you, but these are all serious accusations. The police kidnapping you, a museum director committing murder. You must admit, even for Venice, it does sound . . . rather fantastical, no?"

"It happened." Julia leaned back and crossed her arms.

"Do you have proof?"

Nick exchanged a worried glance with his wife. He combed his memories. With everything the Order had done, all their crimes, they didn't have a shred of evidence. And half the things they did were tied to events that were preposterous at best. As if any jury in the world would believe a painting came to life or that a five-hundred-year-old man had been alive up until a few days ago.

"I have a witness," Julia said.

"Do you?" The detective widened an eye. "And their name?"

Nick squeezed Julia's leg before she answered. Though Lacasse seemed by-the-book, his demeanor, or perhaps line of questioning, didn't sit well with him, as if Lacasse knew more than he should've. He eyeballed the detective's face, but the man countered without altering his expression a hair. Whether he was legit or working with the Order, this guy was a pro. Nick needed to up his game.

"We have multiple witnesses and plenty of proof," he said. "But we want a lawyer."

"And have you contacted the American embassy?" Julia asked.

"We sent an email informing them of your transfer. You'll have the opportunity to contact a lawyer once in Venice."

Nick and Julia stared in quizzical silence at Lacasse. Nick wasn't sure if he'd heard right. And if he did, he couldn't put his finger on his internal reaction. Was it fear? Elation? Trepidation? Anxiety? All the above? Whatever the sensation, it had nothing to do with the police and everything to do with the Order. And more to the point—Isabella. He was reasonably sure Julia was thinking the same thing when she finally spoke in a barely audible whisper.

"What?"

Noticing her quivering hand, Nick took it and held it tight.

"The crimes occurred in Venice." Lacasse spoke to Julia. "You'll need to be returned there to process your arrest. Excuse me. *Monsieur* O'Connor, I mean, not you. You, madame, are not under arrest and, of course, free to go. As a courtesy, you are welcome to accompany your husband to Venice."

Nick wasn't even looking at Lacasse. Seeing Julia's face redden more, Nick's wave of emotions was replaced with a whole new set—sympathy, empathy, guilt, protectiveness. And a rapidly rising pulse.

"I can't go back to Venice," he said, his voice cracking.

"It's not a choice, Monsieur O'Connor. And I assure you, your cooperation will make it a much more pleasant trip."

"But the consulate is *here*," Nick said.

"That's irrelevant. And far too early in the process. As I mentioned, they've been informed of your transfer. We're leaving in five minutes. I'll give you time to say goodbye to your wife, if she chooses to stay."

With that, Lacasse gathered his photos and file and left the room. Whether the transfer confirmed Lacasse was with the Order or it was just standard protocol didn't make a difference. Either way, Nick was going back to Venice. He shut his eyes for a moment, then turned to Julia.

"Babe, I'm so—"

She whipped her hands away. "Don't fucking even, Nick." Tears welled in her eyes. Nick's moistened, too. He tried to fight them but surrendered to it all. As they rolled down his cheeks, the flood released from Julia. She threw her arms around him.

"They're minor charges," he said. "We'll get through this."

"I know. I—I, we were so close. I just feel so far from home. And it's such a steep hill to get there, like we keep slipping down."

"Babe, you're not. Like he said, *you're* not under arrest."

She pulled back. Nick wiped her cheeks. She did the same for him.

"Does it matter? Of course I'm coming with you."

"You should go home. I *want* you to go home."

"Who'll get your lawyer? Keep della Porta away? Keep us both sane?"

Nick couldn't help but offer a sad smile. He truly wanted her safe and happy, but he'd never convince her to go home. He hugged her again. "I'm so sorry."

"You should be."

THE UNMARKED BLACK BMW X3's tires massaged the cobblestones of the alley behind the police station garage before turning onto Milan's paved streets. Nick sat in the back behind Julia. To his left, Lacasse sat behind the driver, another plain-clothed officer whose name he wasn't told.

Nick kneaded his shackled hands on his lap. He couldn't remember how it felt being cuffed as a teenager, but now, the metal seemed unnecessarily tight and restrictive. The flip side was that this luxury cop car didn't have ripped seats or a stench of stale vomit. "How far is the airport?" he asked Lacasse.

"We're driving to Venice, Monsieur O'Connor. It's only three hours."

Patently unhappy with the situation, Julia cleared her throat with a vengeance and gazed out the window at a Gothic cathedral.

"We haven't been in one of these in a while," Nick said to her, trying to lighten the mood.

"A horrible situation?" She snapped her head at him.

Nick shifted in his seat. "A car. I meant a car."

"Uh-huh." She turned her attention back to the city passing by. As they exited the old city center, the buildings became more contemporary and spread out, a dramatic contrast to tightly wound, ancient Venice.

He didn't blame Julia for being pissed. They'd made it so far—just a few minutes more, and they would've been home free. Now, they were being dragged back to the lion's den—by the lion's teeth. Still, despite their predicament, driving in a car through modern northern Italy brought him back to the present, the real world, and crucially—his old self. Maybe they'd get out of this. He was only accused of minor crimes, after all. Figuring he could use the three hours to his advantage, he spoke to Lacasse again.

"What did the consulate say?"

"We have not heard back, monsieur," the Interpol detective replied, scrolling through his phone.

"Don't I have the right to be brought there?"

"Why would you have that right?"

"Because I'm an American citizen."

With an irritated exhale that betrayed his typically calm demeanor, Lacasse turned to Nick. "So you can commit a crime and not be charged here?"

"Well, I didn't commit a crime—"

"You've forgotten the photographs?"

Nick shut himself up.

Lacasse relaxed his countenance again and fixed his gaze on Nick, showing a softer side. "Monsieur O'Connor, you have only been charged at this point. You have not gone to trial. You have not been found guilty."

"Good to know," Nick said, cracking a smile to hide his anxiety.

"But when you *are* found guilty, at that point, our countries' governments can discuss extradition."

"You mean I'll be rotting in an Italian prison either way."

"You're a smart man, Monsieur O'Connor." Lacasse's accent seemed to intensify his smugness. The man's haughty grin nearly reached his ear as he went back to his phone.

Julia discharged one of her now-trademarked low, guttural growls.

Nick's shoulders sagged. "How'd you find us, anyway?" he asked Lacasse.

The Interpol detective scoffed.

"Come on," Nick said. "Best case for you, I eat pasta behind bars for the rest of my life. Worst case, I get off, and we fly back to America. What's the difference?"

Still not looking up, Lacasse whistled through his teeth.

"A three-hour drive, right?" Nick continued. "A hundred-eighty minutes, it takes two seconds to ask the question each time, that's roughly . . . five thous—"

"How do you think? Facial recognition technology."

Julia turned around to Nick, shaking her head with an indignant hoot.

They didn't need to exchange a word—he knew exactly what she was thinking. The whole situation was absurd. Not just the cops and the Order, but everything. Talking to a painting, running for his life, Paganelli, Tintoretto. A remarkable stat hit him. In his life as Angelo, he'd been with Isabella—physically, in her presence—for a total of less than 24 hours. They needed less than that to reach the consulate. He released an angry half-laugh, half-growl of his own. They never stood a chance.

IV

"OPEN IT." DETECTIVE FANELLA APPROACHED the bars that sealed della Porta's corridor, her auburn hair brushing the front of her fitted, yellow linen blazer, her posture and expression as sharp as a steel blade. A short, uniformed guard marched in front of her. Behind them strode della Porta's attorney—a thirty-year-old woman in a plain black business suit, her brown hair tied into a tight bun. Several birthmarks dotted her face. From beneath her tortoise shell glasses, her clinical eyes commanded the look of someone who expected they'd win from the get-go.

Salvatore della Porta should've felt more pleased. But he'd been in the cell for nearly three days—three days too long. A series of formalities needed to be completed before he'd be released. He removed his rectangular Gucci eyeglasses and polished the lenses with his handkerchief.

One task was already accomplished. His attorney had convinced Venice's *Procuratore della Repubblica*, the district attorney—a man he'd known for twelve years—that there wasn't enough evidence to press charges.

Though half his age, della Porta's attorney was one of the top criminal defense lawyers in northern Italy—and a member of the Order. They'd strategized about going up the ladder with connections, starting with the mayor, but his attorney was confident they wouldn't need any string-pulling. A barrage of counterevidence would prove a raving lunatic's accusation that della Porta murdered the countess was not only unfounded, it was downright laughable. Not to mention, they'd yet to find a body.

Della Porta returned the glasses to his Roman nose and used his hands as best he could to comb his salt-and-pepper hair. He tucked his tieless white shirt into his gray wool slacks and donned his suit jacket.

He should've been overjoyed. He'd gotten away with murder—the murder of someone who needed to be removed. True, the countess's death was hardly a crime. It was a necessary action to advance a higher purpose that would transform the world for the better. So then why wasn't he elated? Why did feelings of uncertainty percolate in his gut? Perhaps, he rationalized, he'd hoped her murder would be pinned on O'Connor. The district attorney had no choice but to drop the charges since, without a body, there was no evidence of a murder at all. At this point, she was just unreachable—not even missing. Perhaps on her yacht. Alas, O'Connor couldn't be charged . . . yet.

As the guard inserted the key into his cell's barred door, della Porta sat on the cot, watching, listening. The key turned, and the mechanism opened. *A lock and key,* della Porta thought. It was one of the most transformative inventions in history, yet the genius had long been forgotten. This particular lock was from the 1960s—ancient by most security standards; relatively brand new in the three-hundred-year-old building. The holding cell was dismal, but he survived his ordeal by thanking his lucky star he wasn't living in centuries past, when the pathetic bastards sentenced to the *Pozzi* in the bowels of the Palazzo Ducale lived in darkness, pissed and shat in a hole in the corner, and dined on a wedge of stale bread.

The modern-day guard clasped the lever and opened the poorly oiled door. The loud creak was a fitting metaphor—an unquestionable announcement of della Porta's return to freedom. He wouldn't be slinking out, just like he wouldn't be tiptoeing to the future that lay in store.

Only when the door was fully open and the three waited for him did he rise from the cot. He smoothed his suit and bid *arrivederci* to his involuntary hotel room. Striding into the hallway, he didn't look anyone in the eye.

"Lacasse?" he asked. Fanella knew the question was for her.
"They're on their way now." She fell in step behind him.
"Excellent."

V

"PLEASE," LACASSE SAID, MOTIONING FOR Nick to board the idling police boat at the quay.

Nick wondered if all cops in Europe were this courteous or if he was getting special treatment. Despite the Frenchman's manners, he was coaxing Nick toward an undesirable fate that seemed more inevitable with every step.

A hundred yards away, Liberty Bridge connected mainland Italy with Venice and was symbolically the last sense of modernity before entering the city. It struck Nick as odd they wouldn't drive over and get as close to their destination as they could. He gazed back at the parking lot; he hadn't yearned to be behind the wheel of a car this much since he got his license on his sixteenth birthday.

"We take a boat from here?" he asked.

"This way," Lacasse replied, gripping Nick's cuffed arm.

The driver gestured for Julia to walk ahead of him as he took up the rear, his hand resting on his sidearm.

Seagulls squealed overhead.

Nick's stomach lurched. He'd been cognizant of his mood, shifting rapidly between confidence and distress. Seeing the driver's gun and three officers waiting on the police boat, distress won the battle and the war. He turned back to Julia. It was in her eyes too. Everything suddenly got real.

And on top of being arrested, they were returning him to Venice. Though Nick retained his ability to speak Venetian and Italian, Angelo had been quiet since the flashback to the Festa della Sensa. But now, with the skyline of Venice in full view across the lagoon, his former self eased his way into the front of his mind, not saying anything—but lurking, waiting, grinning.

The ten-minute ride was choppier than expected on the high-speed police boat. It could've been the noise or the need to stifle bouts of nausea emanating from multiple sources, but Nick didn't say a word the entire trip. Neither did Julia.

The boat pulled up to a large, red brick building that rose from the water. If it wasn't for the docked police boats and Nick's ability to read the signs, he would've thought the building was a 1930s insane asylum, not the Venetian headquarters for the *carabinieri*—Italy's state police. Lacasse led Nick onto the pier and toward the entrance. Julia followed, with the driver and three officers in tow.

When they reached the door, the driver stopped Julia. "No entry, signora," he said.

"What do you mean?" she asked.

"I'm sorry, madame," Lacasse replied, "but you're not permitted in this entry. It's for police and prisoners."

"Dove la dovarìa andàr?" Nick blurted out in Venetian. His command of the language took everyone there by surprise, including Lacasse, who seemingly couldn't speak the dialect. "Sorry," Nick said, switching to English. "Where's she supposed to go?"

"Why'd you even take me here?" A frantic timbre crept into Julia's voice.

"You came on your volition." Lacasse pointed around the corner. "The main entrance is on the street side."

"How am I supposed to speak to my husband?" Julia asked. "I need to get a lawyer."

"There's no shortage of them," Lacasse said. He nudged Nick along. "Let's go."

"It's okay, babe," Nick said, calling back. "Find Carlo. He'll help you get a lawyer. They'll know what to do."

And as they pushed Nick through the door, the last thing he saw was his sweet, beautiful wife standing there, looking more lost than he'd ever seen another person look.

"Go to Carlo's," he yelled.

As had been the case for the last few days, Nick's desire to free Isabella had subsided. He wanted her and the others released from *Paradise*, despite their alleged crimes, but he realized it was an unwinnable fight. After the torture room, Julia's safety and his future with her eclipsed everything else. They just needed to get on a plane. It seemed so simple, yet so increasingly difficult.

Inside the station, the long, concrete entryway had the impression of walking from an arena to a locker room. The corridor led to a gate, where a guard in a bulletproof booth processed new arrivals. As they relieved Nick of his few belongings—his wallet, watch, and beloved belt—the booth guard turned to his right and pressed a button, which emitted a loud buzz.

Nick's heart skipped a beat. His skin grew cold. The blood drained from his face.

The guard hadn't opened the gate for his entry, but to discharge the last man he wanted to see—Salvatore della Porta, who strode out with an air of supreme confidence. Nick's shock segued to the realization that della Porta had been arrested, and that understanding led to a fury since the man was now being freed. Detective Fanella, whom he'd last seen chasing after della Porta from the Palazzo's torture room, guided him through the double gate. She noticed Nick and averted her eyes. Della Porta, on the other hand, grinned at Nick victoriously.

"You were right after all," della Porta said.

Nick didn't answer.

"This wouldn't 'end well for one of us,' Mr. O'Connor. Or should I say . . . Siòr Angelo Mascari?"

A tempest fueled within, a wrath generated by centuries of wrongdoing, culminating in a present-day heat. Only after the surprise and anger of seeing his nemesis did Nick interpret the implication of della Porta's release: the man was no longer a suspect in the countess's murder.

JULIA STARED AT THE station's rear door for what seemed like an eternity, her numbed mind enveloped in the fog of disbelief. She worried Nick's sorrowful gaze would be the last image of him she'd see. And what about her? What would she do? All alone in another country, her husband arrested, with one friend in Venice—Carlo, whose allegiance was questionable, at best. At worst, the artist was loyal to the very people responsible for their predicament.

The rumble of a train entering the city drowned out nearby church bells.

She stood at the door hoping this was all a mistake—a dream perhaps, or even a sadistic practical joke. But when a cop came out for a smoke break, the man leered at her and perked his lips. Discomfort replaced her numbness. She closed her eyes briefly and shuddered her body to scatter her nerves. This was real; it was happening. She picked at her fingernails, then rubbed the rosemary tattoo on her inner left wrist, a memento she got when her grandma Rosemarie died three years earlier.

A red Vespa zoomed past her toward the bridge. Julia caught a glimpse of the driver—a girl about her age with long, fiery hair blowing behind her like a dragon's tail. Clutching her for dear life, a guy about the same age closed his eyes, strands of hair whipping his face. Unbothered by the ride and unafraid of any danger, the girl barked out words in Italian—in full control of every aspect of the situation.

Julia stared at the motorbike as the couple sped out of Venice. At first, she thought the image was a sign. But then she noticed a swarm of Vespas riding to and from the city. But it didn't matter; seeing the redhead on the bike sparked a 180 in her thinking. Her life was her own, and she was in charge.

She promised herself she would stop being the victim.

With that, she headed to the front of the building to obtain the station's contact info and visiting rules. The brisk walk refreshed her and helped adjust her psychological state. It even felt strangely nice being back in Venice. Even on the outskirts where cars were allowed and despite the unimaginable circumstances she was in, she had to admit—she loved this city.

With a clear head, she made a mental list: find a new hotel; call Carlo; get the stuff she and Nick had left behind; hire a good defense attorney; call the consulate.

Her brief confidence vanished. *Shit*. The Order had taken her purse and cell phone. She had nothing other than a melted stick of lip balm in her front jeans pocket.

VI

DRIVING A PAINTBRUSH INTO HIS INNER ear canal seemed like a reasonably good idea.

The souls screamed at Carlo in a deafening cacophony that sounded like a blend of a million cicadas, ten thousand fingernails on a blackboard, and a dozen cruise ship horns, all amplified to eleven, and all emanating within his head.

Bits of Venetian, Italian, and Latin words snaked their way through the noise: *liar, child, traitor, pagan, justice.* But he couldn't isolate their specific source in *Paradiso*.

Unable to take the pain, he burst out of the otherwise empty Great Council Room, shut the door, and dashed ten meters down the hall to an open window overlooking the courtyard. He sucked air in. As he distanced himself from the painting, the voices diminished. Watching the spattering of tourists in the courtyard below helped, as well. This wing of the Palazzo was still closed to the public due to the fire, so few visitors showed up with the main attraction inaccessible.

He cracked his knuckles and caressed his arms.

For the second time in as many days, Carlo had experienced the unbearable. As a pleasure-seeker who questioned how people enjoyed S&M, Carlo avoided pain almost religiously; he had ventured into the room to confirm that what he'd heard the previous day was real. He had made it a meter before turning around.

"Thank you for coming, Carlo."

He turned to find Bernardo strolling toward him, his buzzcut and bruiser face belying his soft eyes. The left sleeve of his navy-blue suit was fastened at the elbow in place of a missing arm.

"Shall we sit in the Great Council Room?"

Carlo took three long strides, grabbed the Bernardo's suit jacket collar, and slammed the powerfully built man against the wall. Though the Protector was twice his mass, Carlo's anger propelled a strength that made him feel like he was pushing an empty body.

"Carlo!" Bernardo unsuccessfully tried to knock his hands away. A surprising expression of genuine fear passed over the man's face. Though Carlo had his talents and attributes, physical size and strength had never been one of them. Always thin and never a good athlete, he'd been on the losing end of the handful of fights he had in his life. To be able to throw a man Bernardo's size against the wall, and to instill a sense of anxiety in him, fueled Carlo with power.

"Did you know?" Carlo spoke through gritted teeth.

"Let me go. What's gotten into you?"

Carlo released his collar but jabbed a finger into his chest.

"Thank you," Bernardo said, straightening his jacket. "You're lucky I'm not as young as I used to be."

"Damn it, Bernardo. Did you know?"

"Know what? What are you doing?"

"The voices. Could Tintoretto hear them? Could he hear *all* of them? All at the same time?"

Bernardo glanced at the Great Council Room.

"Tell me the truth," Carlo yelled, his veins pumping blood on overdrive. He'd always respected Bernardo and though he was twenty years older, considered him a friend. He never suspected Bernardo had lied to him, but now, as memories flickered through his head, the idea that the man never fibbed seemed a childish whimsy.

"It's complicated," Bernardo said.

"It's a yes or no answer."

"It's a yes *and* no answer."

"What the hell does that mean? You're giving me a worse headache than the souls."

"It means Tintoretto was five hundred years old, nearly deaf, and probably said fifty words in the last fifty years. Yes, there was a rumor—lore, even—he could hear the imprisoned, but nobody knew for sure. And we never suspected he heard them all at once. Though..." Bernardo peered at the floor.

"Though what? Look at me."

Bernardo met his eyes. "It may explain... his ears."

"What do you mean? You just said he was deaf."

"Carlo, his ears were always bloody."

Gasping at the inference, Carlo shut his eyes and pictured the one night he saw Tintoretto. Even in the presence of a five-hundred-year-old man, to say there were distractions was an understatement, but he'd never forget seeing the Renaissance master. His face appeared in Carlo's mind. Pink hair, presumably white and stained with blood, grew wild from scabbed ears. Was the man digging his own eardrums out? Or did that happen decades prior? After all, Tintoretto spoke to him directly and answered his questions. Perhaps he read lips. Or perhaps he managed to control the voices—or at least tune them out.

"I am truly sorry," Bernardo said when Carlo opened his eyes. "About many things. I never wanted this to happen—that is to say, I *did* have faith in you to be the next Painter and always thought you were the best and most competent choice. I meant nobody intended for the transition to be so... quick and..."

"Violent?" Carlo had never known the stoic Protector to be at a loss for words.

Bernardo nodded.

"You said nobody knew," Carlo said. "What about Salvatore? Did he know I'd be able to hear them all?"

"I believe his answer would be the same as mine. It seems impossible he'd know more."

"But Tintoretto could've told him. Or it could've been mentioned in some book."

Bernardo didn't have an answer.

Even if nobody in the present-day knew the truth, Carlo felt betrayed by the situation. He'd be gifted a great power, only to discover after the fact that it came with a greater curse.

"So ramming a paintbrush into my ear canal *is* a good idea," he said.

"A bit extreme, don't you think? Can you hear them now, away from *Paradiso*?"

"A little." Carlo paused, listening to the faint voices assaulting his head. "It's a whisper from here, like angry wind. I think most of them have stopped yelling."

"Let's walk, then. It's not why I summoned you here anyway."

Bernardo placed his one good hand on Carlo's back and guided him away. Carlo had always pitied his friend for losing his arm in a boating accident at twelve. He took three steps with Bernardo and halted, doing a double-take at the object strung over the shoulder of his good arm—a white leather purse.

"A new fashion statement?" Carlo asked.

"What a comedian." Bernardo handed it over. "I believe you'll recognize this."

The purse seemed familiar. When Carlo opened it and saw the Nikon DSLR inside, he knew who it belonged to.

"We'd like you to give it to Signora O'Connor."

Confusion beset Carlo. He held his hand up, trying to sort the myriad of questions swirling through his brain, but no rational answers arrived. "Okay, why do you have this? And do you mean *send* it to her? Julia's in America."

"Come, Carlo. Let's get some fresh air."

Carlo followed Bernardo through the Palazzo, down the Giants' Staircase flanked by twenty-foot-tall marble statues of Mars and Neptune, and ambled the courtyard through the trickle of tourists. Even with Carlo's thick hair, the mid-afternoon Mediterranean sun felt as though it singed his scalp.

"Are you going to answer my questions?" he asked.

"Signora O'Connor is in Venice."

Carlo stopped in his tracks. "What? Why? When?"

"Her husband was arrested by Interpol and transferred back here."

The anger boiling inside Carlo erupted. "You couldn't just let them go? After all you did to them? Is Julia under arrest?"

"No."

"Then why do you have her purse?"

"Keep your voice down."

Bernardo glanced about at the tourists eyeing their conversation. The man must've been conflicted as Chief of Security for the museum. A guard approached them, but Bernardo waved him off. Carlo couldn't care less that he was causing a scene.

The Protector cleared his throat and spoke in a whisper. "She left it behind."

Now Carlo was really pissed. "You mean you took it when you *kidnapped* her."

"Come with me."

He brought Carlo to the empty far edge of the courtyard. They stood in the shade of the large Gothic building. Bernardo continued speaking in hushed tones.

"I was not part of that decision," he said. "I am making peace. I suggest you broker that peace."

"What are you saying?"

"Nick O'Connor has been charged with very serious offenses. There are photographs, video, many witnesses. Including yourself. And . . . you are also a witness to the unfortunate circumstances Julia O'Connor was subjected to."

"So are you." Carlo pulled out a pack of cigarettes and lit one while Bernardo answered.

"And I would talk to her and even apologize, if she'd let me. She'll listen to you. There's no need for any of this to escalate. It'll quickly become an international incident that nobody will win. Except the press. And we'll all be caught in the middle."

"If Julia lets it go, keeps everything quiet, the police will drop the charges against Nick?"

"Exactly."

Rubbing his jaw, Carlo contemplated the man's proposal. Though he was furious with della Porta for what he did to Julia, Nick was a friend. Julia would be in the middle of both cases. So would he. It could drag on for years. What would be the outcome? His mentor or friend—or both— would be in prison. For Carlo's whole life, he was never one to fight. He had always found reason and middle ground. And while he'd sought to soothe arguments of his own or between two friends, those arguments never had real significance. Now, he was presented with a choice that had far-reaching consequences that would turn lives upside-down. He took a long drag. Bernardo was right. There was no reason for this to escalate on either side.

"I'll talk to Julia," he said, smoke escaping his mouth. "She's a rational person, and I think she'll accept your proposal."

"Of course she will. Take her purse. Their passports are inside. Their luggage has been brought to your flat. And as a show of good faith, their hotel bill has been paid."

Carlo smiled at the gesture and lifted Julia's purse. "So where is she?"

"Oh. I have no idea. But without a phone, identification, or a euro, I'm assuming she'll find you."

VII

UNSURPRISINGLY, THE INTERROGATION ROOM was similar to the one in Milan. Except here in Venice, they'd handcuffed Nick to the steel table. Were they that scared of him? What was he going to do? A camera watched from the ceiling corner. It all seemed over the top for minor charges, even if they occurred at a UNESCO Heritage Site. A sense of foreboding rippled through his body, and yet, he couldn't take his mind off Julia. He hoped she was safe and had found Carlo.

After sitting in the interrogation room for thirty minutes without answers, that sense of dread transitioned to boredom. With no phone, nothing to read, and unable to pace the room, the stillness became a form of torture worse than the physical kind he previously endured. The last time he remembered being so bored was when he was six, in a department store, waiting for his mother while she tried on clothes. Since then, he'd always been busy. Whether studying, coding, working, playing hockey, or spending time with Julia, friends, or family, every minute had been occupied with some activity.

The thoughts sparked another memory of boredom—but not quite monotony as much as care-free relaxation. He was Angelo, reclining in a hammock on the deck of a large ship, a hat over his eyes, a perfect autumn sun warming his tanned skin. He couldn't recall the precise memory but sensed he was in the middle of a long voyage, perhaps across the ocean, in tune with the rhythm of the waves. And while there was little to do to pass the time, the serenity of the experience soothed his present self.

Closing his eyes, Nick warily allowed himself to lapse into a regression so he could depart from his present circumstances. The vision of lying in a hammock switched to another one that always brought serenity—Isabella. Angelo pictured her smiling, in his cousin's skiff, that perfect day in the Venetian Lagoon when she agreed to run away with him.

"When we last met, you were reporting a crime," said the Italian woman's voice, her sultry inflection gift-wrapping each word.

Nick's eyes snapped open. Detective Fanella entered the room and closed the door. Angelo was annoyed to be jostled from the memory, but Nick straightened, relieved to get things moving in the present day. Julia needed him; they needed to get back to America. Back to their lives.

"Actually," Nick said, "when we last met, you were committing a crime. *Crimes*, really. How many was it? I lost track."

Fanella took the seat opposite Nick, her lips twisted in a smirk. The first time Nick met Fanella, when he and Julia had reported her camera stolen, he had found the Venetian detective to be remarkably attractive. Now, knowing she was della Porta's lackey with a badge, it was as if her inner self had slithered out and consumed her exterior. Nick wouldn't have been surprised if her skin turned to scales and she revealed a set of fangs.

Nick swallowed his repulsion and continued. "Kidnapping, assault, false imprisonment, unlawful restraint. Am I missing something? Those are illegal in Italy, right?"

"Certo. Of course. And who committed these crimes, Signor O'Connor?"

"You. Salvatore della Porta. Bernardo. The bald guy with beady eyes in the pin-striped suit. What's his name?" Nick drummed his fingers on the table. "Zotti?"

Fanella laughed, and it wasn't fake. The woman genuinely thought his comment was funny. Composing herself, she said, "A police officer and respected members of the community kidnapped you and tied you up?"

Nick pushed back from the table until the chain obstructed his motion. He spoke through clenched teeth. "You were there. Why am I wasting my time, as if you're gonna arrest your boss?"

"Signor della Porta is an acquaintance," she replied with another chuckle. "Being a member of a museum or social group is not a crime. Killing a member is."

And there it was.

"You know damn well della Porta killed the countess."

"Interesting. Can you confirm she's dead?" The detective removed a notepad from her suit jacket pocket and scribbled something in it.

Nick clammed up. Once again, he felt four moves behind and should've known she and Lacasse would've coordinated.

"Nobody has suspected she's been murdered." Fanella clicked her tongue. "Nobody but *you*. But that's not why I'm here." The detective placed a file folder on the table and opened it. She spun the paper around for Nick to see. "This is your arrest document for the murder of Jacopo Comin three nights ago."

If Nick felt four moves behind before, now he was playing a different game altogether—and didn't know the rules. Fear replaced his anger. Noticing his hands shaking, he pressed them together. He racked his brain. So, he *wasn't* being charged for the countess, but who the hell was Comin? Between all the events in the present and past, his thoughts were already muddled. Was there someone he accidentally killed? Maybe as Angelo—could they do that? Did *they* kill someone and were they trying to pin it on him? Shit, Paganelli, the old kook who gave him the blueprint. The bastards must've found Paganelli and killed him. But if so, why the fake name? Nothing made sense.

He raised his eyes from his hands to meet her gaze. "Who's Jacopo Comin?"

"The elderly gentleman you killed in cold blood, in front of nearly fifty witnesses at a reception at the Palazzo Ducale."

And then it hit him. Jacopo Comin was a man he knew almost intimately. Isabella knew him even better.

"I WANT A LAWYER." It was the first thing out of Nick's mouth, the only thing he managed since Fanella's new accusation—*charge*—of murder.

Fanella read from a sheet of paper: "In addition, willful destruction of an Italian landmark and UNESCO—"

"I want a lawyer." This time, Nick said it through closed teeth.

"We have dozens of witnesses who saw you stab Signor Comin to death before lighting the fire, assaulting a half dozen other people, and detonating the explosion in the Great Council Room."

Nick steadied his breathing in a near-fruitless attempt to control his temper. "And you let della Porta go?" he said, attempting to deflect. "I told you about the murder weapon. He bludgeoned the countess to death. That poor woman." He tsked and sighed sadly for effect.

Fanella answered without emotion. "We found that paperweight on his desk, perfectly clean, as was his office. But that also raises the question of how you knew about it. Was it an additional instance of trespassing?"

"I've never been to his office."

"You have an accomplice, then? Perhaps your wife?" Fanella flourished her hand and grinned.

If she intended to provoke a reaction, it worked. Nick's breath caught in his throat. Once again, he felt out of his element. He wasn't a fish out of water; he was a fish on Mars. Fanella already knew Nick would do anything to protect Julia—including implicating himself, if need be.

The door opened, and Lacasse strode in, his brown leather dress shoes nearly stomping the floor. "Detective Fanella. A word, please."

Fanella scowled at the Interpol agent. "Detective Lacass—"

"Outside the room, if you please."

As Fanella exited with Lacasse, Nick pondered the Frenchman's demeanor. He certainly wasn't fuming, but Nick sensed a hint of anger in his register. Assuming he'd been watching the interview, what did Fanella say that would cause another cop to barge in like that? Though unlikely, maybe Lacasse wasn't part of the Order. Whatever it was, Nick needed to think of himself and Julia. Even if Lacasse was pissed about one charge for whatever reason, all the others combined seemed like an impossible mountain to conquer. Other than exonerating Julia, it was pointless trying to explain anything or defend himself, especially to the very people who perpetrated the real crime.

A ping of hope touched Nick. He could use Italian bureaucracy and Lacasse's by-the-book nature to his advantage.

Nick shook his head. Who was he kidding? He was an amateur playing a team of pros, and he didn't know the game's rules. A sudden urge to flee overtook him. He'd run so much the past few days, and he was ready to do it again. He glanced around the room; there wasn't a single thing he could use as a weapon. Like the interrogation room in Milan, the chairs were lightweight plastic, not like the wooden chair he smashed in Fanella's office. Nick could overpower her. Lacasse would be another story, not to mention an untold number of cops and guards, plus getting out of Venice. And Julia. How would he get to her? He banished the thought of escape from his head. He may as well have been on Alcatraz. Or Mars, flopping around.

The door opened again.

As he did in Milan, Lacasse glided silently into the room. Whatever had bugged him was resolved. With her eyes narrowed, Fanella dragged her seat back with a loud scrape, dropped into it, and cleared her throat. Lacasse walked to the corner behind Nick, blending in with the walls.

"For the third time, I want a lawyer," Nick said. "And I also wanna talk to the U.S. embassy."

"The consulate in Milan has already been informed of your arrest," Fanella said.

"Then why hasn't anyone shown up or contacted me?"

She shrugged. "Ask them. In the meantime, we can appoint a public defender for—"

"No. No. No. I want Julia to find one. Not you. Please, ask her. I'll know if you don't." Getting two cops to ask his wife to find an attorney felt like a prudent move. And any paper trail would help protect Julia.

Fanella looked to Lacasse, who signaled affirmation.

"Certo," Fanella said. "But first, we have some questions."

"Good luck with—" Nick cut himself off, realizing he could play his own game. His favorite hockey move was a deke feint, whereby a player would fake out an opposing player and draw him out of position while maintaining possession of the puck. Sure, he just said he wasn't saying another word without an attorney, but knowing her questions could help him craft a strategy. He just needed to be careful with his answers. "I mean, what are your questions?"

Detective Fanella adopted a stony demeanor. "We understand you were searching for a book. What book were you looking for?"

Again, Nick felt flustered. Not only did her question seem random, della Porta himself *knew* the answer. Nick figured it couldn't hurt to play along if they already knew and cooperating could pay benefits. "The criminal record log from 1589, confirming the existence of Isabella Scalfini, which della Porta is fully aware of. He read it to me."

Lacasse's soothing French voice drifted into Nick's ears from the rear wall. "There was another book."

"No," Nick said, craning his neck around. "We found the criminal record log. Della Porta found it, really."

"What about a black book? A small, black book. One that has been lost to the ages."

Nick smiled. Lacasse may've been a pro, but his single question confirmed he was with the Order and revealed what they were digging for. And it gave Nick leverage. He'd keep that card close. "I'd like my lawyer now." He relaxed in his seat. "No more answers without one."

Fanella eyed Lacasse again. Neither detective replied.

"I could say it in Venetian or Italian." Nick stared Fanella down, then leaned back to Lacasse. "Or ninth-grade French. Contact Julia. Have her find my lawyer. Then I'll talk."

"As you wish," Lacasse said.

VIII

THOUGH IT HAD ONLY BEEN THREE DAYS since della Porta was last in his office, he felt as though it'd been months. He hadn't experienced this type of time stretch since the early days of coronavirus, when quarantine seemed like years. Venice was no stranger to plagues—they invented quarantine—but the whole city reeled in a collective heartbreaking meltdown. As the head of two organizations reliant on gatherings of people, della Porta took two bullets, but he knew the Palazzo and the Order would be fine. The former was well-funded with a sizeable endowment; the latter collected annual membership dues, plus other more lucrative sources of income.

Hundreds of other businesses, from restaurants to deliverymen, weren't so lucky. Those occupations were the lifeblood of Venice. Della Porta rarely felt pity, but to see hardworking men and women have their incomes grind to a halt overnight prompted an atypical tear. Despite the economic downtown, once the lockdown was lifted, it was truly remarkable to experience the city as it would've been before it became the tourist capital of Europe.

When Venetians poked out of their doors to find their streets empty and canals crystal clear, it created a bond that lifted the spirits of each resident, undeterred by their losses. For della Porta, it reminded him of the Order's past and potential. At the first Convocation after the lockdown, he planted the seeds of his vision in a nostalgic sermon, glorifying their past and elevating their future. At the conclusion of his speech, members approached the dais, expressing their agreement.

In the past three days, nothing in his office had changed, but Fanella and two police officers had performed a perfunctory search. With the Koons dog clean on his desk, the Persian rug no longer there, and the floor spotless, not a hair from the countess was present. And if there was, so what? She came to his office all the time.

With a satisfied grin, he gazed out the window to absorb the view of the Venetian Lagoon he cherished. Except for the motorboats, the vista wouldn't have been that different two hundred years ago. He tugged on the lapels of his favorite suit—a custom charcoal gray wool-cashmere blend. His lavender tie projected both freshness and power. With the countess out of the picture, della Porta once again at the helm, and Order members more loyal than ever, he was on his way to bridging past and present—and creating a future no man had ever dreamt of before.

The world's one veritable religion.

The door opened behind him with a knock. He never understood that move. Why knock and open the door at the same time? Clearly, he'd know if someone entered the room. Then again, he hadn't heard the countess enter his office that fateful night. Tonight, though, he expected his visitor: his always punctual, always faithful, always reliable Head of Security for the Palazzo and Enforcer of the Charge, the chief Protector of the Order.

"Come in, Bernardo, my friend," della Porta said in Italian without turning. "Please, close the door." He watched his chief Protector follow his instruction in the window's reflection. "Did you know the Casinò di Venezia is the first and oldest public casino in the world?"

"I knew it was old, but I never knew it was the oldest. Is it really true?"

Della Porta faced his friend. Bernardo wore his standard navy-blue suit, white shirt, and black tie that people often mistook for a security guard uniform. "Do you think I'd state such a claim if it weren't? Please, sit."

As Bernardo adjusted his large frame on the brown leather Chesterfield sofa—the last piece of furniture to be graced by the countess's regal ass—he appeared flustered. "No, signore. I didn't mean—"

"Relax, my friend." Della Porta headed to the bar and poured two glasses of a 2018 Valpolicella he'd decanted earlier. The fresh and fruity red was the perfect choice for new beginnings. "I know you weren't questioning the veracity of my statement but rhetorically, given the implausible nature of the claim, since gambling dates back thousands of years. The casino used to be private, of course. Owned by the Order, as you know. In 1638, they made the wise decision to open it to the public. Sometimes to attain money and power, you need to take a gamble. But when you're the house, you make the odds." He handed Bernardo a glass of wine and took the armchair opposite him. "I'm assuming Carlo agreed?"

"You should know, signore, Zotti—"

"Besides the fact that he has something of mine, I honestly don't care what Zotti thinks. Did Carlo agree or not?"

Bernardo cleared his throat. "Yes. He'll speak to Signora O'Connor. I expect they'll take our offer."

"Why wouldn't they? It's as generous an offer as they'll get." Della Porta took a sip, letting the flavor of the grapes caress his tongue. "Despite that American pest wreaking havoc and injuring four Protectors."

Bernardo shifted in his seat and wiped his brow. "They'll recover. The incident is over. Even if he takes the deal, O'Connor will spend the rest of his days in prison or be extradited to the U.S."

"Other than his knowledge—which we'll get soon enough—O'Connor is a barnacle. We currently have twelve Protectors. I want you to begin recruiting more from our ranks. We'll be adding to our membership, and I expect you to quadruple the Protectors in sixty days."

"Quadruple?"

"To start. The Order is going to achieve great things. And you're in an ideal spot, my friend."

Bernardo's lips curled up to an almost smile. "Thank you, Exalted Master. I'll review membership today and craft a plan." He glanced at his watch. "Signor Zotti—"

"I told you, Bernardo, I do not care about him."

Without so much as a knock, the door opened. A tall, bald man in a brown double-breasted pin-striped suit waltzed in. Davide Zotti. The man himself. "Do not care about whom?" he asked. Without permission, he strode in and sat next to Bernardo. As usual, the man's lack of etiquette was outshone by his lack of fashion sense.

Bernardo offered his open palm and a light shrug to della Porta, indicating this is what he'd been trying to say.

"Nick O'Connor," della Porta said flatly. He reminded himself to start locking his door.

Zotti raised an eyebrow and cocked his shiny head. "Why wouldn't you care about a man who committed major crimes against the Order? Congratulations on your exoneration, by the way."

Della Porta noted Zotti didn't bother to hide the sarcasm behind his smirk. "I do not need to explain myself to you, Davide."

"No, I suspect your role as Exalted Master has been reinstated."

"Correct. So please return what belongs to me." Della Porta held his hand out.

"It belongs to the Order." Zotti loosened his tie and removed the Exalted Master's pendant from beneath his shirt. But he didn't hand it over. "Of course, nobody has seen the countess nor heard from her."

"What are you implying?" Della Porta's veins tightened. Zotti positioned himself to be a problem—a problem he couldn't dispose of as easily as he did the countess. One councilmember out of five was suspicious enough. As she'd been a frequent world traveler, he could milk the old bag's absence until he found a way to pin her murder on O'Connor. Zotti, on the other hand, rarely left the city and was exceedingly social, butting his bald head and beady eyes into every party and function he could find. And a second councilmember disappearing may as well be a guilty plea in the eyes of the others.

"I'm stating that our senior councilmember knows the rules." Zotti eyed their wine glasses. "Are you going to leave me sitting dry?"

Bernardo rose for the bar. "Allow me," he said.

Della Porta narrowed his eyes and adjusted his glasses. As transparent as it was, he respected Zotti's cover tactic. "*I* know the rules. And this is the same as in every other facet of business or life. Interim means an intervening time. Provisional. Until the norm has returned. As you can see, I have. I am the duly elected Exalted Master. Now, the pendant."

"Of course. . . Exalted Master. That's why I'm here." Zotti handed the necklace to della Porta, who took it, feeling as if he reunited with a lost child.

Bestowed upon each Exalted Master, the golden pendant was carved with a taijitu, more commonly known as a yin-yang symbol. The black dot was replaced with an amethyst and the white one with a jade. Surrounding the symbol were seven sunrays. Della Porta kissed the pendant, then placed the chain around his neck.

"There was also something I wanted to ask you," Zotti said. He gestured his thanks for the wine from Bernardo, who sat back down.

"Then ask, Davide. Out with it." Della Porta crossed his legs and splayed his arm over the chair back.

"The night in the interrogation chamber, you asked Signor O'Connor about a book. A black book. What book is this, and why would an American have knowledge of it?"

Della Porta didn't hesitate in his response. "A book containing secrets that could propel the Order to heights never seen."

Not surprisingly, Zotti's eyes widened, and his eyebrows perked up. "Go on."

"As you know, Nick O'Connor is the soul mate of a prisoner in *Paradiso*. In a past life, he was a swordsman from the late 1500s who murdered a senior councilmember of the Order, a confidante of the doge. That councilmember was Renzo Scalfini."

"I've never heard that name," Zotti said.

"Nor would you. But that he was so trusted by the leader of the Republic shows you his degree of influence. I believe you've heard whispers of a book, which was in Scalfini's possession, given to him by the doge himself, to protect. A book that definitively connects the Order to the Church."

Both Zotti and Bernardo were rapt with attention, like children on their first day of school.

"Connects in what way?" Zotti asked.

Della Porta grinned. Though the conversation was happening sooner than expected, it was so far going as he anticipated; he intended to tell Zotti first. A benefit—the *single* benefit of incarceration is time. Time to think. Without life's numerous distractions, della Porta was afforded a wealth of hours to formulate a strategy. When he revealed his plans to the countess, he didn't have time to calculate her reaction. In short, he misjudged her. It was a mistake he wouldn't make again. Zotti was infinitely more ambitious than the countess—and thirty years younger. And he'd appreciate being brought in early.

Of everyone on the Council of the Sun Crystal, Zotti would be the most likely to challenge della Porta. So della Porta needed to flip that script and make him a useful ally, one who had notable business and political connections throughout Europe.

It was time for Bernardo to be brought up to speed, as well. He was more conservative, but he was faithful to della Porta, and his presence could subconsciously help persuade Zotti. If della Porta could recruit Zotti, he'd soon have the whole council behind him; the mayor and Trevisan wouldn't refuse. From there, it would be a matter of convincing the councils in Madrid and Paris. And with Bernardo as his loyal general, they'd be unstoppable.

To attain power, you need to take a gamble.

Della Porta released three quick exhalations to steel his nerves. "My friends, it's time for the Order to claim its rightful place"—he captured their gazes—"as the world's one veritable religion. *Veritism.*"

They had identical reactions, gawking at della Porta before turning to each other. Surely contemplating the idea and what it meant for the Order—what it meant for *them*—Bernardo gazed at the floor while Zotti regarded the ceiling and whistled.

The single sentence, the seed of a plan, may have been simple in its construct—but imbued with so massive a power that if successful, it would trigger world-changing consequences. It was an alluring proposition. Who could decline such promise? Della Porta basked in the glow of the dominion he'd govern. Everyone the world over would venerate him. Even dissenters wouldn't be able to deny the glory of the achievement.

And when he finished explaining how they'd become the dominant faith and how the doge's book would help them achieve that lofty goal, Zotti reacted as predicted. With dancing eyes, the man clapped, stood, and shook della Porta's hand. Bernardo sat on the couch with a rare smile.

When you're the house, della Porta thought, *you make the odds. For any game.*

IX

CARLO'S LOFT WAS SITUATED IN THE CORNER of a quiet, enclosed square. Two boys and two girls, all about six or seven, kicked a blue rubber ball around. On the far side sat a lonely restaurant with three empty outdoor tables, enticing Julia's rumbling stomach.

She sat hugging her knees with her back pressed against Carlo's door, picking at her fingernails. She refused to cry. She didn't want to pity herself. She didn't want pity from anyone. She wanted to *fight*. She was angry and had every right to be.

"God, this sucks."

Leaning over to Carlo's small herb garden on his tiny stoop, she plucked a basil leaf and inhaled the scent. The freshness of the herb reinvigorated her senses. Crushed between her fingertips, the oils released a stronger aroma that reminded her of what she loved most about Italy and the Mediterranean—a zest for life. That zest was part of her *and* her marriage. She rubbed her rosemary tattoo. She and Nick would get back to a life worth living. They just needed a couple of allies and wins on the books.

A sweet mewl brought her attention to a striped, gray tabby. At first, she thought it was a stray, but then she noticed the collar.

"Hello, Olivia," she said, reading the tag. "Aren't you a sweet girl? I wish I had something for you."

The cat lay next to her and purred, so Julia scratched it behind its ears.

If only she had her phone to research lawyers. Or a camera to capture the tableau of the square. Or a bag of chips. But with no money or phone, all she could do was wait, pet a cat, and think.

The ball bounced over to her. It startled the tabby away but brought a young girl skipping over. Julia snagged the ball and handed it to her.

"Grazie, signora," the girl said with a singsong voice. Her toothless smile had Julia wishing for her camera more than ever.

"Prego." Julia gave herself a gold medal for completing a full Italian conversation with a child, who ran back to her friends. The game brought her attention to the scene's backdrop—the restaurant. Guided by her grumbling stomach, she held her head high, circumvented the soccer game, and approached a brunette about her age wiping down the outdoor tables.

"Scusa," Julia said. "Do you speak English?"

"A little," the waitress replied without looking up. She seemed annoyed by Julia's intrusion, as if knowing Julia had no intention of being a customer—at least not a paying one.

"Sorry to bother you. Do you know Carlo Zuccaro? He lives over there." Julia pointed to Carlo's building.

At Carlo's name, the waitress gave Julia her attention. "Sì, certo. He eat here many time."

Julia smiled with relief. "Oh, good. Well, I'm his friend, and. . ." She didn't know why she was so nervous, but she had trouble stringing her sentence together, perhaps because she'd never asked such a thing. "Do you think I could order some food, and when he gets here, he'll pay for it?" She raised her open palms. "I lost my purse, my wallet, everything."

The waitress's English wasn't the best, but she clearly understood Julia's predicament. Empathy shone in her eyes. "Un momento." She went back to the restaurant door, calling out, "Papà," as she entered.

Julia smiled, unable to resist crossing her fingers. At this point, she'd take a mint.

A few minutes later, the waitress returned with a small bundle wrapped in takeout paper. "Prego," she said, handing it over to Julia.

"Grazie, grazie, thank you so much," Julia said, beaming. She took the package, truly grateful. "I'll pay you when Carlo gets here."

"No need. Please sit, eat." The waitress gestured to one of the tables.

"That's okay. I don't want to bother you any further. Grazie mille."

With another smile and wave, Julia went back to Carlo's stoop. She unwrapped the package to find a small roll with prosciutto—which she devoured in five bites. Meager, but the sandwich filled her belly. And obtaining it raised her confidence.

Finally, after twenty more minutes of nibbling on basil and oregano, she saw him striding into the square from an alley, wearing a black t-shirt, black jeans, and his black leather Converse All Stars. The accessory slung over his shoulder didn't thrill her: a Palazzo Ducale tote bag. With his eyes glued to the ground, Carlo looked as angry as she felt. His oval face, without a hint of facial hair, was red and pinched in a tight scowl beneath his mop of dark hair. But when he lifted his gaze and saw her, his mouth broke into a wide smile.

She popped to her feet. They didn't say a word—just exchanged the warmest and longest hug she'd experienced in ages. Other than holding her husband's hand, the last physical contact she had was Nick spooning her at the hotel the night they fled Venice. She wished she didn't push his arm away. Feeling a little uncomfortable, she broke free of Carlo's hold.

"I thought I'd never see you again." He kissed both of her cheeks.

"Tell me about it. At least not in Venice."

Carlo gazed at Julia. His attentive, light hazel eyes conveyed a mix of ecstasy and warmth. While it was comforting to have a friend, it also felt over the top. It had only been two days since they last saw each other. Though, considering Carlo had been helping Nick and Julia escape from a torture room, maybe an over-the-top reaction was called for. Still, he should've been more shocked.

"Come inside. You must be exhausted. Are you thirsty? Hungry?"

"Thanks. Yeah, all the above."

"Where are your suitcases?" he asked while inserting his key and scanning the vicinity. He rolled his front door open.

"What do you mean? You know we didn't have them." She followed him inside. "Wait, were you expect—"

She cut herself off. Just inside his loft, she spotted her and Nick's suitcases, along with Nick's backpack.

"What the fuck?"

"Julia, I—"

"You need to explain this. Now."

"I can. I can explain."

"Now!"

Carlo placed his hand on the small of Julia's back. She shimmied away, in no mood for his gigolo routine. An intense need to run assailed her. She wanted to take her bags and get the hell out of there. In fact, she didn't even need her stuff.

"Tell me, Carlo. Why are our bags here? If you don't answer in five seconds, I'm taking them, and then you're *really* never seeing me again."

"Okay, okay, sì. Let's sit."

Julia threw her hands up. Emotions that had been simmering beneath the surface of reason began to bubble over. "Forget it." She grabbed the carry-on.

"Bernardo brought them here," Carlo said. "I thought they'd be outside."

Julia released the handle. Her desire to leave was split by wanting to know. Or did she even care? She could take her bags and leave this place. Except . . . *Nick*. Again, she felt so far from home. Here was a chance for a getaway. But she couldn't abandon Nick, even after what he did; it wasn't his fault. She collapsed on her carry-on. The tears flowed, stinging the raw skin around her eyes. The anguish erupted. She stifled a wail with her fist, then pounded the bag.

Out of the corner of her watery eye, she noticed Carlo reach for her, but he stopped. At least the guy was learning. She wiped her tears, composed herself, and stood.

Without a word, he pulled her white leather purse out of the tote bag and handed it to her.

A sensation she hadn't felt in days nudged her heart: optimism. Rifling through her purse, she found her camera, both passports, her phone, and her wallet. She figured their belongings were searched, but other than the invasion of privacy, it didn't matter—they had nothing to hide. Chuckling, she hadn't even realized she couldn't escape before. But now, with everything she needed, she could've, in theory, been on the next plane to Boston.

With a final wipe of her eye, she said, "Why? Why'd they bring everything? And don't give me some crap story that they're just being nice. They had Nick arrested."

"I thought you'd be happy."

"Fuck happy, Carlo. They stole my purse, kidnapped me, and almost killed me. None of this ever should've happened. This was supposed to be a vacation. Now answer the question."

"Can we sit?"

About to scream until she lost her voice, Julia caught herself. Her legs ached. Her stomach growled. Her tongue felt like sandpaper covered in cotton balls. "Fine. And I'd love a glass of water."

The moment he turned, Julia unbuttoned her jeans and wiggled the blueprint out of them, doing it quickly, but careful not to rip the fragile parchment. Her skin breathed again. Though Nick thought the document could be used as evidence against him, she felt otherwise. If anything, just the fact that he obtained it could somehow validate his claims. She hid the document in the garment bag's side pocket, then made her way through the loft's long studio area and living room to the open floorplan kitchen.

Sitting at Carlo's butcher block counter table, Julia scrolled through her phone, overwhelmed by the volume of messages. At least she had 8% battery life left. She deleted as much spam as she could but stopped on an email from Lionel Benton, the English art critic and conspiracy theorist who provided Julia with valuable information about Tintoretto and the Order's black market art dealings.

"Ah, here we are," Carlo said before she opened the message.

She put the phone away and nearly salivated at the platter of cheese, charcuterie, and bread he set before her, along with an espresso and water.

The coffee's rich, nutty essence may have been the best thing that had ever graced her taste buds. Coupled with the energizing caffeine, its warmth coated her internally and soothed her restless spirit. After she devoured the carbs and protein, she finally looked at her friend. He sat across from her with a glint in his eyes. She had issues with Carlo, but his kindness was a refreshing break from everybody else she'd dealt with recently, and more importantly—he'd saved hers and Nick's lives.

"Thank you, Carlo. For my stuff, too. But this food doesn't let you off the hook. You owe me an explanation."

Nodding, Carlo said, "They'll drop the charges—"

"What?!" Julia couldn't contain her excitement.

He held up his hand and explained what Bernardo had told him. At first blush, each side letting it go was a tempting proposition. But could she trust them? And was it even a fair deal? The answer to the first question arrived in a half-second. Though the proposal came via Carlo and Bernardo, it really came from della Porta. No way could she trust them. And that was the answer to the second question. Vandalism, even of a UNESCO site, did not equate to kidnapping or attempted murder. Sure, these guys had the upper hand, but they were obviously nervous; otherwise, they wouldn't have proposed a deal. One thing she was always good at, especially as a journalist, was causing a fuss. She could bring this to the press. In fact, they probably knew she used to be a reporter.

Julia felt Carlo's regard as she nibbled on a chunk of bread.

"A court case can drag on for years, for each charge," he said. "And there are photos, video evidence."

"What about *your* evidence?" She tossed the bread onto the plate. "You're a witness."

He placed his palm over his heart. "Julia, I'm in the middle."

"If you're in the middle, you're on the wrong side. You don't have to be, Carlo. You know the truth."

"You're right. That's why I advise you to move on. It's not worth it."

She slammed the table. "Justice is always worth it. Always."

Carlo's nostrils flared. Though she'd known him a short time, she sensed he understood she wasn't letting it go. That said, she still wasn't sure of his loyalties. He may not have been in bed with the Order, but he shared a room with them. But *that* said, she had no one else to turn to, and Carlo's proximity to della Porta could be an asset.

"Do you know any lawyers?" she asked. "Criminal defense?"

"Julia. . ." He lit a cigarette, this time without bothering to ask if she'd mind. With a puff of smoke, he said, "Yes." As he powered on his laptop a few moments later, he explained, "A friend had some trouble a few years back. He sold gondola ride tickets. But there was no gondola."

"You're friends with a guy who scammed tourists?"

"It was a terrible thing he did, and we are not friends now. The important thing is this attorney, how do you say, helped him to be innocent."

Clicking on the staff page of a law firm website, he scrolled down through photos until he stopped on one attorney: a mid-thirties woman with heavy birthmarks on her cheeks, her brown hair in a bun, tortoise-shell glasses resting on her nose.

X

THE DINNER OF CALF'S LIVER AND ONIONS served with polenta blew Nick away. They even gave him a glass of red wine. He wasn't sure if this was typical for an Italian prison or if he was still getting special treatment, but he decided not to rock the boat. If they wanted to butter him up, they could try. He'd take the butter. They could have his dirty dish. If there was one thing Wade taught him from extensive travel and camping trips, it was this: eat when you can, sleep when you can, shit when you can. Nick chuckled. What are older brothers for?

A week earlier, Nick wouldn't have touched liver. But at the first whiff of the gaminess, he knew *fegato alla veneziana* had been a common Venetian dish for centuries. He savored every bite, mystified it didn't spark a flashback. Though he was relieved he hadn't had one since Milan, a part of him was concerned. Not *concerned*, but certainly curious. Nick assumed returning to Venice would've brought Angelo out in an unstoppable flood. His past life had eaten a similar variation of this dish at his family's dining table centuries ago, but it ended there—like knowledge of a memory, rather than retaining the memory itself.

He tapped his plastic knife on the plastic tray, then rotated his wrist and jabbed his arm out, as if the utensil was a rapier. The soreness in his arm and lat persisted, but Nick smiled, knowing he hadn't lost any technique. Yet, like the food, the movement did nothing to trigger a regression. He pondered if he'd succeeded in burying his former self. Or perhaps the thick police station walls acted as a suppressor. Or maybe Angelo was still in his brain, lurking, waiting, strategizing a plan of attack.

With no answer and his mind and body firmly planted in the present, his thoughts zipped to Julia. He hoped she'd found Carlo and had a good dinner herself. Remembering she didn't have any money, his stomach plummeted. He couldn't believe he'd forgotten to give her his wallet before they confiscated it. He made a mental note to ask the police to hand his belongings—a grand total of a watch and wallet—to Julia. At least she could use his credit cards. There'd be no point not to now.

Shortly after Nick finished his meal, a lanky guard took the tray, refusing to answer questions. The quiet of the jail gnawed at him; they'd stuck him in a cell in a hall with zero neighbors. Needing to move, Nick paced the floor. Twenty steps into what was going to be a very long night, Nick asked the guard for a pen and a piece of paper. The cop hesitated, but Nick claimed it was for a confession. He filled both sides of the page with a letter to Julia. He'd never written her a love letter before and was amazed at how the words flowed out.

"I need a second page," he called without looking up.

"You have a visitor," the guard replied.

Nick folded the paper and hid it under his mattress. No doubt his visitor would question him again, now that his hunger was satiated and he had some wine in him. Would it be Fanella? A prosecutor? Someone new from the Order?

To his surprise and overwhelming joy, a blonde-haired beauty he knew and loved speed-walked toward his cell with an expression forged of elation and apprehension. Even in the moment, he couldn't help but find her gorgeous. And those eyes—those emerald eyes were always imbued with tenderness. When Julia looked at something or someone, it was as if nothing else in the world existed.

Nick clasped his wife's hands through the bars. He kissed them, then kissed her lips and hugged her as best he could. Her warmth blanketed him, despite the cold steel separating them, pressing against their skin. He'd never been so happy to see her, and he could tell, she felt the same.

"I found a lawyer," she said. "And there's so much more."

"I've missed you so much." Nick let his eyes dampen.

"I know, me too," she said through tears. "And it's only been a few hours, but we need to talk fast."

He kissed her again and wiped her cheeks.

"Honey, they're giving us ten minutes."

"That's it? Can we sit somewhere?"

Julia shrugged.

Releasing her, Nick turned to the guard and asked the request in Venetian.

"No." From ten feet away, the guard clicked his tongue and shook his head, as if Nick should've known.

"It doesn't matter," Nick said. "We have nothing to hide. Are you hungry? Maybe he'll get you something."

Julia composed herself and got serious. "I'm all set. Before anything, I need to know. How—how are you feeling? Are you . . . you know, still Nick?"

He knitted his brows. "I've always been Nick, babe. And I always will be. I feel fine, actually. I haven't even thought about the past." Nick itched his beard growth. He didn't know why he lied. "It's surprising, to be honest. I figured returning to Venice would bring a tsunami of memories. It could be these walls. Maybe it's a good thing I'm in this cell."

"It'd be a good thing if we were landing in Boston right now."

Taking her hands again, Nick gazed into her eyes. He choked up a bit, feeling as full of emotion as he did when he proposed to her four and a half years ago. "Jules, I want you to go home—"

"It's not happening, honey."

"Please. I know you wanna help, and that's how you can. By giving me the peace of mind to know you're safe."

Julia weighed his request. "I can't. Honestly, I—I don't even want to."

Nick lowered his head and wiped his eyes. He knew she wouldn't leave, but the stress of her safety was wearing him down. She wouldn't even be safe in police custody. "Can you at least register with the U.S. embassy? You can do that."

"They said they told them—"

"I don't trust them for a second. Do it yourself. Please. And don't go out at a night."

"That, I can do. It'll get expensive, but I'll order in every night."

"You know I don't give a shit about the money. Grab my wallet before you leave. And tip as little as you want."

Julia offered a light titter. She cleared her throat and shook her head. "God, this whole thing is so crazy. I feel like when we're old and retired—"

"Traveling the world taking pictures?"

She choked up, then awkwardly hugged him again.

"Everywhere but Italy, of course," Nick said. "What were you gonna say?"

She released her hold. "Oh, just that I think we're gonna wonder if all this ever happened. It's so surreal."

"You're telling me. As much as I wish we could hug each other this whole time, we probably have five minutes now. Did you find Carlo?"

"Yeah, he helped me find a lawyer."

"That's fantastic. Tell Carlo I said grazie."

A thought hit Nick. It wasn't ideal, and he felt like he might regret his words later, but if Julia's safety was paramount, then she needed someone to watch over her. He ran the calculations of different outcomes in his head. On the one hand, she could be alone in a hotel room. What would stop the Order from bribing a manager to access Julia's room? For all he knew, hotel staff could be Order members. On the other hand, there was someone he wasn't sure he could trust, someone who was *definitely* with the Order, someone who checked out his wife in front of him... "Actually," he said, "stay with Carlo"... someone who seemed to genuinely care about her well-being.

Julia cocked her head and bit her lip. "Sure that's the best idea?"

"Definitely not. I don't know who he has allegiance to. And he's got a serious case of gigoloitis—"

"Inflammation of the gigolo?"

"It's a painful condition." Nick laughed. "But I know he wouldn't let anything happen to you. *That's* what's key. Just take the couch, eh?"

"I will." She glanced at the guard. "Listen, there's something else—"

"I have something else, too. There's a new charge."

"What?"

"Don't worry, it's more B.S."

"What's the charge, Nick?"

He ran his fingers on his stubble. There was no point in beating around the bush. "They're saying I killed someone." He raised his hand to preempt her shock. "But it's ridiculous. It's literally impossible."

Julia eyed him between stunted breaths, attempting to read his expression. "That could explain my news. Carlo met with Bernardo. They'll drop the charges against you if I forget everything they did. But they never mentioned a murder charge."

Alarm bells clanged in Nick's head. He eyed the guard again, who pretended to be minding his own business. Either way, what was the guy going to do, tell della Porta something he already knew? "We're not seeing their whole strategy. Seems like a huge gambit. They'd know you'd speak to me at some point, especially with an attorney involved."

"I agree, but you know how secretive they are. Or maybe they want to get the ball rolling with the smaller charges. They want to avoid an international incident."

"True. What did you say?"

"I said no fucking way."

He smirked. "That explains the lawyer."

"I never trusted them for a second either. And now we know. They'd drop all the small stuff, but you'd be in jail for decades for a bogus murder."

Nick deliberated Julia's words—and the bigger picture. Everything clicked. Julia still couldn't bring herself to believe that Tintoretto had been alive, and it didn't matter because no court would believe it either. Della Porta could just go to a morgue, find the oldest John Doe there, and pin it on Nick. No, that was far too easy. It wasn't that they wanted him in jail for decades—they wanted him out of the way *forever*. He met Julia's eye. "Take the offer."

"Um, what? Did you just hear what I said?"

"The murder charge is a bluff. They can't possibly prove it."

"They can fake the evidence."

"Not when they're claiming the victim's name is Jacopo Comin."

"Due minuti," the guard called.

"Two minutes," Nick said to Julia. "Listen, babe, I *did* kill him—"

"What?" Her head quivered, like a cheetah shaking off water.

He eyed the guard, whom Nick didn't doubt understood English and was listening to every word. He wanted to explain more about his innocence, but also knew that with Julia's journalism background and inquisitive nature, she was more than capable of discovering it on her own. "There's more, much more. Don't forget that name. *Jacopo Comin*. Remember a place I said there was something kooky? We had stopped somewhere before I threw something away?"

Julia swallowed, then blinked her eyes slowly to indicate a yes.

Nick placed a finger on her lips. "If I'm taken, find. . ." Nick mouthed the next word: 'Paganelli.'

She squinted, trying to piece it together.

He took her forearm and traced the letters for 'P' and then 'old man' on her skin. He yearned to touch her whole body but kept his attention on her arm. She nodded her understanding of what he wrote. He brought her ear close and whispered as quietly as he could: "Either on Poveglia Island or an abandoned kosher butcher shop. They want Renzo's book. Renzo's black book."

Julia pulled back. She clearly heard but didn't comprehend what he was talking about or why he was telling her.

"Don't forget. Repeat what I said to yourself."

"I got it, honey. I was a journalist, remember? Why are you telling me?"

Nick drew in a ragged breath. The puzzle pieces that had clicked a moment earlier presented themselves as a complete picture in vivid, HD clarity. The Order didn't need to sentence all their adversaries to *Paradise* to rid them for eternity. For some, there was a far simpler solution. Della Porta could do the math as easily as anyone—this was Nick's seventh and final life. They could lock him up and pry Angelo's information out of him until they got what they wanted. And then what?

"*Adrift, lost at sea,*" he sang in a mumbled whisper. "*Baby, you're my world. The only girl for me.*"

"What are you doing, Nick? Talk to me."

He couldn't bring himself to meet her gaze. "I think they'll kill me."

"What!?"

"Un minuto," the guard called with an all-too gleeful grin.

Julia blanched. "But we have a lawyer. We'll get outta here."

"I hope so, Jules. Of course I do. I just wanna be prepared."

Tears cascaded from her eyes again. The sight had Nick crying a moment later. But talking about his imminent death wasn't the reason. If anything, it felt like relief. He was actually content. Julia was on the opposite end of the spectrum—and that's what really got him. That, and the thought that he'd never see her again. What would she do? He hoped she'd move on and find happiness. Nick brushed these notions aside; the clock was ticking. "Finish my work. You'll have help."

"Finito," the guard said, walking over. "Time to go, signora." He prodded her away from the bars.

Nick held her warm hand until their fingertips grazed each other's.

"I'm gonna finish my own work and get you out of here," she said through the tears. "I'll be back with our lawyer."

"I know you will. I love you so much."

"I love you, you idiot."

A smile twitched Nick's mouth. "Get my wallet. My watch, too," he said as she was escorted away. "Give her my things," he called to the guard.

Without turning, the guard flicked his hand up in response.

"Look up Jacopo Comin!" Nick shouted to Julia. They were the last words he managed before she was led through the gate.

XI

CARLO PACED THE LENGTH OF HIS STUDIO area in his loft, running his hands through his hair, wanting to punch through every painting. He mustered every ounce of rational energy to resist doing so. Julia would be back soon, so he needed to relax, but his conversation with della Porta incensed his veins.

Calm yourself.

His inner voice had been louder lately. And he listened to it. He stopped pacing, closed his eyes, and stretched his entire body—each limb, each toe, each finger. The motion worked. He was still riled up, so he poured himself a glass of wine and sat on a stool at the kitchen table. The sangiovese was a bit sharp, but he let it rest on his tongue to accelerate the alcohol's effect. With his steam ratcheted down a notch, he thought back to his meeting with della Porta.

After Julia left to see Nick, Carlo canceled a date with Jordan and used the opportunity to run over to his once-father figure. Banging on the door unannounced, della Porta answered in a suit, as if he'd just returned home, yet he held a bag of birdseed. He extended his free hand for an embrace, but Carlo avoided his arms and barged into the flat he called home for six years as a teenager. He had fond memories of the spacious four-bedroom, but now it may as well have been a sterile hotel suite.

"I understand you're angry at me, son," della Porta said, closing the door.

The word 'son' enraged Carlo. He was in della Porta's face with a speed that surprised himself—and clearly della Porta more so. The fear was evident in the man's eyes. Carlo pointed a finger at him. "Don't you call me that. Not ever. I am *not* your son."

"I'm sorry, Carlo. It comes out naturally to me." Della Porta's anxiety was palpable, but he maintained control. "Have a seat. Would you like a drink?" He remained standing at the door, seemingly waiting for Carlo to do something.

Carlo backed off but didn't sit.

Tori Amos's *Past the Mission* coated the room through brass Bang & Olufsen Beolab pillar speakers that glorified every note of each instrument as if it were played live.

Two sun conures flew over to della Porta and landed on his hand. The orange, yellow, and green parakeets were beloved pets; Carlo had to admit he admired how the older man doted over them.

As della Porta returned the songbirds to their open-air wooden cage and fed them, Carlo gazed about the flat. Recessed lighting illuminated dark woods and leather furniture. Pre-modern paintings, all worth more than anything he'd created, decorated the walls. The place was immaculate and sophisticated—a mini-museum, designed more to be a showpiece than for comfort. Other than the birds and music, it was cold, uninviting, and everything seemed to be cast in a different light than what he'd remembered. Everything. Not just the décor but his entire upbringing since della Porta had entered his life seventeen years ago. When Carlo attended university—for which della Porta secured a scholarship—in addition to art, culture, and history, della Porta had insisted Carlo take an online pre-law class at Oxford in English, as well as one from the University of Rome. Della Porta said it was good knowledge to have and could be useful. Then there were the frequent meals, the prominent guests who'd join them, and della Porta's not-so-subtle habit of pointing out Carlo's need for manners.

The music ended, and della Porta tapped on his mobile.

"Have you heard the new Billie Eilish song? It's stunning, so powerful. Their styles are vastly different, but her raw talent reminds me of Tori Amos—"

Carlo shot his hand out as if halting oncoming traffic. For a man who relished the past, della Porta was remarkably current, but Carlo didn't want to hear any music. He didn't want to hear della Porta's voice. He didn't want to hear *anything*.

He stroked his jaw and widened his eyes as he scrutinized the flat. There were also the constant links to the past, as evident in the 16th-century reproduction wallpaper in the living room. The orblike chandelier over the oak dining table looked like a large Sun Crystal that had illuminated the Great Council Room. Della Porta's frequent mentions of light and lighting—how it would affect art now made sense. When Carlo lived with della Porta, there were arguments and disagreements, but they were always borne from typical teenage angst, or, more likely, Carlo's reaction to the traumatic childhood event of losing his father to death and his mother to a mental breakdown. In truth, he had been blessed that della Porta took him in.

But now, it all clicked together: this entire time . . . his so-called guardian had been grooming him for the Order.

He peered at della Porta's bedroom door, which even now was closed. He snuck in once as a teenager. Every drawer and closet door had been locked. He'd mock della Porta's obsession with secrecy, blaming it on the man's OCD and eccentricities. But it was all part of the plan—a plan in motion. And not just to make him a member of the Order, but to be their Painter. Carlo thought back to the night he met the countess.

'*You're an integral piece of a picture still being sketched,*' della Porta had said. '*Despite all your playing around, your destiny promises great things.*'

At the time, Carlo chalked up his hyperbolic art metaphors to the atmosphere of the mayor's party and the introduction to the countess. The countess. His father. Paganelli, his father's killer. Nick. Nick was desperate and not in his right mind, but Carlo had nagging questions about his friend, too.

"Have a seat, Carlo. Wine?"

"I don't want any wine." Carlo faced della Porta with a constricted gaze. "I want answers."

A loud knock on Carlo's door snapped him back to the present in his own flat. He hurried over and opened it to find Julia. The late evening humidity had teased her hair, and her face was flushed. When she raised her red eyes to look at him, she looked more despondent than ever.

XII

STARING AT HIS PRISON CELL CEILING IMBUED a strange sense of calm in Nick. Besides discussing his imminent death with his wife and being pissed at himself for forgetting to give her the letter, he felt at peace. He didn't *want* to feel at peace. He wanted to dig through the wall, free Isabella and the other souls, grab Julia, and jet back to Boston. There was no way he could be with Isabella, but he could certainly ease her suffering—and Julia's. But he didn't budge from the cot. He didn't lift a finger. It wasn't that he didn't have the fight or the energy. Sure, he was tired, but that wasn't it. Maybe after all that had happened in all his lives, he was *prepared* for his next— and final—chapter.

He smiled with affection at this notion, but his lips morphed into a sneer, overtaken by an inner chuckle that grew so maniacal, he couldn't help but laugh out loud. Whether this reaction was Angelo's or Nick's didn't matter. He cackled at his absurd thoughts of being ready for death. In reality, in this, his seventh and ultimate life, his soul wasn't remotely ready to go.

"Is something funny, Signor O'Connor?" said a gruff voice with a light Italian accent.

Nick shot up from the cot to find a heavyset man in his late fifties at the cell bars, flanked by two guards. With his beige linen suit, receding hair pulled into a ponytail, gray goatee, and brown briefcase, the man could've played a sort of opera singer-slash-colonial businessman.

"Depends on your point of view," Nick answered. "You are?"

The stranger pushed his small, round glasses up his fleshy nose. "Avvocato Alberico Gulotta," he said with a confident air, as if he were world famous.

Nick studied the man, curious if they'd met. There was no way; Nick would've remembered him. He shrugged.

"Signore, I am your attorney."

"Oh, sorry. She didn't tell me your name. I wasn't expecting you until... I don't know, tomorrow at the earliest."

Gulotta spoke as much with his free hands as he did with his mouth. "You don't want to be imprisoned any longer than you need to be, I presume?"

"Definitely not. Are you gonna get me out of here?"

"You have friends in high places, as they say. You are to be released into my custody and transferred to the American embassy in Rome."

Stunned, Nick's jaw popped open as Gulotta motioned to the guards, who promptly opened the door and gestured for Nick to exit. He stood stock-still. This didn't add up. There weren't even numbers entered into the equation. It was like car plus tomato equaled horse.

"Please, Signor O'Connor, if you will. There is much paperwork."

"Adesso," said one of the guards. "Now."

All of Nick's contentment with death vanished out the six-inch window over his cot.

This is it. They're gonna torture me, then kill me.

Chills scurried up and down his spine. There was nowhere he could run, not this time. Not that he could physically, if he wanted to. His knees buckled and shook. But there was no sense postponing the inevitable—it was a long time coming. He had his chance to say goodbye to Julia. He regretted not being able to free Isabella, but he tried. At least he tried. He squared his shoulders. Closing his eyes for a moment, he drew a mile-long breath and then said goodbye to his cell, to his life, and tentatively stepped out.

Gulotta wasn't kidding about the paperwork. The documentation appeared legit and probably was, but Nick figured it was all for show so they could cover their butts. The official ruse took over forty minutes to finish with the two guards, the station chief who'd been called back in, and the Italian equivalent of a desk sergeant who'd been interrupted having a late dinner.

It made perfect sense—make it appear as if he were legally freed, then kill him when he wasn't in police custody. It was brilliant, actually. Nobody would've believed he'd hanged himself in his cell. Let people comb through the paper trail and conspiracy theories for years, so long as Nick was out of the way. The single time he said anything was to voice his disbelief at the email Gulotta presented from the Deputy Prime Minister of Italy, who had demanded Nick's immediate liberation.

Nick scoffed and shook his head when he read the printout. "Nice touch." The attention to detail impressed him. Whether it was an outright forgery or the more likely scenario—that the politician was a member of the Order—didn't matter. The outcome would be the same. Gulotta preempted the cops' questions about the authenticity of the letter and got the supposed Deputy Prime Minister on a Zoom call from his bed. Nick didn't know who the guy was, but everyone else in the room bowed down to him. When the call ended, all four cops acted pissed as hell. Everyone deserved an Oscar.

Even Lacasse was in on the act in a second phone call, confirming to Nick his front-and-center role in the Order. No way any honest cop would let this happen—he'd be in the station, doing whatever the hell he could to hold Nick until the Deputy Prime Minister himself walked through the door.

"Sì, Investigatore Lacasse," the station chief said into his cell. "It is happening now. My hands are tied."

Lacasse yelled something into the phone, but Nick couldn't decipher it.

"I will try," the station chief said before ending the call. He turned to Gulotta and switched to Italian. "You'll need to wait for the investigatore."

Gulotta pointed to the final signature line. "Sign here, Signor O'Connor."

Nick rubbed the back of his neck, then scribbled his name on the paper.

"My client is a free man," Gulotta said. "He does not need to wait for anyone."

A free man who won't be waiting for the guillotine, Nick thought.

Two minutes later, when Gulotta escorted Nick outside the station door with his belt back on his jeans and his wedding ring on his finger, he expected Bernardo, Dante, and at least three other Protectors, but the street was empty. Hot, humid air that smelled like a mix of rotten fish and exhaust smothered him, but he reveled in the freedom. He gazed at the night sky; a layer of clouds obscured the stars.

Bewildered they were alone, every urge in his body screamed at him to dash away from this fat guy as fast as possible. Though he and Julia had taken a water taxi from the airport when they first arrived in Venice, Nick knew where he was. *Ponte della Libertà*, Liberty Bridge, led straight to the mainland. Or, he was one hundred yards from the train station. Of course, Julia had his wallet. And he needed to get her. He could sprint to Carlo's, and now that he was free, they could board a train for Milan. Or better, another country. That was the plan, and it was a good one.

"Please, signore," Gulotta said. "We don't have much time." Gulotta hustled to a black Vespa waiting across the street, hopped his hefty body on, and started the engine. "Come, please." He repeatedly glanced back at the police station, but nobody came out.

"You're kidding, right?"

"Your questions will soon be answered."

"Where are you taking me?" Nick asked in Italian.

"There's no time, please!" The man was near frantic. He continued to check the station entrance.

Nick followed suit. A gray rat climbed a drainpipe on the side of the building.

The station chief barged out. Something wasn't right. Was Nick wrong about his lawyer? With his curiosity and a sudden sense of urgency getting the better of him, Nick squeezed onto the back of the scooter. Gulotta didn't hesitate; he revved the throttle before Nick was situated. The Vespa sputtered off beneath the weight of the two men. It wasn't the getaway Nick would've wanted, but it beat running.

With his briefcase clamped between his knees, Gulotta drove for less than two minutes until they reached the literal end of the road at Piazzale Roma, the final place in Venice wheeled motor vehicles were permitted.

Hopping off first, Gulotta glanced behind him and hurried down the street. Again, Nick fought the urge to race to Carlo's, but his gut ordered him to follow. He matched the lawyer's brisk clip. Four blocks and three footbridges later, Gulotta paused at the edge of a canal, in the shadow of a building. He scanned the area again.

As Nick watched the man's nerve-rattled demeanor, the germinating thought Nick had on the Vespa was confirmed: this was a jailbreak. Opening his briefcase, Gulotta pulled out a Yankees hat, which he handed to Nick. He removed his suit jacket and jammed it into the briefcase.

It was one thing to fight every urge to run; putting on a Yankees hat was like sliding down a giant razor blade into a pool of alcohol. The hat wasn't the world's greatest disguise, but it would prevent instant recognition, potentially buying them a few precious seconds. He definitely would've fooled any of his friends in Boston. With a cringe that aggravated every pain in his sore body, he donned the cap.

"Hey, can I use your phone?" Nick asked. "I need to call my wife."

"Soon, soon. We are not safe here."

Gulotta peeled off a fake goatee and tossed it into the water. He undid his ponytail and removed his glasses, which he was also about to drop into the canal, but Nick grabbed his wrist and took the specs from him.

"False breadcrumbs," Nick said. He sprinted to the next alley and hurled the glasses in the opposite direction.

After another few minutes of a circuitous route, Nick followed Gulotta into a narrow alley. They stopped at an old, black metal door at the end of it. The attorney produced a key, and with a final scan over his shoulder and even up, he unlocked the door and slipped inside.

Nick was surprised to find a spacious interior courtyard with a wide staircase leading to the upper floors. A running birdbath-style stone fountain stood in the center with a few plants at the base. Opposite the alleyway, a set of double French doors served as the main entrance.

"Where are we? And who are you?" Nick asked.

Without a word, Gulotta used a different key to unlock what appeared to be a closet embedded underneath the staircase. Nick followed him into the small storage room. Using his cell phone's flashlight, the lawyer found yet a third keyhole, which he opened. A latch on what Nick thought was a solid wall next to him clicked. Gulotta pressed on the wall, which opened to reveal a short corridor. Nick followed the man inside, who sealed the secret passage. In the dim light of Gulotta's phone, they came to a spiral staircase, hidden within the bowels of the building.

Climbing the stairs for what felt like four floors, Nick felt physically safe, but with each step, he sensed he rose toward a potentially bigger predicament. *Out of the frying pan and into the fire?*

"Seriously, where the fuck are we going?"

"Almost there, my friend."

At the top of the flight, they reached another metal door, which Nick hoped would be the last, though he had to admit he enjoyed the cloak and dagger mystery. Gulotta rapped five times on the door in a distinct pattern. After an agonizing wait in dark silence, it opened.

XIII

BLOWING HER NOSE FOR THE UMPTEENTH TIME, Julia tucked another dirty tissue into her jeans pocket. She sat on the couch in Carlo's living room area and eyed him in the kitchen, opening a bottle of wine. He was being a true friend and gentleman, so she reminded herself to be appreciative of the little things. If she'd been alone in a hotel room right now, she'd be an inconsolable wreck. What was Nick talking about? Did he really think they'd kill him? Why was he so defeatist? He wasn't being the fighter she so dearly loved. Had his former life taken over? It didn't seem like it, and from what she'd heard, he was a fighter in that life, too.

"Is a table red okay?" Carlo asked, walking over with two full glasses.

"As long as there's alcohol in it, fuck yes." Julia took the wine and chugged it.

Carlo perked his eyebrows with a smirk. "We both had bad days."

"Bad? Getting chewed out by your boss is a bad day. Locking yourself out of your apartment is a bad day." More than annoyed, she stood and walked to the narrow window next to his front door.

"What are you doing?"

"Opening a window. It's a million degrees in here." She wound the ancient iron crank. A mosquito dive-bombed her face; she swatted her hands wildly.

"You and your husband are much alike," Carlo said. "He did the same thing here."

"Well, you're not the only European I've met who likes stuffy rooms with no air. And when are they gonna invent screens on this continent?"

"What do you mean, like a TV?"

Unsure if he was kidding but lacking the mental strength to explain something so banal if he wasn't, she returned to the kitchen and refilled her glass, then plopped down on the couch next to him. "Thanks for letting me stay here, Carlo."

"It is my pleasure. There's no door, but you can sleep in my bed." He pointed to the doorless bedroom at the end of his loft.

"What? No."

"Alone, I mean." Carlo raised his hands defensively in what seemed like an honest misunderstanding. "My couch is a bed. I'll sleep here."

Julia caressed the leather she sat on. It didn't have a hidden mattress and didn't seem like it converted into anything. "This is a sofa bed?"

"A couch bed, sì. I sleep on it."

Again, Julia wasn't sure if he was kidding, but she didn't care enough to ask. She rubbed her eyes. Her husband was sleeping on a hard cot and probably couldn't open his window. Their last conversation haunted her. Would she ever see him again? She stared into her wine, as if the answer was hiding at the bottom of the glass. Her disheveled hair fell over her face as she hung her head. *Enough.* Once again, she ordered herself to stop being the victim. Taking charge of her brain, she pushed her hair back and sat upright, hoping it would wake her up a bit.

"Do you know someone named Jacopo Comin?"

Carlo did a double-take and shot his body back. His reaction was so severe, it startled Julia.

"Who is he?" she asked.

"Why are you asking?"

"Don't play games with me, Carlo. I'm in no mood. Who is he, and how do you know him?"

"I don't—I mean, I . . . Julia, that's Tintoretto's real name."

Julia nearly spat out her wine. That couldn't possibly be true. Or maybe it was. "But obviously there was someone else alive now with that name."

"Why are you asking about Tintoretto?"

"I'm not. Your pals are full of shit. Nick said they pressed charges against him for murder. *Murder*, Carlo. They probably thought we'd make that deal, and then they'd slam him with the murder charge."

Carlo shook his head. "But what does this have to do with Tintoretto?"

"Nothing. It's just a coincidence. Or maybe he's a relative or something, I don't know."

He spoke in a near whisper. "That's who they said he killed? Jacopo Comin, are you sure?"

"Are you gonna tell me what happened or not?"

"Julia," he started, but paused a moment. "There are things about Venice you do not, as an outsider, understand. I am only beginning to. This city can do things to a man . . . change him. Make him into someone he never would have believed he could become. I think that is what happened to Nick. He has fallen under Venice's spell." He shook his head and rubbed his forearms. "Even if I could explain it correctly, you would not understand. But trust me when I say Nick needs serious help."

Now Julia was really pissed. Wanting answers, she narrowed her eyes. "Venice's spell? You sound like a cheesy tourism poster. The help Nick needs is the support of his family and friends. And a lawyer. Answer the damn question."

Carlo gulped down his wine and lit a cigarette. Julia wasn't thrilled with the smoke, and even less so that it seemed as though Carlo was going to finish the whole thing before speaking again. After his third drag, he blew a cloud of smoke toward the ceiling. "There was an event—"

"What event?"

"For Venetians, held at the Palazzo. Nick disrupted the whole thing. People tried to subdue him, but he fought them, and then, yes, he killed an old man. Jacopo Comin."

Julia peered into the Italian artist's hazel eyes. She chewed her cheek. "Bullshit, Carlo. Stop lying."

"I'm *not* lying."

"Tell me the fucking truth, or I'm walking out that door!"

Carlo took another drag. "Okay, okay, okay. But remember, everything I said was true." Standing, he paced the room, stopping at one of his abstract paintings propped against the wall. He cocked his head at it. "Is there too much red in this?"

"Carlo!"

He sat back down. With an uncharacteristic seriousness, he took her hand and met her eyes. "Jacopo Comin *is* the real name of Tintoretto. Well, technically it was Jacopo Robusti, since that was his father's name, but the family name was originally Comin." Perhaps it was his demeanor or perhaps it was his touch, but it all clicked for Julia. In shock, she didn't pull away. "All of it is real, Julia—all of it. I did not believe it either until I saw it. Tintoretto, *Paradiso*, the souls. Tintoretto—*the Painter*—is like . . . the keeper of the souls. The maintainer of justice. When Nick tried to free them, he killed him."

A rush of emotions engulfed Julia. It was all too much. Her first instinct was to again fight her own cognizance and dispute Carlo's claim, but so much had transpired, and everything he said matched what Nick had told her. Even the things della Porta alluded to now added up. She'd been fighting it for too long. Letting herself accept the impossible, a wave of guilt swept over her—she hadn't believed her husband. And instead, she believed a guy she'd known for less than a week. But pushing her shame aside, she dialed up her journalist self and zeroed in on fact-finding. "How did he do it?"

"Does it matter? What I want to know is how they intend to charge him for the murder of a man who shouldn't have been alive."

XIV

"ANY TROUBLE?" ASKED THE GIRL IN ENGLISH, as she guided Nick and Gulotta through a coat closet and into a stark white space.

"None," Gulotta replied in Italian.

Emerging from the dark staircase, Nick squinted for a moment to allow his eyes to adjust. They walked into a living room, furnished with nothing but a modern white leather couch, matching side chairs, and a glass-top coffee table. Bright recessed ceiling lights lit the bare white walls and bleached wood floor. With an odor of fresh paint, sawed wood, and new furniture, the space seemed to have been recently renovated. Crisp, cool air caressed his sweaty pores. The light, the room's colorless interior, and the air conditioning gave Nick the impression he'd just walked through a portal into a spaceship.

The girl, who was in her early twenties, thin, and an inch or two shorter than Julia, kissed both his cheeks and welcomed him inside. Her bobbed hairstyle was different shades of molasses, like the swirl of a cinnamon bun, with pink tips. A round silver pendant rested in the hollow of her throat, but Nick couldn't make out the design engraved on it. Between her hair, retro 80s jeans shorts, tucked-in technicolor shirt, and black & gold studded Nikes, a new idea formulated in Nick's head: he'd entered the VIP room of a club. But the silence—and being on the fourth floor of a Venetian apartment building—mocked that hypothesis.

"Thanks for coming, Nick. I can't believe this. This is dope A.F.," she said in fluent English with an indecipherable accent that sounded primarily American, but blended with British and French, dusted with a sprinkling of Italian. Displaying a high-beam smile of perfect teeth, she gawked at him, as if starstruck by her favorite celebrity.

Super uncomfortable, Nick ventured deeper into the room. The moment he did, a remarkable sense of recognition hit him, though he'd never set foot in this apartment—or any place like it. He wondered if he'd been here as Angelo in the 16th century. That's when he saw a familiar seventy-something man rushing toward him from the open kitchen.

Black oval-frame glasses rested on the older gentleman's clean-shaven face beneath perfectly cropped white hair. His khaki pants and tucked-in baby blue Polo shirt both had packaging creases, completing the look of a recent makeover. He wrapped his arms around Nick in a massive bear hug.

"Nicholas," he shouted in English. "I was certain I'd never see you again. And I've never said that and meant it for eternity." Nick had heard that heavily accented, papery voice before.

Nick released himself from the man's hold and took two steps back. "Do I—?" The air of familiarity suddenly made sense. "Holy shit." Nick probed the man's tawny eyes, which spoke of experience. He looked him up and down, side-to-side. "No way. Paganelli?"

The man stood tall and smoothed his shirt. He raised his chin, proudly displaying himself. Gone was his scruffy brown robe and frowzy white beard. Paganelli's previous aroma of incense and stale air had been replaced with soap.

"You are *Enzo* Paganelli, right?" Nick asked. "Not his brother?"

Releasing a raucous howl that sounded like his throat was chopping wood, Paganelli slapped Nick on the back. "In the flesh, Angelo. I've had brethren, but never a brother."

Nick gawked, finding it difficult to believe. "You've come a long way from a condemned hospital kitchen on a haunted island. You clean up nice."

"Grazie, my friend." It was Paganelli's turn to size up Nick. "You look . . . about the same, I suppose. I've seen worse."

"You sure have." Nick chuckled. "Where's your rat?"

An affectionate smile spread across Paganelli's lips. "Chewbacca's sleeping in a beautiful little shoebox in the other room."

"Where it's gonna stay," said the girl, crinkling her nose. The diamond stud in it blinked at Nick. She grinned at him again. "It's really you. The truly one and only Nick O'Connor." She gave him a surprisingly firm handshake.

Perhaps it was the lighting, but it took him a moment to notice her allure. The nose stud, along with multiple ear studs and loops, accentuated her sharp features, particularly her big brown eyes that were highlighted with dark eyeliner. Not necessarily his type, he'd be surprised if she weren't a model, like the face of French perfume trying to crack the New England private school market. Her eyes carried a vague resemblance, and she recognized him, but Nick summoned zero recollection of her and didn't think she was the basis for his strange, persistent sense that he knew her or this building. "Have we met?"

"Nope. The name's Fosca Elizabeth," she said, tucking a lock of pink-tipped hair behind her ear. "But you met my nonna-mère."

Nick's déjà vu refused to give him a break. It gave him chills that distracted him from everything else, including Fosca's bewildering response. He gazed around the apartment; this place was throwing him off. He'd thought he retained all of Angelo's memories, but obviously not. If he'd been here at some point, the renovation was blocking a clear recollection. He shrugged the feeling off; the priority was understanding why these people brought him here and what they wanted.

"I give up," he said, pointing back and forth between Paganelli and Fosca. "Is she . . . are you her grandfather?"

Stepping to Paganelli's side, Fosca put a warm arm around him. "Uncle Enzo's well, he's not my real uncle, but he's more like . . . well, an uncle. My nonna-mère—my grandmother—is"—she choked up—"*was* . . ." Her words trailed off into a sob.

Nick wondered if he said something wrong.

Clearly distraught, she raised a finger, requesting a moment. Nick thought she'd dry her eyes, but instead, she scrolled through her phone and handed it to him. A text in English from a European number lit up the screen:

'NOC is the key. DP is done.'

"It was the last one she sent. I tried texting and calling her a hundred times," Fosca said through her tears. "When that son-of-a-bitch was arrested, I knew it was true."

The rabbit hole led straight to Wonderland. Shaking his head, Nick figured NOC stood for Nick O'Connor and DP for della Porta, but he had no clue who sent the text, why, or how he was the key to anything. "I'm more confused than an average Yankees fan," he said.

Paganelli kissed the girl's head with more tenderness than Nick had ever thought the man capable. "Nicholas, this is Fosca Baldesseri. Her grandmother was the countess."

XV

WITH THE REGRETTABLE CONVERSATION WITH Carlo rumbling in his head, della Porta needed to relax. He poured himself an amaretto and brought a bag of seed over to his sun conures when his mobile rang. *Richard Lacasse*, the screen announced. Della Porta answered on the first ring.

"Monsieur Lacasse, it's quite late," he said in English. "Everything okay?"

"Signore, it is Fanella," the Venetian detective said on speakerphone. "There has been a problem."

Della Porta thought something happened to his friend from Interpol. "Where is Lacasse?"

"Doing pushups on the street."

Before della Porta replied, Lacasse joined the call. His typically soothing voice was short of breath, agitated. "The carabinieri," he said with his nasally French accent, "in their infinite wisdom, believed an order from the Deputy Prime Minister of Italy to release Nick O'Connor."

"Is this a joke?" Della Porta stepped away from his beloved birds.

"Everything was legitimate." Fanella clicked her tongue. "It was the DPM. Maybe he was compromised, or maybe he was tricked, but what would you have us do? A head of state—"

"What would I have you do?" Lacasse butted in, angrier than della Porta had ever heard the man. "You do what every competent police officer in the world does. If Jesus himself calls, you hold the suspect and delay, delay, delay, for as long as possible. Especially under such questionable circumstances." He lowered his voice to an angry whisper. "She let the key to finding the doge's book walk out that door."

"How is it possible the DPM could've known about O'Connor," della Porta asked, "let alone be persuaded to order his release?"

"We're working through that," Lacasse replied. "The American government was involved."

"I see," della Porta said, before pausing again. He wondered how high O'Connor's connections went. Whoever they were, it made sense that Julia contacted them. "Find out. In the meantime, perhaps we can turn this into a fortunate circumstance. I'll instruct the Protectors to go to the Palazzo and surveil the Great Council Room."

"Why would he risk returning?" Fanella asked.

"He's tied to *Paradiso*. He can't resist. You two, meet the Protectors there. Stay out of sight and observe. If O'Connor leaves, follow him. But do not apprehend him unless he attempts to flee Venice. He must be taken alive."

"You think he'll lead us to the book?" Lacasse asked.

"Or at least have another conversation with his soul mate. Record every word he says."

"Okay, we'll see you there," Lacasse said.

"No, there's a slim chance he may go elsewhere," della Porta replied.

"You need support," Fanella said. "Where should I meet you?"

"I'll have Bernardo," della Porta said. "You go with Lacasse to the Palazzo."

XVI

"SO, I REALLY DO HAVE FRIENDS IN HIGH PLACES?" Nick asked Gulotta, who returned from the bathroom and sat in one of the mid-century side chairs in the living room. Nick had taken the other, while Fosca and Paganelli sat on the sofa.

"More than you know," Gulotta replied. He reached for his espresso and took a sip.

Nick followed suit. He was wiped and needed the caffeine. A bottle of white wine sat on the coffee table, along with a sliced baguette, two types of cheese, and a tapenade in a takeout container.

After the revelation about her grandmother, Fosca's mood brightened, and the group seemed to meld into a natural, familial vibe. Though he was pissed at Paganelli for drugging him and smashing his phone on Poveglia Island, Nick had to admit—between everything he'd been through with Paganelli, his brief but meaningful encounter with the countess, and his recent adventure with Gulotta, it almost felt like some ragtag group of orphans bonding. He yearned to return to Julia but figured she was safe at Carlo's. He'd go to her soon—an hour or two wouldn't make any difference. Plus, the Order was likely combing the city for him; if they were going to escape Venice yet again, they'd have to do it in the middle of the night.

"What time is it?" he asked Gulotta.

The lawyer checked his watch. "Almost 22:30."

10:30. Not late enough. The best move was to wait until three or four in the morning. He already planned on asking Gulotta for his scooter. He'd buy it outright, then go straight to Julia, ride across the bridge, and not stop for anything but gas until they reached the American embassy in Austria.

Though the continuing sense of déjà vu haunted him, Nick relaxed; he was with friends and had a solid plan. He took another sip of espresso and turned to Fosca.

"How in the world were you able to do this so quickly? I mean, your contact in the EU government can just pick up the phone and call the U.S. Secretary of State?" He spoke faster to her than he did to the other Europeans. She was fluent in English, if not more comfortable speaking it.

"You make it sound like it was easy," she replied, clipping a barrette into her hair to keep it from falling over her eye, "but basically, yeah."

"Must be nice being royalty."

"*Nobility*," Fosca corrected. "Not royalty. The titles are in name only."

"And money," Paganelli said, joining her laughter with a woodchop from his throat. "And they certainly open doors."

"I'm blown away," Nick said, stifling a yawn. "The U.S. Secretary of State jumped on the phone and called the Italian Deputy Prime Minister to request my release? And wait—are you a countess now?" Nick helped himself to some bread and dipped it in the tapenade.

Fosca laughed. "Yes to your first question, and that's a good question to your second. I'll have to ask my mom."

"You've advanced from baronessa to viscontessa," Gulotta offered.

"Your mother is now countess," Paganelli added.

Fosca shrugged apathetically. "Good to know."

"Jeez, I just realized I owe you an apology," Nick said to Fosca. He took a napkin to hold the bread, careful not to let crumbs fall on the pristine white rug.

"What on Earth for?" she asked.

Nick chuckled as he used a small knife to spread some brie onto another slice of bread. "Wow, you sounded so much like your grandmother just now." He didn't intend to cause her grief, but Fosca frowned and twisted her shirt. "Sorry, and this might be worse, but I, um, apologize for . . . killing your ancestor."

She widened her eyes. "You mean Tintoretto? We haven't thanked *you* yet. My family's been trying to kill him for centuries."

Nick stopped himself from taking a bite. "Say what now?"

"Technically, it's my turn to apologize. We haven't been formally introduced. You're sitting with three members of *Il Gilda di Silvanus*, the Guild of Silvanus."

Paganelli held his fingers up. "*Two* members, Fosca."

"Oh, please, Uncle Enzo. Give it a rest." She pivoted to Nick. "He thinks he's Han Solo. Without a monetary reward."

"Wait," Nick said to Paganelli, recalling their conversation on Poveglia. "The resistance. *This* is what you were talking about?"

"Like I said, not what we call ourselves."

"See that?" Fosca said with amusement. "You all heard that, right? 'Not what *we* call *our*selves' he said."

"He did indeed," Gulotta concurred.

Feeling like this insane adventure suddenly became animated, Nick placed the bread on the coffee table and waved both hands. "Okay, hold up. The Guild of Slytherin? Han Solo, Harry Potter, you guys are messing with me, right?"

Fosca cracked up and smacked Paganelli on his shoulder. "You didn't tell me he's hilarious."

Not finding it funny, Paganelli cleared his throat. "*Silvanus*. The Guild of Silvanus. Remember it because you are also a part of it."

"I am not." Nick recoiled at the conversation's direction. He succumbed to exhaustion and slumped into the chair, melting into the leather—and away from more confrontation.

"Fighting the Order, trying to free the souls," Gulotta said. "Does that sound like someone you know?"

"Yeah, him." Nick pointed a thumb at Paganelli.

"Very true," Fosca said, smiling at her uncle. "He finally decided to come out of the shadows and join us."

"Join is a generous description. Your grandmother and I ran a perfectly good operation."

"That yielded zero results." Her eyes moistened. "Worse than that."

Paganelli patted her shoulder. "Della Porta killed her despite the plan. Prudence is still the best course of action."

Fosca shook her head, and Gulotta scoffed. Nick sensed the dynamic in the room shifting.

"How big is this Guild?" he asked, genuinely interested, but also hoping to steer the subject back to the friendly atmosphere from a few moments earlier.

"Big enough," Fosca answered, her chin raised with pride. "It's the quality of our members that counts."

"And I suspect your contact in the government is a member?"

"They are," Gulotta said, slicing a chunk of cheese, "but we fed them faulty information to protect them."

Nick wiped his mouth. "How big are we talking? Fifty? A hundred?"

"Sixteen," Paganelli said. "*Not* including me."

Fosca groaned unabashedly.

"Sixteen?" Nick blurted out. "Seriously? Della Porta's gotta have sixteen Protectors chasing me alone. How many people are in the Order?"

Paganelli shrugged. "Between here, Paris, and Madrid, probably a thousand."

Blinking, Nick wasn't sure which bit to process first. "There are three chapters?"

"Did I not tell you that, Angelo?"

"Who knows? Maybe you did in the middle of all that crap about angels or giving me laced tea."

"Ancient history."

"It was three days ago! And the name's Nick."

"As you wish, Nicholas." Paganelli fluttered his hand, as if shooing the past into the wind. "But remember the tenets that govern the awesome power of the Seventh Sun are as real as your Isabella and my wife. For in light, there is truth." He kissed his lips to his thumb and forefinger pressed together, like he was holding an imaginary trinket.

"Doesn't change the fact that you're all out of your mind. They have a thousand? And you're seventeen?"

"Sixteen. I am advocating a different path."

"Eighteen with you," Fosca said to Nick. "But who cares? We're not charging them in a field in open warfare. Cut off the head, and the army is irrelevant."

"The head," Nick said. "You mean della Porta?"

Gulotta answered. "It's more of a metaphorical head. A conceptual head."

Paganelli cleared his throat, not masking his dissent.

"Come on," Fosca said, "we don't need a thousand people to bring them down. We need the *right* people. The right people to go through the right doors that we can open. We're well-funded." She pinched the fabric of Paganelli's shirt. "Isn't it nice not to be on your own?" She turned to Nick. "I think he enjoyed pretending to be a bum."

Paganelli squeezed the bridge of his nose but stayed silent, letting her win that one.

She had a point, Nick thought. But it led to a different point. "Alright, fair enough. But the Order has money, too. Probably more. And with your grandmother's access, why didn't she ever go in and do the job herself? Or get someone else to do it, like the EU person or the other"—he pointed to Paganelli and Gulotta and winked— "quality people in your group?"

"As you know first-hand, Nicholas," Paganelli said, "there are many challenges and obstacles."

"Yeah, but the countess was on the council. She had access."

Fosca shook her head. "It's not that simple. Even if it were a suicide mission, which she'd never do because her family would be ostracized and destroyed, the Painter himself, even at that age, was incredibly powerful. Remember, he traded seven bodies for one. Imagine that strength. And he's protected." Her explanation was imbued with reverence and a hint of weariness. "In the 19th century, two of my ancestors tried but were killed. They concealed their identities, but it's known in my family. That's why my parents didn't want to be involved. Why my grandfather divorced her."

Nick chowed down on his bread and cheese while Paganelli jumped in.

"So we came up with a new plan," he said. "Replace the Painter with one of our own. Zuccaro. But della Porta killed him, took the boy, and forced me into hiding."

"It's been a long, bumpy road." Fosca jabbed a finger into Paganelli's chest, admonishing him. "And you never needed to literally go underground."

The elderly man's brow clouded over his deep-set, dampening eyes. "You were a child. And you still are."

"You don't think I miss her, too? Both of them? You don't need to be blood to be family. We can find Elena." It was Fosca's turn to comfort Paganelli. She massaged her uncle's shoulder.

Nick recalled Paganelli's story about his wife. Not only did della Porta have Carlo's dad sentenced to *Paradise*, but he convinced the Exalted Master of the day to do the same to Paganelli's wife—out of spite. Given Fosca's phrasing, he guessed Elena was Paganelli's daughter—whom he hadn't seen in fifteen years since he went off the grid.

Though Fosca expressed genuine concern for her surrogate uncle's welfare, the two of them scowled at each other, and the vibe shifted again. They'd both lost family to the Order and were rightfully torn up about it, but an underlying disagreement seemed to be brewing.

"What's this really about?" Nick asked.

Silence fell for a moment, but Paganelli spoke first. "There's a belief that some information can take down the Order, but my feeling is that's a distraction—"

"Not a distraction," Fosca said. "It's real."

"Freeing the souls is the only way," Paganelli continued. "Kill the Painter."

"We tried that," Nick said. He turned to Fosca. "What's the information?"

"It'll expose their secrets and corruption," Fosca replied. "Or we can use it as leverage."

"What she means," Paganelli said, "is nobody knows, as it's been lost to time."

Nick snickered. He'd had this conversation—and regression—too many times already. "Of course. The book. Renzo Scalfini's secret book that contains all these juicy tidbits that can either destroy the Order or make them omnipotent."

Fosca's eyes lit up. "We knew you'd know it!"

"Know *of* it," he answered. "But I never saw it, I have no idea what was in it, and it's probably dust by now. I'm going with Paganelli on this."

With a smug grin, Paganelli leaned back and crossed his arms and legs, as if resting his case.

"It's real," Fosca said, her eyes narrowing. She stood and scrutinized the elderly man. "Far older books have survived. The fact that Nick knows of it corroborates its existence."

Nick shook his head. "Even if it contains exactly what you hope, people distill information differently now. They'll dispute it, contradict it, or just plain not believe it. Especially coming from an ancient book. People don't even believe video and audio. Have you seen deepfake tech?"

"There are plenty of old books people believe. Ever hear of something called the Bible? Now is the time to strike before they regain strength. We get the book, we cut off the head. Then we cut off the hands and free the souls."

Now Paganelli raised his voice. "If we release the souls, there won't be a head. The Painter is real. We know *exactly* who he is."

The former Protector's statement sent a jolt through Nick. They *did* know who the Painter was—and Nick sent his wife to the guy's loft. He still had trouble accepting that della Porta somehow managed to transfer Tintoretto's power to Carlo, but there was no reason to think it wasn't successful. And if Carlo was now in a position of influence, did that mean Julia was safer? Or in even more danger?

Gulotta stepped to Fosca's side and interrupted Nick's thoughts with another disturbing one. "Killing a Painter is a temporary measure without destroying the Sun Crystal, also no easy task. *If* you succeed," he said. "If killing Carlo fails, or worse—della Porta installs a new Painter and gets the book—the head will become so strong, we won't be able to cut it off."

"But if we get it first," Fosca added, "we'll have leverage. We'll own the Order. We'll shut it all down, and they'll never start it up again."

"You don't even know what's in it." Paganelli waved his hand, as if shooing away gnats.

Fosca folded her arms. "It's worth a shot."

"Della Porta's looking for that book too, you know," Nick chimed in.

"We know," Paganelli said. "We should take advantage of his preoccupation."

"*He* obviously thinks it's real. At the very least we need to prevent him from getting it." Fosca huffed and paced the rug. "My nonna-mère believed the book could destroy the Order. It's another reason she didn't kill the Painter. She hoped Nick had the information to find it."

"And look what happened," Paganelli said. "Be happy she wasn't sentenced."

Nick offered a nod of condolence to both of them. He couldn't imagine the weight of the family burden over centuries, especially Fosca's. He respected those that walked away, but knowing the truth about *Paradise*, he would've stood in her shoes given the chance. *Wait—stop.*

He rattled his head, needing to bring his train of thought to a screeching halt. By joining the discussion, he was one step closer to joining them. A noble cause, but not *his* cause. He had an obligation to *Julia*. Whether Carlo was friend or foe didn't matter. As much as he wanted to save Isabella, he couldn't get even more involved in a centuries-old struggle. The sense of déjà vu was crushing him because he'd been through all this before. The future with his present-day wife, being with her, building a family—*that's* what mattered. He wanted kids with Julia. They couldn't be forever tied to a weight at the bottom of the Venetian Lagoon. Screw escaping in the middle of the night. It was late enough. They needed to get out of there. Now.

With a burning resolve, Nick sprung to his feet. "Look," he said to the group, "you know I'm on your side, but I'm not the guy for this." They glanced at him and each other, taken aback, but not as surprised as Nick expected they'd be. He turned to Gulotta. "Can I grab your scooter keys? I'll Venmo you the money for it."

Gulotta turned to Fosca, who spoke with a brazen sharpness. "You're just gonna hightail it out of here? You know the stakes."

"There are *personal* stakes, too. You're not drafting me into your war with the Order."

"But your beloved, Nicholas," Paganelli said. "Do you not want to liberate her?"

"Of course I do." Nick spun to him. "I'd like to free your wife, too—and all the souls. You know that more than anyone." Physically and emotionally spent, he scratched the back of his neck and rubbed his temples. "Look, I tried. You also know better than anyone what can happen. I can't risk my life or my wife's anymore. You said everyone has a soul mate, right? I'm sure someone else will come around."

"In a hundred years." Fosca's volume rose, her expression darkening.

Nick faced her, remorse filling his chest, Julia and home occupying his mind. "Open warfare or not, seventeen to a thousand? I'm not your guy, Fosca. I'm sorry." He turned back to Gulotta. "Come on, buddy, let me get those keys. I'll pay you double what it's worth."

"Nick, please," Fosca said. She raised her hands to him but fell short of clasping them together. "Do you know the risks we took to bust you out of prison?"

"I do. And I'm grateful. Eternally grateful, but I'm not joining your fight. Fuck no. Gulotta, keys."

"Just do it." Fosca scowled at Paganelli.

Sighing, Gulotta moved to stand.

"Wait, Nicholas." Paganelli rose from the couch. "Before you go, I have a gift for you."

As Paganelli opened the door of an adjacent room and disappeared inside, Nick wondered what kind of gift it could be, and then realized he didn't give a crap. A crushing urge to rush out and reach Julia overtook him. He shuffled from foot to foot. "Come on, Gulotta. Now."

"Patience, friend." Gulotta raised a finger and relaxed into his seat.

A moment later, Paganelli reappeared.

Nick's eyes grew wide. Dizzying palpitations erupted in his chest.

Nestled in the old man's arms was an object Nick had seen in the Palazzo tunnel and the true source of his overwhelming déjà vu: a clay urn.

Isabella's urn.

XVII

HE TAPPED HIS CANE ON THE BRICK BRIDGE and whistled an upbeat ditty. A pigeon cooed, seemingly in time. The last sunrays of the day twinkled off the peaceful canal water. A perfect evening, for the day's events proved he would join the Council of Ten at the next opening.

The punch to the skull came without warning. A ringing detonated between his ears. A kick to his calf sent him to the ground. His head smacked against the stone balustrade. Large hands lifted him up and spun him around. "*Paradise* awaits, Senator Quattrone," said a large, grinning man with an unruly brown beard. Another man forced a sack over his head. The strike to the gut impelled a saliva gob from his lips into the cloth.

"CARLO, WHAT THE fuck is this?"

Julia stood at one of his easels, the sheet pulled back to reveal the artist's latest work. A man, naked beneath a blanket, lay sprawled on a pile of books and wine bottles. Standing over him were two women, both clad in ancient garb. One held the man down, while the other slit his throat, drenching the scene in blood. The man and the woman wielding the knife looked all too familiar. Chills flurried her spine.

"You can at least answer." She'd already asked three times.

He lounged on the couch with a glass of wine precariously perched in his hand. Finally, he snapped back to reality and turned to her.

"I recognize this," she said. "It's a variation of *Judith Slaying Holofernes*."

He righted his glass and took a sip. "On metallic glass. A silly name, don't you think? Not fragile at all. Good for painting, of course. I love how reflective it is."

"Don't change the subject. Is that me with the knife, cutting off Nick's head?"

Carlo looked away.

"And let me guess," she continued. "The maidservant is supposed to be Isabella?"

He brought the glass to his lips. Sensing he wasn't going to answer, she joined him on the couch again. Carlo's laptop on the coffee table switched to a screensaver shot of a random tropical beach. With his help, she'd been researching Italian criminal law and if Nick could be extradited to the U.S. She figured it wasn't too early to dive in and get the ball rolling in the morning. Too tired to wake the computer up, she grabbed her own glass and chugged half of it.

"I'm not mad. It just took me by surprise, is all. It's pretty creative, to be honest."

Again, he didn't answer. Given his total lack of reaction, she got the sense that an entirely different topic occupied his thoughts.

"Carlo, what's going on? It's like you went to another planet." As she said the words, she realized she'd said a variation of the same thing to Nick a dozen times over the past week. *Too weird.* And he was staring at her, though really, he was staring *through* her. She snapped her fingers.

"Scusami, Julia," he said before taking another sip of wine. "I've been having . . . visions."

"Now you? You're kidding, right?" The coincidence was too much. She wasn't going to accept a new virus that caused people to hallucinate. Though, she conceded, a brain-eating parasite would explain everything. She shuddered at the disgusting thought.

"No." Carlo shook his head. "They come without warning."

Julia eyed him, trying to discern if he was ill. And if so, how did he and Nick contract the parasite? "What kind of visions?" she finally asked. "Please tell me they're not back to a 16th-century swordfighter."

He reacted with a sharp laugh, as if he genuinely thought she told a good joke. "They're to different times, different centuries, different people. The one I just had. . . I've heard that name before. Quattrone. Senator Quattrone." He gazed at the ceiling. "I remember. My first year at university, I took a course in Venetian folklore. Senator Quattrone had disagreements with the doge and disappeared under mysterious circumstances in the early 1600s. It's believed he haunts a bridge in Cannaregio; on certain days at dusk, one could hear a whistling coming from beneath it."

"Have you ever been to that bridge?"

"Sì, with that class. Ponte Vendramin, it's nothing special." He smiled. "I didn't hear the whistle, but it was a fun class."

"Okay, so you're having a weird daydream. You've been under a lot of stress, not much sleep. Lots of wine. It's easily explained."

Carlo shook his head. "You always make good points. That is all true and probably part of it. It was like a memory. But not a memory. I was there, for all of them. It's like I'm experiencing these people's lives. Reliving them. I *was* Quattrone. I saw it through his eyes. I felt it through his senses. And I didn't see it, but I know what happened to him. . . ."

"What?"

"He wasn't murdered. He was taken. And sentenced to *Paradiso*. All the people I'm having visions of—all of them were sentenced to *Paradiso*."

Julia gasped. Even with all she'd heard, it was an unsettling piece of news. Then it hit her—once again, another piece of the puzzle was missing. "How do you know they were sentenced to *Paradise*?"

Carlo's eyes widened as if he'd just been caught.

"I. . . I just feel it."

"What are you hiding, Carlo?"

"Nothing. What do you mean?"

"You're having visions of people sentenced to the painting. Why would that be?"

Jerking his head backward, Carlo softened his voice. "They're dreams,

Julia. I can't say for sure why I feel it, but like you said, they can be explained by everything that's happened, don't you think? I saw a painting come to life."

Julia settled down. It didn't fully explain it, but his statement solidified a different thought that had been nagging at her. The words she was about to say were the subject of fantasy, but she eschewed reality for a moment. "You said earlier that when Nick tried to free the souls, he killed Comin, I mean, Tintoretto." She gauged his reaction. There was none. "Isn't that what's supposed to free them? Killing the Painter?"

"I don't—I think—I don't really know. That's what I heard, too."

"So why aren't they free?"

Carlo shook his head. "I don't know."

Time seemed to disappear over the next hour. Between two additional bottles of wine and Carlo's story, the minutes blended together. He told her everything about the Order, everything that happened to Nick. Everything about his family and past. But was it everything? She couldn't be sure and at times felt he was withholding information. His father's death came up again, how he perished in a horrible fire. She reminded him there was never an investigation, but the discussion veered back to della Porta and how he became Carlo's guardian. That conversation circled back to the Order.

Coupled with what Benton had told her, a clear picture of what Nick was up against emerged. She woke the laptop up, ready to research ways to help Nick other than a lawyer but didn't have a solid place to start. The wine clouded her thoughts, but she enjoyed the feeling and started to believe all the impossible things Carlo had told her. She also began seeing him in a different light. He was more than an Italian wannabe gigolo and talented painter. He was multifaceted and thoughtful. And damn good-looking.

Julia jumped. His hand landed on her thigh with such quickness, she didn't notice him moving his arm. The sting of his slap was brief, dampened by the alcohol. Startled by his speed and that he'd even put his hand on her leg, she stared at it. She hadn't noticed his paint-stained fingers were long and his fingernails seemed manicured—an unusual thing for an artist. Finally, Carlo lifted his palm and showed her the dead mosquito. He flicked the carcass onto the floor.

"Oh," she said, feeling her cheeks burn. "Thank you." She took another sip of wine. Half a glass from being totally wasted, she cut herself off. She savored the golden moment of intoxication—when one's senses were dulled enough to let inhibitions sail away, but not enough to lose the capacity to function. She wished Nick were there. It'd been a week since they last had sex. And she was dying for an orgasm.

XVIII

HIS HEART POUNDED SO RAPIDLY AGAINST his ribcage that Nick worried he'd go into cardiac arrest. Isabella's urn sat on the white granite countertop between the Jack and Jill sinks. Save a roll of toilet paper, it was the lone item in the otherwise never-used chalk-white bathroom. *Isabella.* There, alone with him, inches away. His hands vibrated uncontrollably, as if his body resonated with the urn's frequency.

He didn't recall saying a word when he took the vessel. He regretted not asking how Paganelli got a hold of it, but that fact was irrelevant in the moment; there was no way Nick was leaving the bathroom yet.

Hyperventilating, he willed himself to close his eyes and rested his head against the cool clay.

An image came into view: Isabella, the two of them relaxing in Angelo's cousin's skiff, bobbing in the Venetian Lagoon beneath a perfect cobalt-blue sky.

The memory settled him enough to maintain some semblance of control. His heartbeat slowed to a manageable rate.

Opening his eyes, he examined the urn. For the most part, it was unremarkable—about a foot high, it looked like a terracotta vase with a wax-coated cap. Hand-painted on the side was 'CXLIV.' *144.* A low number given the thousands imprisoned, but Nick remembered his regression to Angelo during Isabella's sentencing. *Paradise* was a work in progress when she was imprisoned in July of 1589.

He reached for the urn, but halted himself, first checking if the door was locked. It was. He picked at the wax, but it was slow-going, crumbling under his fingernails. Quickly checking the vanity and sink drawers and finding them empty, Nick glanced about the bathroom until his eyes settled on the hand towel hook. With a quick thrust, he snapped it off the wall and used the screw to cut through the wax seal, scraping enough away. Staring at the vessel again, he rubbed his hands together, before exhaling into them. He messed up his hair, then smoothed it back.

Nick hesitated, acutely aware that two roads lay before him. If he stepped onto one, there may be no turning back. And no happy ending. But what of Isabella's ending? If he chose the safe path for himself, she'd be destined for no end, let alone a happy one.

A faint whisper left his lips: "We are of the same heart."

Angelo reached out...

...and opened the cap.

1589

ISABELLA'S SCREAM PIERCED ANGELO'S EARS, despite the leather strap clamped between her teeth. He held her head, caressed her hair, and kissed her forehead as she lay on the dirty wooden table, stained with every kind of bodily fluid from an untold number of people. The doctor crouched at the end of the table, maneuvering the iron Tire-Tete inside of her.

"Pàr piassèr, dotor," Angelo said. "Stop hurting her. I beg of you."

"You should be begging the Lord for forgiveness," the doctor replied. "As should I."

Isabella spat out the strap. "You took the ducats," she shouted. "Just hurry and finish!"

Her eyes rolled up to the black rafters, where pigeons made their home with rats. Hemp-cord sheets obscured the windows, the door was shut, and the medico insisted on only three candles to light the small space. Even with the cover and being in the shipbuilding yards, Angelo was sure Isabella's cries could be heard all the way to San Polo.

"Stop," Angelo yelled. "For all that is holy, stop!"

The doctor withdrew the bloody tool from Isabella. Angelo was on him in a flash. He grabbed the man's throat and slammed him against the wall.

"I will snap your neck if you continue inflicting pain." Angelo's saliva sprayed his face.

"You supplicate for that which is holy," the doctor said. "Her pain is Jesus absolving her sin, siòr."

Angelo didn't loosen his grip. "And what of my sin?"

"It is not the man's to bear."

"Please, my love," Isabella said. "It's almost over."

The doctor's words didn't sit well with Angelo, but he released his neck.

As Angelo knelt next to his love, the doctor returned to his work. Isabella squeezed Angelo's hand so hard he thought she might crush it. He placed the strap back in her mouth and covered her head with kisses. Though the doctor administered the pain, Angelo felt responsible for it. The man's words repeated in his mind. The sin was entirely on his shoulders, entirely his to bear. He wanted to drive the Tire-Tete through his own abdomen. He swore he'd never let her experience this type of pain—or any discomfort at all—ever again. Renzo dispensed beatings more frequently and harshly on Isabella than on anything in the stables. It was astounding that his treatment didn't abort the baby. On second thought, taking the iron tool from the doctor and cracking it into the back of her brutish husband's ugly head when he returned from Trieste would kill two birds with one stone.

Isabella wailed again, the strap useless in stifling her cry.

The doctor twisted the Tire-Tete. As he extracted the tool, Angelo shielded his beloved's eyes with a dusty gray blanket, lifting it over their heads, as if the two of them were in a private tent, on the other side of the world. With no words to utter that could soothe her, he pressed his forehead against her sweaty brow. Their tears mingled. He gripped her hand, desperate to absorb her suffering.

Only when the doctor announced, "Finìo," did Angelo lower the blanket.

After placing a clean cloth on Isabella, the doctor stood and gathered his tools. He wrapped everything, including a bloody bundle, in a large satchel. "Leave here before dawn. Then she must rest for three days."

"What shall I tell my maidservants?" Isabella asked in a weak voice.

"That your cycle is unusually severe. You will heal. But do not let them see you until you do." He placed a small green glass vial on the table. "Theriac for the pain. No more than a half spoonful each night."

The doctor made for the door.

"Not a word of this to a soul," Angelo said. "Or I will slit your throat from behind."

Without turning, the medico bowed and left. A late winter dusting blew into the room. Angelo began placing an additional wool blanket over Isabella, but she stopped him. "You need to stay warm."

"I want to feel cold. I *need* to feel cold. Please, open the door."

Angelo did as she requested. The breeze brought in airy snowflakes that drifted about the room like restless fairies.

He returned to his love's side, wiped her forehead, then took her hands in his. "Are you in pain, 'mòre mio?"

"It is better now," she said with a sharp huff. "Do not worry yourself."

Though Angelo had faced the tip of a sword countless times, never had he been put in such a situation as Isabella, physically or mentally. The courage his beloved displayed astounded him. "How could I not worry? The doctor's words were false. A fabrication to ease me in the moment. I am to blame for this. It is my burden."

"Everything we did, we did together. We made the right choice. It was our *only* choice."

Angelo hung his head. "I feel this sin will haunt us for our days."

"It's more agony than anything my body can endure, tesoro. But Renzo would've known. He would've known. . ." She shivered and caressed her belly with a profound sadness. "The outcome would've been far worse for the three of us."

Burying his head on her bosom, Angelo sighed. "You are right, undeniably. I wish there'd been a third course. We risk ex-communication."

"God does not punish love. He understands."

"God willing, there will be a penance we can pay."

"The child was conceived by love, but under . . . grievous circumstances. Renzo would've killed it *and* me. I know this. Our penance will be to free ourselves from his grasp. We'll have another child someday—a child we can raise and love without fear of persecution or abuse."

The tears streamed down Isabella's face. Angelo couldn't hold his back any longer. He joined her in her sobs. He took her hand and kissed it over and over

XX

... AND OVER AND OVER. BAWLING UNCONTROLLABLY, Nick planted kisses on the urn.

"Tuto, 'mòre mio," he whispered. "Everything. Everything."

An irrepressible urge to be one with Isabella consumed Nick, like a raging forest fire devouring the spark that lit the inferno. Placing his nose over the urn, he closed his eyes and fanned the air toward him, as if smelling a boiling soup. He expected a scent of ash and dust, but it was the opposite. Though Isabella's cinders were from over four-hundred-thirty years ago, the vessel had always been sealed. An aroma of cinnamon mixed with rose caressed his nostrils. The sweet flowers combined with the peppery spice awakened his essence, coiling nearly orgasmic shivers up his spine that popped goosebumps over his body. He swallowed, wanting, needing, craving more than just fragrance.

Throwing caution and rational thought into his inner blaze, the wind picked up, and Nick did the only thing that made sense in the moment—he fed the fire. He dipped his forefinger into Isabella's ashes, closed his eyes, and licked. Her incinerated body melted into a paste of rose and cinnamon—a tonic of spiritual nourishment. He shuddered as he brought Isabella inside of him. Again, it wasn't enough; the small taste prompted an instant addiction. He needed all of her, to return to her.

He plunged his fingers into the cool ash and ladled a handful, which he fed himself like a starving grizzly bear.

When he did it again, his fingers lighted on something unexpected—a hard, foreign object. He pulled it out to find Isabella's onyx and ruby rosary. Sensations Nick had never experienced flooded his body all at once, at full blast. Everything washed over him—joy, sorrow, guilt, relief, hunger, satisfaction, exhaustion, exhilaration.

With tremoring hands, he placed the rosary around his neck and kissed the beads. Moving to cross himself, he stopped. Instead, he held a large onyx bead and whispered in Venetian, "Forgive me my trespass... I will *not* forgive those who've trespassed against us. Lead me *not* from temptation. Deliver me ... to my love."

Nick realized his former life drove his actions.

Angelo was in control. Nick surrendered.

He dug his hand back into the urn and wiped Isabella onto his forehead, cheeks, and beard growth. He scooped more of her and spread her into his hair, tussling it, then smoothing it back, careful not to shake the ashes out.

Pining to be closer to her, he removed his shirt, followed by his shoes, socks, pants, and boxers. Handful after handful, he coated his body with Isabella, pausing only to consume more of her. And when he was finished, he was one with his soul mate—outside and in.

AFTER DRESSING, ANOTHER person's reflection stared back at him in the mirror. Gray skin, gray hair, gray clothes. It was a fitting hue for someone caught between two worlds—and for another living in purgatory for centuries.

With a satisfied grin, he kissed the ash-covered rosary hanging from his neck and opened the bathroom door.

"Even if they're severely wounded," Paganelli said, "we can look for the book later, if need be."

Fosca shook her head. "What if you fail—again? We can't afford to lose any more people."

Alberico Gulotta, standing behind the couch, was about to speak to Paganelli, but when he turned toward the bathroom, his glass dropped with his jaw. Wine splashed across the white rug. Gulotta backed away from his ash-covered body, likely thinking it filth, when in truth, it was beauty. Paganelli and Fosca, both on the couch, turned at the sound and gasped.

"Nick..." was all Fosca could mutter.

He walked over and sat in the free side chair, covering the white leather with ash. Everyone in Venice knew the myth of the phoenix, as the city itself had experienced a rebirth many times. As he flicked his gaze across the people gawking at him, he knew he was the legend come to life.

"Nicola sè morto," he declared.

"Morto...?" Fosca whispered with an air of comprehension.

Paganelli grinned. "Yes. Nicholas is dead. Welcome, Angelo."

Gulotta remained behind the couch, staring at Angelo in astonishment.

"No stà a preòccuparte," Angelo said to Fosca.

She turned to Paganelli for help with the translation.

"Do not be alarmed, Fosca," Angelo said, preempting Paganelli. "I can speak your English and some Italian. I retain all of Nick's memories." He was aware his voice was different—a slightly higher pitch and inflected with his true Venetian accent—but it felt natural to be his original self and simultaneously in command of his present-day life.

"In light, there is truth." Paganelli raised his arms and gazed at the ceiling before speaking to Angelo again. "I trust you enjoyed seeing Isabella again?"

The comment sparked a frenzy in Angelo. He pounced on Paganelli, gripping the old man's throat. "How did you get the urn? Why didn't you get it for me before?"

"Nick, stop!" Fosca screamed.

"I couldn't possibly," Paganelli managed with limited breath.

Angelo sensed Gulotta jumping up from behind him. As the attorney moved to restrain him, Angelo elbowed him in the jaw. Gulotta cried out and stumbled back.

Fosca gripped Angelo's arm, trying to pry it away. "It was my idea," she yelled. "Uncle Enzo never would've had access to the book."

"The doge's book? What book?" Angelo asked.

"Another," Paganelli wheezed. "Let me go. I'll explain."

Angelo released his hold. He should've felt gratitude toward Paganelli and his friends, but he mistrusted them. Sitting back in his chair, he folded his arms. "I'm listening."

Paganelli rubbed his neck. Gulotta sat in his own chair, massaging his jaw.

Though the tension in the room dissipated, Fosca's hands shook; she was clearly not used to seeing people fight. "The Book of Names," she said with a rattled voice. "All the victims in *Paradise* are in it."

"How did you get it?"

"When della Porta was in prison," Gulotta replied.

"I found the urn number," Fosca said. "Uncle Enzo went under the Palazzo and got it."

"We needed to move fast," Paganelli said. "I fear they'll seal the tunnel, if they haven't already."

Angelo returned his attention to Fosca. "How would you have access to such a book? One that is surely kept locked away."

"How do you think?" Gulotta asked.

"You're in the Order," Angelo said to Fosca.

"We all are," she replied.

"Or *were*," Paganelli added. He cleared his throat. "We're on your side, Angelo. As you know."

"Apologies, siòr. As you would imagine, my emotions are . . . running high."

"Water under the proverbial bridge, my friend. I'm sure I would've done the same in your shoes."

Paganelli poured a glass of white wine and handed it to Angelo. The wine soothed his parched throat, still glazed with ash. He followed with some olives, which helped to settle his stomach.

The old man's gaze fell on Isabella's rosary. "Before a soul is sentenced," he said, "the Order divests victims of Earthly possessions on their person. But after incineration, it's the custom to bury any such items in the urn."

Angelo caressed the beautiful beads hanging from his neck.

Fosca continued to gape with a shaking hand. Angelo realized it wasn't the fight that bothered her, but *him*. She was clearly scared of him, unsettled by his transformation, or both.

"You said you recall Nick's life," Paganelli said. "And all of your own as well, I presume?"

"Of course. My life beyond Venice was remarkable. But now, I have returned, and I will free my beloved. This time, I shall succeed."

"You will." Paganelli pointed his bony finger at the Renaissance-era swordsman come to life. "You'll destroy the Sun Crystal and kill the Painter."

"Uncle Enzo," Fosca said, her apparent anger and frustration supplanting her fear. "You're a stubborn old goat."

Paganelli chuckled. "Do all millennials use tired expressions? My mother used to call my father the same thing."

"Then it runs in your family, doesn't it?" she said. "And it's not funny."

As she, Gulotta, and Paganelli rattled on in low voices, Angelo ignored them and walked to the kitchen. He opened the drawers, searching for a knife. All of them were empty. The only knife of any sort was the cheese knife on the cutting board.

"Why do you have nothing here?" he asked.

"Because nobody lives here," Fosca replied. "It's a temporary apartment. A safe house."

"Even safe houses need utensils." Angelo left the kitchen and headed for the door. "It matters not. I know where I can obtain a better weapon."

"Wait, Nick—I mean, Angelo." Fosca rushed over and took his arm.

Annoyed, Angelo stopped and faced the girl.

"You know the Order is bigger than the Painter. Much bigger. He's a tool, the Order's hand. Killing him would be a setback for them. Renzo's book will destroy them forever."

"Severing the hand will free Isabella. *That* is my mission."

Paganelli and Gulotta hustled over. Fosca continued. "You can help us in our mission, too. You must remember something."

"That book is the cause of all my sorrows."

"It's also the reason you met Isabella," Paganelli said.

The old man spoke the truth. Angelo conceded this point with a nod. "As I said, I don't know where the book is. I told this to della Porta. It's possible it was in a box in the Scalfinis' armoire, but I cannot say for sure. The people who would know are the Bird Brothers."

"Who?" Fosca asked.

Angelo placed his hand on the doorknob but paused before turning it. He owed these people a debt. "Vito and Ivan Uccello. They hired me to find it before they betrayed me. They may have found the key to the lockbox." He opened the door. "You should know della Porta knows of them as well."

Fosca took his free hand and squeezed it. "Grazie, Angelo."

"What are you going to do?" Gulotta asked.

"His job," Paganelli replied. "One I should have accomplished years ago."

Angelo shook his head. "It's my mission now. May God help you with yours."

XXI

THE LAST TIME NICK CREPT TO THE BRIDGE beyond the northeastern corner of St. Mark's Basilica, it was to retrieve the boat in the tunnel beneath the Palazzo so that he and Julia could escape Venice. She had feared for her life, thinking her husband had a psychotic break. Angelo shook his head, scattering a dusting of ash. It wasn't a break, but a restoration, a homecoming, a reinstatement. A return to the real. Though he retained all of Nick's memories and emotions, his present life—including Julia—was not a concern.

She is. She's more than a concern.

Nick crawled forward from the recesses of Angelo's mind.

Julia's alive. Flesh, breathing. In the here and now.

Ignoring Nick's voice, Angelo focused on the current reason he returned to this spot—he needed a weapon. On the way, Angelo had surveilled the Palazzo, which brushed against the Basilica's southern wall. He'd seen four men strolling about St. Mark's Square, but he knew they were plain-clothed guards patrolling the building's perimeter. There were likely more inside the compound, so he needed to stay in the shadows. Lacasse would've informed della Porta of Nick's release; they expected him to go to the Palazzo, and he wouldn't be surprised if their patrol extended this far out. He wondered if della Porta was aware of the secret tunnel. Though the bastard was the Exalted Master, the tunnel was hundreds of years old, and the rusty gate clearly hadn't been used for decades. It didn't seem like new urns had been placed there for some time, either.

That said, Paganelli knew about the tunnel, and if della Porta wasn't aware of it before, they'd be searching for how Nick entered the building. They knew he entered the Great Council Room through the secret door beneath *Paradise*. There could be multiple means of ingress, so it may take some time before they discovered the hatchway in the Painter's room.

It's a trap, you fool.

Angelo pondered this. When he rushed in to kill Tintoretto, it didn't go well. Then again, in *that* attempt, Nick had nothing but a small knife and had never killed a man. Angelo, on the other hand, had drawn blood on countless occasions. He was once the best swordsman in Venice. After leaving his most serene city, he improved infinitely over the years, struck down dozens of enemies, and never received a serious injury. With his skill and Nick's strength, combined with his knowledge of past and present, he'd be unrivaled. He'd strike the new Painter down, then find the Sun Crystal and destroy it. Isabella would finally be free.

He shimmied over the bridge down to the narrow canal ledge where Nick had given Julia a gun to wait for him. That gun would've been useful now, but Nick had tossed it overboard when they rowed to the mainland.

They have guns, moron. And they're not muskets. Go to Julia, live a happy life.

Angelo paused, allowing Nick to make his case. But a broader view of his life as Nick—being with Julia, cooking in their Boston home together, driving to Home Depot to pick up supplies for another project, even making love—felt like watching a play. Objectively, it was his body moving through the scenes, but the sentiment behind his actions was foreign. A different person lived that life. Angelo and Isabella were real. Nick and Julia were fabrications. Had he absconded with Isabella a day prior—*five minutes prior*—they would've lived their days together. Nothing but numbness inhabited Angelo's mind as he turned the pages of his current life's memories.

His thoughts sailed to Isabella. Even in his hyper-alert state, she soothed his heart with a calm and peace. The gun would've been useful, but it wasn't necessary. He severed any attachment to this life, tucked the rosary into his shirt, and slid into the water.

Her ashes floated off. With a deep inhale, he submerged his head into the canal. The cold water cleansed and bolstered his skin, as if recoated with his first life's body. When he raised his head above the water's surface, any vestiges of life to which Nick had been clinging dissolved.

Though the bottom of the canal was near pitch black, Angelo had an excellent idea of where Nick had tossed the Protector's sword. He'd anticipated needing multiple dives, but a shimmer on the steel enabled him to find it in one breath. He popped up from the murky depth with the weapon, victorious. The champion swordsman in him wanted to pump his hand in the air, but he caught himself. A lone man paced onto the bridge. Angelo recognized his stature and graying hair.

Detective Lacasse.

Swimming silently to the abutment beneath the bridge, Angelo sunk to his nostrils to maintain a vantage point. The French Interpol detective crouched and peered into the canal. Angelo cursed himself. He must've heard a splash—or worse, awaited his arrival.

A trickle of rain pattered the water, causing small ripples. Lacasse remained motionless, then shined a light into the canal. Angelo submerged himself, keeping his body pressed against the stone. A muffled voice carried through the water. The light scanned the area one more time before switching off. Angelo floated up and sucked air. The detective was gone.

With all the Protectors and guards on-site, Angelo was right—they expected him and set a trap, but it didn't matter. Though he yearned to see Isabella in the Great Council Room, he'd return to the Palazzo later.

FIFTEEN MINUTES LATER, Angelo crept up to Carlo's front window and peered inside. Every sense heightened. The hairs on his neck stood on end as raindrops pelted his body. His hearing and vision distilled to a pinpoint target: Julia and Carlo on the couch in the center of the loft, their backs to him, looking at a computer on her lap.

The window was open but barred and far too narrow for Angelo to fit through. Reaching in, he stretched for the inside door handle, but it was just out of his grasp. Squashing the urge to smash the window, he checked the door from the outside. Ever so quietly, he gripped the handle. Angelo froze at the voices behind him. He crouched and turned his head surreptitiously. A young couple, arm-in-arm, traversed the small square. When they entered the connecting alley, Angelo returned his attention to the door handle. Planting one hand on the wood to dampen any sound, he pressed down on the latch. To his surprise, the handle moved. He turned it as slowly as possible, feeling the cylinder rotate and the pin tumblers fall into place. He silently thanked Carlo for having a modern door and rolled it open, just enough to squeeze through.

Julia talked over acoustic folk music with a raspy-voiced singer crooning in Italian. Of course, she couldn't understand the lyrics, but Angelo wondered if the song about unrequited love was intentional. The thought only fueled his anger. The Painter shimmied closer to Julia. He draped his arm over the back of the sofa, tucked under her blonde ponytail, his hand inches from her shoulder.

Mindful to limit all possible sounds, Angelo kept the door slightly open to avoid the latch startling them. He was so focused on his stealth entry, he didn't even listen to what Julia was saying. And he didn't care. Here she was, Nick's wife, on the couch, enjoying wine with another man. For all she knew, Nick was in prison, agonizing in fear that the guards would kill him the moment they had the chance.

Angelo tiptoed toward his target. Drawing the sword from his belt, he raised the blade and crept up behind them. He disliked the heavy weight and clunky balance of the Mongolian short sword—and worse, that it was the Order's weapon—but gripping a hilt energized his senses and strengthened his resolve.

He pressed the tip against the back of the Painter's neck.

"Don't move," he whispered in Venetian, the words seeping from the darkest cavern of his heart.

Julia screamed and spun around.

Neither Carlo nor Angelo flexed a muscle.

"Nick!" Julia's eyes flicked from the sword in his hands to his face to Carlo. "What—why—how'd you get out? Why are you holding a sword?"

Angelo caught a glimpse of his reflection in the TV mounted on the wall. He vaguely resembled her husband. Eyes wild, unshaven, unruly hair, wet clothes; he didn't recognize himself.

"Nick is dead," he growled in English.

With a gasp, Julia covered her mouth, surely not only at the words, but at Angelo's changed voice and accent.

Do not hurt her.

"Nick—Nick. You . . . you're standing right here. I don't know how, but you are, and you're you. Put the sword down, honey. Please."

Carlo remained motionless.

"You thought Nick was locked away." Angelo's chest heaved; the stress on his bruised ribcage felt like a punch with every breath. "So you ran into the arms of your lover?"

The sword pressed firmer into Carlo's neck. Blood trickled at the point.

"Nick, stop," Julia shouted. "I'm not with him. This is crazy. Nothing happened!"

"You'd stab your friend in the back?" Carlo asked.

"You're not my friend."

He is. Nick spoke to Angelo in his head.

Carlo stiffened more. "Have I ever done anything against you?"

He saved us.

"You're part of the Order," Angelo said to Carlo.

"Sì, now I am. But I have done everything to help you."

"Then tell me where the Sun Crystal is."

"The Palazzo, I suppose."

"Honey." Julia slowly placed the laptop on the coffee table and clasped her hands together. "Please believe us. All we want is what's best for you. You need help. Please, Nick."

"My name is *Angelo*," he said, turning to Julia.

"Help . . . me," Nick whispered coarsely.

Shaking his head to rid himself of the mental intruder, Angelo lowered the sword a hair.

Carlo didn't hesitate. He rolled forward onto the table, inadvertently knocking the wine and the laptop onto the floor.

Angelo lunged but was far too slow. With remarkable speed and agility, Carlo popped up, vaulted onto the couch, and leaped, catching the hilt and tackling Angelo to the floor. Angelo crashed hard on his back;

Nick's physical wounds ricocheted through him. With fierce eyes, Carlo grabbed Angelo's hand and smashed it with unknown strength, causing Angelo's fingers to pop open. The Painter snatched the sword and bounded to his feet. Staring at the tip of a blade pointing down at him, the swordsman was stunned that his adversary had defeated him in seconds.

He attempted to shuffle backward, but Carlo leveled the sword inches from his nose, pinning Angelo down. Carlo's speed was mesmerizing. He glided in a streak like a sailfish—faster than the Whip Snake or any opponent Angelo had ever faced. His chances of besting the Painter were nil; Fosca had warned him of his agility and strength, and so had Isabella.

The young Painter is extremely powerful,' Angelo's beloved had said the final time he saw her in *Paradiso*. '*Commit a crime, not hostile to the Order, but against another. Supplicate for mercy. They'll sentence you to Paradise. You must kill a loved one.*'

If he couldn't kill the Painter...

"No," Nick cried out, the words reverberating in his mind.

"Sì," Angelo yelled.

'*We'll be imprisoned for eternity,*' Isabella had said, '*but we shall be together.*'

"Carlo... before it's too late..." Nick pried his way into the forefront of Angelo's mind, forcing the words out. "Save Julia..."

"I already have," replied Carlo.

"No..."

"Siènsio," Angelo screamed, shoving Nick back into his hole.

But the younger owner of the body refused to go.

"Kill me," Nick muttered with waning strength. "Please."

Julia gasped.

Carlo leveled the sword at Angelo's eye. "You make me want to."

"Carlo, no!" a voice hollered from the open door.

Craning his neck, Angelo's stomach constricted at Bernardo running into the flat, with della Porta standing in the doorway. Both wielded Mongolian short swords.

"This is not our way," della Porta continued. "You must remain a pure soul. Put the weapon down."

"He tried to kill me," Carlo said, in a voice that sounded like a plea.

Angelo seized his moment and suppressed Nick. He whacked Carlo's sword away with the back of his hand. Disregarding the blistering pain and blood splattering from the open gash, he rolled forward and tackled Carlo's skinny knees, causing him to collapse backward. Angelo retrieved the sword, but instead of attacking the Painter, he lurched to his feet and pursued Julia, who scrambled away.

CARLO JUMPED UP to aid Julia, but before he could, something else caught his attention. Something unfathomably horrible.

A new, unexpected visitor—an elderly man with short, white hair in a soaking wet baby blue Polo—bounded up the stoop and into his home.

As if in slow motion, the white-haired man drove a pair of scissors into della Porta's right shoulder.

The air in della Porta's lungs discharged. Without looking at his assailant, he said, "Paganelli. Forever the betrayer." He collapsed to his knees, attempting to reach the scissors in vain.

"Paganelli?" Carlo exclaimed, unable to yet process how his father's killer could be there at that moment.

With an almost childlike glee, the old man towered over della Porta and relieved him of his sword. "You have some twisted notions to call *me* the betrayer."

Carlo snapped out of it. This man who murdered his father and upended his life was in *his* home, moments away from repeating the past with *his* father figure. Carlo couldn't let that happen. Della Porta needed him. Julia, still evading Nick deeper into his flat, needed him. It pained Carlo to be unable to help Julia, but if he went to her aid, Paganelli could kill della Porta and Bernardo. He charged Paganelli. Bernardo followed.

"Eh, eh, eh," Paganelli said. He brought his blade to della Porta's neck. "You control his fate now."

They stopped in their tracks, two meters away.

"Drop your sword and kick it over," Paganelli ordered the one-armed Protector.

Bernardo grimaced but obeyed the command. Keeping his weapon pressed against della Porta's skin, Paganelli crouched and claimed Bernardo's.

"It's nice to be able to do this." Paganelli snickered, holding a weapon in each hand, mocking Bernardo's armless shoulder.

"You don't deserve to wield a Protector's sword," Bernardo replied. "You disgraced it long ago, and you disgrace it now."

Clenching his fists, Carlo desperately wanted to charge. But even with his newfound agility, the old man would have ample time to slide his blade across della Porta's neck.

"I am the only one who has ever wielded it with honor," Paganelli said. "Divina Protectores, remember? A protector *of* the divine does not make one divine, despite delusions of grandeur."

Carlo glanced to the rear of his flat. Julia dodged Nick, scrabbling between furniture. The dilemma was torture, but she seemed to be fending off her husband—or, more accurately, the man possessing him. Carlo returned his attention to the other men, horrified by the blood streaming from della Porta's shoulder. "I know you," Carlo said to the white-haired man. "You came to my house. You knew my parents. You madman, what have you done?"

Paganelli spoke to della Porta. "You didn't get that chance to kill me. But you had the chance for Carlo's father, didn't you? And my wife. Yet, I am branded the madman, the outcast. Won't you finally admit the truth?"

Carlo stilled. He yearned to rush to Julia's aid, as well as help della Porta, but Paganelli's statement rendered him motionless.

Bernardo seized the moment. With Paganelli's attention diverted, he dove for the old man's sword on della Porta, and at the same time, he attempted to wedge himself between the two men. The move failed.

Paganelli's weapon glanced Bernardo's hip, striking him off balance. He toppled into both men, and the three of them crashed out the door and off the stoop.

Carlo chased after them to find the men lying in the wet courtyard, illuminated by Carlo's lights and a lone streetlamp in the hot, rainy night. His herb garden littered the cobblestones. Bernardo stretched and retrieved a sword, but with della Porta's body on top of Paganelli, the old man maneuvered his blade beneath della Porta's chin. Slowly, Paganelli hoisted the injured man to his feet.

Hustling to Bernardo, Carlo helped his wounded friend up. Blood gushed from his pant leg.

"A foolish move," Paganelli said, who seemed to be unscathed.

"Just do it already." Della Porta coughed. "What are you waiting for?"

Paganelli snorted. "Angelo, of course. I prefer a fighting chance." He jeered at Bernardo and della Porta with contempt, his wet white hair gleaming beneath the streetlight.

He looked at Carlo but averted his eyes, and Carlo saw it in that instant: remorse and torment. This old man wanted to kill della Porta and even Bernardo, perhaps for revenge, but his task was to kill *him*, the Painter. And there could be only one reason for such an action: he wanted to free the souls.

"STOP," JULIA SCREAMED.

At the far end of Carlo's loft, Angelo loomed toward Julia. She darted past him and positioned her body on the opposite side of the sofa.

Angelo's insides waged holy war as he continued his pursuit. "Leave her be," Nick screamed, roaring from within. Angelo's fingers tightened around the sword's hilt.

"Nick, don't do this." Her body quaked.

"Find it in your heart, Julia. Forgive me," Angelo said through clenched teeth.

"Forgive you for what? Come back to me, honey."

"Your death will bring me to my love. They'll sentence me."

Julia backed away, shaking.

"Nick loves you, Julia," Angelo offered. He said it to calm her, but the words came out with malice as he buried Nick. "He does, but you're not soul mates. There is no other way." He lumbered toward her.

"No other way for what?" She dashed behind the side chair. "You're scaring the shit out of me!"

Though Julia's death would lead to Angelo's reunion with Isabella, frightening her disgusted him. The sword weighed heavy in his hand as he focused on the outcome, not the act. He convulsed his head to clear his thoughts.

You must kill her, my love.

Isabella's voice wasn't audible in his mind like Nick's, but Angelo imagined his beloved's soothing tones as a sweet respite from the drama and confusion in front of him. His heart surged at the thought of her, but he found himself unable to take the next step. "No. No ti pòl farlo."

You must do it for our love. There is no other way.

The conviction was unwavering for Angelo; Nick tried to fight him, but as Angelo's control grew, Nick's command of his body and mind waned. "I love you, Julia," he whispered, conscious his voice took on an eerily soothing cadence.

"But it's not *true* love," Angelo said. "We must sacrifice one love for true love."

"You *are* my true love, Nick O'Connor!"

Her words pushed Angelo closer to the truth, closer to her. Nick began to slip away. "I am Angelo Mascari."

Julia backed into the wall between two abstract black and white paintings. There was nowhere to go. Tears rolled down her face.

"Snap out of it, honey! You're Nicholas O'Connor. An American. We live in Boston. We went to BU together. You're the man I married, the man I love. *My* soul mate!"

No, Angelo Mascari was first.

I am Nicholas O'Connor now.

No. We are one. And one with Isabella.

The muddled cocktail of voices and thoughts discombobulated his senses. In a moment of blind confusion, the glint of Nick's wedding ring on his finger caught his attention. The true owner of his present life wasn't done.

Angelo's hand rose to his mouth. He kissed the ring, then bit his fist, trying to shock himself into some sort of reality. Nick's nightmare persisted. He punched himself repeatedly in the temple.

Wake up wake up wake up wake up!

The urge to conclude his task did not abate. Julia stood stunned, and with each blow, she cried out as if she, too, was wounded.

"Nick, stop! Angelo, whoever you are, please!"

Angelo shook out his fist. He ripped off the ring and chucked it to the other side of the loft. He leveled the sword at Julia again. This was his path. "They'll sentence me. They'll sentence me."

Julia's an innocent. There's still time.

This was true. Angelo's eyes shifted to Julia, who cowered in front of him. She grabbed a floor lamp and held it out in a feeble attempt to protect herself. Her watery eyes blinked with fright. It was so pathetic, so meek. He felt his heart go out to her. She would never survive. He didn't want to kill an innocent. The decision weighed heavy on his heart, but it wasn't a choice.

"Julia," Carlo called from outside.

Julia took her chance. She tore through the kitchen, eluding Angelo in his distraction.

It was but a moment, a blink that prolonged fate. He followed her, where she searched the space, found the knife block, and slid a large carving knife out. Her courage prompted a woeful smile.

It is the one way, 'mòre mio.

Again, earnest resolution bolstered Angelo.

So much carnage, so much bloodshed. It should've shaken him more. All this violence. But in his mind, driven by Isabella's words, driven by centuries of anguish, he could not be deterred.

"It will be done. They will sentence me."

He tightened his grip around the sword.

"What can I do? What can I do?" Julia cried out, but her words were like a tattered umbrella in a hurricane. Her voice rumpled into itself, forming a pile of pleading drivel before Angelo's feet.

He sympathized with her yearning for a sensible resolution. But there was none. "I'm righting an age-old wrong."

It was time. He raised the sword, grasping it to bear down on her. He aimed and thrust at her.

But he was met with an unexpected parry. Julia gripped the carving knife with both hands, blocking Angelo's attack.

Do it. Do it now.

The unrelenting voice crushed his head. But more than that, it throbbed in his chest, permeated his being. Determined strength welled through him.

Isabella. Isabella. Isabella.

He swung. Julia screamed. Again, she parried, but the sword knocked the knife out of her hand. It flew across the kitchen and landed with a clatter.

Julia scuttled away into Carlo's studio area. She stumbled over boxes of paint tubes and cans containing brushes, moving between various easels, knocking them and paintings down behind her, but it was futile. Finally, Angelo couldn't take it any longer. Isabella's voice overpowered him.

Do it, my love.

He attacked, over and over, the tarnished steel blazing through the air.

Julia backed away, ducking and dodging, slamming into an easel. A sheet-covered painting toppled to the floor and landed with a clatter. Julia snatched the painting and held it in front of her body like a tragic shield, cowering before the man she thought was her husband. Angelo smirked at the artwork—a disturbing depiction of his wife and soul mate severing his head.

"Not very prophetic," Angelo mumbled.

He lunged at the painting, but to his surprise, it deflected the blow. Julia cried out in pain and dropped it, the sides slicing through her palms. Angelo recalled Carlo painted on metallic glass.

"Carlo, help!" Julia shrieked as her bloody hands flailed in front of her.

CARLO SPUN FOR JULIA. Bernardo inched forward.

"STAY WHERE YOU ARE!" Paganelli bellowed.

Carlo pivoted back to Paganelli and della Porta. Bernardo froze. Rain drenched all three men.

"Let them be," Paganelli continued. "If either of you move again, della Porta dies. We shall wait for Angelo."

Carlo hungered to save Julia, but fear froze him in place. Her rescue would be the death of della Porta and possibly Bernardo.

"Before della Porta dies, we'll learn the truth," Paganelli said.

Della Porta coughed and met Carlo's gaze. "You *know* the truth."

"For only when judged in light will thy true demon be shown," Paganelli said to Carlo with surprising tranquility. "I had no motive to kill him. He was my friend."

Bernardo spoke, his voice gritty. "Do not listen to him, Carlo. He murdered your father, for reasons known only to him."

"Who killed him?" Carlo demanded with such force that it caused Paganelli to take a step back, dragging della Porta with him.

"I would've done anything for your father," Paganelli shouted with desperation. "I would've done anything for my *wife*! He took *everything* from me. The Order destroyed my family." Paganelli pushed the blade into della Porta's skin, drawing blood. "To allow evil to walk on Earth sets evil onto oneself."

Carlo didn't know who to believe, but this man—raving, causing chaos, was a stranger to him, moments from committing murder, potentially again. Della Porta's death would bring Carlo no closer to answers, no closer to justice.

Julia screamed from within his flat. Waiting another second was no longer an option. Carlo lunged for the sword pressed against della Porta. He caught the hilt as the blade glanced della Porta's skin. Paganelli struggled as Carlo wrested the weapon from his grip. Della Porta crawled away.

Unflinching in the opportunity, Bernardo grabbed Paganelli's second sword from the man's fingers. He flourished the weapon into position and swung for Paganelli's head.

Paganelli dodged. The sword missed, and the old man tripped forward, landing on top of Carlo. Carlo crashed hard on the street, the cobblestones smacking his spine.

Bernardo was ruthless in his attack and on Paganelli a half-second later. He drove his sword into the back of Paganelli's neck.

The tip jutted through the old man's throat; blood sprayed Carlo's face.

In shock, Carlo stared at the elderly man's open, pale blue eyes as blood and rain poured from Paganelli's lethal wound, dripping into Carlo's eyes and nose, the liquids and disgust of the moment doing nothing to wake him from his frozen state. The old man's blood trickled onto Carlo's lips and tongue. Unable to reach his mouth with his arms pinned, he knew he'd remember the bitter, coppery taste for the rest of his long life.

"I'll live," he heard della Porta say to Bernardo. "Help the Painter."

The Protector did as he was told. He rolled Paganelli's body off Carlo onto the dirty cobblestones, blood pooling around the corpse. Carlo spat, then wiped his face with the back of his sleeve. On his knees, he crawled over to della Porta.

"Carlo," Julia screamed from inside. "Help me!"

Della Porta panted in quick spurts. He whispered to Carlo. "You must know, my son, my words are true. Go. Save her."

Carlo peered down at della Porta. There was an exchange of understanding. And then, all sound and emotion clicked off—everything but Julia's scream. He bolted for her, bounding into the loft. Nick had backed Julia against the wall on the far side, next to his bedroom.

"I must be with her," Nick—*or Angelo*—pleaded to his frightened wife. He detonated a primal scream that ricocheted off the walls, ceiling, and floor.

Carlo sprinted through the space, jumping over the fallen easels in his way. Six meters . . . five . . .

"Forgive me, Julia," Angelo cried out.

Faster than he'd ever run, Carlo charged. Four meters . . . three . . . two . . .

And then Angelo drove the sword into Julia's gut.

Carlo dove and tackled Angelo to the floor.

Angelo's body fell limp beneath his own, as if he'd surrendered completely. "I'm so sorry, Julia," he bawled. "Please forgive me. It is for love. Perdonìme."

Rushing over, Bernardo pressed his knee on the madman's neck. Carlo jumped up and hurried to Julia.

The blade had moved through her organs and exited her back, lodged in the wooden beam behind her.

"Carlo," della Porta called from the doorway. He'd crawled up the stoop, his face twisted in obvious pain. "Embrace apotheosis, my son."

Barely alive, the blood seeped from Julia's wounds, like a red sunset blushing the horizon. Her eyes widened, and she attempted to speak.

Careful not to disturb the blade, Carlo wrapped his arms around her and brought her to the floor.

"Call an ambulance boat!" he yelled.

Bernardo was already on his phone, his knee cemented on Angelo's back; the reincarnated swordsman's face was directed at Carlo and Julia, forced to watch them.

Her face was pale and sallow, her head sunken in her chest. He lifted her chin. Tears pooled in her eyes and in his, as well.

"What do I do?" Carlo's hands trembled in his frantic state.

Nobody answered, and there was no way to tend the wound, but Carlo tried anyway. He cupped the steel between his fingers and pressed on her skin to make a seal at the front and rear entry incisions. She offered him a weak smile. Tears coursed down his face.

"Yours is a young life," Carlo whispered. "You will find your soul mate."

"You . . . need. . ." It was as if she struggled with all her might to utter the words. "You need . . . to pay the restaurant."

She gazed at him with what seemed like gratitude, then closed her eyes. Carlo had no idea what she meant, and it didn't matter in the moment. This beautiful woman—this radiant soul—one caught in a tornado churned by the actions of others, deserved the full life of her dreams, even if he weren't a part of it. He shut his own eyes, converging all his inner strength, pressing on the wounds, the blood warming his palms. Unknown vibrations from lives he'd yet to live resounded from his core. The energy flowed within him, meshing with Julia's weakening lifeblood.

Sorrow tugged at his chest. The anger, the pity, the disgust, the wretchedness of it all.

"E'l gabìa misericordia de mi, Carlo," Angelo begged. "Pàr piassèr per favore. I confess to my sins of today and years past. Show mercy, sentence me to *Paradise*!"

His pleas bounced off the Painter's consciousness as if they were hitting a cement wall.

XXII

IT HAD BEEN NEARLY FORTY-EIGHT HOURS, and della Porta was still unaccustomed to the restrictive bandages fastened around his torso, hindered by the sling that held his arm.

After the hospital discharged him, he went to his office to plug any holes in the Order's bilge. Despite his leg wound, Bernardo had paid off Carlo's neighbors, taken care of Paganelli's body, and brought Nick to a cell in the Palazzo. The latter two were little worry, and they could be used to his advantage. Carlo, on the other hand, was a pressing concern. Between his attachment to Signora O'Connor, the unsavory events, and hurled accusations, he worried for the young Painter's state of mind, as well as for their fractured relationship. Della Porta didn't believe either was irreparably damaged, but there was too much to accomplish in too short a period. Should Carlo be unstable or unwilling to be guided toward the grandeur that awaited him, della Porta would have no choice but to replace him with a more suitable alternative.

The recent turmoil had also led to rumblings within the Order. Zotti was firmly on della Porta's side, but the mayor was unconvinced. He openly questioned della Porta's ability to lead. The countess's extended absence was an additional impediment, and not just within the Order. There was significant anxiety regarding her disappearance; family members had convinced Interpol to put out an APB throughout Europe.

Equal attention had been placed on the whereabouts of Nick O'Connor. Not only for his welfare, but because he was the prime suspect in the murder of Jacopo Comin. Della Porta and his team were unable to determine O'Connor's connection to the U.S. Secretary of State and why she demanded his release, but by all accounts, it was legitimate. However, that he evaded his attorney and had since been on the lam cemented his guilty appearance.

Della Porta had asked Lacasse to also charge O'Connor in the countess's disappearance, but unable to establish a connection between the American computer programmer and the Italian octogenarian socialite, he only remained a person of interest. Either way, della Porta was pleased with the turn of events. The police and media on both sides of the Atlantic would be guessing until they found something or moved on to the next story.

When the time was right, della Porta would plant indisputable evidence implicating O'Connor. A suicide note would be found, as would clothes in a canal to indicate he drowned himself. And nobody would miss Enzo Paganelli, who had already been long forgotten. Claiming the disgraced Protector's body was Jacopo Comin was an option, but della Porta deemed it too great a risk should someone recognize Enzo.

He released three rapid exhalations, calming his pulse.

Cautious not to exacerbate his wound, della Porta reached for the pen on his desk. So much had happened, but there were invoices and checks to be signed, paperwork to review. Life went on.

A knock rapped on his office door. "They're doing it now, signore," said a timid voice from behind the wood. "The Painter and Enforcer of the Charge will meet you in the furnace room."

His hand tightened around the pen. "Grazie," he called, with more exuberance than he felt. "Have them start without me. I'll be there shortly." Earlier, he had every intention of joining them and witnessing the proceedings, but an emotional plea for monotony surged through him. He needed a moment.

BERNARDO AND CARLO STOOD in the corner of the small room, their backs against the ancient stones. Carlo had been told few people knew the space existed, and he wasn't surprised when he saw it.

The furnace felt like hell's oven; a waterfall of sweat rolled down his back. On the cart was Enzo Paganelli's corpse. He wouldn't have any embalming, wake, or ceremonial burial. A man his father had once called a friend would be incinerated.

Carlo stared ahead expressionless, observing the scene. Two men wearing heat-resistant gloves rolled Paganelli into the furnace and shut the door. He sensed Bernardo looking at him, searching for a reaction or a clue to his thinking. Did it matter to the Protector?

In truth, thoughts of the situation and everyone involved bombarded Carlo in a mental blitz—especially Nick. There was no other way to slice it: his American friend was lost. Nick and Angelo shared a soul, but their psyches diverged due to time, circumstance, or environment. The Venetian swordsman had taken over fully, and what he did to Julia was unforgivable. Seeing what that man was capable of had Carlo wondering if it would've been better if he was captured by the Order in the 16th century. Yet, if Angelo was sentenced to *Paradiso*, Carlo never would've met Nick and Julia. Angelo also acted out of love and desperation, but he'd gone too far. How could Carlo call himself Julia's friend if he let the actions go uncontested?

Bernardo turned to the incinerator, its red glow reflecting off his skin.

"Paganelli was your friend, wasn't he," Carlo said, more a statement than a question.

"At one time."

"And a friend of my father's?"

"At one time."

Carlo fell silent for a moment. "All souls deserve a proper burial," he said. "Even when impossible."

One of the men pulled a lever. The furnace erupted to life, engulfing Paganelli's corpse.

"Still," Carlo continued, turning to Bernardo and scrutinizing his averted eyes. "Didn't this man at least deserve true judgment through the Sun Crystal? That's the Order's way, is it not?"

"You were there, Carlo. There was no choice."

"Had he lived," Carlo inquired, "would he have been sentenced to *Paradiso*?"

"I believe he deserved that honor."

"That doesn't answer the question."

Staring straight ahead, Bernardo exhaled without answering.

"Is it possible Paganelli was telling the truth?"

The Protector remained silent, gazing into the flames.

XXIII

A TSUNAMI OF FEAR SHOULD'VE OVERWHELMED ANGELO. He was moments from being sentenced to a ceaseless purgatory, yet he made no effort to free himself from his binds. His wrists and ankles were shackled to a chair in the Great Council Room—the same chair that had held Isabella captive all those years ago. They'd divested him of his Earthly belongings and gave him nothing but a thin, white gown.

Della Porta occupied the pulpit before *Paradiso*, rambling on about the everlasting sins Nick and Angelo had committed: killing Renzo; murdering the Painter; stabbing Julia; threatening the very existence of the Order.

These were great crimes without question. But all Angelo felt in his heart was a vast sense of serenity.

The Exalted Master adjusted his purple robe with ermine fur collar and raised his arms to an otherwise empty room. On the stage stood Bernardo and Lacasse, the only other people there, both wearing black robes. They'd brought Angelo in, as well as the Sun Crystal, mounted in its five-foot candleholder, which they had set behind Angelo.

He'd seen the candleholder when they sentenced Isabella, and though it had been over four hundred years, the memory was an eyeblink. The golden holder was engraved with Latin and Asian etchings and stood on three wrought lion's feet. Three swirling prongs at the top held the Sun

Crystal, about the size of a young boy's head. He remembered being mystified then, as now, that though nothing illuminated the orb, it glowed and cast hypnotic silver light across the room.

The urgency with which della Porta had moved to sentence Angelo brought a sense of relief; the time had come. He overheard them saying it wasn't a full moon, but the Sun Crystal had yet to be moved from Venice, so della Porta called an emergency Convocation.

Still, it struck Angelo as peculiar that della Porta would go through the whole ritual, let alone give a sermon to an empty room. It was also strange that security was so lax. With della Porta's arm in a sling, if Angelo could free himself, he'd only need to face Bernardo and Lacasse, though additional Protectors patrolled the premises. That's if he'd desired freedom—which he did not.

The prism and camera obscura lowered from the ceiling. Bernardo and Lacasse secured them to the floor between him and the new canvas.

Della Porta raised his uninjured arm to Heaven as he continued his homily. "The Order itself will embrace apotheosis," he said, "and betrayers will not be tolerated. We are humbled by the Supreme Painter as we are instructed to guide his brush. He is a just deity, and we ask for peace for Angelo Mascari and Nicholas O'Connor's soul as it is removed from our Earthly realm and unable to cause any more dissonance."

Angelo couldn't help but laugh. Peace for his soul was not something della Porta worried about in earnest.

Unlike when Isabella was sentenced and faced the room, Angelo had been positioned to view *Paradiso*, which exhilarated him. He nearly thanked them for being merciful. Above the council chairs, Isabella's portrait was fixed in the glorious masterpiece, yearning toward the Mother Mary. His soul mate's love gushed through him as she whispered with tears of joy, *"I love you, Angelo. I have waited for this day for too long."*

Della Porta approached Angelo. "One last chance, Signor Mascari. Reveal the location of the book, and we'll show mercy."

Angelo's lips pressed together in a wry leer. What could be more merciful than finally reuniting him with his soul mate? It was his last chance—not for mercy, but to torment della Porta. "Of course I know where it is," he lied. "I've always known. But *you* never will."

The angry contortion of della Porta's facial features made Angelo cackle, assuaging any concerns that his enemies would win in his absence. He'd enter *Paradiso* and be with Isabella, content on all levels.

Della Porta whispered into Angelo's ear. "I expected your answer. I didn't think your visage would do *Paradiso* justice. Carlo begged me to spare your life and honor your plea."

"How gracious of you."

With a snicker, della Porta straightened. He began chanting in an unknown tongue Angelo couldn't understand but had heard five centuries prior.

As his heart warmed, Angelo craned his neck to watch della Porta. The Exalted Master cantillated his mantra and lit the wick of a large braided black and red candle in the holder. The fat wick sparked, and a vigorous flame swelled, as if drawn upward, abnormally high. Its heat burned bright, and the Sun Crystal above it glowed a heavy purple, then indigo, followed by rich unearthly green, encircling a coal-black center.

"Soon, 'mòre mio," he said in Venetian to Isabella. "Your heart sets mine ablaze."

"Now and forever." Her voice cracked with joy.

All the years, all the centuries, all the fighting, the yearning, the regrets, the second-guessing, it all led to this moment. In the end, nothing could keep soul mates apart.

Nothing.

Destiny could not be fought. He gazed at Jesus and the Mother Mary with blurry eyes—wet from tears of love, joy, and gratitude. Their divine hands had guided him and Isabella together. "Gràssie," he whispered to them. "Gràssie." He smiled at Isabella, so awash in happiness to spend eternity with his beloved, so caught in such a euphoric state, it took a moment to realize what unfolded before him.

Bernardo and Lacasse carried in a new, fifteen-foot-long blank canvas. They placed it on two supports on the dais in front of him.

Carlo entered the room from one of the main doors adjacent to the stage. He winced and adjusted the white Painter's robe, which once graced Jacopo Tintoretto's shoulders. On his ears were headphones, the electronic dance music so loud, the thumping bass line accosted Angelo's ears. A pained expression contorted Carlo's face. He rushed to the center of the new canvas. Bernardo and Lacasse joined della Porta's chant, the intensity rising.

The new Painter lifted a palette and hurriedly grabbed a brush from a box. He scrutinized Angelo, then dipped the bristles in a small pot on a table.

Angelo recoiled and shifted in the chair. His hands tugged at their restraints. "Wait, what's going on?" he demanded.

Carlo didn't answer. He studied Angelo again, then readied his paintbrush at the canvas.

Let me out, Nick screamed internally. *Julia needs me. It's not too late. I'll get us out of here.*

Angelo stifled his present-day life. Nick was the last thing he needed in a time of crisis. Angelo twisted in his seat. The Sun Crystal behind him glowed brighter. A green light emanated from it, spiraling toward him.

"Give . . . me . . . control." Nick's voice struggled to be heard from his mouth. Angelo panicked, unsure what to do. Nick jerked his hands against his binds, the metal chafing his skin. He rubbed his wrists against the shackles, shaving the skin away so he could free his hand. Searing heat rose as the skin tore, and blood poured forth, lubricating the steel. Suppressing the pain, Nick heaved his right hand with all his might. It started slipping through. One more inch and he'd have it out.

"It's not supposed to be like this," Angelo shouted. "Paint me into *Paradiso*. We're soul mates!"

"That does *not* mean you're destined to be together," della Porta replied with seething vindictiveness. "Our sins separate us from our loves." He continued the chant with Bernardo and Lacasse.

"Stop. I beg of you. Carlo, show merc—"

Angelo's words were sucked from him. The light engulfed him.

His chest pitched forward. It felt as though he forcibly shed his entire body's skin with one motion. His life's soul was wrenched through the camera obscura. His eyes bulged as the Sun Crystal's light sucked his being from every cell.

"*Nooo*," Isabella cried. "*No, my love!*"

Half of him appeared in front of him and half left behind. His translucent self was drawn into the box. It inverted, passed through the second lens of the camera obscura, and refracted through the prism. He squinted his eyes as his own image projected on the blank canvas awaiting Carlo. The manifestation was terrifying.

Carlo had his brush ready. He worked fast, solidifying Angelo's destiny.

The Painter paused, his face contorted, almost as if in more pain than Angelo. He squeezed his eyes shut, then pressed the headphones against his ears. Hyperventilating, with a shaking hand, he stroked paint across Angelo's projected face, adhering it for eternity.

"No," Angelo's ethereal form shouted. "Isabella!"

"Julia!" Nick echoed.

But it was too late for both. Angelo's brain commanded his fists to pound on the walls of this invisible cell, but he was powerless, as Carlo confined his soul to an entirely new canvas.

The Painter dropped the brush and bolted for the door.

Angelo and Nick would forever be separated from their loves.

XXIV

CARLO STRETCHED HIS ARMS AND ACHING BACK on the love seat. He wiggled his bare toes hanging off one side and rolled his head on the rigid edge of the other. A week of contortionist sleeping had folded his body into origami.

He glanced at Julia on the hospital bed. The doctors said it was a miracle she lived; the nurses crossed themselves every time they entered the room.

Still asleep, Julia's breathing matched the EKG machine's rhythmic beeping. How many times had he heard that sound? Half a million? A million? More than once, he wanted to shake her awake, but the doctors warned him not to. Her body had been through intense trauma and needed to heal.

Ospedale SS. Giovanni e Paolo, named for Saints John and Paul, was the best medical center in Venice and watched over by the patron saints of hospitals and the sick, so Carlo knew she was in good hands here and above.

By the third day, thoughts of another person he knew under medical care weighed on him like the city of Venice itself. For over a decade, his poor mother had been in a private assisted living facility that offered psychiatric support just outside Montebelluna, a quaint town nestled in the foothills of the Italian Alps. The annual bill was paid by della Porta, for which Carlo was grateful. He didn't want to miss Julia if she woke, but Montebelluna, a town known for its production of ski boots, was a ninety-minute train ride away. Earlier that morning, on the fourth day of Julia's coma, Carlo took the opportunity to see his mother, hoping the trip to the countryside would also help clear his mind. Unsettling thoughts of Paganelli's incineration and Angelo's sentencing had been haunting him.

On most days, his mother was fairly normal—whatever that meant—but she suffered from what her doctor called *sporadic shell shock syndrome*. Without warning, whether she was sitting, standing, eating, watching TV, or walking, she'd rock back and forth, repeating a phrase over and over. It could be "Turn it off, turn it off, turn it off," or "Stay here," or "He did it," or a simple, "No, no, no." The frequency and length of the episodes occurred arbitrarily. Medication did little to suppress them. Though they may have been random, she always seemed to have a fit every time her son visited. And whenever she muttered the word, "he" in whatever phrase she repeated, he sensed it wasn't about his deceased father, but *him*. "You," on the other hand, was certainly a reference to his father. "You left me, you left me, you left me."

Considering he'd be lucky to have a ten-minute conversation with his mom before she lapsed into her shell-shocked state—one which more often than not included the word "he"—Carlo's visits grew scarce over the years. It had been four months since his last, and sitting in a hospital beside a woman he'd known a week bore a sharp sliver of guilt through his heart. Their bond was so close before the fire took his father; he yearned for that tenderness—or even for a conversation with her.

He had to see his mother. He *needed* his mamma.

The visit went exactly as expected, unfortunately. Joy wrapped him like a baby-soft blanket when he laid eyes on his beloved mother, still beautiful, her dark hair graying at the temples. Her oval face looked as healthy as ever. Her lips were a bright pink, and he wondered if she put on lip gloss and mascara. They drank cappuccino in the lounge, at a window with a view of the Alps. Sitting there with her, Carlo had forgotten everything that had happened with his family, as if he'd been transported to an alternate reality—the one that was *actually* real. But after a few minutes of small talk about his art career, it started. First the rocking, then the muttering.

"He did it, he did it, he did it," she whispered in Venetian.

Uncontrollable tears welled in Carlo's eyes. Was it talk of art that triggered the episode? The coffee's aroma? Carlo's resemblance to his father? He sprung from his seat and hugged her. He kissed her forehead, but she continued unabated. He smoothed her hair, desperate for her to return to him, but it was useless. The nurse guided Carlo away, stating his mother could be like that for hours. He didn't want to leave, but as his sweet mamma swayed and murmured the phrase, she met his eyes. Her hardened gaze turned his body to ice.

She knew. Somehow, she knew Carlo had snuck into his father's workspace all those years ago. She knew he'd seen the prism. And shortly after, it had all burned, with his father inside. Carlo never should've stolen the key. He was warned many times to mind his business, or he'd be punished. His father's work was private—and Carlo lost two parents because of his actions. He was wrong to view the prism, and though he wasn't quite sure how the indiscretion resulted in so much suffering, he couldn't help but believe he was to blame.

The disappointment and anger in his mother's expression caused his inner self to shatter. His knees buckled. He instinctively raised his guard and stepped back, thankful when she looked away. Carlo took the nurse's cue and jetted from the facility.

With a heavy heart, he returned to Julia that afternoon, and his guilt was equally palpable, if not more so. At least in his parents' case, he could rationalize that he was a child at the time. With Julia and Nick, though, he was a grown man. Ramifications had yet to reveal themselves, but Carlo knew they'd come, so he promised himself he'd protect Julia.

While she was in a coma, the only thing he could do was wait.

And wait, he did. Three more days passed. He caught up on dozens of messages from friends who missed him but hit the clubs and taverns without him; checked to see if there was any update on the countess, which there was none; searched on news of the fight outside his flat, also which there was none; contacted a Venetian art gallery, to which he sent images of his work and arranged an in-person meeting; and ended things with Jordan by phone. She pretended to take it well, but the hitch in her voice gave her away. She'd be okay. It could never work long-term since she was flying back to Sydney at the end of the summer. Carlo had declined a final romp, which he now regretted and contemplated calling her multiple times. But every time he found her name in his contacts, he'd invariably glimpse Julia and not make the call.

Most of his time in the hospital was spent in sheer boredom. He enjoyed the silver lining of being able to sketch with colored pencils, catch up on movies and TV, and read a book on his phone. Wanting to practice English and learn more about American women, he opted for a fun present-day novel about the ghost of legendary writer and satirist Dorothy Parker, which did not disappoint and offered insight into American sarcasm he often missed.

With boredom came thoughts—thoughts that continued to plague him. Enough time had passed for him to consider, reconsider, question, and bury the punishment he enacted on Angelo. Those thoughts were accompanied by vindication, relief, sadness, horror, and most of all, that incessant, relentless culpability. Angelo's punishment was righteous, but he was in *Nick's* body. For all Carlo knew, Angelo could've been extracted or suppressed. Nick and Julia could've potentially returned to America without incident. With a lurch in his gut, Carlo speculated that he subconsciously removed Nick to free Julia from her marital constraints. No matter what the reason or justification, the guilt would return. So, Carlo blocked those thoughts. Angelo deserved the sentence. For Julia's sake, it was the right thing to do. He *hoped*.

Reaching to the floor, he grabbed his sketchpad and a handful of pencils. He flipped through the book. Almost every picture was one of Julia transposed into a classical scene he drew from memory, on top of which he layered modern imagery, from technology in trees to graffiti on walls. He planned on painting most of the sketches and had enough ideas to fill a solo show.

A flicker of movement caught his eye in the morning sun cracking through the blinds. Almost not believing, he raised his eyes to Julia's bed. Nothing. She slept peacefully, with an intriguing half-smile whose meaning Mona Lisa would ponder. She'd been through so much; he hoped she dreamt sweet thoughts. He realized he knew little about her, especially her life before their trip to Venice. He had checked her LinkedIn, Facebook, and Instagram accounts and was pleasantly surprised to see that before she became a professional fine arts photographer, she had been a journalist for the *Boston Globe* and now contributed articles to some in-flight airline magazines. Her last Facebook and Instagram posts were from Venice before they met. Before that, it was what he expected—her photography and articles, along with outings with Nick and friends, trips, and a handful of humorous, yet pointed political posts. In all the pictures of her and Nick, the common thread was that they beamed from ear-to-ear. He couldn't recall being that happy with anyone. And now, she and Nick would never smile together again.

Though he wasn't solely to blame, a large part of the O'Connors' travails weighed on his shoulders. More than a large part—the *majority* of it. After all, he encouraged—*enabled*—Nick to speak with Isabella, brought him to the library archive, and, as Painter, he actively prevented Isabella's release. He didn't regret that one too much, as he also thwarted the liberation of thousands of evil souls. Freeing the O'Connors from the torture room was another source of comfort. But still, if he hadn't approached Nick in the Great Council Room, Nick would've been kicked out for climbing on the council seats, and Carlo never would've met Julia. Truth be told, he was horrified by his own actions. Carlo had never thought of himself as one who'd exact vengeance, but that's precisely what he did. And as far as he knew, it was irreversible. True, it was for Julia, and perhaps he was under duress, especially with Paganelli's death. He'd always wanted the chance to confront his father's killer, and Paganelli's last words made the truth murkier than—

THE REFLECTION IN THE oval vanity mirror told the story of a tired woman, too tired for her age, yet unable to rest. She fixed her brown hair with a blue kingfisher feather hairpin, an exotic Chinese gift from the director of Teatro La Fenice. She had made the right decision; no singular group should wield so much power.

She dabbed the ointment on the dry rash on her cheek. The apothecarist swore it was a tried-and-true remedy, but it seemed to have worsened over the past week. Though, it could've been a physical incarnation caused by the stress of her husband's philandering, drinking, and anger. Or, from the stress of her own actions. After applying the ointment, she covered her face with a whitening mixture and spritzed perfume from the atomizer on her neck. Placing it back on the table, she had a half-second to notice the shadowy figure in the mirror's reflection before he yanked a black sack over her head.

"*Paradise* awaits," the man whispered into her ear.

CARLO'S EYES BLINKED OPEN. The flashbacks had been coming more frequently, always unexpected to the point that he wondered if he, too, suffered from *sporadic shell shock syndrome*. His visions usually had a violent ending that left him feeling the physical and emotional effects of the moment. He prayed his mother didn't have similar experiences. He committed the image of the woman at the mirror to memory; he'd sketch it later. Needing to bring himself back to the 21st century, he stretched for his mobile on the floor. He sneered at a text from della Porta, a dinner invitation.

Julia coughed.

Carlo shot up and raced to her side. Her face twitched, and she wiggled her fingers. That wasn't a trick of the light.

As if a newborn, she opened her eyes halfway.

She coughed again and smacked her lips.

"Julia, it's okay," he said softly. "You're safe."

She tried to swallow. Her mouth opened but emitted only a hoarse whisper. Realizing she hadn't had anything real to drink in a week, Carlo snatched the apple juice box on the bedside table. He punctured the straw through the top and placed it between her cracked lips. She drank it all.

Finally opening her eyes completely, she turned her head and gazed at him. Filled with grief, Carlo smiled at those green orbs flecked with gold. Even in her weakened state with pallid skin, her beauty radiated around her. It was so good to see her again. A tear rolled down his cheek.

"Nick?"

"It's me, Carlo. How are you feeling?"

"No," Julia said. She rolled her head on the pillow, gazing about the room. "I know it's you. I meant where's Nick?"

Her unexpected first words brought a frown to Carlo's face—and, he had to admit, a little jealousy. She'd ask about her husband at some point, but he hadn't thought it would happen the moment she woke. He'd had a week to think about the answer; he'd yet to decide what to say. "I'm going to call the doctor, Julia."

"Where's Nick, Carlo?"

He couldn't bring himself to look her in the eye. He gazed at the floor. "What do you remember?"

XXV

"Forty-three," della Porta said, with an uncontainable grin. Even with his bandages, he yearned to interlock his hands behind his head and kick his feet onto the table but maintained his professional composure. He sensed Bernardo wanted to do the same, as he hadn't seen the man smile so in . . . well, ever. Bernardo had just informed him he'd recruited forty-three new candidates for Discipuli, all of whom would be groomed to be Protectors. The plan was coming together. He never expected it to be this quick.

They sat in Ristorante Ai Stagneri's wine cellar, which the restaurant used as a private room. The owner was an Order member, so they could count on the staff's discretion. Della Porta wasn't a fan of avant-garde food, but Chef Maurizio's lauded interpretations of classic Venetian dishes were true culinary artistry that reminded della Porta of Carlo's work. *Perhaps this is the future*, he mused—reinterpretations of the classics.

The one thing missing from the dinner was Carlo. Della Porta had invited him to meals every day in the past week. He'd yet to receive a response. Time heals all wounds. He'd give Carlo the space he needed, but the young Painter would come around soon enough. Quite simply, he didn't have a choice.

"Fanella helped, of course," Bernardo said, deftly using his one hand to slice a fried sardine and add red onion, snow peas, avocado, and lime mayonnaise to the fork. "Thirty-four are police officers. Dante brought in four friends who are fellow security guards and bouncers, Lacasse, another three, and Manuel, the remaining two." Bernardo took a bite and luxuriated in the flavors della Porta knew were dancing on his friend's taste buds.

"Manuel's redemption has been impressive. And all have been properly vetted?" Della Porta grinned, more at his friend's reaction, as he'd already tried the *aperitivo*.

Bernardo finished chewing and released the breath that accompanies life's pleasures. He wiped his mouth before speaking. "We're working through that, but nearly. And of course, we'll need ceremonies. Signore, given that we'll have over fifty soon, I was thinking we should initiate them en masse."

"Excellent idea, my friend," della Porta said. "I've been thinking the same thing. Do it as soon as possible. In the next two or three days."

"But the next full moon is two weeks away."

Della Porta dismissed Bernardo's comment with a wave of the hand. "That's folklore nonsense that ancients like Paganelli believed."

Bernardo's mouth dropped. "I . . . I never knew that."

"What does the moon have to do with anything? It's a giant rock in Earth's orbit. The full moon's just an arbitrary day to enforce traditions, like the Sabbath."

"But it's full. Tides are affected. . . ."

The response didn't please Della Porta. It had nothing to do with intelligence. His Chief of Security and Enforcer of the Charge had one of the soundest minds in his employ. In fact, many people in the Order and the world over had notions like moon phases so entrenched in their heads that they didn't even know a loose blanket covered their eyes. What bothered della Porta the most was how so many people lacked the wherewithal to think for even half a second. He let it go with a flourish. "Come, Bernardo. There are two high tides each day. I don't need to tell you the moon doesn't actually change shape. How we see it is a mere reflection of light. You can have a mass on any day, and so, we can have a Convocation on a Tuesday, if we want. Set it up."

Seemingly embarrassed, Bernardo took a long drink of his spritz. Della Porta seized advantage of his reaction to broach a subject that had been plaguing his mind for almost two weeks. Someone had knowledge of his altercation with O'Connor in the Marciana archives and told the countess of the incident.

"Bernardo, you may recall we were in your office when you received a red flag that Carlo was in the Marciana Library before I went to see him."

"Certo."

Della Porta probed his man for a reaction. There was none other than curiosity. "I'd wager you were unaware that Nick O'Connor was with him."

"What? What was he doing there?"

"Researching his soul mate in the archive. Carlo was helping him. Of course, this was before Carlo was a member. And there wasn't much to discover. Not until O'Connor tied me up and forced me to talk."

Bernardo leaned forward, his eyes wide. "Signore? I had no idea. Were you hurt?"

Della Porta glanced at his watch. He needed to wrap this conversation before Lacasse and Manuel arrived. "It doesn't matter now. And rest assured, I never suspected you knew. The countess, however, *did*."

"How could she? There are no cameras back there."

"That's exactly my question."

The door opened, and a server admitted Lacasse in his light gray suit, followed by Manuel wearing a variation of his maroon tie, this one striped with blue. Della Porta signaled to Bernardo that they'd resume their discussion later.

"Manuel, Monsieur Lacasse, thank you for joining us," della Porta said, switching from Venetian to English. "Please, have a seat."

Both men moved to take their chairs.

"Not you, Manuel."

Lacasse accepted the instruction without emotion. Manuel remained standing.

"Much of the Order's tenets center around redemption," della Porta said to Manuel, then upon the man's inquisitive look about the word added, "Redenzione in Italiano. You know this about the Order. Redemption, yes?"

"Sì, signore," Manuel replied.

"And redemption is achievable. You've shown that since you botched your surveillance of the O'Connors. How you could've lost two tourists is beyond me, but. . . I'm impressed you've brought in new Protectors."

"Grazie, signore. They . . . will honor il oath and service il Order well."

Manuel's English was pathetic, but della Porta forgave this minor trespass. "As will you," he said. "You're here for two reasons. First, I want you to continue watching Signora O'Connor. Report back everything. And do not lose her this time."

"But, signore, she is with Carlo, no?"

"She is, but that doesn't mean another set of eyes cannot be on her."

Bernardo and Lacasse nodded their agreement.

"Additionally," della Porta continued, "I have special projects for you. Your sister-in-law is the assistant to Silvio Navarro, the editor-in-chief at MediaStatuto, correct?"

"She is."

"MediaStatuto is the perfect outlet to spread positive news about the Order. Their print and digital news media. Their blogs, podcasts, too. Do you have a problem with providing her with articles of interest?"

"It would be my pleasure."

"I trust you can accomplish this task without sitting on your own testicles?"

Manuel cleared his throat, visibly understanding that English. He parted his lips to say one thing, but came out with a meek, "Sì, signore."

Della Porta wished Manuel had the actual balls to counter the insult. Rather than demeaning the man further, he feigned sympathy. "Speaking of testicles, how are your wife and new baby?"

"They are both wonderful, signore. Grazie mille," Manuel replied with widened eyes. "Little Camilla is three months now."

"I hope to meet her one day," della Porta said with a forced grin. "Now go home, spend the night with them."

As Manuel made for the door, a server entered, carrying three plates of burrata with heirloom tomatoes. Not seeing Manuel, she nearly collided with him, but the Protector snatched two plates from her and allowed her to steady herself before he handed them back. Though the girl was mortified by the near disaster, Manuel relaxed her with a warm hand on her shoulder, then left the room. Though Della Porta didn't want to give Manuel too much credit just yet, he was pleased he had offered the man a chance at redemption.

"What's the news?" della Porta asked Lacasse.

When the server left, the Interpol detective opened a folder.

"Not good," Lacasse said with his soothing French accent. "We've had zero leads on the countess. Interpol has extended their search to Portugal and Greece."

"Zero? What about O'Connor?"

Lacasse remained calm, but della Porta could sense irritation in the man's eyes. "As you know, Monsieur della Porta, without the ability to apprehend and question O'Connor, any charges would be based on circumstantial evidence. My colleagues have a hard time believing he's connected at all, but the fact remains, they don't have any other suspects besides..."

"Besides whom?"

Lacasse cleared his throat. "Yourself."

"Are you suggesting a raving madman's accusations should be believed?"

"Of course not."

"Then you said it yourself. You have no other suspects. Even if you can't physically detain him, you can charge him, can't you?"

"Monsieur," Lacasse said with calculated precision, "please understand I have an obligation to two organizations. Two sets of laws, if you will. One must be followed to the letter. While you may stretch the other, problems arise when they overlap."

"Is it really that much of a stretch to connect O'Connor to the countess?"

"Oui. And not just her. I should've been informed about the Jacopo Comin charge. I never would've agreed."

"It was a ruse. Designed for leverage."

"And if looked into, it'll be a ruse that casts doubt on every charge."

Self-reproach buzzed through della Porta. He sipped his spritz. He needed to remedy the situation and return the focus to charging O'Connor for the countess's disappearance. "You are right, my friend. We should've consulted with you. I'll instruct Fanella to drop the murder charge. But there must be ways to connect him to the countess. Perhaps Manuel's sister-in-law can be of assistance in this regard, as well. I believe one of their outlets must've had an article or two about the countess. Leak some information to whomever their source is with the police in different towns from here to Milano. O'Connor is the perfect scapegoat for her murder."

Lacasse raised an eyebrow. "Monsieur, the countess is missing, not murdered."

"I know that, Lacasse." Della Porta's ire swelled—at himself for his slip. "I want to find her more than anyone. But it's been over a week with no contact and no sightings. We need to assume the worst. For all we know, O'Connor *did* kill her. Her granddaughter seems to think so."

"She's constantly messaging me on LinkedIn for updates." Lacasse shook his head with genuine annoyance. "I never should've connected with her."

"She can be a badger," Bernardo said.

Della Porta laughed. "Maybe I *should* set her up with Carlo."

"What's that?" Lacasse asked.

"Oh, I jokingly suggested it to the countess. But now it's not such a bad idea. It would take Carlo away from Mrs. O'Connor."

"Or Carlo could take Mrs. O'Connor on a vacation back to America," Lacasse said.

The three men cracked up.

Bernardo raised his hand to interject. "With all due respect, signori, I know this is a council decision, but with the countess and O'Connor, we now have two high-profile individuals missing. I don't think it wise for us to hold O'Connor's body any longer. I think we should stage a suicide. By fire, or a drowning."

"I've been thinking this, as well," Lacasse added. "But the body would need to be discovered in a couple of months. It would throw off the Guild."

Della Porta snarled at the word 'guild.' It amazed him that some of the Order's most loyal followers would question the existence of the Doge's book yet take as gospel a group that supposedly had been fighting from the shadows since time immemorial. "The Guild," he snapped, "if you should even dignify it with an organizational name, died with Paganelli. As far as I'm concerned, he was their one and only member since 1926."

The young female server reentered the room and displayed a bottle of pinot grigio to della Porta. After she poured him a taste and he signaled his approval, she filled the three men's glasses. At the same time, another server entered, carrying plates of ravioli filled with saffron butter and Cantabrian anchovies.

When they left, Lacasse began eating as though he hadn't all day—which may have been true.

"And in any event," della Porta continued, "you're both right. We can fake O'Connor's suicide, but it's too early to do so. We can use this situation to our advantage. Hopefully, I pray, Contessa Baldesseri will be found, but people are searching for O'Connor, as well. It's exactly why it's in our interest if he's the prime suspect."

Lacasse tapped his fork in the air, as if ringing an invisible bell. "Let's see if MediaStatuto finds anything. The moment we have any evidence, we'll press charges."

After a nod of agreement, Bernardo checked his watch, dabbed his mouth, and stood. "If you'll excuse me, signori."

"Where are you going?" della Porta asked.

"Carlo asked me to meet him. Apologies, I said I would."

Not for the first time in recent days, the blood in della Porta's veins switched from exuberant to furious. He placed his glass on the table with more force than intended. "Carlo was supposed to meet us here. He—" della Porta needed to prevent further embarrassment. He required Carlo for Order duties but also worried about their relationship. He loved Carlo like a son. All sons lash out at their fathers from time to time. Carlo would realize that della Porta had always had his best interests at heart. But for now, he had to maintain a face of leadership and show everyone he had control, including the control of Carlo and Fosca. "He should've informed me. As you should have, as well."

"I apologize, signore. Shall I call him and tell him to come?"

"What does he want to meet you about?"

"I believe the souls."

"The souls?"

"He wants to meet in the Palazzo. For my help."

Della Porta raised an eyebrow. "What are you saying, Bernardo?"

"You do know he can speak with—well, *hear*—them, yes?"

Lacasse dropped his fork and snapped his head to the conversation.

Della Porta was just as surprised but contained his reaction. "Yes, of course." His anger switched to worry. The rumor that Tintoretto could hear the souls was pure speculation. Everyone always assumed the old Painter was deaf as a doornail, though auditory faculty wouldn't affect hearing the prisoners in *Paradiso*. His infirmity was thought to be from his advanced age. He must've been able to tune them out. Regardless, the rumor was true, which suddenly presented a problem of extraordinary consequences. Should Carlo be able to speak with the souls, it would be della Porta's undoing.

"You're saying he can speak with them?" he asked.

"Well, like I said, he can hear them, but I believe he hears all of them at once. The one time I saw him, he ran out of the room in pain."

"And you didn't think it important to tell us this?" Lacasse's tone was smooth and calm, but his words and intent were unmistakable.

Bernardo knew he'd blundered but remained silent.

Another urgent thought hit della Porta. He needed to quash Bernardo's plan. "When we sentenced O'Connor, I thought the headphones were for his usual angst. If he was in actual pain, then he shouldn't go back. I worry for his welfare, for his sanity."

"But signore, he'll need to perform during Convocations. I was thinking I could help him relax and concentrate. I thought you'd be pleased."

"Why would I be pleased?"

"He could speak with Isabella Scalfini. Possibly others may know the location of the doge's book."

Della Porta wanted to kick himself for not thinking of this earlier. How did the most obvious answer slip his mind? He blamed it on having too much on his plate. Getting Carlo to speak with Isabella and avoid certain other souls was a challenge in itself, but the proposition of being led straight to the book was too great to ignore. "Yes, absolutely. That's an excellent idea. I'll go with you." He put down his fork.

"With all due respect, Exalted Master," Bernardo said, "I don't think he'll be okay with that."

Della Porta sighed. Bernardo was right, of course.

"Very well. But keep it brief, and make sure he focuses only on Isabella Scalfini or people from her time. Keep me posted."

Bernardo reached the door.

"And Bernardo, one more thing. Do not tell Carlo about the mass initiation." If Carlo refused to keep della Porta in the loop, then he'd quickly learn what that meant.

"I doubt he'd attend anyway," Bernardo replied. "It'll need to be in the Great Council Room."

WAITING FOR BERNARDO, Carlo paced the corridor of the Palazzo, thirty meters from the entrance to the Great Council Room. It seemed to be a safe distance from the voices in *Paradiso*.

He gazed out at the starlit sky.

Leaving Julia was a loathsome action, but her doctors had instructed him to take a break. They were right—he needed time away from the hospital. Since he'd brought Julia there, other than visiting his mother, he'd left only to let the cleaning crew into his flat, retrieve Julia's suitcases, and pick up a change of clothes for himself. And besides needing a physical break, so much was on his mind, he felt like it would burst, especially with a week to do nothing but think—along with the all-too-frequent interruptions of random past lives. Though the visions were snippets, he was convinced that becoming the Painter had given him not only the capacity to hear the souls, but that he could glimpse pieces of their memories, as well. Being in their presence was excruciating, but he hoped he'd be able to mute them and speak with one or two.

Bernardo didn't have any experience helping someone isolate a single voice out of thousands, but who did? If there was one man who could help facilitate the extreme focus Carlo would need, it was Bernardo.

As if on cue, the one-armed chief Protector strode toward him. Carlo cocked his head—was that a bit of a skip in his step?

"Sorry to keep you waiting," Bernardo said in Venetian, with an expression Carlo could only describe as a stoic smile. But for Bernardo, it was as if he was jumping for joy.

"You're in a good mood." It was infectious, too. Carlo couldn't help but grin.

Bernardo waved him off. "Why shouldn't I be? You missed a sublime meal."

"I've tasted food before."

"You know he wants to see you. You can't hide from him forever."

Carlo raised his hands. He was in no mood for this. "You're here to help me with voices in my head. I don't need an actual verbal lecture."

Bernardo shrugged apologetically, then eyed the door to the Great Council Room. "Can you hear them now?"

"Inaudible whispers from here. A muted buzz."

"I don't know how I can help you with this, Carlo. I feel like a blind man helping someone who can see."

"You're the most level-headed and balanced person I know." He clasped his friend's armless shoulder. "An impressive feat for a one-armed man."

The Protector shot him a pointed look.

Carlo scrutinized the door again. An overwhelming sense of dread filled him, like the morning his wisdom tooth was extracted. The pain was inevitable; there was no sense in putting it off. And like the cruciality of that dental procedure, so was the necessity of standing before *Paradiso*. For in some strange, masochist way, he knew it was the first step toward a penance for what he did to Nick. "Ready?"

"You're not wearing the headphones?"

"They helped, but barely. It was excruciating. If I'm going to do this, I must learn how to tune them out."

Bernardo furrowed his brow and tracked Carlo's gaze, still on the door. "Maybe it makes sense to run in."

"Almost like jumping the first hurdle." Carlo nodded. "I like it. See, you're helping already. Okay, let's do it." He stretched his neck.

Bernardo hustled to the door and readied his hand on the nob. "Three. Two. Go."

Carlo sprinted for his target. Bernardo opened the door, his timing perfect.

As the Painter skidded to a stop before *Paradiso*, the souls erupted when they saw him. It was as if a thousand people simultaneously screamed at him from an inch away. He couldn't make out a single word. Summoning all his mental strength, he focused on the top of the painting, struggling to tune them out.

"Bernardo. . ." Invisible claws sliced his brain. Spikes skewered his ears.

He collapsed to his knees and clasped his head. "Stop! Make it stop!" But their volume grew. The aural hurricane accosting him dampened his vision. *Paradiso* blurred, but he could've sworn in that moment, he saw a slight man emerge from the secret door. The man gasped at the Painter, pushed his glasses on his nose, and hurried out of the room. Carlo cried in pain and punched the marble floor. With cloudy eyes, he gaped up at Bernardo.

Bernardo didn't need to hear his plea for help. The Protector wrapped his arm beneath the Painter's armpits and helped him out, kicking the door closed as they entered the hall. Carlo stumbled further down the hall and leaned against the open window. He sucked air in. As the quiet engulfed him, he steadied his body, cognizant that Bernardo had been watching him. It must've been a strange scene without the full soundtrack.

Carlo lit a cigarette and exhaled out the window. Smoking was forbidden here, but Bernardo ignored the violation.

"What did you hear?" he asked.

"Everyone." Carlo coughed and cleared his throat. He took another drag, which made his throat worse, then pinched the cherry off and watched it float down to the courtyard. "I can't do it. It's not possible."

A countenance of concern passed over Bernardo's face. "You're the maintainer of everlasting justice. You must be able to see *Paradiso*."

"I don't know what to tell you."

"Tintoretto learned to do it."

Carlo narrowed his eyes. "By scratching his ears out," he snapped. He threw the rest of the cigarette into a nearby trashcan. "Even with headphones, I can't do it again. It gets worse each time."

Bernardo shook his head. Maybe he didn't know the solution, but he seemed to know more than he led on. Carlo also remembered Tintoretto had some hearing; it was brief, but he had a conversation with the man. And besides, going deaf would do nothing to stop voices in one's head. Tintoretto dealt with it, but he had hundreds of years to learn how.

"What aren't you telling me?" Carlo asked.

"I always figured it was because of his age, but I got the sense he could tune *everyone* out. In the painting *and* in the flesh." Bernardo gripped Carlo's arm. "Either way, Carlo, you're right. You're right about all of this. But there is a way. You *can* learn."

"Not in there. No way." He yanked free from Bernardo's hold and paced the hallway again. "Tintoretto experienced it slowly, soul-by-soul. Maybe that's how he was able to cope. I can start a new painting. Or continue on the one I started."

Bernardo tilted his head, seemingly thinking it was a plausible idea. "Or perhaps you can work on one of the other variations of *Paradiso*. I wonder if you'd hear those souls. We could potentially arrange for a cross-museum exhibition."

Stopping, Carlo cracked his knuckles and gaped at Bernardo. He wasn't sure he heard right. "Variations? You mean the studies?"

"Did you think *Paradiso* happened overnight?"

"Bernardo, stop." Carlo's pulse quickened. He didn't bother to calm himself. "The studies. The one in the Louvre and the one in the Thyssen-Bornemisza, they're both . . . filled with souls?"

"As I said, it didn't happen overnight. There was experimentation and quite a bit of debauchery in those days."

The revelation was nothing short of mind-blowing. "But those paintings, they've been out of Venice for decades. Did they—are they—is the Order also in Paris and Madrid?"

Bernardo massaged his jaw and cleared his throat. "Apologies, my friend. I thought you knew all—"

"I didn't."

"This shouldn't have come from me, but it's nothing important anyway. Many organizations have multiple chapters."

"Nothing important?" Carlo screamed the question, the words echoing off the marble walls. "Are they active? Do they still sentence souls?"

Bernardo appeared to understand what Carlo was getting at but avoided his gaze.

Carlo answered for him. He couldn't determine why he was so angry, but he felt duped more than ever. Or, he conceded, perhaps he felt as though he wasn't unique anymore. "So . . . two more paintings mean two more Painters, yes?"

Bernardo finally looked him in the eye. "Yes. But it does not affect your work here or what you do. Signor della Porta will tell you more."

Carlo cracked his knuckles again. He recalled Nick punching the wall in the archive. He felt like doing the same but stopped himself only because he didn't want to break his hand.

"Why didn't he tell me?"

"You'll need to ask him, Carlo. But like I said, it's not important and doesn't affect you."

"What about the Sun Crystal? Are there three of them?"

Bernardo shook his head. "It's transported for Convocations."

Carlo knew della Porta and Bernardo were withholding far more than he'd been privy to, but he rationalized that he'd been Painter for less than a week. He closed his eyes and forced himself to breathe. And that's when a blurred memory presented himself.

"There was a man."

"What man?" Bernardo asked.

"In the Great Council Room. He left the secret door that Tintoretto had come through. Who was he?"

Bernardo continued to look at Carlo but didn't answer.

"You're my friend, Bernardo. Tell me."

Gnashing his teeth, Bernardo looked like a bull reluctant to enter the ring. "An appraiser."

"Of?"

"The master had ample time to paint."

Carlo felt his eyes widen. In all this time, the furious painter must've painted hundreds of works. Maybe thousands. His indignation switched to giddy schoolboy excitement. "Tintoretto? You're talking about undiscovered—no, *unseen*—Tintorettos. I want to see them," he said, his voice cracking a bit.

"In due time, Carlo."

"Why? I want to see them now."

Bernardo turned away again, as if unwilling to reveal vital info. "They're in his room."

"So? I'm the Painter now, right? Let's go."

"I said no."

"Why not?"

Bernardo's stare prompted Carlo to take a step back. Realizing he was on the defensive, he straightened his back and broadened his shoulders. Friend or not, Bernardo—and della Porta—had treated him like a child for too long.

"Carlo," Bernardo said, with a reassuring tone that preempted further conflict, "you'd have to go through the Great Council Room."

The fact presented an unsavory quandary. Though Carlo would trade almost anything to see hundreds of never-before-seen Tintorettos, an acoustic vise squeezing his brain again was on the exception list. Perhaps Bernardo had his best intentions at heart after all. Carlo softened his voice. "There's no other way in? Can't you take them out?"

Bernardo again cleared his throat. "In due time, Carlo. You'll see them in due time."

WALKING THROUGH A temporary exhibition of medieval pillars with Corinthian capitals, Carlo reached the end of the hall and unlocked the wooden door. His conversation with Bernardo sparked numerous questions that swirled in his head, and he wanted to return to Julia but felt compelled to make a quick stop. Bernardo had given him a key a week ago, the one time he'd set foot in the Palazzo's storage room. He flipped on the lights and surveyed the vast space filled with overflow paintings, sculptures, arms and armor, and Palazzo operational materials, such as brochures, chairs, and more. The most valuable works were crated, but dozens of paintings were stacked on shelves, organized by century and artist. During his previous visit to this room, he was in a different frame of mind, angry and desperate to return to the hospital. He'd thought it more of a prison cell and hadn't realized what a remarkable place it was. He could spend the rest of his life among the artwork, though it wouldn't be quite as enjoyable if he couldn't walk around.

Stopping at the near-empty section of the shelves for 21st-century art, he pulled out the two-meter-high by five-meter-long canvas and propped it against the scaffold before removing the sheet.

A lone figure against a white backdrop stared at him. With the subject's dark hair and eyes, Carlo had to admit the near-actual size representation was remarkably accurate and eerily lifelike. He'd yet to decide on a background but was pleased with his choice to pay homage to Tintoretto; Carlo clothed his subject in the same magenta tunic worn by

Saint Mark in the artist's masterpiece, *Miracle of the Slave*. Carlo's subject was barefoot, an expression of unrequited longing on his face, reaching for the viewer with his left hand. His right palm was held upward, symbolically empty.

"*You woke me up,*" the subject said in Venetian.

"Nice to know souls sleep. Hello, Nick," Carlo said.

"*It's Angelo. I've always been Angelo.*"

XXVI

WHEN SHE WAS NINE, JULIA AND HER friends held a schoolyard contest. They took turns standing on the monkey bar ladder and jumped to see who could catch the furthest rung. Julia won by nabbing the fifth. But she wanted to cement her status in schoolyard history, so naturally, she sought the sixth bar. With twenty kids cheering her on, she sprung off the ladder, extended her hands like Supergirl—and missed. She landed hard, with her elbow slamming into her gut. Gasping for air, unable to scream, tears pouring down her face, she'd thought she punctured her lungs, broken every rib and maybe her spine. The gym teacher looked her over and dismissively reassured her that she'd just gotten the wind knocked out of her. Sure enough, she was able to walk away and was fine—except for a dull pain and bruise in her gut that persisted for weeks.

Her parents had promised her it'd be the worst injury she'd ever experience. Little did they know.

The hospital mirror reflected Julia's image, but she felt as though she stared at a stranger. The stitched-up, three-inch laceration on her abdomen was a new addition, but the moment of incision wasn't the only thing she couldn't recollect. Such a bizarre experience, to slumber for a week. She didn't remember any dreams or even sleeping, for that matter. It was as if seven days had been extracted from her life. She'd heard about people who experienced missing time because they believed they were abducted by aliens. It was the best way she could explain being in a coma—*missing time*.

Even breathing heightened her disorientation, as the aroma of the hospital accosted her nostrils. She recalled the same odor after Nick's hockey accident just a few short months ago, though it seemed like another lifetime. Maybe it was.

Her room was clean and modern, and an Italian hospital smelled the same as an American one—bleached sheets, sterile *everything*. The unmistakable stench of life hanging in the balance pervaded the air, even in her private room. Unless that was her.

Julia wasn't surprised that her childhood dog always freaked out in the vet's parking lot. If humans could sense the cusp of death, for an animal who could find hidden treats in a dark house, it must've been like being thrown into a morgue without electricity.

A much-needed shower helped to level-set her place of mind, but it didn't help with the hospital's odor, and a fresh bandage highlighted the injury. Everything that happened before she received it was fuzzy, though she recalled her husband chasing her around Carlo's loft with a sword. But it wasn't her husband. A deranged, desperate soul from another time committed the act. From what she remembered, her poor Nick did everything he could to fight his former self and save her. It all seemed like a dream. But every twist and turn of her body brought a painful reminder that the scar—and the incident—was very real. Angelo was to blame. Or perhaps Isabella. No, it wasn't either of them, she thought, not really. Blame landed squarely with the Order.

If she thought getting kidnapped, brought to a torture room, and escaping Venice in the dead of night was a bad experience, waking up in the hospital with what could've been a fatal wound took the cake.

She didn't think Carlo was lying, but when he filled in the gaps for her, it almost seemed as though he were mistaken—or trying to fault Nick for something he didn't do. After all, she remembered Carlo rushing outside, so how could he know what happened? Even in Nick's deranged state, there was no way he would've stabbed her—it was unquestionably Angelo who assaulted her. Nick tried to protect her but was overpowered. Then Angelo managed to flee, according to Carlo. If only she could reach Nick and bring him home. She tried calling, texting, emailing, and messaging through three different apps, but no luck. That sure felt like déjà vu.

Her doctor and nurse had examined her all morning. They were amazed her vitals had returned to normal and how fast the laceration had mended. Apparently, her scar appeared four months old, rather than a week. They couldn't explain how she healed so rapidly, especially with so much blood loss. She was lucky to be alive, let alone up and walking. Without knowing how severe the wound was in the first place, their astonishment left little impression on her. It felt as though people were raving about a movie she never saw—and from the description, didn't want to. Perhaps death had been close. Did it matter? Did she truly recover quickly?

Physically, the pain told her she hadn't healed at all. Mentally, she felt as though she'd pulled an all-nighter, taken a sleeping pill, and then was awakened for a surprise exam. Emotionally, she should've been a wreck, but between her recent experience with trauma and her sleepwalking mindset, it was as if she'd been zombified—and that numbness was a welcome coping mechanism.

She took photos of her scar and emaciated naked body to document the experience before rifling through her suitcase. Carlo was wonderful and had brought her stuff to the hospital room. He even charged her camera and cell phone batteries. Tittering at her outfit choices, she shook her head. Since it was the middle of what was supposed to be a three-week trip, everything was clean—though she guessed most of her clothes would hang off her rail-thin frame; she'd lost fifteen pounds. She was so famished, she felt as though she could eat her weight back in one sitting. Most of what she had packed was sensible, comfortable travel clothing, but in desperate need to feel . . . *alive*, she opted for a knee-length pink floral summer dress she picked up on sale at Nordstrom Rack before the trip. She planned on wearing it one hot night to an outdoor restaurant. Ripping the tags off, she put it on and admired herself in the mirror. She felt alive again—or at least a semblance of a living person. And wanting to feel as much herself as possible, she decided to forgo all makeup, though the bags under her eyes screamed for it. *Strange, to have bags under one's eyes following a week's worth of sleep.*

Her doctor was also bewildered by her memory loss, but said it was psychological; the brain had a way of blocking traumatic events. That was enough for Julia since she had lied to the doctor out of fear of implicating Nick in yet another crime. The official diagnosis: she needed to take it easy, but otherwise, there was no reason for her to be there. Her discharge was for noon, at which point, the police were coming to talk to her. She had forty-five minutes. She'd intended to be out of there in thirty. The Venetian police meant Fanella, which meant the Order.

After a final glance in the mirror, Julia packed up her belongings and headed to the admitting desk. The process was straightforward, if not unceremonious, and rather lonely. The only surprise was how inexpensive her hospital bill was—less than her deductible, so she charged the whole tab to get the airline miles.

Waiting for the paperwork, Julia prayed the cops wouldn't arrive early. Then again, leaving the hospital alone scared the hell out of her. Angelo tried to kill her, but she knew she could reach Nick if she could just get him out of Venice. Then they could return to America and get him the therapy he needed.

She called her husband for the who-knows-what-time and didn't bother leaving another message. She also checked her emails and texts, which were few. Everyone she knew thought they were in the middle of their vacation. She replied to three: a follow-up regarding dinner from Pierre Gold, the New York gallery owner, to which she replied she'd get back to him; to Delta, apologizing for never sending the Biennale article and that it wouldn't be coming; and a check-in from Wade, Nick's brother, who asked how their trip was going. 'You'll hear all about it,' she wrote back, adding a few crooked and upside-down smiley emojis. She regretted the cryptic nature of her response a half-second after she clicked send.

"Julia," the young male voice called from the hall toward the entrance.

"Signora O'Connor," the older male voice called from the opposite end of the hall.

On one side, Carlo rushed toward her, looking disheveled. From the other side came her gray-haired doctor, clipboard in hand. Carlo arrived a step ahead. "I'm so sorry, Julia. I overslept."

"Signora O'Connor," the doctor said, "I have a test result for you."

"Yes?"

The doctor glanced at Carlo and took Julia's arm to bring her aside. "One of your blood tests was slightly irregular—"

Julia gasped. "Am I okay?"

"Yes, yes," he said with his thick Italian accent, adjusting his eyeglasses. "You're relatively fine, which is remarkable, but because of this test, I did another to confirm a suspicion. While you were in the coma, you had heavy vaginal bleeding. I'm sorry to tell you but... you were pregnant."

CARLO HELPED JULIA with her suitcases as they exited the hospital. Its gothic facade differed dramatically from the antiseptic interior, but the remarkable architecture was a fleeting glimpse in the downpour that matched Julia's frame of mind. She held an umbrella, doing her best to shield them from the rain. Even holding a simple object above her head was an agonizing task for her abdomen, but she powered through it. She was determined to power through everything. After hearing she lost the baby, Julia barely said two words. Carlo's silence spoke volumes—he had heard the doctor. She was glad he didn't try to talk about it—what was there to say? Though the news hit her like a ton of bricks, it was an *unexpected* loss. She had no idea she was pregnant. As hard as it was, it was another thing that couldn't weigh her down. That bastard Angelo inflicted more damage than he'd intended, but she and Nick could try again when they were ready.

"Mrs. O'Connor." A middle-aged woman with a British accent and a raised finger approached them across the square. In her other hand, a black umbrella shielded her shoulder-length, brown wavy hair. A camel-colored trench coat protected her clothes. "May I have a word?"

Who was Julia kidding? All she wanted was to be in her actual husband's arms, sobbing into his shoulder. With limited energy, she stopped and heaved a sigh, unintentionally providing the Englishwoman with an opening. She eyed Carlo suspiciously, then leaned into Julia's ear.

"My name is Maggie Yorn. I'm from the Times," she whispered, before returning to normal volume. "I'm glad to see you well."

Julia raised an eyebrow.

"My colleague is a mutual friend," Ms. Yorn continued. "He works in the arts section."

"Signora," Carlo said, taking Julia's arm, "she's exhausted. Perhaps another time."

Despite Carlo trying to nudge her along, Julia held her ground. It took a few seconds, but she realized who Ms. Yorn was referring to. Lionel Benton, the art critic.

Ms. Yorn must've noticed Julia's expression because she pointed at Carlo with her eyes.

"Carlo," Julia said, "give me a second, okay?"

Without waiting for him to answer, Julia handed Carlo her umbrella and ducked under Ms. Yorn's. They stepped a few feet away, and Ms. Yorn angled the umbrella in Carlo's direction. Julia noted how sly she was about it—she lowered the umbrella just a few inches so Carlo wouldn't be able to hear their conversation, but not enough to make it appear she was overtly blocking him out.

"We just want you to know we have your welfare in mind," the reporter said. "And resources, should you need them." She reached out and placed a hand on Julia's to emphasize her sympathy.

Julia smiled but couldn't help thinking it wasn't her well-being they cared about. "Is Mr. Benton back in Venice?"

"He thought it best to remain in London. But that doesn't mean he hasn't been following your story, Mrs. O'Connor."

"How could he?"

"Well, that's where I come in."

"And what do you do, Ms. Yorn?"

"Call me Maggie. We also know you need to be *exceedingly* cautious."

Julia glanced back at Carlo. Holding the umbrella and her suitcase, he looked like an outcast friend—staring at them. Julia tipped Ms. Yorn's umbrella down a bit more and turned her head. "Can I trust Carlo?"

"You tell me."

"I think so. Can I trust you?"

"You have no reason to, but you also have friends in short supply. And I believe you know you can trust Lionel."

Julia nodded. "Do you know what happened to my husband?"

"Nobody has seen him. We think they're holding him in the Palazzo."

Though she thought Nick was on the run, the answer didn't surprise Julia. Even if he'd been on the move, he would've found a way to visit her in the hospital or contact her. She cut a look at Carlo, who continued watching them hard.

"I should go," Julia said.

Again, Maggie motioned her eyes toward Carlo. "Did you ever tell him about his father? That there was never an arson investigation?"

"Mr. Benton told you?"

"I told him. Did you tell your young artist friend?"

Julia positioned her body so Carlo couldn't see her lips or hear her whisper. "Yes. Well, the first time under duress. The second under the influence."

Maggie squinted, not happy with that answer. "Doesn't change the knowledge. Has he looked into it?"

"I have no idea. Why are you asking?"

"The facts of a life-changing event have been locked away. Curious, no?"

Julia had wondered about it herself. She wanted to bring it up with Carlo, but it was such a personal, sensitive subject. She peeked back at him; he continued to watch them. "I really need to go."

"Della Porta is planning something. We don't know what, but he's recruited dozens into the Order, mostly cops." Without another word, Maggie turned on her heel and headed down an alley.

The reporter's words were like freezing darts that impaled Julia. If they were true, then helping Nick just got significantly more difficult. She hustled back to Carlo and joined him under the umbrella. "Sorry about that," she said.

He didn't answer. Julia realized he hadn't been staring at them—he was in a trance—an all-too-similar daze she'd seen before. "Carlo!" Julia snapped her fingers in front of his face. He shook his head and returned to the present. "Another flashback?"

"So strange," Carlo said. "The rain triggered it. I was a woman. I'm not sure where, maybe Venice, in a boat, in the rain. And the strangest thing . . . it was the same time with a memory of camping. A red and blue tent. Stuff was stolen. Like two dreams at once." He rubbed his eyes with distress.

"I don't know, Carlo. But it's raining here, in real life."

He shook his head, scattering whatever thoughts were in his head with the rain, and then took the umbrella to hold over Julia. The two walked from the hospital.

"What did that reporter want?" he asked.

Everything Maggie Yorn said lingered in Julia's mind. This wasn't the best time to broach such a delicate subject with a friend who'd been bending backward to help her, but when Julia debated it, she realized that the truth would help him. It was the least she could do, so why put it off?

"Carlo," she said as gently as she could, "do you remember when I told you there was never an investigation into the fire that destroyed your parents' house?"

Carlo cocked his head. "Is that what the reporter wanted to talk about?"

A businessman hurried past them, holding a newspaper over his drenched head.

"No," Julia replied. "Well, does it matter? I'm just wondering if you ever checked it out."

A somber sigh was Carlo's answer.

XXVII

CARLO STRODE THE PALAZZO'S FAMILIAR HALL with a heavy burden and a sleep-deprived brain. His sofa was like slumbering on a godsent cloud compared to the loveseat in the hospital, but his mind plagued him. Waking at dawn, he found a text Bernardo sent the night before, asking him to join a pre-breakfast meeting. His shoulders sagged. He had zero inclination to be there, but Bernardo wrote that it was critical. He yearned to be with Julia, to make sure she was okay, to feed her and help her convalesce. A note on the table, along with bread, jam, and instructions for the Nespresso machine, with a few capsule choices would hopefully be a nice welcome in his absence. She'd gone to bed after an early dinner the previous night; it surprised him that she was tired after waking from a coma, but her body needed to heal. And in truth, he'd been thinking about what Bernardo had said during their last meeting. Carlo wasn't required to like della Porta, but he needed to make amends with him. Combined with the time and urgency, it seemed compulsory—he was the Painter and had obligations to the Order. And that would lead to propelling his career to new heights. Working with della Porta was an inescapable task. And . . . he wouldn't be able to figure out the mystery of his father and Paganelli otherwise.

He opened della Porta's office door and halted on the threshold with widened eyes. He expected just della Porta and Bernardo, but the chief

Protector wasn't there. Instead, della Porta stood in front of his desk. On the couch and side chairs sat Mayor Giovanelli and a tall, bald man in a double-breasted suit. Carlo recalled Davide Zotti, one of the councilmembers. Also on the couch sat an attractive girl with pink-highlighted brown hair, about his age. Mounted on the wall where there once was an 18th-century tapestry, hung a large flatscreen monitor, with two men and one woman on the screen, none of whom Carlo recognized, each in their own window.

"Ah, Carlo, so good to see you, my so—er, friend," della Porta said in English. He rushed over and gave Carlo a warm embrace before closing the door. "You're right on time."

He brought Carlo over to the group.

"You've met the mayor and Signor Zotti, but I'd like you to meet Francesca Elizabeth, the countess's granddaughter who lives in Paris."

"Fosca." The girl stood to shake Carlo's hand. "And London, though I'm thinking of moving here."

"Really?" della Porta said with genuine surprise.

"So you're the famous Carlo Zuccaro," she said, blatantly ignoring della Porta.

Intoxicating tendrils of jasmine and citrus notes, layered over hints of ginger and vanilla, teased Carlo's olfactory senses. He guessed it was Dolce & Gabbana's classic perfume, a scent he'd succumbed to on multiple occasions. He resisted the temptation to kiss Fosca's hand as he did her grandmother's, sensing the move would be inappropriate in this business-like setting.

Though the girl carried a strong resemblance to Countess Faustina Baldesseri, her smooth skin, piercings, and lively grip energized his sullen mood—and his libido. Her large brown eyes, darkened by eyeliner, bored into him with a curious look that Carlo couldn't pin. A sudden urge to paint her filled him, but instead, it was almost as if she studied *him* . . . which he didn't mind in the slightest.

She gazed at their fingers with a sly grin, compelling his own eyes down. Realizing he held her hand for far longer than was appropriate, he released hers and chuckled to divert attention.

"I'm hardly known in my neighborhood, Fosca. But I appreciate the sentiment. It's lovely to meet you. I only had the chance to meet your grandmother once. She was a remarkable woman who will be dearly missed—"

"Miss-*ing*," della Porta said. "She's *missing*, Carlo."

Carlo bowed his head in apology to Fosca. "Forgive me, Fosca. Is there any news?"

"None." She frowned. "It's why I'm here. And to handle her affairs."

"Come, there are people you need to meet." Della Porta guided Carlo to the empty side chair but held his arm to prevent him from sitting. He pointed to the monitor. "On the left is Bianca Trevisan, a member of the Venetian Council who resides in Milano. You spoke briefly on the night of your ascension to Painter."

"A pleasure to meet you again, Signora Trevisan," Carlo said.

"Likewise," the middle-aged Trevisan replied, her short curly brown hair reflecting in the glow of her computer monitor.

"In the middle," della Porta continued, "allow me to introduce Christophe François, head and Exalted Master of our Order's esteemed Paris chapter."

Carlo whispered into della Porta's ear. "Why didn't you tell me about the other chapters, the other paintings?"

"It never came up," della Porta hissed through clenched teeth. "Now's not the time. Say hello to François."

Carlo nodded to the nearly bald, bespectacled octogenarian on the monitor. "Very nice to make your acquaintance, Monsieur François."

"Bonjour, Carlo," François replied.

Della Porta simpered and pointed to the computer window on the right. A man about della Porta's age with a thick beard and salt and pepper hair scowled with undisguised annoyance. "And on the right—"

"Enough with the endless formalities, della Porta," said the man in Spanish-accented English. "You're not the host of a dating reality show. Carlo, I'm José Vasquez. Head and Exalted Master of the Spanish chapter."

"Very nice to meet you, Señor Vasquez." Carlo proffered a warm smile.

"Let's hope so," said Vasquez, with his yawning, guttural voice. "You're filling massive shoes. Esteemed, massive shoes."

Carlo took his seat. "I think about that fact every day, Señor Vasquez. It still seems like an impossible dream. All I can say is that I will never fill Tintoretto's shoes. But I will try to walk in his footsteps."

Everyone concurred with the sentiment.

"As you can see," della Porta said with a wide grin, "he is more than up to the task. More than the perfect choice."

"It's nice he possesses a morsel of humility," said Vasquez.

The man's statement was laced with obvious derision that took Carlo aback, making him question where Vasquez's antagonism sprang from.

"No response?" said the man. "We've all heard about your womanizing exploits, so we know you have a pair of balls. But it seems like you hide them between your legs when faced with the slightest conflict."

The room murmured and cleared their throats.

Carlo couldn't fathom why a total stranger would chastise him. And though it was true he disliked conflict, he disliked being humiliated even more. "I have no problem with conflict, Señor Vasquez, even if it's out of the blue and designed so obviously to provoke a response. I just need to know what I'm getting into. Would you prefer to discuss my humility? Or my balls?"

"Ha," hollered Vasquez. "At least he has a sense of humor. This isn't a fight, Carlo. Keep your knives in your belt. Just know that there is no margin for error."

"So I've heard," Carlo replied.

"José," della Porta said, "give Carlo a break. You've only just met him—"

"It'd be nice to meet him in person."

"And you're always welcome in our fair city. Call my secretary, and she'll arrange a good time. But now, let's move onto the second item on our agenda." Della Porta stepped over to Zotti. "As everyone knows, our Order has accomplished the literal fantastic. Yet, the power and secrets we hold have been in the shadows—"

"Is this about the O'Connors?" Christophe François asked, all-business.

"And I thought we were going to discuss my nonna-mère's interim replacement on the council," Fosca added.

Della Porta cleared his throat. "Yes, I mean no, this is not about either of those points, but yes, both items shall be discussed."

"Let's discuss them now," said the more emotionally driven François.

"I concur," Trevisan added. "We should've wrapped them up a week ago."

"Ladies, gentlemen." Della Porta held his hands up. "Agendas are fluid." He turned to Fosca. "Regarding an interim replacement for your grandmother, Fosca, as much as we'd love to have you, we're going in another direction."

"Isn't that what this meeting is about?" Trevisan asked.

"In part, yes. Fosca is family and a wonderful contribution. But she's been in the Order a mere few years and is based in Paris—"

"London." Fosca glared at him. "And I'm thinking of moving here."

"If we practiced nepotism with every member of the Order," della Porta said, "then the Council of the Sun Crystal would comprise hundreds of our children, siblings, and cousins. I'm sorry, my dear, but some members have been with the Venetian chapter for longer than you've been alive. It's logical sense to go with someone more experienced and senior."

Fosca's cheeks burned red. "Is that what everyone thinks?"

Carlo pitied her. He must've been in her shoes not long ago, when the council voted on a replacement for the Painter. He also felt a little guilty, since he got the job. Della Porta had been championing him for the position, but the mayor, Zotti, and others were jockeying for their choices. It was only by circumstance that Carlo ascended to Painter.

"I'm with della Porta on this," Zotti said.

"Same," the mayor added.

"As am I," said Trevisan.

"Thank you all," said della Porta. "Fosca, you're more than welcome to attend our Convocations and non-council meetings, such as this one. You'll be on a council before you know it."

"I could see a spot opening on the Paris council in the next decade or so," François said. "You'll be first in line for consideration."

Fosca straightened her posture and crossed her legs. The redness subsided, and her face resumed its previous golden glow. "Thank you, everyone."

"Now what about the O'Connors?" Vasquez stroked his beard.

Della Porta returned to his desk, prompting everyone in the room and on the monitors to crane their necks awkwardly. Carlo sensed it was a tactical move.

"As you know," della Porta said, removing his glasses, "the official story is he's missing and the prime suspect in the countess's disappearance."

"This is unprecedented territory for the Order." Vasquez took a drink of water.

"Insightful." Della Porta held his glasses to the light, then cleaned them with his handkerchief before putting them on again. "And since he hasn't been formally charged yet, *we're* holding him. He potentially has information."

The announcement caught Carlo by surprise, and that surprise quickly shifted to anger. Why would della Porta lie to the group and put Carlo in the position of needing to back up that lie? Was he testing him? He knew Carlo couldn't reveal the truth.

Vasquez slammed his fist on his desk, causing his monitor to quake. Even over a video conference, his action startled the room. "There are two people of note missing. On your watch, della Porta." He pointed his finger at the camera. "Plus, there's been chatter, people asking questions. I suspect it's the Guild."

Della Porta raised his hand. "The Guild is a non-issue, my friend. Their one and only member is deceased."

"You underestimate your opponents as you overestimate your protégé. You need to do something about O'Connor. How long do you think you can hold an American prisoner before word gets out?"

"Why?" della Porta demanded. A nerve had been struck; a vein engorged in his forehead. "Why would word get out? Other than Bernardo, nobody beyond this room knows of this. And why do we need to be involved with O'Connor's story at all? A man is missing—a man who visited this museum but otherwise with whom we have zero involvement. As long as none of you leaks it that he's in our custody, it shouldn't matter. For all anybody knows, he met an Italian girl and they eloped to Sicilia. Who knows, who cares? It's not our problem."

The room fell silent, apparently appeased by della Porta's statement. The whole meeting, Carlo questioned why he'd been brought there. Perhaps it was to hear della Porta's lie in front of everyone. Would that lend credence to it?

"The important thing," della Porta continued, "is that O'Connor can be useful to us, which brings me to the final item on our agenda. The Order's future. For too long, we've been in seclusion. It's time we enact our calling. Veritism."

Della Porta waited for a response. Other than Zotti, the rest of the room shrugged.

"And what's Veritism?" Trevisan asked.

"Truth. And, more to the point, *us*," della Porta replied with extreme confidence. "You, me, everyone here, every member of the Order since it began. Since those brave Benedictine monks and our forefathers created the world's one veritable religion. The *Order* is Veritism."

As della Porta explained his grand scheme of bringing the Order to the public and revealing long-hidden truths to the masses, Carlo couldn't help but agree it was an enticing idea. All religions were based on faith. If the Order revealed facts—*verifiable* facts—about life and the afterlife, it would change everything. As one of the Painters, he'd be in a remarkable position. He gazed about the room. Everyone wore broad smiles but three people: Fosca, who was visibly dismayed but trying to hide it; the mayor, who was either processing the information or holding in a massive dump; and Vasquez, who had a ticking timebomb behind his eyes.

After almost a minute of silence, François was the first to break it.

"Bravo," the Parisian said, applauding through his monitor. "You've outdone yourself, Monsieur della Porta. This is a revelation."

Della Porta's grin consumed his face. Though Carlo just met Christophe François, as the eldest present, he sensed he'd be the most likely to disagree. That he approved of Veritism and della Porta's plan with such enthusiasm must've been nothing short of a coup. "Merci," said della Porta. "I am truly humbled."

"You're insane," said Vasquez.

Della Porta's pleasant expression vanished.

"This is preposterous," the Spaniard continued. "How can any of you support this? What this man proposes goes against every tenet of our Order. Not to mention we'll be ridiculed if we go public. Even if we showed them proof of the souls, nobody would believe it. They'd think it's special effects."

The mayor signaled his agreement. "My son can make those effects on his computer."

"That's where O'Connor and the doge's book comes in," della Porta said. "In O'Connor's past life, he was tasked to purloin the book from a councilman called Renzo Scalfini."

And as della Porta explained his plan, Carlo realized how little he knew about the Order. He expected della Porta to withhold information and didn't fault him for seeking power. But at what cost?

Vasquez bellowed, breaking Carlo's inner thoughts. He could tell the man was getting under della Porta's skin; he had already burrowed under his own. Della Porta's face reddened at the laughter, and he paced the floor.

"Am I the only one here," della Porta said, with a manner seeming to castigate his colleagues, "who believes so fully in our mission, in our charge, that he is willing to take it where it should go?" He stopped moving and pointed at Vasquez and the mayor. "Why should just three cities have the benefit of the Seventh Sun? At a time, it was only Venice." He spoke to Vasquez. "Would you have objected when the Order expanded to Madrid?"

The Spaniard didn't answer.

"I'm with you," Zotti said.

"As am I," added François.

"Thank you, my friends. And many more will join us. Our numbers will swell. We've recruited an additional fifty Protectors in less than a week. We're expanding throughout the Veneto and will have five hundred by summer's end. Señor Vasquez, Monsieur François, I hope you will do the same."

"To what end?" asked Vasquez.

"Once we obtain the doge's book, we'll . . . *convince* the Church to recognize the Order publicly."

Vasquez cleared his throat. "None of the senior members in this room would dispute the fact that the Church has known about us and worked with us. Obviously, there were ledgers and journals kept. None would deny the existence of that. If they haven't been lost, the questions are how you expect to find them and why you think they'll sway a single person that they're real?"

"Excuse me," Fosca said with her hand raised. "For the benefit of the junior members, could you please tell us what books these are and what's in them?"

"It's a single book, Fosca. The private journal of Doge Pasqual Cicogna. It contains proof the Church not only has known about our secrets for all these years, but that many bishops, cardinals, and possibly the pope were secret members. We simply need to obtain it."

Vasquez shook his head. "And four hundred years later, they'll just step aside for you?"

"We will not seek to supplant them but unify with them. Once we have the support of the Church and its followers, we'll show the world our true power—and the truths of this world. God's people will no longer be kept in the dark."

After a moment of pensive thought, Carlo broke the silence. "Who are God's people?"

Della Porta grinned. "Ah, good catch, Carlo. The *Supreme Painter of the Universe's* people is more accurate. *We* are, of course. Those who have been ordained with the secrets of the Seventh Sun. You, especially. But, more broadly," he said, outstretching his arms, "every person on Earth."

"You haven't answered my question," interrupted Vasquez. "Even if you find the doge's book, how will you leverage it? What makes you think the Church will say, 'Sí, it's all true, we'll kneel before you, Lord della Porta?'" He cracked up at his joke.

"With proof," della Porta replied steadily. "We will show them truths. The search is already in the works. My men are looking for the book as we speak."

"How?" asked Fosca.

"Research. Starting in the archives, searching for clues. No doubt it will take time, but it *will* be found."

As della Porta continued explaining, Carlo turned his attention to Fosca. Though she sat listening and smiled when everyone else did, her jaw was locked, a hatred kindling in her eyes. She was hiding something. And it made her even more alluring.

"Carlo," della Porta said, "I said, isn't that right?"

Carlo forced himself back into the conversation. "Yes, signore, of course."

Vasquez laughed again. This time François joined in. "Your new Painter isn't much for attention, is he?" François said.

"We have an Exalted Master making major decisions on his own and a Painter with ADHD." The mayor shook his head in disparagement.

Della Porta cleared his throat. "Once again, Mayor, you make unfounded accusations. I have made no decisions on my own—"

"Yet you did it," said Vasquez.

"Out of necessity," della Porta replied. "I called this symposium precisely for discussion." He stepped over to Carlo and placed a hand on his shoulder. A chill bristled Carlo's skin, but he indulged the man. "Carlo exhibits tremendous focus. If he didn't, he wouldn't be able to create spectacular paintings. He's a phenomenal artist, like his father."

"It's essential I review the Painter and his work," replied Vasquez.

The mention of Carlo's father sparked a stick of dynamite within Carlo that obliterated della Porta's compliment and support. With all of della Porta's methodical planning, how could he be so consistently blind to Carlo's feelings? The dynamite exploded and cleared a mountain that had been the source of Carlo's own sightlessness.

Yet you did it.

Vasquez's words circled in Carlo's head.

"He did it, he did it, he did it," his mother had mumbled in Montebelluna. "Stay away from that man," she had said years earlier when he was a boy.

Della Porta wasn't the only blind man in the room. Had the truth been standing before Carlo all this time? Was his own guilt projecting self-blame? His mother wasn't referring to him. The look in her eyes wasn't disappointment and anger toward *him*. Or, at most, she was disappointed that Carlo let himself be taken in by della Porta.

Stay away from that man.

When he and Julia left the hospital, Carlo had dismissed her mention of the arson investigation, but he couldn't deny the question had stalked him. If the police never looked into the fire, it meant someone was covering up what could only be one thing—murder. But more than that, the coverup explained *how* he was murdered. And it wasn't immolation.

Another memory bit the back of his mind. When he was alone in the Great Council Room, he'd heard the souls screaming at him: *liar, child, traitor, pagan, justice.*

His head was a jumble, and he'd thought he heard the Latin *'filius,'* which could be translated as 'child.' But now, his memory cleared. It wasn't *filius*, but *'figlio,'* the Italian word for 'son.' And it was uttered by a voice he knew.

He did it.

Carlo jerked away from della Porta.

There were a million other questions, but at that moment, just one mattered. "Why is he in there?" he blurted out.

The entire group turned to him.

Carlo glared at della Porta. "Why is my father in . . . *Paradise*?"

XXVIII

CARLO'S INHALES POPPED IN SHORT SPURTS. A deluge of rage overwhelmed him. Though he knew he was reaching and had no solid proof, the microexpression of guilt in della Porta's eyes confirmed the allegation was true.

His supposed father figure—a man who once legally held the status of Carlo's *guardian*—averted his gaze and adjusted his glasses. "We've been over this, my son—"

"What did I tell you?" Carlo shouted, tears welling in his eyes. He didn't care that everyone stared at him, mouths agape at his outburst. He wanted them to hear this. "Do not call me that. Now tell me. Tell *all* of us. Explain, in the finest detail, with everything you've planned... if Paganelli killed my father, then why is he in *Paradiso*? Sentenced to *Paradiso*? Explain."

The group turned to della Porta, expecting a response, though Carlo figured some of them knew the answer. Of them all, Fosca was on the edge of her seat, her complexion reddening in anger. With a deliberate gait, della Porta took his place in the center of the room. "You're the Painter," he said. "You have the right to know."

The statement infuriated Carlo. Blood rushed to his head. His nostrils flared. "I have a right to know because I'm his *son*!"

Della Porta arched back a bit and swallowed. "It was Paganelli. He had already swayed the Exalted Master of the day that your father was evil. I tried to convince him otherwise, but it was too late. We were all too late. Paganelli had fooled us, so your father was condemned. Afterward, sì, his body was burned in the fire."

Carlo shook his head. "But you said Paganelli killed him. That he locked him in. You lied to me."

"Paganelli *did* kill him. A mere technicality whose hand—"

"You lie!" Carlo's scream startled the room.

Della Porta nodded forlornly. "I did. And I apologize, Carlo. I didn't tell you to protect you."

"You didn't tell me because you were grooming me, and you didn't want me to screw it all and move to New York."

"His story is true, Carlo," Christophe François said. The man sounded like he had gravel in his elderly throat.

A silence passed over the room, allowing Carlo a moment to absorb the revelation. Though he was expecting the truth, it came as a shock nonetheless, and François's corroboration of della Porta's statement surprised Carlo more than anything. He forced his body to steady itself.

"My father is in there, unjustly imprisoned for eternity."

"It's a stain on the Order," François admitted. "A most regrettable error. Having you as Painter, I hope, can heal those wounds."

Nobody responded, again giving Carlo time to process. He skimmed his gaze about the room. Though not all may have known, they seemed to share a collective blame—except for Fosca. His eyes landed on della Porta, who looked away. Perhaps della Porta told the truth now, but that didn't absolve him from lying for years.

"And now I," Carlo whispered, his voice eluding him, "am the one responsible for his imprisonment."

Finally, della Porta broke the silence.

"Understand," he said with a timbre that Carlo took as sincere, "if we could turn back time, we would. If there was a way to extract a single soul, we would. But neither thing is possible. However, you've seen the evil with your own eyes. What happened to your father pains me, all of us, to no end, but we must preserve *Paradise*. This is about the future. Your father knew this. The Zuccaro family has been in the Order for centuries. There has never been so ideal a choice for Painter as yourself. Please forgive me, but it wasn't a full lie—and not one without good cause."

Carlo didn't know what to believe. "So I should thank Bernardo for killing Paganelli?"

Fosca gasped. Everyone turned to her.

"You seem distraught by that news, Fosca." Della Porta crinkled his brow.

Composing herself, Fosca cleared her throat. "Of course, I'm distraught. He was a family friend when I was a kid. I knew he went rogue, but I didn't know he died"—she threw a scowl at chief Protector—"or that Bernardo killed him. You were friends with him too, weren't you?"

"I was. And I was misled," della Porta replied.

Fosca sat back in her chair, regaining composure, her chest heaving.

Della Porta faced the group again. "It was an unavoidable outcome. Nobody is happy about it. But it's done, and it's time to lead this conversation back on track."

"How am I supposed to trust you?" Carlo asked.

Della Porta's face reddened. He turned slowly back to Carlo. "Carlo, enough. How can you trust me? Look at where you are. Where would you be without me, eh? New York? Hah. You'd be on the Rialto Bridge selling cheap watercolors. You want to talk about trust? We all know you befriended the O'Connors when I specifically asked you not to. That entire mess is your fault, isn't it?"

Falsehoods regularly spewed from della Porta's mouth, but he could not be argued with when he spoke the truth. Carlo had no response.

"Not only did you befriend them," della Porta continued, "you encouraged Signor O'Connor to explore his past and enabled him to speak with Isabella Scalfini. And look what happened. Look what happened to his poor wife. Her condition is *your* responsibility. In fact, *she* is your responsibility. You need to tell Signora O'Connor to go home."

Carlo gazed at the floor, ashamed of his behavior. Though he faulted della Porta for the origin of his story and for being deceitful, everything the man said about Nick and Julia was true. "She won't do that, and I can't force her," he said softly, still with his head down.

"Then it's your job to keep her in check. Have her chase loose ends until she goes home. Because she's never going to find her husband. Now, let's stay on point."

Vasquez's guffaw cackled from the monitor. "Your hand-picked, undisciplined Painter is responsible for the wife of your prisoner? How soon until they're in bed and he's whispering in her ear?"

Carlo shifted, as if sitting on barnacles. He cleared his throat and locked his gaze on Vasquez's monitor before saying the one thing he could think of that might appease the Spaniard and the room. "I am committed to the Order. There is no margin for failure."

WITH AN UNNERVING MIX of anger and despair, Carlo entered the storage room and flipped the light on. He needed to process that his father was in a purgatory for which he was now the warden, but that could wait. At that moment, he was angry at della Porta, but more upset with himself. He let della Porta get the upper hand at every turn. If that was a fight, Carlo didn't even show up.

On top of that, his confrontation with José Vasquez left him feeling like he lost six pints of blood. And the Mayor breathing down his neck caused him to squirm. At least della Porta was supportive, despite his deception. Carlo appreciated the man's honesty about his father and was relieved by the truth, but he couldn't make Julia go home; he owed a debt to her. Della Porta's words in the archive rang true:

'Fate is a funny mistress. She tantalizes us with the illusion of control, but she has us all by the balls.'

Carlo had dismissed the sentiment as colorful hyperbole. Now, he felt the vise of fate squeezing so hard, it was difficult to walk. But he vowed not to dwell on what happened. He'd been too dejected of late and missed his cheery self. The past could not be undone, but the future could be made. He was a firm believer in fate—a fate that one made *oneself*. In spite of della Porta pulling strings his whole life, Carlo had put himself in positions where he wanted to be. He wasn't della Porta's marionette; he was his own man and would continue to be, even more than ever.

A closed door meant nothing more than a new direction.

No longer did Carlo dread visiting the Great Council Room. Now, he wanted to find his father and speak to him amidst the madness, if possible. If he could isolate his father's voice, he could learn the truth.

It appeared della Porta was unaware Carlo could speak with Nick—or Angelo. He had to know he could hear the souls in *Paradiso*. Could it be possible that della Porta hadn't realized Carlo could converse with his new prisoner? Or was he allowing him to and scheming against him? Whatever the reason, Carlo was alone now, and one thing was certain: nobody but he could hear Angelo.

"Now what do you want?" Angelo asked before Carlo had removed the sheet completely.

"I want to talk," Carlo replied.

"*As if there's anything else for us to do?*"

Carlo cocked his head; he pitied the man. "What do you do all day?"

"*What do you want, Carlo?*"

"Very well. When you were Angelo—"

"*I am Angelo.*"

"In the 16th century, did the Order betray you?"

"*You heard the criminal report. I was with you in the archive, remember?*"

Carlo paced a few steps. Angelo wouldn't be forthcoming with information. "You have Nick's memories, too?"

"*What do you want, Carlo?*"

"I want to know the whole story."

"*Talk about betrayal. You committed the ultimate one. We were friends.*"

"You tried to kill me." Carlo did a double-take, realizing Angelo's words. "*Nick* was my friend, not you."

"*I had no choice. You're the warden of the souls. I begged for mercy, Carlo. Begged.*"

A troubled sigh didn't absolve Carlo's burden. He'd yet to come to terms with what he'd done to Nick. Since the two men shared a soul, it meant they shared the punishment; the soul deserved peace. Not honoring Angelo's request to be painted into *Paradiso* alongside Isabella compounded Carlo's remorse. It was della Porta's idea and as Exalted Master, his ultimate decision, but Carlo didn't refuse. In the end, he was no better than Paganelli—or whoever sentenced his father. "It was an act of passion. I wish it hadn't ended this way."

"Has it ended?"

"No. And I'm the only one who can remedy the situation."

There was a pause. *"You can transfer me into Paradise?"*

"There are options." In truth, Carlo didn't know what he could do. Della Porta said they couldn't extract a soul, but if you could put one in, why couldn't you take one out? At a minimum, Carlo could bring this painting into the Great Council Room. Even if it happened at night, it would be something, so Angelo could converse with Isabella. "But no matter what, I can't do anything without your help."

"I can't be much help as an immobile two-dimensional work of art. And by the way, you could've painted my jawline a little stronger."

Blinking, Carlo peered at his artwork that seemed to be a spitting likeness of Nick, from what he could remember. "It's perfect. Wait, can—can you see yourself?"

"Again, what do you want, Carlo?"

Angelo's sense of humor was remarkably similar to Nick's. Carlo got down to business. "You can help me find the doge's book."

"You and the rest—"

A faint shuffle pattered behind Carlo. He spun toward the sound. Angelo must've heard it, too, since he cut himself off. "Anybody there?"

No answer. He walked toward the door and glanced down the rows of shelving but didn't see anybody. It could've been a rat. He returned to Angelo.

"Yes, exactly. Me and the rest of the Order."

"And the Guild."

"I just heard of the Guild. It's a group fighting the Order?"

"It doesn't matter. I don't know where the book is."

"There must be something you remember, something that can help me find it."

"You want to find it before della Porta?"

"Don't you?"

Angelo chuckled. *"You've given me zero reason to trust you."*

"You also have zero to lose by doing so. I'm the one person who can help you."

He laughed again. *"This is true. Are you a relation to Giuseppe Zuccaro? He was a cheesemonger in Campo San Stin."*

Carlo couldn't tell if Angelo was serious. He shook his head and shrugged.

"*An honorable man. Sold the finest Morlacco in the sestieri.*" Angelo paused again before speaking. "*I do not know if this will aid you, but I believe the book was in a brass lockbox with a design that must represent the Seventh Sun. A split circle with sunrays and other symbols. You heard the police report by the Bird Brothers. Ivan and Vito Uccello. They paid me to find the book. After Renzo died, it would make sense that they scoured the room and took the lockbox. But I am certain that Ivan didn't die with it in his possession.*"

"How can you be sure?"

"*Because he didn't have it when I killed him. On the mainland. Severed the bastard's throat as he lay in the muck. I regret not doing the same to Vito.*"

The story took Carlo aback. He knew Angelo had escaped, but what became of him remained a mystery. The information could prove to be useful. He had a lead. Vito Uccello. And the design of the box.

"*You now know things nobody else in this living world knows.*"

Carlo was obliged. Still, he couldn't help but ask, "Where did you go after Venice?"

"*The New World. A nobleman aided my flight. He died because of my actions.*"

"Who was he?"

"*I never knew, and it's not the time for that story. I can't say if Vito gave the book to anybody else, even to the doge. For all we know, it's in this very room.*"

"It could be. And Ivan may've had a wife and children."

"*It wouldn't surprise me.*"

"What about the Scalfini residence? Could it have been hidden somewhere inside?"

"*It's possible it was not in that lockbox.*"

"Do you recall the address?"

"*Homes in Venice did not have addresses then. But I can tell you it was a three-story yellow villa on the Grand Canal, near Campo San Polo. On the corner was an engraving. A saint, maybe. Holding a shovel and a branch or a leaf. I do not recall.*"

"Thank you, Angelo." Carlo grabbed the sheet but stopped himself. "I am sorry, Nick, Angelo. You will be reunited with Isabella. You have my word."

"*We'll see if it means anything.*"

Carlo threw the sheet over the canvas.

"*IF I COULD KILL YOU, I would,*" Nick said.

"*That would mean killing yourself,*" Angelo replied.

"*If it means release, then sign me up.*"

"*You were our seventh life. Release does not guarantee ascension.*"

"*Does it matter?*"

Frozen in the dark was a slow way to pass eternity. Before Carlo had arrived, Angelo had allowed Nick to resurface. Talking to oneself—even when one's self hates his other self—is preferable to talking to no one at all. Though he wished he could kill Carlo, he found himself yearning for the conversation. And it was true—Carlo was his only possible means of ascension or better, somehow being reunited with Isabella. He didn't know if Carlo lied, but did it matter?

A soft glow from behind the sheet interrupted his thoughts. Usually, all the lights would turn on when someone entered the storage room.

A moment later, hands pulled the sheet halfway off the painting.

Fosca stood in front of him. She shined her cell phone screen on his painted face and gasped. In the dim light, she covered her mouth, nearly hyperventilating, blinking rapidly.

A warmth imbued Angelo's soul.

"*It's nice to see you, Fosca.*" She couldn't hear him, for his speech was all cerebral, but his statement was sincere. "*Turns out you were right. Carlo's pretty strong.*"

"Ni . . . Nick? Or Angelo? Are you really in there?"

"*I've been in worse places. I contracted scurvy and dysentery on the crossing to the New World.*" He paused. "*No, this is definitely the worst.*"

Angelo felt Nick yearning to speak, but he subjugated his other self and eyed Fosca. It was as if two panes of glass pressed him together, with the piece facing her allowing for one-way communication. When Carlo came, it was as if the pane became more porous, so they could communicate, even though his voice was in Carlo's head.

"Can you hear me?"

"Every word." If only he could give her a sign. But it was impossible.

"I can't believe they did this to you. I . . . I feel responsible."

"I'm a grown man. Men. No matter how you slice it, I'd be in prison or dead."

"Please know, I'm gonna do everything I can to figure out how to save you."

"Kill the Painter."

"Even if it means killing the Painter. But . . . there may be a way to reverse the process."

"Reverse the process?"

Fosca couldn't hear him, but she continued speaking to the inanimate representation before her.

"To be honest, I have no idea if it's possible, but I'm pretty sure they haven't incinerated your body yet. What I'm saying is . . . there's hope. But you know, don't get your hopes up."

Angelo pictured Nick's body, ancient and disheveled, crammed in a deep freezer somewhere.

"I'll also watch over Julia for you."

With an exquisite countenance of remorse that Angelo thought should never grace such a pretty girl's face, she brought the sheet down and enshrouded the imprisoned swordsman in darkness.

XXIX

"Grazie," Julia said to the bubbly server as she refilled the fresh-squeezed orange juice. The glass sat next to Julia's cappuccino, nearly finished broccoli rabe frittata, crumbs of a cornetto, and an empty dish of strawberry jam. Waking ravenous, she had devoured the bread Carlo left for her, withdrew five hundred euros from the nearest bank, and stopped at the first restaurant she found with outdoor seating, Wi-Fi, and a breakfast menu. The server had thought it funny when Julia requested a typical large Italian breakfast.

"A cappuccino and hard roll," the server had said. Thrilled that tourists had returned to Italy, she made some recommendations, which triggered Julia's salivary glands and made her stomach rumble.

While waiting for her food, she chatted with an American family of four, deflecting questions about her traveling situation with sightseeing tips, including the Palazzo Ducale. It felt strange to recommend a place that caused her so much grief. Still, it was a spectacular sight, and she was glad a family could enjoy it under normal circumstances. Her lost pregnancy lingered in her head; she couldn't wait to take family trips with Nick and their future children.

Though her situation hadn't changed, Julia felt more recharged than she'd been in ages—perhaps not since her and Nick's vacation to Key West three years prior. Compared to the narrow hospital bed, sleeping in Carlo's queen revitalized her body. She owed him one. A few, actually. Or was he paying her back? Maybe they were even at this point. She'd texted him when she sat down and told herself they'd get down to business when he arrived—tracking down Nick and returning him to a semblance of normal.

She knew in her heart she'd be able to coax Nick out of Angelo long enough to get on a train. He'd told her that the farther he was from Venice, the more he felt like his real self. Unfortunately, locating him was like searching for Rumpelstiltskin's magical spinning needle in a million haystacks. The impossibility of the task be damned—Nick wouldn't give up on her, and she wouldn't do it to him.

Embarking on such a difficult undertaking alone made it even harder. An ounce of emotional support would've worked wonders. She wanted to call her sisters or a friend, but it was 4:30 in the morning. Instead, she texted the goofy photo of Nick in front of St. Mark's Tower to his brother Wade and emailed Lionel Benton in London to ask about Maggie Yorn. She was curious why the British reporter would've felt compelled to investigate the Zuccaro housefire.

After a few sips of cappuccino, she polished off the zesty frittata and snapped some photos of her empty plates and the restaurant before pulling her iPad from her purse. She had a lot of work to do, but it was good to have her camera in her hands again. Unable to resist, she took a shot of the diners at the three other tables with the winding *calle* behind them before her attention was captured by a man and his prepubescent son struggling with boxes of onions balanced precariously high on a cart. She uploaded the best to Instagram. The first post in two weeks had her feeling nervous, but the tiny return to the mundane was a godsend for her psyche when it was done. It was as if she'd been trudging through quicksand with ankle weights and suddenly learned how to fly. Other weights remained, and the only way she could remove those was to tackle them one by one.

Briefly considering contacting the attorney she and Carlo found, Julia decided she had let others get involved too much. It was time to take matters into her own hands. And though a part of her screamed to just forget it all and go home, or at least call her parents and friends until someone answered, would that solve or change anything? Would returning to Boston help her beloved husband in the slightest? Would hearing a familiar voice get her one step closer to justice? No, it would prolong the problem and his suffering—*her* suffering, too. Nick needed help. Della Porta and his cronies needed to be in prison. She took a healthy gulp of juice, downed the remaining cappuccino, and recounted everything.

The last thing she remembered was Angelo pointing a sword at her. She also recalled della Porta, Bernardo, and a mystery man entering Carlo's loft. After that, Maggie Yorn told her that della Porta was holding Nick and planning something big. And the final thing Nick told her from his prison cell: "Find Paganelli. Finish my work." Not much to start with. Julia's favorite journalism professor at Boston University taught her to question everything and everyone, and don't let go until you have answers. She stuck with the process as a city reporter for the *Boston Globe*, and by the time she left three short years later, it had become an engrained habit she hoped she'd never shake. Though she left her job to pursue fine art photography, she had a knack for journalism, especially investigative stories. There wasn't much to go on, but she knew she could find her husband. Unfortunately, checking Maggie's theory that Nick was being held in the Palazzo was nearly impossible, but she could investigate other possibilities and rule them out one-by-one. She typed out her questions:

1) How did Nick get out of prison? Was he released? Did he escape? In either case, who helped him?
2) How did Angelo possess Nick's body?
3) How did Nick/Angelo get to Carlo's? Where did he get the sword?
4) Who and where is Paganelli? Was he the mystery man? On Poveglia Island? What abandoned kosher butcher shop?
5) Where is Nick?????
6) ~~Why am I alone?~~

After deleting #6 and vowing to herself she'd dump the self-pity once and for all, she re-read the list. Of all the questions, the only searchable answer was Poveglia Island. Though she didn't know the island's name she'd seen in the rowboat when Nick tossed the gun overboard, it wasn't hard to find on Google Maps. Was Nick there with Paganelli, the kooky guy he mentioned? Even if he wasn't, it was by far the best lead, if not the only one. All she knew was that he was missing before, and he'd returned to rescue her then. She'd find him. Or he'd find her.

"Ask him where he was."

Julia jumped at the quick whisper into her ear, then pressed her hand on her heart to calm it. Maggie Yorn stood behind her.

"Maggie?"

"Just ask him."

"Who—?"

The reporter hurried away, disappearing behind a tour group.

"Espresso e cornetto," a man called to the waitress.

Julia turned to find Carlo striding to her table. He took a seat opposite her, looking rather frazzled.

"Did you see a ghost and get into a fight with it?" she asked. A bit unsettled herself, Julia realized Maggie was referring to Carlo.

Without the slightest reaction to her joke, his eyes darted to the other diners and the noisy foot traffic streaming past their table. The routineness of the scene seemed to settle his demeanor. "You're feeling better"—he eyed her empty plates—"and hungry."

"Was," Julia said. "Where have you been all morning?"

"The library."

"The library? Why?"

"I also had a meeting. At the Palazzo."

Julia slammed her fork down. Carlo looked at it but didn't flinch. She felt her face constrict into a scowl. His answer explained Maggie's covert action. And she couldn't believe it. How could Carlo, who'd done so much for her, go to a meeting where her husband was being held? "Did you see Nick? Have a beer with him?"

Carlo glanced around, then pulled a crumpled pack of cigarettes and a plastic lighter from his pocket. Still not used to all his smoking, she backed away when he lit up. The American family did the same, towing their kids' chairs away from him—or perhaps away from the crazy lady still gripping a fork like a weapon. She placed the utensil down and folded her hands on the table.

Speaking in a hushed, measured tone, Carlo said, "Nick is not tied up or *behind bars* at the Palazzo, Julia. I know this because I saw him run out of my flat while I was holding your wounds."

"That doesn't mean della Porta and his men didn't capture him."

"They didn't. I'd know."

She laughed. "Are you serious? You're Mr. Order now? Della Porta has been keeping secrets from you for years."

He reached for her hands, but she pulled them away. She appreciated everything he'd done for her. He saved her life, but she had to face facts—he was playing both sides. Maggie was right about the arson investigation. Would he have volunteered that he went to the Palazzo if Julia didn't ask?

The waitress returned with Carlo's coffee and croissant, along with an ashtray.

After quashing his cigarette, he added a sugar cube to his espresso, stirred, and took a long sip.

"Who was your meeting with?" Julia asked. "Della Porta?"

"With many people. I had to go."

Julia's gaze narrowed. "Are the police looking for Nick?"

He shrugged. "I suppose."

"Isn't it strange they haven't questioned me?"

"I do not know, Julia."

"The answer's pretty obvious. They're controlled by your pals in the Order. They were supposed to see me in the hospital, and I haven't heard from them since. There's a reason della Porta stopped them, which means he knows something. So, what do *you* know?"

"I'm in the middle, Julia." He stared her square in the eye, then bit into his croissant.

As usual, nothing added up. There was no question Fanella was with the Order, along with plenty of other cops. She couldn't trust them. She could go back to the consulate, but they did nothing last time. Come to think of it, wasn't the consulate supposed to contact her? Could they be in on it, too? The likely scenario was that Lacasse was also in the Order, and he never called the consulate as he said he would. She could contact them again, but either way, it seemed like a waste of time. Regardless of the question, she kept returning to the same conclusion: she was on her own. That said, even though Carlo joined the Order, he was her one friend in Venice. Hopefully, that friendship meant something—and he could use his inside connections to help her cause.

"Please understand," he said, seemingly reading her thoughts, "I have an obligation, but I also have an obligation to you." He nibbled at his croissant.

"Do you?"

"Of course."

"What obligation is that?"

"To keep you safe."

The sentiment caused her to reevaluate her earlier thoughts. Maybe it wasn't that he was playing both sides, but as he said, he had conflicting obligations.

"Thank you," she said. "For everything."

He bowed his head in return. "Friends again?"

She offered a sorrowful smile and finished the OJ before wiping her mouth with the cloth napkin. Carlo followed suit with his croissant. She wasn't sure why he felt obliged to protect her, but she had an inkling. After all, he was a large part of why she and Nick were in this mess. And the sole reason she still breathed. She wished he also felt obliged to help her find Nick. If he wanted to keep her safe, then finding Nick was part of that job description. She did a quick search on her iPad for Poveglia Island and displayed the results to Carlo.

"Have you ever been here?"

He raised an eyebrow and scanned their surroundings again. "No, why?"

Julia glanced around, as well. Ever since they were followed by the Order's goon—the creepy guy with the maroon tie—she'd gotten into the habit of looking over her shoulder, but nothing was out of the ordinary. And she doubted anybody wanted to watch her gorge her depleted body on breakfast and take a few photos of ordinary life.

"There's a chance Nick might be there," she said in a normal volume.

He took another sip of espresso before speaking again. "Why would he go to Poveglia? It's the most haunted island in the world."

"Good thing he doesn't believe in ghosts. He told me about a guy who might be there. Maybe Angelo would want to go, too. It's my only lead. Do you know how I can get there? Are there ferries?"

"What guy?"

"Paganelli. I don't know his first name."

Carlo nearly spit out his coffee. "Enzo Paganelli. He's the man who killed my father."

Julia jutted her head back and raised an eyebrow. She recalled the story

Carlo told her and Nick when they first embarked on this adventure. They went to Carlo's that day because she thought she smelled a story about a black-market art ring—a decision she regretted more every day. When Carlo told them his father died in a fire, he said it was an accident. "That's a switch. You said your dad fell asleep with the generator on in his workspace."

"I learned that wasn't the case."

"Oh, and I'll take one guess at your source. The man who runs the Palazzo and the Order."

"He didn't tell me before to protect me."

Julia snorted her incredulity.

"Paganelli was on the run all those years, *not* della Porta. Paganelli has done horrible things. I know this."

"Then come with me. You can ask him yourself."

The intensity of Carlo's gaze caused Julia to shift backward. "He's dead," he said.

The news hit Julia like an autumn gust sweeping every leaf off a maple in one blow. She'd never met the man, but it didn't seem possible. "What? How?"

He spoke in a slow, reflective manner. "That night, Julia. He came into my loft, stabbed della Porta. You don't remember?"

Shit, she thought. Paganelli must've been the mystery man. "I remember della Porta and Bernardo, but I only glimpsed them. And then you all went outside."

"Because the fight took us there. He almost killed Salvatore. He would've killed me if he had the chance."

"But why?"

Carlo shook his head and kicked at a loose cobblestone to the side of the table. He lowered his voice. "He was crazy, Julia. He thought. . . he thought I'm the new Painter. Nick, or Angelo, or both thought—*thinks*—the same thing."

"Why would he think that?"

"I just told you. They're crazy." He glanced around again to make sure nobody was eavesdropping. "But I'm on your side. You know that, right?"

"I think so." In truth, Julia didn't know what she knew, but she didn't appreciate Carlo's assessment of Nick's mental state. Being controlled by someone else didn't make him crazy. "Who killed Paganelli?"

"Bernardo," Carlo answered in a clipped whisper.

Julia knew Carlo had to be involved in the fight but accepted that Bernardo dealt the final blow. And it was all in self-defense. It also tied in with Carlo's story that he rushed to her aid before Angelo escaped.

"Now what? Do you think it's possible Nick went to Poveglia Island anyway?"

"I have no idea," Carlo said, still whispering. "But there's new information. We could help Nick by finishing his job."

Julia matched his volume. "He asked me to do that for him."

"For good reason. If we do it, then he can . . . be free. Free to come out."

"What's that supposed to mean?" Julia really questioned if it was a language barrier or if he was hiding something.

"We stop the Order."

"You want to destroy them?"

"I didn't say that. These people are my friends, my family. But we can root out corruption and return it to its true mission of keeping Earth a place of good and beauty. And maybe we can liberate the souls. Even the evil souls have been imprisoned long enough. Redemption must be real."

Not wanting to enter a philosophical conversation at the moment, she measured the aspects that affected her and Nick. She'd prefer to destroy the Order and bury della Porta, but if stopping them meant finding Nick and ending this nightmare, she was all for it. One step at a time. She'd even be happy seeing della Porta rotting in a prison cell—this time for the rest of his life. "What's this information?"

XXX

FOR A NUMBER OF YEARS, DELLA PORTA HAD admired MediaStatuto, the largest mass media company in Northern Italy. They owned a television station, three newspapers, numerous podcasts, and dozens of websites. While arts and culture baked their bread, they regularly delved into politics, often through their arts programming, but always with a cultural angle. Though they had programming for both sides of the political spectrum, it always veered left, which suited della Porta just fine. It could've been a Communist or Fascist organization; as long as they disseminated his message, it would serve his agenda.

Located forty kilometers away in Padua, his driver took thirty-five minutes to deliver him and Bernardo to the car park. Though della Porta detested contemporary design, he had to admit the modern office with large glass windows was spacious and airy. Silvio Navarro, the editor-in-chief, heavyset with red hair that matched his cheeks, had a jovial demeanor, an enviable trait given the stress of the industry. As he and Caterina, Manuel's sister-in-law, gave della Porta and Bernardo a tour, della Porta envied Navarro's ability to watch most of his employees across the open floorplan.

Despite the business at hand, for the whole morning, his confrontation with Carlo gnawed at him like wood rot eating away a hull. He had been so focused on the council and the other Exalted Masters' response to his plan, that he neglected to consider Carlo. In retrospect, he should've informed him of the other chapters and paintings to mitigate the blow. Vasquez was a rabid badger. Della Porta had never gotten along with Vasquez and was thankful he only had to interact with him once or twice a year. The spectacle embarrassed all present. His protégé's treatment was despicable; it was no wonder the boy lashed out like a cornered animal.

Della Porta sighed. Carlo was like a son to him. Why wouldn't he think of della Porta as a father? He practically raised the boy, gave him everything. Carlo was lost. It was the only answer, and in truth, della Porta couldn't blame him for feeling that way; he needed to put himself in Carlo's shoes. He had thrust him into a role with no preparation and scant knowledge. Carlo was family.

Those who are closest to us are those we take for granted. Yet they're often the most vulnerable.

Della Porta should've learned that from his own upbringing.

As they toured the facility, the other person troubling della Porta returned to his head: the countess. Or, more specifically, how the countess knew about his altercation with Nick in the library archive.

He didn't think the young Painter could've told the old bag about the incident. When would he have had the time or access to her? Or the inclination. No, Carlo's only concern with the countess was how she could influence his career. It had to be someone else. There was a mole in the Order, and della Porta would get to the bottom of it. Still, Carlo's indiscretion presented another problem. He hated that Carlo was spending all his time with Julia O'Connor. He had to agree with Vasquez and the mayor on this point. It would only be a matter of time before he slipped up—or worse, slipped into bed with her—if he hadn't already. Della Porta suddenly appreciated Manuel's redemption more than ever. Not only did he secure this meeting with Navarro, but at the moment, he was keeping tabs on Carlo—hopefully, the *right* way this time. If only Lacasse didn't need to return to Paris.

They reached the conference room and took their seats at a large, oval wooden table. A platter of antipasti waited for them. Della Porta tipped his head to Caterina. The selection of bresaola, grilled vegetables, and anchovy fillets on a bed of arugula was the ideal choice for a late-morning business meeting. She set glasses before the three men, then served pinot grigio.

"Grazie, Caterina," Navarro said.

"Prego." Caterina smiled and left the room.

"Any word from Manuel?" della Porta whispered to Bernardo who surreptitiously checked his phone.

Bernardo tucked the device into his inner suit jacket pocket. "He's on them. No significant movements."

"Thank you for your gift to the foundation," Navarro said in Italian. He was on the board of Save Venice, a U.S.-based non-profit dedicated to preserving Venice's artistic heritage. Though an American organization, they did imperative work, and Della Porta donated every year; he made a recent sizeable contribution that he expected would be noticed.

"Certo. Our interests are aligned, of course."

"Caterina filled me in on the overview of this meeting," Navarro said, "but as you know, we already cover any relevant cultural or arts stories."

Della Porta selected an anchovy and grilled bell pepper, which he ate slowly. He rinsed his mouth with the tart white wine, then touched his Exalted Master's pendant beneath his shirt. "When I was a teenager in Chioggia, I helped my father run the family apparel company in the summer months. It gave me my first business experience, but more than that, it provided me with an appreciation for family. Sure, my family was lovely, with delightful meals and Christmas and the rest, but working with a relative or friends, building something together that you love, there's nothing like it, am I right?"

Navarro gazed about the conference room with nostalgia. Various mementos from the company's history made their home on the bookcase against the far wall. "I couldn't agree more. My grandfather started MediaStatuto in 1949. It was one of the first major businesses founded after the war."

"And you've brought it to heights your grandfather and father could never have fathomed."

"Oh, sure they did. They just didn't have the technology."

Della Porta clapped his hands together. "Even better. You helped them realize their dreams. You're modest, but let's admit, much more so."

Navarro nodded in thanks but also implied for della Porta to get to his point.

"One day," della Porta said, eager to do so, "in August, I'll never forget because it was scorching, my father had left home before me to go to the shop. That morning, I was drenched in sweat, that's how hot it was, I arrived to find three imposing men in the store. I didn't want to intrude, but my father saw me, and I could see he was apprehensive. He called me over and introduced me. Perhaps he thought my presence would give him some sort of protection, I never asked. I don't remember the men's names, but they left an indelible impression. They wanted my father to help them with something. I could tell he didn't want to, and to this day, I'm not sure what they wanted. But I wanted my father to *refuse*. I didn't want him to go into business with men he feared, men who seemed to be extorting him."

"Mafia?"

"That's what I assumed. For years. But you know what happened? The men lived up to their word. They helped support the business with referrals and new customers. We had zero thefts, supply lines were always smooth, and our sales tripled in five years."

Navarro raised his glass as a toast. "And then your father sold the business and made some wise investments."

"You've done your homework."

"It's no secret, Signor della Porta. I don't mean to be rude, but is there a reason you're telling us this story?"

Of course Navarro knew the point of the story. Instead of answering, della Porta raised one corner of his mouth and stared him down.

After a pause, Navarro spoke. "Is there something you believe I can do for you?"

"Kind of you to ask. And if you do, it can benefit you greatly. If you don't, well, who can say? The business world is so difficult these days."

"*Quite* difficult," Bernardo added as he filled his plate with a selection of antipasti.

For a man in the communications business, Navarro's silence was an entire Sunday paper. He didn't need to ask if it was a threat. But della Porta didn't want to force the man. He wanted him as a true ally, just as he learned from his father's benefactors all those years ago.

"Your grandfather was a member of our Order," della Porta said.

"He was."

"Have you not wanted to join? You've always been welcome."

"Certo. But my grandfather lived in Venice. I'm in Padua, I'm not sure about the time commitment..."

Della Porta raised his hand to reassure the man. "Times have changed, my friend, as you well know." He gestured to the workers beyond the conference room glass wall. "All these people worked from home not long ago. We have members who don't live in Italy and come to Convocations once a year or less."

"Convocations?"

"You'll learn all about them," della Porta said with a grin.

The media mogul cleared his throat. "I've been asked to join in the past."

"I'm aware, my friend. And also that you declined. The Order is changing. You'll like the new direction." Della Porta smacked the table. "Consider yourself in, Silvio. I'll send you the details."

Navarro swallowed but bowed his head. "Grazie, Signore."

"It's my honor. Caterina should join us, as well. Everyone is welcome. I'll speak to Manuel." Della Porta slid his plate away. "Now, I assume you've read some stories about Contessa Baldesseri's disappearance?"

"Terrible thing. We've run a few ourselves, but there isn't much to go on."

"I'm here to give you a lead. An American named Nick O'Connor was seen with her, quite agitated. He's a person of interest in the investigation. You can check with Interpol yourself. A few select articles would cement him as the prime suspect."

Navarro ground his teeth together, clearly mulling over the ramifications if he didn't oblige—and the benefits if he did. The man had no choice.

"And perhaps you can run a feel-good piece about my donation to Save Venice. Remember, Silvio. Our interests are aligned."

He tipped his head in agreement.

"Excellent," della Porta said with another clap. He raised his glass and clinked it to Navarro's before drinking. "I can see this is the first of many meetings. Our relationship will flourish, especially once you're officially one of us. After all, those that are closest to us are like family."

As della Porta said the words, he nearly coughed them up. He loathed to think a similar conversation with Carlo was necessary.

XXXI

"IT WOULD BE NICE IF I COULD PINPOINT THE FLASHBACKS—I mean dreams," Carlo said as he led Julia past outdoor restaurants on the *fondamenta* running alongside the Grand Canal. "Or just see Angelo's."

They had just crossed the picturesque Rialto Bridge, which she and Nick had visited on a sunnier day. She gazed up at the thick cloud cover. It felt like it was going to rain again, and neither of them had an umbrella. Carlo's comment struck her as odd. "You said the visions or dreams or whatever were from people in the painting."

"They are."

"So why would you have Angelo's?"

Carlo cleared his throat. "I'm tired. I meant Isabella's. It's hard to keep track." He scrutinized the masonry of every building they passed.

As they navigated between a hotel on their right and outdoor seating and a gondola launch on their left, Julia glanced over her shoulder to make sure no one followed them before checking her phone again. Even if Angelo was shunning modern technology, Nick would've found a way to contact her. Unless he was hurt, on that island, or he really was being held in the Palazzo. She shook her head and dropped her phone back into her purse—nothing from Nick or Benton.

"And you had this vision in the Palazzo?" she asked, recalling their conversation at the café. When they crossed the bridge, he had revealed his information was about some sort of book last seen at the Scalfini residence. It was curious, but she didn't see how it could help Nick.

"No, I mean a little of it. But the important thing is the doge's book. And I know for sure della Porta doesn't know where Renzo and Isabella lived. I also think he doesn't think a Bird Brother found it, or if so, which brother."

"Wait, Renzo? I know that name."

"That was Isabella's husband."

"Okay, I don't know about any Bird Brothers, but Nick mentioned something about Renzo's book. A black book."

Carlo stopped and faced Julia with the look of a curious skeptic. "Renzo's book *is* the doge's book. They're one and the same. What did he say?"

Shrugging, Julia continued walking. "I had no idea what he was talking about. Nothing except that della Porta wants it."

"This isn't a book he can buy on Amazon, Julia." Carlo caught up to her. "You know he'll do anything for it. You were in the torture room."

"Your lunatic stepfather wasn't speaking English half the time, Carlo."

"He's *not* my stepfather. The doge's book is why he kidnapped you. He thinks it will bring him great power. Enough power to make Veritism the world's dominant religion, with him in charge."

"What?" She didn't like the sound of that.

"Don't you see?" Carlo said. "This is much bigger than any of us."

"What could possibly be in this old book that would enable him to rule the world?"

"To be honest, I don't know. I don't think della Porta knows either, but if it's true, I can't risk him getting it. If we find the doge's book first, we can stop him, turn the tables. Use it as leverage to exonerate Nick. And maybe simultaneously expose the corruption. Not just della Porta, but so many. The police, too. They'd have no choice but to drop all charges. And I can return the Order to a force for good."

It was a captivating proposition. And finding a book was easier than fighting della Porta's men. But were they going to locate it? Especially with della Porta looking too? She stopped and snickered at the ridiculousness of chasing a four-hundred-fifty-year-old mystery. "You think the book will still be there after all this time?"

"It's worth a look, no?"

"A murder site and my husband's former life's lover's home wasn't on my must-see list of Venice."

"Almost every place in Venice is a murder site."

"That's reassuring. I don't know, Carlo. I just wanna find Nick, go home, and get him the treatment he needs."

"Until della Porta's grasp reaches America. Besides, Nick needs to be free of Angelo *and* the Order. And until he is, they'll have him extradited to Italy. Even if he's innocent."

Carlo glanced over his shoulder again. Julia did the same. His incessant searching was contagious, and she hoped to have learned a lesson from when she and Nick were followed. The street teemed with tourists and Venetians, but no one seemed to be trailing them.

She had to admit Carlo had a point. And she certainly didn't want to let della Porta run around seeking absolute power with impunity if she could somehow prevent it. "The last time we teamed up, you said it would be an adventure."

"*You* said that." Carlo chuckled.

He stopped short at the corner of an alley. A restaurant housed the bottom of a three-story building. About eight feet above street level, a bas-relief carved into the building's corner watched over the people below, reminding Julia of an inverted version of her photograph of the dinner scene from a spider's perspective. It appeared to be a man holding what looked like a sword and either a giant feather or a huge paintbrush. All the tourists walked right by, not even noticing it, as countless others likely did throughout history.

"What's that carving? Is that guy notable?" she asked.

"Wealthy Venetians would have patron saints engraved into their homes like this. But this isn't it. He told me that the saint on the Scalfini residence would have a shovel and a branch."

"Who told you?"

"I mean in my vision. Not really 'told,' I don't know how to say it. See it, I guess? Please, Julia. This is not easy to explain in Italian, let alone English." Carlo pulled out a cigarette and lit up.

Julia had a dozen questions. For a guy who spoke three languages fluently, he struggled at peculiar moments, but she let it go. Delving into

Carlo's visions and their source could lead her off their current road; she had no desire for that. They continued walking, needing to bypass the Grand Canal by traversing two covered alleys, a courtyard, and a third alley until they emerged on an unusually wide *fondamenta* with a *vaporetto* stop, Venice's public waterbus. Bordered by the water, the canal-side walkway felt like half a piazza, enclosed by four stately homes, accessible by water or the one alleyway. She scanned the spattering of people waiting for the *vaporetto*; it didn't seem as though any of the people who'd already been standing there could be watching them.

Julia joined Carlo in the scavenger hunt, checking the sides of buildings for carvings. They found only one other on a cornerstone—a kneeling saint holding a cross.

"The good news is San Polo isn't that big," Carlo said. "It must be on the other side of the Rialto."

Julia cocked her head at the last house—a fading terracotta-colored three-story building with cathedral windows. On the corner, about ten feet up, was a bas-relief, smaller than the others. "Could that be it?"

Carlo followed her gaze. "Leave the hawk eye to the photographer."

"It comes in handy from time to time."

He dropped his cigarette and stomped it out. They walked over for a better look. The carving depicted a man wearing a saintly robe, holding a shovel and a book. He grinned.

"I thought it was supposed to be a shovel and a branch," she said.

"Things change, memories fade. Focus on the shovel."

"Who is that?"

"Like I said, the patron saint of something or other. Who knows?"

Julia respected her husband's religion, but never got the whole saint thing. She once heard there were ten thousand of them.

She gazed about the vicinity. They were surrounded by water, boats, and stone. "Not too much shoveling going on around here." The building had a balcony between the cathedral windows. The bottom floor windows were barred and curtained. A sudden queasiness told her this was it—and it repulsed her. Isabella's home cut too close to the bone—too close to the origin of a series of events that led to a travesty in her life. She ingested the bile and hid her reaction from Carlo. That travesty needed a happy ending. Apparently, returning to the scene of a past crime may solve a present predicament. She had to stay the course and power through. Taking out her cell, she Googled 'patron saint with a shovel.'

"Saint Fiacre," she said.

"Never heard of him." Carlo continued examining the home.

"Are you sure this is right? He was the patron saint of gardeners."

He turned his attention back to her with a frown.

Julia continued reading, "He got his sainthood because he built a hospice for the poor after single-handedly clearing an entire forest in one day."

Carlo's eyebrows shot up. "A forest? He must also be the patron saint of forests. Or maybe he was. This is it."

She shook her head and raised her hands. "You're kidding, right? We're literally in the opposite of a forest. None of these houses are even made of wood."

"They all have wooden beams. And there's a petrified forest beneath our feet."

Julia recalled watching a YouTube video about the history of Venice. In order to build the city in marshland, Venetians had driven millions of huge wooden stakes into the seabed and then built on top of them. Without exposure to oxygen, the logs petrified.

Carlo squeezed her shoulder. "When Nick and I were in the archives, we found the record log. Renzo Scalfini owned a timber company."

"That's different from gardening."

"Maybe there was a different interpretation back then. This is it."

Carlo climbed the short stoop.

"Wait," Julia said. "What are you gonna do, just ring the doorbell?"

"Sure, why not?" He shrugged.

"And then what, just ask to snoop around their entire house, look for secret compartments? Rip out their walls?"

"We'll see how it goes."

"We need a—"

He rang the bell.

"—plan."

Julia rolled her eyes. It was like being with Nick—which she wished she were. With a combination of melancholy and frustration, she joined Carlo at the front door.

Being so close on the property was almost too much to bear. Of course, Nick wasn't cheating on her with Isabella, but Julia couldn't help the jealousy creeping in. And resentment—she didn't know Angelo's whole story, but it had far too many unhappy endings for her taste. Her queasiness rolled into a wave of nausea, but she couldn't pull away. With a tentative hand, she closed her eyes and touched the door with a single finger. She didn't feel a connection and figured the door was replaced many times over, but her skin prickled nonetheless.

"They're not home," Carlo said, ringing the doorbell again.

Julia examined the window. A half-inch crack in the curtain enabled her to peek inside. The living room appeared modern, with kids' toys strewn about. A small tent sat in the corner. Besides the fact that the house used to be Isabella's, Julia was entirely uncomfortable peeping into a family's home. "This is too much of a longshot. Ready to go to Poveglia?"

Carlo shook his head. "We'll come back later. There are better clues than Poveglia. There's a man on Murano."

Julia turned to survey the vicinity. "Murano? What clues—" Her spine seized. She twisted back to the house. A chill ran through her—and not because of Isabella's home. "Fuck."

"What is it?"

"Don't look. Not yet. Act casual." She caught her breath. "There's a man. On the vaporetto launch. Leaning on the rail looking at his phone." It was the same guy who watched her when she photographed the dove. He didn't wear his maroon tie, but there was no question it was the same handsome creep with bronze skin. She described him to Carlo in a whisper. "Take out your phone and pretend to be on it."

He did and turned, inconspicuously searching.

"Do you see him?"

"Merda," Carlo said. "I've seen him before. At the Palazzo."

"Shit, we led them right to the house. How did we not notice him?"

Carlo was pissed, and she didn't blame him. They'd been so caught up in their conversation, they didn't think to take more precautions, like circling around or doubling back. *Amateur hour in Venice, thank you very little.* They had to do something, and had to do it fast. A brief thought of rushing over and shoving the guy into the canal—maybe under a *vaporetto*—occurred to her. The move would give her enormous satisfaction, but with numerous witnesses, it would also land her in jail.

"Follow me," she said. "My actions, too."

Summoning everything she remembered from her high school acting classes, Julia released a genuine laugh and patted Carlo on the back to nudge him forward. Bewildered for just a moment, Carlo picked up quickly and joined in the faux mirth. They hurried down the steps and walked right past the man.

"That's why you don't let the tourist lead the way," she said in a loud voice. "Why wouldn't Marco Polo's house be a museum?"

"It is. And the worst museum in Venice," he said with a convincing chuckle.

Julia took a furtive peek over her right shoulder as they continued into the alley. She didn't see the man, but she suddenly felt something pressed into her left palm. A moment later, the man dashed ahead of them. Bringing her hand up, she opened it to find a slip of paper. She and Carlo exchanged a curious look. Turning it over, they discovered it was a ticket for a boat tour—departing in thirty minutes.

ARRIVING OUT OF BREATH at the wharf not far from the Santa Lucia Railway Station, Julia and Carlo searched for the Panorama Island City tour boat.

"There," he said, pointing to an idling white and blue motorboat.

Julia had expected a large vessel, filled with dozens of passengers. They raced over to find the bearded captain—the epitome of a grizzled Italian tour guide in a black and white striped shirt—staring at his watch. Sitting in the stern was a solo passenger: a young woman wearing a white t-shirt, tweed skirt, black knee-high socks, and cherry red Doc Martens ankle boots. Her black beret, paisley scarf, and large, round, blue-tinted sunglasses obscured her face, but Julia sensed she was in her mid-20s. An orange Fjällräven backpack sat at her feet.

Tourists streamed both ways on the *fondamenta*, heading to and from the train station. The recent rain had brought the water level to just a foot below the top of the pier.

As Carlo headed toward the boat, Julia grabbed his wrist. "Are we sure this isn't a trap?" she whispered. As a *vaporetto* motored past, its wake impelled the water onto the dock. She stepped back to avoid soaking her sneakers.

He paused. "No. But the Order would never try anything against you with me here." He shook his head. "It isn't how they operate. Come."

The captain took Julia's ticket. As she boarded, Carlo and the captain had an animated conversation in their language. After being in Italy for two weeks, she could at least recognize Italian when she heard it. Though, for all she knew, it could've been Venetian or another dialect most Americans never knew existed.

"He said I was supposed to buy my ticket in advance," Carlo said.

"Who cares," Julia said to the captain, pulling her wallet from her purse. "We'll pay now." She selected a credit card but stopped, opting for cash. She fingered the bills with hesitation. On the one hand, if this was a trap, leaving a trail was a smart move. On the other, if this boat was headed for unknown allies, cash would be the prudent move. Though she prayed it was for the latter, she decided to play it safe. She offered the captain her card.

Instead of taking it, he looked at the other tourist. She said something Julia didn't understand, wagged her finger, then waved Carlo aboard. The captain spoke to Carlo, who translated for Julia.

"He said he can't take credit cards. He made a mistake. The ticket is for two people."

Julia didn't buy that for a second, but she took Carlo's proffered hand and stepped onto the boat. Carlo followed. After unmooring the ropes and jumping on, the captain, who apparently spoke zero English, showed them the lifejackets and pointed to a cushioned bench where they took their seats.

"Get all that?" the tourist woman asked in English, with an unusual European-tinted American accent.

"Almost," Julia answered with a polite smile. It struck her as odd that a tour boat captain didn't speak English, but she guessed the creepy guy who handed her the ticket wanted them to take a ride to meet someone.

The tourist girl gazed at the clouds. Her diamond nose stud and multiple earrings glistened under the overcast sky. "At least it isn't raining."

As the captain took his seat and throttled away from the dock, panic set in. What in the world was she doing, hopping onto a boat that a man in the Order gave them a ticket for? She reached into her not-so-distant memory. Though the creep in the maroon tie never actually did anything, if he hadn't followed her, she wouldn't have researched the Palazzo and wouldn't have convinced Nick that a ring of art corruption would be a fun story to pursue. *Fun.* She shook her head at the enormity of her miscalculation. If she and Nick hadn't returned to Carlo's, they would've been enjoying their vacation in Cinque Terre right now, almost ready to head back to their normal lives in Boston.

Your decision, she reminded herself. Just like boarding this boat. And if going deeper into the rabbit hole brought her closer to the rabbit, what choice did she have?

The captain was separated by a canopy that covered the center of the boat. She cautiously popped her head in and checked it out. Other than two additional benches on either side, there was nothing else and no place anybody could be hiding.

Settling into the seat next to Carlo, the boat ride itself seemed danger-free. Whatever peril may be lurking, it waited at their destination. Navigating the busy Grand Canal, the captain joined the traffic heading away from the city center.

"Can you believe that with all the times I've been to Venice," the tourist said, "I've never taken a boat tour?" She lowered her sunglasses and fixed her gaze on Carlo.

His jaw popped open. "Fosca?"

"We all have secrets, don't we, Carlo?"

XXXII

THE BOAT HEADED UNDER THE BRIDGE Julia had seen when Lacasse brought Nick to the police station. As the captain cut north to circumnavigate the island, Fosca told them she'd hired this boat so they'd have a private place to talk. She and Carlo explained how they knew each other, along with more about della Porta's grand plan and how it hinged on finding the doge's elusive book. While all of it was a lot to take in, Julia had one question for her:

"You met Nick?"

They turned to her with guilty looks. Though the captain maintained a slow speed, the salty ocean breeze whipped her hair back and elicited a sense of clarity. Of course Fosca met Nick. And it had to have happened in the few hours between Nick being his normal, albeit melancholy self in prison and when he showed up at Carlo's as a sword-wielding psychopath from the 16th century.

As if reading her mind, Fosca finally spoke. "Julia, please know. We asked him to join our cause, yes. But I—we—had no clue what would happen. It was . . . extraordinary."

Carlo wore a gloomier expression than Fosca.

Julia sensed the girl's words were true. "How did it happen?"

"We gave him something of Isabella's," Fosca said, pinching her shirt.

"What?"

Fosca flashed imploring eyes, then threw her gaze at Carlo. "Does it matter? It was just supposed to inspire him."

Julia considered the question. It was a horrible situation and outcome that pissed her off any way she sliced it. Whatever caused Nick's transformation didn't matter.

Knowing Fosca and her pals triggered it didn't sit well with Julia, but what was she going to do, fight this chick? Fosca clearly was filled with remorse. How could anyone know what would happen? Julia told herself she'd bring it up later, but one thing was for sure—Fosca was on her side and could help Nick. Right now, they needed to discuss the task at hand. Regardless of Nick's condition, Carlo was right—getting him out of trouble was the top priority. If the book would accomplish that by bringing down the Order, then they had to work together. That said, motoring around the north of Venice, instead of going south to Poveglia, made Julia feel like she was traveling backward again.

"What's your big plan, then?" she asked.

"Well. . ." Fosca wrapped her scarf tighter around her neck. "Della Porta and his minions have been combing through the wills of Renzo Scalfini and his heirs."

"I thought he and Isabella were childless," Carlo said, scratching his face.

"They were. But Renzo had two sons with his first wife, both already adults when he died. His estate and belongings were split between them and two nephews. They're tracing the wills through all the heirs to the present day." She cascaded her manicured tangerine fingernails down like neon raindrops. "You can imagine how everything the family has owned and lost has spread over centuries. My family is similar. I have a cousin who owns a vase dating back to 1480. And as of yesterday, a great aunt threatening to sue for artwork that had been in nonna-mère's possession since *their* grandmother passed away in the 1960s." She shook her head with exasperation. "Knowing my family, it's the first drop of a tsunami."

Julia crossed her legs. It felt good to be on a boat again. "So it'll take a while to track down who got the book."

"Right," Fosca said. "Which is why I wanna start at the source. There's a huge chance the book was hidden before Renzo was killed. Let's find the original Scalfini house and pay the current owners—"

"We were just there," Julia said.

Fosca's eyes widened. "What?"

"Yeah, your boy interrupted us."

"How in the world did you find it so fast?"

"It doesn't matter," Carlo said resolutely. "Della Porta's on the wrong track, too. This is what I was telling you, Julia." He turned to Fosca and pointed his thumb at the captain. "How much time do we have him for?"

She shrugged. "All week, if you want."

Carlo glanced at Julia. He opened his mouth but turned back to Fosca. "Can we trust you?"

Fosca jutted her head back. "Can I trust *you*? I know I can trust Julia, but what about *you*, Carlo? Whose side are *you* on?"

It was Carlo's turn to be offended. He contorted his face. "I'm on Julia's side. You're with the Guild, aren't you?"

"Do I look like I'm with the bad guys?"

Julia held her palm up. "The Guild?"

"Yes," Fosca said. "We've kept the Order in check, but now it's time to bring them down."

"And the countess?" Carlo asked. "Your grandmother?"

"She was our leader. If you were going to tell her something, you can tell me."

He rubbed his arms. "The Bird Brothers would've taken the doge's book the day Renzo died. That was their chance. I admit it's unlikely the book still exists, but if the box it was in was passed down through generations, the highest probability is that it's on Murano Island."

"How do you know all this?" Julia asked.

Carlo scratched his face again. "I had a lot of time when you were in the hospital. And I told you, I went to the library this morning. Like the Scalfinis, there have been thousands of descendants. But the eldest living male through the male lineage directly from Vito Uccello is a man named Isacco. Isacco Uccello. He lives on Murano."

JULIA HAD READ ABOUT Murano before their trip. The island was famous for its patchwork quilt of polychromatic buildings and artisan glassblowers who created souvenirs and jewelry in a myriad of bright colors. Nick had purchased a Murano-made bracelet after their first fateful visit to the Palazzo as an apology gift. She had hoped they'd visit together.

In an increasingly rare tourist moment, she used her Nikon to snap a dozen shots of the island—which was a tenth the size of Venice in the middle of the Lagoon.

As the captain entered the traffic lane and slowed the boat, Julia's conflicting feelings grew. She was excited to see this quainter, rainbow-esque version of Venice, but she knew she wouldn't be able to enjoy it.

The captain piloted toward an empty dock, then jumped out, and moored the craft. He uttered some words and tapped his watch, suggesting that he'd wait. Cheery tourists milled about, following tour guides, snapping pictures, and shooting videos with their phones.

On the pier, Carlo checked Google maps on his phone and headed off.

"So that creepy guy is with your group?" Julia asked Fosca, as they caught up with Carlo.

She laughed. "You mean Manuel? He's pretty nice once you get to know him."

"I don't know about that. He has a constant lecherous way of looking at people. Or at me, anyway."

"Not just you. But he's harmless. And really, an invaluable asset. He helped you and Nick behind the scenes."

"What do you mean? When?"

Fosca eyed Carlo and stopped walking at an empty alley between two artisan glass shops. "Hold on. Before we go any farther, we need to clear the air and show our cards." She glanced around and walked a few feet into the alley that led to a small footbridge over a canal.

Julia and Carlo followed. "What are you talking about?" she asked. "Pretty sure you know all my cards. Which are none."

"Not you. *Him*. You haven't said a word since the boat, Carlo."

He raised his hands and shrugged.

"The question still stands. Whose side are you on?" Fosca said flatly.

Carlo seemed sheepish next to her indicting glare. "It's what I've been thinking about. I'm on the side of truth."

"That isn't good enough. Della Porta knows the truth. He knows what he's done."

"I'm on the side of good."

"Nope, still not enough. White supremacists think they're doing good. You have secrets, Carlo. Della Porta has secrets. I know you feel some sense of loyalty to him, but that man is not your friend. And he's damn well not your father."

A cackle of amusement erupted from the street, echoing off the alley walls. Julia turned to spot a group of American college kids passing by.

"Are we going to Isacco Uccello so you can get back in della Porta's good graces?" Fosca asked.

"No," Carlo replied. "It's the other way around. I am not happy with him."

"'Not happy' doesn't cut it."

"It's more than that, and you know it. You saw."

"You're pissed at him, sure, but you're also loyal. If you think he's fucked in the head, trust me, he's way worse."

"I agree," Carlo said. "Salvatore has too much power. But you should know I don't want to destroy the Order. I took an oath. I want to return it to its original intention, solely for good."

Fosca rolled her eyes at the word 'oath' and wagged her finger at him. "It's a package deal. You were at that meeting, too. If we don't stop della Porta, he's going to rule the world."

"We can stop him," Carlo said.

An older lady with a cane hobbled over the footbridge on the other side of the alley and headed toward them.

"Come on," Fosca said. They exited the alley and continued walking.

She spoke in hushed tones. "Even if we bring della Porta down, the seed has been planted. Someone else will take over."

Julia furrowed her brow. Though her mixed background provided a diverse exposure to Christianity and Judaism, as well as presents for both Christmas and Hanukkah when she was a kid, her secular family was living proof of harmony through union. She was also raised to give credit where credit was due. "I'd like to see della Porta rule his pinky toe from behind bars," she said, "but a single religion that unites the world sounds like a pretty good thing to me."

Carlo smiled at Julia.

"If you frolic among the daisies in Utopia," Fosca said. "They don't want to go public to unite the world. They're doing this to *control* it. Half the Order is corrupt, but even if you find someone with truly good intentions, absolute power corrupts absolutely."

"It doesn't need to be the case," Carlo said.

"I'm not willing to find out," Fosca replied. "The Order itself started out with good intentions, and look what happened."

Julia and Carlo agreed. She had a point.

"The Ancient Order of the Seventh Sun," Fosca continued, "will imprison millions of souls without a trial, just as they've already done with thousands in three paintings. That will spread throughout the world. No way can you control all of them and all the people in charge."

Julia held a finger up. "Wait, did you say *three* paintings?"

"There are three variations of *Paradise*," Fosca replied. "One in Paris and another in Madrid."

"But what if the souls *are* evil?" Carlo asked.

The news of three paintings floored Julia. She wanted to ask more about them, but Carlo's postulation about the souls superseded any conversation about quantity. Her questions could wait.

"The Guild believes in redemption," Fosca replied.

"So do I," he said. "But I saw them come to life. It wasn't a pretty sight."

Fosca continued. "Because they're pissed off as fuck. If someone's soul is judged to be evil in one life, that person may not necessarily be bad in another—or even harm the world at all."

"Is it worth the risk?" Carlo asked.

"Wake up and look around the real world." Fosca's tone heated up. "Does the crime rate go up every time people get out of jail?"

"It's possible."

"And it's also possible people make mistakes. Or are incarcerated unjustly. You know that more than anybody. Everything about della Porta's plan sucks ass. Not to mention, having multiple religions and diversity is a good thing."

"Fair point," Julia said.

As they spoke, they followed the map on Carlo's phone, leaving the main touristy streets and arriving on a quiet, residential one, with a row of connected two-story homes. They all had similarly tiled roofs and rectangular windows, though each was painted a different color. Still old, the homes felt a few hundred years newer than those in Venice and were set back from the smooth cobblestone sidewalk, separated by a foliage-covered chain-link fence. It amazed Julia how this island village, also with no cars and filled with canals and bridges, was like a suburban Venice. The peace of Murano struck Julia. It was considerably quieter than Venice; seagulls and lapping water were the dominant sounds. It was lusher, too, with more trees and even a grass strip running along the sidewalk. If only she could enjoy it more. But the weather wasn't great. The dark clouds appeared as though they'd burst at any moment.

After checking his phone and pocketing it, Carlo stopped at the gate of a pale-yellow house with a red door. "Ready?"

"No," Fosca said. "You never answered the question. Are you with us or against us?"

Carlo clinched his jaw. Julia could tell the gears in his mind were working overtime. "I'm with you," he finally said.

"I have a witness." Fosca indicated Julia. "So don't cross us."

Taking charge, Fosca opened the gate and knocked on the door. Julia and Carlo followed. She liked this girl.

A few moments later, a man in his mid-sixties around Nick's height, wearing blue-tinted round glasses and a tie-dye Grateful Dead t-shirt answered. With his shoulder-length scraggly hair, multi-day scruff, and AirPods planted in his ears, Julia got the impression the man was a modern-day Italian hippie. Carlo and Fosca exchanged a few words in Italian and introduced themselves and Julia. The man, who Julia determined was indeed Isacco Uccello, was entirely irritated by the interruption. He closed the door on them.

Fosca stuck her foot in the crack. Isacco scowled at the action, but when she pointed to Julia and spoke with animated hands, it piqued his curiosity.

"Americana?" Isacco said, referencing Julia.

"Da Boston," Carlo replied.

Apparently, Julia's nationality helped relax his guard. "Te piàsea ea tò Nikon?" he asked.

Julia lifted her camera hanging around her neck.

"He asked if you like your Nikon," Carlo said.

"I love it."

"Bèn," Isacco replied. With a big smile, he invited them in.

Julia gasped as she entered Isacco's home, relieved he didn't see her reaction. The man's living room looked as if a pack rat married a tech geek who couldn't care less about his living conditions. Other than a small wooden dining table with two chairs—one covered in catalogs—and a ratty blue couch on a worn green carpet, boxes of all sorts of electronics occupied the space. Additional open boxes, cell phones, and accessories littered a desk in the corner, along with two monitors and two cameras with ring lights mounted on tripods.

The man said some words to Fosca, and Carlo and bowed his head.

"He apologizes for the mess," Carlo said. "He was working."

"Is he in a band?" Julia asked.

Carlo turned back to Isacco and asked in Italian. Isacco cracked up, then replied.

"Not a band," Carlo translated, "but half his fanbase is in America."

"Fanbase?"

"Product reviews on YouTube. He hires people to dub his words or use subtitles."

Isacco bobbed his head with a goofy grin.

Julia was astounded. The guy must've been damn good at reviews because he took work-from-home to another level.

He continued speaking as he removed a half dozen boxes from the couch and offered the space to the trio. Carlo sat in the middle. Isacco carried his clean dining chair over.

"He said his show on your camera has the most views of any review he's done."

Julia wondered if she'd watched it but didn't think so. "I'll have to check it out," she said. Carlo interpreted for her.

"Gràssie," Isacco said, pressing his hands together.

The three Italians proceeded to have a vivacious conversation for the next few minutes. Julia tried to pick up a few words here and there, but after being immersed in the culture for two weeks, she realized the only Italian words she knew were greetings, how to ask for the bathroom, and pasta shapes.

The discourse finally died down. Isacco said something to Fosca and Carlo, in a more resolute tone.

Her friends exchanged glances with each other, then answered Isacco. Still unsatisfied, he folded his arms and clammed up.

"Okay, fine," Fosca said in English. She pulled up something on her phone and showed it to Isacco, swiping through and pointing.

His expression switched to one of pure despondency. He said a few more words, prompting tears in Fosca's eyes. Isacco bit his lip and massaged his stubble. After a moment, he stood, then disappeared into another room. Fosca and Carlo glanced and shrugged at each other.

"Um, is someone gonna fill me in?" Julia asked.

"Oh, sorry," Fosca said. "The three of us"—she circled her finger, signifying her, Carlo and Isacco—"have something in common."

"What's that?"

"Grudges don't die in Italy. All three of our families have been betrayed by the Order. He said his grandfather liked to say his own grandfather always worried someone would come. They lived in fear. But nobody came. The doge's book is a curse for the Uccellos, and he wants the opportunity to move on. He asked for evidence we weren't with della Porta, so I showed him some articles about my family."

Carlo gazed sullenly at the floor, lost in thought.

"Your grandmother," Julia said to Fosca. "You mentioned her before. She's a countess?"

"Was." Fosca cleared her throat with a forlorn eye.

"Nick said something about that. Did . . . did della Porta really kill her?" Julia had trouble believing she was having yet another conversation about murder.

"Like I said, I don't have proof about her or that the Order killed anyone," Fosca said, "but I'd bet money on it. A lot. The Baldesseris are a prominent family in the Order, but many have been screwed over." She threw a glance at Carlo. "And the Zuccaros. And apparently the Uccellos, too." Shaking her head, her expression turned to anger. "Sometimes you just want to see your enemies drown."

Julia widened her eyes. Fosca seemed like she really wanted to kill della Porta and his cronies. She looked at Carlo—he also wore a look of shock.

"What?" Fosca said, reading their expressions. "It's the only way. How long can this go on?"

Isacco returned holding a case of diapers, which he set on the nasty carpet. Julia hadn't noticed signs of a baby or anybody else living there. It didn't seem as though this guy ever left the house.

He said something else in Italian.

"He said he doesn't trust us," Carlo said.

"We did just meet," Julia replied.

"But," Carlo translated as the man continued speaking a mile-a-minute, "he has a feeling about us. He doesn't trust us, but he thinks we're telling the truth."

Isacco cut into Carlo's translation, animating his hands wildly, like he was providing the accompanying sign language.

Carlo translated. "And he doesn't care. He wants this to end for his family. It's been a curse for too long. They need to move on."

For a moment, Julia considered asking how it was a curse but opted to let sleeping, rabid Dobermans lie.

Using a box cutter, Isacco slit the tape on the diaper carton and removed a few diapers. Carlo gasped at what was hidden beneath them.

Julia, too, widened her eyes. Isacco pulled out one of the most beautifully designed brass boxes she'd ever seen. The corners were reinforced with patterned steel. Embossed on the top was a yin-yang, surrounded by seven sunrays and two dozen or more mysterious symbols. In the yin-yang, one dot was a purple gemstone, likely an amethyst. The other dot she guessed was made of jade. Most of the other symbols were engraved into the brass, but four were made of other materials: copper, white, which was probably ivory, something green, and a fourth she was certain was gold.

"I believe inside is the book you seek," Carlo translated.

Fosca's eyes lit up. "Let's open it!" she said in English.

Either Isacco understood what she said or figured it out. He waved her off and uttered more.

Fosca frowned and tucked her hair behind her ear. "He doesn't know how to open it. The combination's been lost to time," she said to Julia.

Julia knelt next to Isacco, who smiled at her. She examined the intricate workmanship of the brass box. The latch didn't seem impressive—just what she would expect from a 16th-century case.

"Can't we just pick the lock?" she asked. "Or bust it open? It's a box."

Carlo translated for her. Isacco said something else. He flipped the latch and opened the lid.

"Not this case," Carlo said. "The one inside."

Isacco removed a smaller, plain brown wooden box the likes of which Julia had never laid eyes upon. Sure, she'd seen plenty of square boxes, but as Isacco rotated it, Julia spied a combination dial on four of the ten-inch sides. The other two sides had identical engravings, so there was no indication of which side was the top. The scruffy Venetian spoke again.

"He thinks the book is inside," Carlo translated. "But this one needs a code, not a key. Maybe four codes. Or a sequence. If we break the seal or try too many times, an acid will dissolve the contents." Carlo said something to Isacco, who replied. Carlo then spoke to Julia. "There *is* a key somewhere. But it doesn't open anything. Carved on that key is the code—or codes—to unlock this box."

Fosca asked Isacco a question.

"Why would they put a code on a key?" Julia asked.

"That's what I just asked him," Fosca said. They smiled at each other. "Seems like a weird thing to do for a combination lock."

Isacco spoke again. Fosca and Carlo nodded.

"Duh," Fosca said. "It's the last place anybody would think to look. They hide everything in plain sight."

Julia leaned over and ran her fingers over the smooth wood. The real key to saving Nick was inside this little box. It was a form of torture knowing that a return to their normal, happy lives was separated by a thin piece of wood.

"Plus," Carlo said. "If it's on a key, it might be too small to read. You may not even notice it."

"I'm guessing he doesn't have the key?" Julia asked.

Carlo translated to Isacco, who replied with a laugh. He patted Julia's back before speaking again.

"Nobody does. After Vito Uccello was betrayed," Carlo interpreted, "his friends buried it with him to preserve the secret. They didn't want some people in the Order finding the doge's book."

"Okay," Julia said. "Where's he buried?"

Fosca interpreted this time. Isacco shook his head. He answered in Italian, but Julia didn't need a translation. He had no idea. Nobody did.

"Wonderful," she said with pronounced sarcasm to ensure the Europeans got it. "We're going on four-hundred-year-old family lore with a dead-end lead. How does he even know all this?"

Isacco spoke to Carlo with exaggerated hand gestures about Julia.

Carlo laughed. "He says his five-year-old nephew doesn't ask this many questions."

"You can tell him I used to be a reporter," Julia replied.

"Really?" Fosca asked. She perked her eyebrows.

"Just for a few years. A local paper."

Carlo translated to Isacco, along with his reply. "Vito's relative kept a journal. The body was never found."

As the three Italians spoke, Julia eyed the box. She yearned to snap some pics of it and the outer box, but given that when the Order kidnapped her, they took her phone and camera, she opted against it. She peered closer. Was there really an acid in there, and did it have a shelf life? She grazed her finger over one of the combination locks. Next to the dials on each side of the box was a small metal tab, which she assumed was a switch. Did it really have a maximum number of tries? Renaissance crafters were incredibly gifted, and this type of thing was common back then. And if it was booby-trapped, how many attempts were already made?

"May I?" she asked Isacco, implying she wanted to pick it up. He gestured approval.

Examining it, she turned it around. The engravings on what she presumed were the top or bottom were smaller versions of the modified yin-yang symbol on the brass box. The other four sides were identical to each other except that the dials on opposite ends were upside-down, making it impossible to figure out which side actually needed the correct combination. She also couldn't locate any seams to determine which side opened; it almost seemed solid. Resisting the impulse to shake the box, she tapped on it instead. It sounded hollow. The combination locks didn't look dissimilar to modern versions. Each had six dials, about the circumference of a quarter, with black capital letters engraved on them. All four showed 'VPTMNO,' clearly a jumble that was no help at all.

Besides not knowing which side to try, how difficult could it be? *Venice?* That's six letters. She shook her head. Too obvious, but then again, they loved hiding everything in plain view. But would they do it in English?

Venezia didn't fit. She hovered her finger over the first dial on a random side, the urge to try a word chewing her up inside. Above and below each letter was half a letter on each dial, and all were visible enough to figure out. Based on the size of the dials and the letters, Julia hypothesized that each dial had ten to fifteen characters. And she couldn't rule out that some of them could be numbers. Going with empirical evidence, if only one side required a combination, she figured it spelled a word, acronym, or abbreviation. Of course, she was flying blind, but using those letters would factor into the possible number of variations and word combinations. *High probability the word starts with a consonant . . . but is that the case in Venetian, Italian or Latin?* She placed her thumb on the first dial.

"Don't even think about it," Fosca said.

Julia lifted her hand. "You're right. But can we take this?"

Fosca translated.

Isacco burst into laughter.

XXXIII

"THE ONLY ONE WHO'S QUALIFIED IS DIEGO BLANCO-Romasanta," della Porta said to Vasquez, whose bearded face once again graced a monitor mounted on his office wall. As della Porta sat on the sofa flipping through a binder of dossiers on his lap—candidates for Madrid's next Painter—Bernardo did the same digitally with a wireless keyboard, perusing their files and art portfolios on the left-side monitor.

"It's not your decision," said Vasquez, waving a fat cigar between his stubby fingers. "That I sent you the files is a courtesy. A courtesy, need I remind you, that you failed to extend to me when you chose a child to replace a glorious master."

"Next time I'm in the middle of a crisis, José, I'll put the world on pause and call you for your approval on a split-second decision."

Vasquez chewed on his cigar while he spoke. "The Sun Crystal was undamaged. You had time."

"Theoretically."

Bernardo looked to della Porta with a raised eye.

"We're moving beyond this conversation," della Porta said. "You were not there. What's done is done. Let's worry about the future. The Spanish Painter is dying. You need to decide, groom the next Painter, and prepare for succession. You've been sitting on this far too long."

"Our Painter is younger than Tintoretto was—"

"By two decades. A blip in their lifetimes."

"More importantly, he's *our* Painter. *We* make the decisions." Vasquez puffed on his cigar.

"The Order is a parliamentary system, as the Republic was for a thousand years."

Vazquez blew the smoke at the monitor's camera. "Except when you decide to take the ship in a radically different direction."

It was an involuntary action, but Della Porta caught himself audibly growling. Vasquez's incessant antagonistic nature was growing tiresome by the minute. What he'd give to rid himself of this annoyance. Della Porta wasn't sure if Vasquez heard the growl, but the man must've sensed his displeasure, for he cleared his throat and continued in a pleasant tone.

"You'll be pleased to know," the Spaniard said, "we've begun recruiting more Protectors, per your advice."

Della Porta raised an eyebrow and felt the corner of his mouth rise along with it. "Excellent. You should know, then, that we're closer than ever to finding the book."

"But you have not found it yet."

"We're going through the descendants one by one and have some promising leads."

"It's only a matter of time." Vasquez tapped his cigar ash.

"Precisely. I'm glad to see you on board, José."

The boisterous laugh the man discharged reverberated like virtual thunder from della Porta's monitor. "I didn't say that. Ah, the fantasies of Italians. It's as if you all live in some sort of waking divine comedy."

Della Porta's blood boiled once again. He hoped Vasquez's reaction was exaggerated, but whether designed to pinch a nerve or not, della Porta tightened his muscles. "Then why are you recruiting additional Protectors?"

"I need to be pragmatic and prepared. When your plan fails dramatically, we'll need reinforcements."

There was no getting through to this man. Della Porta cleared his throat. "Let's wrap this conversation. Blanco-Romasanta's under thirty and has twelve solo shows. His post-impressionist style has the ideal balance of minimalist light and concentrated emotion. It reminds me of Sorolla at night after too much wine. If he's not your top choice, who is?"

"On some things—*many* things—we agree, Salvatore. You'll be pleased to know that El Lobo Blanco is my top choice, as well."

The accord pleased della Porta, but he snorted at Blanco-Romasanta's moniker, attempting—and failing—to match the intensity of Vasquez's previous mirth. He cleared his throat but maintained his sense of belittling amusement. Though Blanco-Romasanta was at the top of della Porta's list, he found self-aggrandizing so distasteful. "I read that in his file. *El Lobo Blanco*. The White Wolf. He actually calls himself that?"

"It's his artist name, and it stuck." He took another quick puff, this time blowing away from the screen. "It's what everyone calls him. Lobo, really. He's gathered some celebrity in Madrid."

"And notoriety," Bernardo added. "Arrested twice for bar brawls."

"Which is what I like about him, in light of his over-inflated sense of self," della Porta said. "We need someone who will be ruthless and take no issues with our charge."

"See?" said Vasquez. "Another thing we agree on. Perhaps we can also agree that Carlo Zuccaro does not possess the best disposition to do exactly that."

"Humility and morality are also essential virtues, both of which Carlo has in abundance," della Porta said. "I have no doubt he has it in him to be implacable . . . yet merciful. You'll see."

"I'd like to."

After a few procedural items to discuss, della Porta ended the call with some pleasantries. He had to admit it was nice seeing eye-to-eye with Vasquez on Blanco-Romasanta. *The White Wolf*, he chuckled inwardly. How narcissistic.

Despite their agreement on Madrid's next Painter, Vasquez and his hostility never sat well with him. Unfortunately, they had to work together. He needed all three chapters on board for his plan to succeed. He'd measured the possibility of going public with only the Venetian *Paradiso*. But with three paintings and hundreds of members loyal to the Madrid and Paris chapters, it seemed impossible without their support. And if della Porta had come to this conclusion, so had Vasquez.

Della Porta stepped to the bar and poured two Camparis over ice. He handed one to Bernardo.

"I've never trusted that man," della Porta said, returning to Venetian.

"Nor have I," his friend replied, nodding his thanks for the drink. "He's loyal, but maybe more loyal to himself. Still..."

"What?"

"... I can't say I don't disagree with him about Carlo."

"Carlo is loyal, Bernardo."

"He is, but he's going to slip. Signora O'Connor's staying with him. For all we know—and we should assume—he's already bedded her. Is that the person you want keeping her in check, looking for the man whose soul he banished? How long before he tells her the truth?"

"Can Manuel confirm their intimacy?"

"No, but he doesn't need to. How many girls have been inside Carlo's flat without him being inside them?"

Della Porta stroked his jaw. He knew the answer: zero. He nurtured Carlo in his formative years, but this thought of Carlo's impropriety with Signora O'Connor—and the potential of his allegiance to shift to her—had been plaguing him of late, more so than the mole's identity. Ever since Carlo's father's death, della Porta had been responsible for the boy. Not only for his well-being, but also for his growth and direction. Now that Carlo replaced Tintoretto, della Porta took pride in knowing that his years-long efforts paid dividends by reaching a critical milestone. To Bernardo and Vasquez's point, Carlo needed to take responsibility for his own actions. That said, there was no denying Della Porta was irrefutably responsible for Carlo's future—which directly affected the Order's future.

Both Carlo and the mole were distractions that interfered with his plans. He met Bernardo's eyes. "What do you propose?"

"Swat two flies at once. Vasquez wants to meet Carlo. Instead of inviting him here..."

"Send Carlo to Madrid." Della Porta grinned. There was a third bird he could kill—preventing Carlo from pinpointing specific souls in *Paradiso*, at least for the time being. "I must say, Bernardo. There's a brilliance in the simplicity. We tell him it's official business, which it is, and he can't refuse. While he's gone—for an indeterminate period—we press Signora O'Connor at every turn."

"Exactly, signore. We don't harm her—"

"No, no, of course not. Carlo would never forgive us."

"But that doesn't mean we can't make her life very unpleasant in Venice."

With a crooked smirk, della Porta clinked his glass to Bernardo's. Bernardo checked the time on his phone. As if on cue, a video call prompt appeared on the center monitor.

"Lacasse is punctual to the second," Bernardo said.

"He's a man who understands the importance of time. And how little we have of it in this world."

Bernardo accepted the call. Lacasse's round, light-brown face appeared in high definition. The Interpol detective sat so close to his camera, his graying wavy mane was cut off at the hairline, and della Porta felt as though his coffee bean eyes watched over the room like Providence.

"Bonjour, Monsieur Lacasse," della Porta said.

Apparently also conscious of how small talk wastes time, Lacasse got right to business. "To the best of our knowledge," he said in English with his nasally French accent, "unless there were illegitimate children, I've tracked down all the remaining Scalfini descendants. I've already interviewed half of those who don't live in Venice or the surrounding areas."

Once again, Lacasse's access to Interpol records proved to be an invaluable resource. "Excellent," della Porta said. "Bernardo and his men have nearly concluded their interviews here. Any promising leads?"

"Nobody had heard of Renzo, but crossing off dead-ends is part of any investigation. If the book wasn't destroyed, it's only a matter of time before we find it."

"That's disappointing, Detective. Any luck on locating the Scalfini residence? I'm certain the book would've been hidden there."

Lacasse whistled through his teeth. "There's nothing digitized. What makes you so sure the book was in the house?"

"Because I believe O'Connor—Mascari, really—never found it. I could tell in his voice. He had nothing to lose by revealing the location." Della Porta raised his hand in a fluttering motion as he spoke. As he said his theory aloud, it further convinced him his thinking was correct. "He had no attachment to the Order, the book, the Guild, none of it. If he thought revealing the book's location would've helped save his wife or perhaps free Isabella—and he did think that—he would've told us. No, he never found it. Which means it was hidden in that house, and its hiding spot died with Renzo."

Lacasse pursed his lips and signaled his agreement.

"My men are combing the records here," Bernardo said to the Frenchman. "But finding a deed is a longshot, especially if Renzo had the house constructed, which is likely, given his wealth."

"It's the same in France," the detective said. "We usually go by architectural records, but that requires an officer to be buried nose-deep in university libraries for weeks. If you're lucky to find a blueprint."

Bernardo snapped his fingers. "The University School of Architecture," he said with an excited glimmer. "Here in Venice. Some years back, they had a student project to scan all the old blueprints they could find."

Typing as fast as he could, Bernardo shared his screen with Lacasse and brought up the university's website. As the two men bickered like students themselves over where to click and what to search, della Porta's mind circled back to something he just said. Needing to focus, he walked over to the window overlooking the Grand Canal. The multitude of ships navigating the channel was like the personification of the grinding gears and firing synapses in his mind.

It stood to reason that Angelo Mascari never found the book. The scoundrel fled after murdering Renzo. But Isabella was captured by two Protectors—two brothers. He had read about it in the criminal record log, as well as in the report written by one of her captors. Those brothers paid Mascari to seduce Isabella and find the book in the Scalfini's bedroom. They would've had time to search the house. After Renzo's death, there was no indication that the quest for the book continued. Della Porta just needed to remember the name of the brothers. And then it hit him.

He spun back to Bernardo and the monitors.

"The book isn't in the Scalfini residence," he announced.

Bernardo stopped typing and turned. Della Porta walked over to ensure he was within the camera's view. Lacasse and Bernardo eyed him with curiosity.

"In fact," della Porta continued, "no Scalfini descendant has it. If anyone living is in possession of it, it would be an *Uccello* descendant."

XXXIV

JULIA JUMPED AT THE SOUND OF HER PHONE'S RING; it had been so long since she heard it. Eating an apple, she'd been enjoying the view of the cloudy, sunset-lit island receding into the distance as they headed back to Venice. Carlo was doing the same, smoking a cigarette on the opposite side. After leaving Isacco Uccello's empty-handed, but with the assurance he'd keep the box safe, the trio stopped for a quick pizza before returning to the captain, who'd been fast asleep. From their snack to the boat ride, Julia once again wished she was with Nick. She'd also been thinking of calling someone—anyone—just to hear a familiar voice, so it was rather timely someone was calling her. Hopefully, it wasn't spam.

On the second ring, she pulled the phone from her purse. It was Lionel Benton. The English art critic would've been the ideal person to speak to—a sympathetic ear to which she could discuss her travails, as he had put it. But despite Carlo and Fosca's seemingly good intentions, Benton was a call she needed to take in private. Other than Nick—the unpossessed version—he was the one person she could trust. She hit 'decline' after the third ring.

"I know where Vito Uccello is buried," Fosca said over the roar of the boat's motor.

Julia and Carlo whipped their heads to her. Fosca's announcement filled Julia's thoughts with pragmatism; there were several dots to connect, but she knew finding Uccello's body could ultimately free Nick from the Order's clutches.

"Where?" she asked.

"I don't know for sure, but my guess is that if he was betrayed by the Order, he's in *Paradise*, which means his body was cremated. Which means his ashes are in an urn."

"Which means the key might be in it, too," Julia added.

Julia's phone pinged. A text from Benton: *'Hope you're well, dear. Maggie is a true friend. She wants to speak, but in person.'* The message sent Julia's mind turning, debating what Maggie Yorn wanted to speak about and when they could meet up.

"Makes sense," Carlo said. "If his friends were in the Order, they would've had time to do it."

"So where's the urn?" Julia asked.

She texted Benton: *'Vacay took a turn. Would love to chat,'* before slipping the phone back into her purse.

Fosca moved from her spot and sat next to Julia. "In a tunnel beneath the Palazzo."

"Great," Julia said. "Let's go."

"I wish it were that easy. They haven't sealed it yet, but they've installed cameras. The only way in now is through Tintoretto's room. Which. . ." She glanced at Carlo.

He cleared his throat. "Is beneath the Great Council Room. There's no way we'd be able to sneak in. It's too great a risk. We don't even know if it's there. In all this time, none of Uccello's relatives had the same thought?"

Julia frowned. Carlo had a point. Still, a secret entrance into the Palazzo sounded all too familiar to Julia. "Where does the tunnel lead?"

"There's access from a canal. Next to the Palazzo."

"I think I know it. I'm pretty sure Nick must've gone into it."

"That explains how he entered," Carlo said.

"And why they're watching it," Fosca added.

A memory slammed into Julia. She grinned. Her friends eyed her with contagious curiosity.

"What are you smiling about?" Carlo asked, his own mouth perking upward.

"Neither of you are wondering how Nick knew about the tunnel? I'm guessing Paganelli told him. But not only that, he gave him a blueprint. Maybe there's another entrance. Maybe the key is in that urn, maybe it's not. But there's one way to find out."

The corners of her mouth rose with her eyebrows.

"And you have that blueprint?" Fosca asked.

Julia bobbed her head, thankful she never threw it away. The three of them smiled at each other.

HE CARESSED HER BREAST with one hand and pleasured her with his other under her sky-blue dress while he drove himself in and out. With moans of ecstasy, she braced herself against the wall. He bit her ear beneath her auburn hair, then gripped his rapier's hilt and planted his seed deep inside her.

AS THEY STOOD IN THE GROUP, he eyed the Minister of Finance hand a parcel to Renzo.

"CARLO," JULIA CALLED with her hands cupped around her mouth.

Standing next to the couch in Fosca's safehouse, he snapped out of whatever reverie had held him hostage and gaped at Julia, then at Fosca in the kitchen. His face turned beet red. He dropped his hands to his groin.

"I need the toilet," he blurted out and hurried off.

"Not that one," Fosca called. "It's filthy. There's another through that bedroom."

She pointed, and Carlo changed direction. A moment later, Fosca brought over three glasses filled with white wine and placed them on the coffee table, then plopped on the couch next to Julia.

"You read my mind." Julia took a glass and clinked it to her new friend's. Before they disembarked the boat, Fosca told them they needed to separate and gave them instructions on how to reach this safehouse. Julia and Carlo went back to his place for the blueprint and a quick bite then left ten minutes apart, with her going first. A mist-like drizzle started falling by the time she found the apartment, which despite its stark white interior, had a welcoming vibe, especially with the deteriorating weather conditions. The lack of color in the space astounded her; it was like the yang to a darkroom's yin. She wished she could stage variations of her prize-winning photograph here, imagining a vibrant group of people eating dinner, as caught by a spider's eight eyes from the ceiling corner.

"Do you live here?" Julia asked before taking a sip of her wine.

"No, I'm staying in the guestroom at nonna-mère's, but I live in London. For now, anyway. Technically, I'm from Paris."

"What does nonna-mère mean, anyway?"

Fosca laughed, though there was an acute sadness in her brown eyes. "Nonna is Italian for grandma and grand-mère is the French. Since I'm both, I mixed the two when I was a little kid, and it stuck. The funny thing is it means 'grandmother-mother,' which is kind of fitting, really."

"So why do you speak with an American accent?"

Fosca took a healthy gulp of her wine. "I went to an American school growing up. Then UCLA."

"Oh. That must've been cool."

"Yeah, I love L.A."

As they waited for Carlo, the conversation lapsed into an uncomfortable silence. Julia got the sense Fosca had something—or *someone*—on her mind, and that someone was Nick. The thought of him and what happened unsettled Julia, but she needed to know. Using her knuckles, she wiped the corners of her wetting eyes, then turned to Fosca. "Nick was here?"

"He wanted to go to you. I'm so sorry, Julia. I had no idea how it would end."

"How *did* it end? You gave him something of Isabella's, and. . .?"

"I mean, he took it into the bathroom. . ." Fosca averted her gaze and drank her wine. "He came out a different person, and then . . . you know. . ."

Julia wasn't sure if she was hiding something or just couldn't bring herself to talk about what Nick did. For a moment, she wanted to check the bathroom out but opted against it. There was nothing else she'd learn; seeing the bathroom would only expand an already-open wound. "I'm assuming you haven't heard from him?"

"I wouldn't have a way to even contact him."

"Contact who?" Carlo asked, rejoining the conversation. He was his normal self again, though his pants seemed slightly wet. He sat on one of the white leather side chairs with a grayish discoloring.

"Nick." Julia checked her phone for the thousandth time. Nothing. She removed the blueprint from her purse and unfolded it on the coffee table, using the wine glasses as paperweights.

Carlo tapped a cigarette from a crumpled pack and pulled it out with his lips.

"Does it smell like a dirty ashtray in here?" Fosca said.

Carlo sniffed the air.

"No, it doesn't," she continued, "so let's keep it that way before I throw the whole pack out the window."

Carlo tried to squeeze the cigarette back into the pack, but it broke. Careful not to let tobacco fall out, he placed the cigarette on a napkin on the coffee table, then joined Fosca and Julia. He helped himself to the third glass of wine. "Have anything to eat?"

"The kitchen at Café Fosca's is closed," she said. "Focus. We'll get food later."

The three of them huddled over the ancient parchment. Julia had seen blueprints before, but she had no clue what she was looking for. Tracing her finger on the lines, she found the Palazzo's front entrance, the Grand Canal to the south, and a small canal to the east bordering the Palazzo's exterior walls.

"How do you know about the cameras?" she asked.

"Because Uncle Enzo saw the equipment when he got Isabella's urn," Fosca replied.

This mysterious uncle piqued Julia's curiosity, but the second half of Fosca's statement caused her to shiver, like she would in a wet Boston winter. But it was June and uncomfortably warm in the stark white apartment. "What are you saying?"

Fosca expelled a mournful exhale and didn't close her mouth, as if the thoughts were there, but not the words. She pinched her lips together.

"Enzo?" Carlo asked, paying attention again. "Enzo *Paganelli*?" Across the three words, his expression shifted from interest to bewilderment to anger. "He's your *uncle*?" To disgust. "You said he was a family friend years ago."

Fosca's countenance matched his. The two of them erupted to their full heights. "He's—was—*like* an uncle to me." Her face reddened, and tears fell. She screamed at Carlo, "Before you killed him."

"Bernardo killed him, not me." Carlo stepped away from the couch and coffee table for more space. He yelled at Fosca. "When your mad uncle tried to murder me. *And* della Porta. And. . ." He spoke through clenched teeth, nostrils flaring. "My father."

"You really believe that crap? Della Porta's lying to you, to everyone." Fosca moved away from the sofa as well.

"François said it was true!"

"He's also been duped."

"I was there, Fosca. Your *uncle* attacked della Porta. He wanted to kill me. He wanted to kill all of us."

Julia was still processing that Fosca thought of the man who helped Nick as an uncle. Worried this argument might come to blows, she also stood in case she needed to intervene, but stayed silent.

Fosca pointed a finger at Carlo, the sapphire on a silver band glistening in the light. "Della Porta left him no choice. You have no idea how torn up he was about what that fuckface did to you."

"What are you talking about?" Carlo's fury diminished a notch.

"Enzo Paganelli had been protecting you, protecting your father, all these years. He was your father's best friend."

"I know. And when my father discovered Paganelli intended to betray the

Order, he murdered him. Your uncle burned my whole house." Moisture filled Carlo's eyes. "My family's house. My family itself. And then. . ."

"And there was never an arson investigation, remember?" Julia said. She felt awful throwing gasoline on the metaphorical fire, but Carlo was too blinded; the veil of truth needed to be lifted.

Carlo glared at Fosca. "Because her uncle covered it up. He had my father sentenced to *Paradise*!"

"What?" Julia exclaimed. It couldn't be true.

"Oh, yes," Carlo continued. "It wasn't the murder that was covered up, but the method."

Fosca tucked a lock of hair behind her ear. Her tone softened. "Did you know della Porta sentenced Enzo's wife to *Paradise*?"

Carlo rubbed his hairless jaw. "Why would he do that?"

"Why do you think?"

"I know what I saw." Carlo rubbed his forearms, then folded them.

"I'm not denying what happened last week," Fosca said. "Believe me, I begged him not to go. And now he's . . . he's. . . I even set his disgusting rat free." She sniffed and crossed herself. "But it's time you realized that every reaction had an earlier action. Della Porta killed your father. And my nonna-mère. Della Porta's the one who had your father sentenced. He's the one who covered it up. Think about it."

Seemingly exhausted, Carlo dropped onto the couch. "Can you prove any of this?"

"I'm working on it."

Julia sat next to Carlo. She put a soft hand on his back. "Carlo, Paganelli wanted to help Nick bring down the Order. It doesn't make sense that he killed your dad."

He rubbed his eyes; his head collapsed in his hand.

"And in the torture room," Julia continued, "I don't know what was said, but I know it had to do with the countess. He ran, remember? And now he's trying to pin it on Nick."

Carlo swallowed hard. He turned to Julia with pressed lips, looking more anguished than ever, almost as if he was ready to confess something.

Fosca positioned herself on the sofa arm on the other side of the Venetian artist. "We're on your side, Carlo. We're all on the same side. Can we all agree to get to the truth? We can agree to *that*, right?"

"I like the sound of that," Carlo said in a low voice. "Let's get the truth before we pass any more judgment."

Feeling a bit like a jerk, if they were on the subject of truth, Julia needed more. Bringing the conversation back to where it started, she asked Fosca, "You were gonna say something before. About Enzo getting Isabella's urn. Why would he do that?" Julia had a sense she knew the answer, but she needed to hear it. "Remember," she added. "The truth."

Fosca's voice cracked when she spoke. "It was her ashes. That's what brought Angelo out. I swear, Julia. We had no idea what would happen to Nick. We thought it was just a powerful memento. I swear." Her eyes dampened again. She patted them, careful not to smudge her plush blue eyeliner.

Julia gulped and sniffed, then pinched the bridge of her nose to force back the tears. She'd been repressing it to an extent, but she knew in her heart something physical caused Nick's transformation to Angelo. And while she held some resentment toward Fosca for enabling it, she didn't blame her—how could she have known? Plus, Fosca and her group had a noble cause, which she respected. Dwelling on the past wasn't going to solve anything.

Julia reached over Carlo and took Fosca's hand. "I believe you."

"I know you do," Fosca said warmly.

The information completed a picture for Julia. There was no question that if Nick was hiding out on Poveglia, he went there by himself—emphasis on *if*. He could've been locked up in the Palazzo. He could've been anywhere. Though she desperately wanted to find him, it didn't seem possible at the moment. And even if she could, Nick would still be in the same boat with the Order and the law. Fosca and Carlo had settled down; they needed to make progress, find the book, and nail della Porta to the wall.

She leaned over the blueprint on the coffee table again and traced her finger along the side canal all the way to the top of the paper, northeast of where the Basilica would be. The end of the trail was where she'd waited for Nick. She shuddered at the memory—standing on that tiny *fondamenta*, a gun in her hand, thinking at the time her husband was deranged. She picked at her fingernails, then pulled her hands apart, and planted her finger on the thin dotted lines leading into the building.

"Here," she said. "This is the tunnel entrance. Where Nick brought the boat out." Running her finger along the lines to the bottom of the page, she stopped at a large rectangle, which she figured was the Great Council Room.

All three of them peered at the paper, their heads getting a little too close for comfort. Julia backed up and stood.

"I don't see another entrance," Carlo said.

"Neither do I." Fosca also backed away from Carlo. She took another sip of wine.

Julia continued gazing at the blueprint. Her bird's eye view helped solidify something in the back of her mind.

"We're SOL," Fosca said.

"I don't understand." Julia chewed her bottom lip. "This has to be the same blueprint, but it's different. There was more writing on it where the Basilica should be. It was dark, but the moon was bright. It was the first thing I saw." She leaned down and tapped a white spot near the secret entrance. "Right here. I'm positive."

"Where were you?" Fosca asked.

"With Nick, in the boat. He'd just thrown. . ." Julia's eyes lit up. She raced to the kitchen and grabbed a glass of water and a napkin.

Hustling back, she wet the napkin and dabbed it where she thought she'd seen the writing. Sure enough, the text appeared.

"Bad. Ass." Fosca's lips twisted into a wide grin.

"Ingresso cortigiano," Carlo read. "Courtesan entrance. Curious it's in Italian."

"I'd hate to be a poor girl going into a castle that way. Do you have a hand towel?" Julia asked.

Fosca came back a few moments later with one. Julia blotted the entire blueprint—careful not to wipe the original lines away.

A few other lines appeared within the complex, but green lines led to the same canal along the Basilica's eastern wall, south of where Nick had entered. Those lines intersected with the urn tunnel.

"There it is," Julia said. "Let's go."

"Whoa, whoa, whoa, Wonder Woman," Fosca said. "It's far too risky tonight."

"Why?" Carlo asked.

"Because of the initiation. Aren't you—?"

"No, I wasn't told," Carlo said. "Who's getting initiated?"

"About fifty Protectors."

Carlo widened his eyes. "Merda."

"Right," Fosca continued. "And I'm guessing they didn't tell you because they suspect something. This isn't good." She turned back to Carlo with a crooked glare. "Maybe you should've attended the meetings they asked you to."

"You're not your grandmother." Carlo ground his teeth.

"No, but she had faith in you. I don't know why. I don't know what della Porta sees in you, either."

Carlo lowered his brow and scratched his neck. Fosca's ongoing aggression toward him surprised Julia. She wondered if there was a history between them, but it didn't seem like it. She didn't think it was jealousy, but the possibility was there. Then again, Julia could've been reading into it more than necessary. The most likely reason for Fosca's attitude was right there on the surface—grief, stress, and Fosca's inexperience dealing with it. Whatever the reason, they needed to move past it. A crowded Palazzo or not, they had the element of surprise.

"We can use this to our advantage," Julia said, needing to force the conversation back to an action plan. "It's the perfect night. They'll all be distracted. We can sneak in, grab the urn, and get out of there while they're occupied with their little get-together."

They both narrowed their eyes at her, unhappy with her demeaning the initiation. Though they had their issues with the Order, they obviously took it seriously.

"You know it's funny," Fosca said to Julia. "Nick refused to join us. He wanted to get back to you. But I didn't even have to ask you, and you're charging full steam ahead."

Julia was glad Nick wanted to return to her instead of joining something that wasn't his fight. "Why is it weird I want to help my husband?"

Carlo and Fosca glanced at each other. "Seems like more than that," Fosca said. "You can go home, call the cavalry."

An unexpected therapy session didn't feel right, but before Julia knew it, her mouth was moving. "When I was a kid, my dog, Domino, would race me to my pillow at bedtime. She'd always win and growl as if I were taking *her* bed. Then she'd wag her tail like she was joking"—she felt her eyes moisten at the fond memory—"which I've always thought she was. Such a good dog."

Fosca and Carlo shared a confused look.

"So," Julia continued, "we had to move, and my parents told me dogs weren't allowed in our new place. It was a rental." The tears streamed from her eyes. "I had to give her up. She was frantic. They needed to sedate her." Julia sniffed and wiped her cheeks. "I found out later that was bullshit. Total bullshit."

"Your parents lied to you?" Carlo asked, a hitch in his voice.

Julia nodded. She pondered why Carlo seemed overly upset but remembered he must've been thinking about his own father and della Porta lying to him. "I never even had to ask. But I knew. I fucking hate liars. I was entering my sophomore year in a new high school, a bunch of extracurriculars, college a few years later, so I'd have limited time, and they didn't want to take care of a dog. Though my younger sister would've if they'd just asked. Before Nick, it was the hardest loss I ever endured."

Fosca took Julia's hand and squeezed it. "Parents can definitely be assholes sometimes."

"And some people need help," Julia said, gazing at Fosca's orange fingernails.

"Nobody was there for you? Not even your sister?" Fosca asked.

Julia shook her head. "No, she was. My older sister, too. It sucked for me, but the truth is, I'm fine. I meant my poor Domino. She was ripped from her family. Worse than that—*betrayed* by her family. Basically thrown into prison with no warning, no reason. She was probably scared shitless, wondering when we'd pick her up, wondering what she did that was so wrong." More tears rolled over her cheeks. "And she was such a good girl. So loyal, so loving. I never found out what happened to her. I hope a nice family adopted her."

Carlo offered a napkin, which Julia accepted. She wiped the tears again, then looked squarely at Carlo and Fosca. "Like I said, some people need help. If I'm in a position to do so, I gotta do it. I don't have time for lawyers and cops who may or may not be crooked. Nick needs me, and I'm not going to abandon him. I will never do that again. And if we can stop an evil megalomaniac in the process, I'm all for it."

Fosca and Carlo smiled at her. It was nice to be part of a team.

"Animals need help, too," Fosca said.

"Damn straight," Julia replied.

"Domino means 'master' in Latin," Carlo said slyly, trying to add some levity.

Julia chuckled at the absurdly ironic name for a dog. With a loaded breath that firmed her resolve, she met her friends' gaze. "We can do this." She pointed to the newly found tunnel on the blueprint. "It's closer and shorter. It'll take less time to get through."

Carlo peered at the lines. "It's also narrower. Much narrower. It might not fit a boat."

"And there are definitely more cameras on the exterior Palazzo wall," Fosca added. "Plus, more guards nearby. Who knows if we can get in, and if we can, who knows if it connects with the urn tunnel? It could be at a different depth, sealed off, or just plain rotting and unsafe. It's hundreds of years old, maybe a thousand, if it was built with the Palazzo."

The three of them fell silent. Julia had to admit, it seemed extremely difficult and likely they could get caught. But that never stopped Nick. He would've done it for her.

"Do we have another option?" she asked.

Fosca and Carlo looked at each other and shrugged. "Not unless we go through the Great Council Room and into Tintoretto's room," Fosca said.

"Which I'm not doing," Carlo added.

"And I have *some* access," Fosca said, "but the Painter's room is off-limits. It's too easy for me to get busted."

Julia cocked her eyebrows. "What time does the initiation start?"

Fosca checked her cell. "Shit. I didn't realize what time it is. It starts in less than half an hour."

"We're cutting it close." Carlo rubbed his knuckles together.

"I have to admit," Fosca said, "it's a terrible idea. But . . . our only idea. I can reach the Book of Names and text you Vito's urn number."

Carlo turned to Julia and tapped his finger on the blueprint. "It's a half moon tonight. I don't think they'll see me. How long do you think you'll be?"

Julia and Fosca exchanged a look. "Are you saying *I* should go into the tunnel?" Julia asked.

"What's the problem?" he replied.

"I'm all for equality," Julia said while Carlo tapped away on his phone, "but I'm more for practicality. You speak Italian, you're stronger and faster, you know the Palazzo and the guards, just in case—"

"Claustrophobic," he said, reading his phone. "I'm also claustrophobic. And I can't swim."

"You can't swim?" Julia and Fosca said in unison.

Julia continued. "You live on an island. There's water going through it."

"There's water *everywhere*," Fosca added. "How can you not know how to swim?"

"Because I never go into the water."

"Yeah, but you take boats all the time," Julia said.

"And you take planes. Can you fly?" He lowered his head, ashamed. "I can swim. I know how, I've been in the water. I'm just . . . better on the ground. With shoes. Where I won't drown."

Julia swirled her wine glass and gazed at the tiny ripples and whirlpool as they settled into a calm surface. She and Nick had gone swimming countless times—in pools, off rental sailboats, in the ocean. The summer after they graduated college, they had gone camping at a pristine remote lake in New Hampshire. They took advantage of their solitude, skinny dipping for hours on end. After making love on the dock, they had a race back to the shore. The winner had to give the other a massage. Nick gave Julia a two-second head start, and she was determined to win. Sure, she wanted a massage, but she wanted to prove she could keep up with his strength, and the water was the one place she had a chance. He gave her a damn good massage.

"Julia," Fosca called.

Blinking her eyes, Julia found Fosca waving her hand at her.

"Still with us?"

"Yeah." Julia quivered at the thought of that weekend. She missed Nick terribly, but she needed to keep her head in the present.

"What do you think?" Fosca asked. "You up for this?"

Swimming in a dark tunnel was yet another item not on Julia's vacation list. But Nick would've done it for her. He *did* do it for her. "I wish I packed more than a couple of bikinis."

XXXV

STANDING ON THE DAIS IN THE GREAT COUNCIL ROOM, della Porta gripped the podium with one hand and caressed his pendant with the other. He wore it over his robe this night for all to see. The souls in *Paradiso* behind him provided an additional surge of strength. Even those who hated him and the Order—and there were many—imbued him with energy. Their grievances caused no consternation. The knowledge of their presence alone fueled his might. And that power would grow. There would be dozens, no, *hundreds* of paintings around the world. Thousands. He'd control them all.

Bathed in the room's amber lighting, four dozen blindfolded initiates stood before him, all wearing white robes with green rope belts. Nearly one hundred members of varying rank, dressed in black with their designated color rope belts sat on the benches lining the room. Many hadn't been to a Convocation in years but turned out for the event on short notice. The Order's largest gathering in his lifetime had the room buzzing, as if the engine had been revved and was raring to go. Repairs from the night O'Connor killed Tintoretto had finally been finished, and the Great Council Room was set to reopen to tourists the following morning.

He turned the typed-up printout to the next sheet, resting on the open parchment pages of the Book of the Seventh Sun.

"In the 16th century," he said loudly to the room, "when *Paradiso* was first announced to those senators not in the Order, as well as to the general public, the imagery of Heaven was presented as a reminder that all laws and decisions were made before a higher power. Little did the uninitiated know it was entirely true."

That higher power behind della Porta resonated stronger than ever. And his own power would explode once he obtained the doge's book.

Assuming the lost book had stayed within the family of one of the Uccello Protectors—the Bird Brothers—della Porta had strategized with Order researchers on how best to tackle the behemoth project. Preliminary research found that Ivan had three children and Vito two. Calculating an average generation of twenty-five years and an average number of surviving children who bore children at two, and taking pedigree collapse into account, which was quite prevalent in Venice, the team calculated that between the two brothers, there were between 250,000 and 1 million living descendants. While the number seemed daunting, it was far less when considering those with the Uccello surname, and whittled into the thousands when looking at adults descended from a male line who still lived in Europe. Additionally, they only needed to find the oldest living heir in each line. He instructed the team to start alphabetically with Ivan. If this search yielded no results, they could expand it. The book would be found.

Once the research plan was strategized, the better part of his day had been spent customizing the rites to efficiently initiate so many people at once. It was the first mass initiation in the Order's history, and with the Venice council unanimously on board, there was no turning back. The two-meter acacia tree stood in its terracotta pot on the stage between him and the painting. After taking the oath together, each candidate would be escorted up the dais to embrace the tree. They'd then be guided back to their spot before removing their blindfolds simultaneously. Reaching for the tree was a physical representation of embracing faith without empirical evidence and a quintessential part of the ceremony. In the future, when they'd have more time for planning, there would be a tree for each.

He beamed at the men and women before him, knowing they'd advance from Discipulus to Protector on an accelerated schedule.

"Though you are unable to yet see the glorious vision of *Paradiso* before you," he continued in an authoritative voice, "and many of you, if not all, have been to this room and have seen it as a beautiful work of art, a masterpiece, when your blindfolds are removed, the painting will look the same, but you will be gifted information that a remarkable few have known. As such, your lives will change. Your beliefs will change. And as with all beliefs, we ask that you take a leap of faith."

Ten of della Porta's most trusted Protectors stepped to the first ten proselytes. Bernardo, Enforcer of the Charge and his most trusted friend, took up the rear, while Dante led the procession, his large frame looming over the woman next to him—and everyone else in the room. A hood obscured Dante's ponytail, but his close-cropped beard and nose were visible—still bandaged from Nick O'Connor's attack. It must've been a vindication for Dante, knowing that his fight with O'Connor ended in a minor defeat, but here he was, leading the fortification of the Order to a strength it had never previously achieved. And Dante was only twenty-nine. He'd heal quickly.

Della Porta continued speaking to the group, his voice rising in volume. "The acacia is the tree of life, symbolic in many cultures and religions, representing the soul and immortality of the spirit. The crown coerced upon Jesus's head was woven from acacia branches. As you know, it has thorns."

Della Porta signaled Dante, who took the woman's arm and led the procession, followed by Manuel and the others up the dais to the tree.

"Strong, sharp, four-centimeter-long thorns," della Porta continued. "If you are here of your own accord, innocent of any wrongdoing against the Ancient Order of the Seventh Sun, be it past, present or future, you shall reach out and take hold of the trunk of this acacia, letting your faith guide your hand, so you will touch the bare wood and not puncture your skin. If the soul is good within, there is an unspoken covenant that cannot be broken. Trust in yourself, reach out with a firm hand, and seize your future."

Dante's initiate kneeled, and with a solemn face, she grabbed the tree, relieved when she didn't spear her palm. They continued on and down the other side of the dais. Manuel did the same with his initiate. Dante went on to the next row, and the process continued in cyclical fashion.

Della Porta thought back to the last initiation, which was Carlo's, on that fateful night. He wished Carlo could be here and was confident he'd come around and grow into the role of the Order's lead Painter, but he did agree with the advice of Zotti, Bernardo, and Lacasse.

He didn't want to send him away; he felt like a vengeful father who, instead of taking responsibility for how he reared his son, relied on punishment as the easy way out. But at this point, it was too late. Sails were full, and the ship of progress couldn't be stopped. And, truth be told, it was an honor and official business for Carlo. He'd meet Vasquez, meet the Spanish Painter, and meet the candidates for their Painter's replacement. Per della Porta's instruction, Carlo would interview them with specific questions designed to provoke a minor reaction. That reaction would determine their disposition, effectiveness, and mental ability to handle the role.

While Carlo's elevation to Painter happened on the spur of the moment, della Porta had to be honest with himself: he could've made better preparations for the enormity of the responsibility now pressing on his protégé's shoulders. Tintoretto himself had years of on-the-job training before *Paradiso* was deemed finished, and he started with a single soul. Carlo inherited thousands. Still, Carlo was the ideal choice, and he would grow into the position.

A meeting with Vasquez was the perfect first business trip. And separating Carlo from Julia O'Connor had become essential. Della Porta needed to rid himself of that distraction and close the book on the O'Connors. Then he needed to figure out the mole and close *that* book, as well. Books. So many books. The Doge's book. The criminal record log. The archive, filled with books...

A flash of lucidity hit him like a lightning bolt striking St. Mark's Tower.

Della Porta slammed the Book of the Seventh Sun closed on the lectern.

He ground his teeth. His veins bulged. He pressed so hard on the book's cover, his hands turned ashen white and left an imprint in the leather. Only when he looked up did he realize everyone in the room had paused. Those who weren't blindfolded beheld him; those who were stared straight ahead, some cocking their heads, as if they had lost their hearing. He considered doing his quick three-breath relaxing technique but opted against it. He wanted to harness this anger, to share it with his flock.

Della Porta caressed the book, then smacked the wooden podium three times. "*Now*, my friends," he called, in as vociferous a voice he could muster without screaming. His words resounded off the walls. "*Now* is the time for unity. For progress. For truth. There is an old expression. The future is but a second away. There is beauty in the simplicity of that statement. Beauty *and* truth. Everyone in this room stands at the doorstep of the future—a future that is a second away. We will soon open the door. Those who are not with us will ultimately join us. Those who are against us"—he regarded every face in the room. So many friends and fellow soldiers at the front. Fanella, Schenker, Zotti, the mayor. He saw Fosca, sitting in the rear. Though she was another person he had to keep at arm's reach, he needed her and was glad she came. Compared to her withered, old hag of a grandmother, Fosca had ambition. "Those who are against us will *never* join us. They will *never* be allowed to experience the transcendence we will. They will rot on Earth." He lowered his voice and spoke to the Protectors leading the procession of initiates. "Carry on."

His mind returned to the archive, to Nick O'Connor, to Carlo, to the mole. Not only was Bernardo loyal, but he was also smart. Even if he had betrayed della Porta—which he was confident did not happen—Bernardo never would've done it so carelessly.

No, it wasn't Bernardo, nor anyone who'd been a member for more than two weeks.

Della Porta had been hiding the truth for too long, shielding the most obvious answer that was always standing in front of him. There was no mole in the Order. Nobody could be that stupid—except a pigeon. A pigeon who flew over his head and now needed his wings clipped.

Carlo.

It could only have been Carlo who told the countess about his altercation with O'Connor in the archive.

As he watched his initiates reach out for the acacia tree, the corners of della Porta's mouth creased up. An overwhelming sense of satisfaction filled him. Bernardo had spoken of killing two birds with one stone by sending Carlo away. But della Porta had three problem birds he needed to resolve: the mole; Julia O'Connor; and he needed Vasquez on board.

Carlo was the mole, sleeping with Mrs. O'Connor and hated by Vasquez. The stone was Vasquez's hand. Della Porta held back a laugh. It was so easy. He'd strike a deal with Vasquez—Carlo's removal in exchange for the Madrid chapter's loyalty. He'd even 'allow' Vasquez to select the next Painter for Madrid. The mayor's choice was a good one for Venice, and then he'd have the mayor's allegiance, as well.

He'd send Carlo to Madrid, where the Sun Crystal was already secured. Once all was settled in Spain, he'd join them and do the power transfer there. Carlo would receive the sentence he deserved: removal from his beloved Venice—and Earth—forever. He was disappointed in Carlo, but for della Porta and the Order, the outcome would be the same.

One-by-one, each initiate had taken hold of the tree. Some were eager, some hesitant, but all did. None seized thorns. When everyone was finished and returned to their places, he spoke again.

"Remove your blindfolds."

They did.

Della Porta beamed at the forty-eight people, prouder than he'd ever been. "The first thing you see is that there are no thorns on this tree. There are *two* species of acacia. This is symbolic that your choice in good or bad may always be obscured or blinded by other factors. Always trust your heart. And always trust the Order."

He had said the same words to Carlo. His choices may have been blinded by other factors, and those decisions took him down a road that led to a singular conclusion: Carlo didn't have a choice anymore.

Della Porta discharged three rapid exhalations to calm himself and grinned at the brilliance of his strategy. All the flotsam and jetsam had been cleared. The waves calmed. It'd be smooth sailing to the horizon.

He began reciting the oath, which the newly installed Discipuli repeated.

XXXVI

JULIA CHECKED HER PHONE TO FIND FOSCA had texted three minutes earlier: '*CDXVI.*' It took her a bit, but she figured out the Roman numerals.

"Four hundred sixteen," she whispered to Carlo. "CDXVI."

He gave a thumbs-up. Keeping an eye out for guards and cameras, the two of them hustled to the bridge that shielded the secret entrance. She wore Carlo's sweatshirt—charcoal gray, loose, but cozy. Pulling the hood over her head gave her a sense of extra protection. They were two bridges down from the tunnel Nick had entered. This bridge was solid stone and buttressed by the rear of the Basilica, with balusters that reminded Julia of giant chess pawns. They hurried to the wide *fondamenta* on the opposite side of the canal. She shuddered. When she stood on this canal the night they escaped, she'd just been kidnapped, she held a gun, and her husband looked like a wet madman.

A whiff of ozone hit Julia's nostrils, presenting them with a new challenge: rain again. They'd been too focused on bringing a crowbar, which he had for art crates, to remember an umbrella. The *fondamenta* was already wet. Either it was lower than others or the canal water was exceptionally high, as the water licked the wall's edge. Julia clicked on the flashlight Carlo had given her and shined it on the bridge, recollecting where the lines led on the blueprint. A stone lion's head hanging off the side observed the canal. She angled the beam to the bottom of the bridge's arch and found her target—a three-foot diameter round grate, more than half submerged in the high water.

Julia shook her body, scattering her nerves. She wasn't thrilled about jumping into the dirty water, but that was the least of her worries. *Nick. He needs me.* She knelt to untie her sneakers.

Carlo grabbed her arm and pulled her back up. "I'm going," he said. "Let's switch flashlights. Yours is waterproof."

"What about your claustrophobia and swimming?"

"Like you said, I live on an island. I need to do this. It's not like I'm swimming to Murano." He kicked the water on the *fondamenta*. "It's deeper than usual. Acqua alta."

"What?"

"High water. From the tides, pressure, rain. It's usually in the autumn, but it's been earlier every year now." He squinted at the sky with worry. "I told you I want to keep you safe. It'll be much safer if I get caught in there. If you get caught out here, you can scream and run. In there..."

Julia was about to protest, but if she were honest with herself, she'd much rather Carlo do it. Maybe he really did want to keep her safe. She swapped flashlights with him. "Just be quick. I'm in no mood to scream and run."

Carlo handed her the crowbar. He removed his leather Converse All Stars, socks, and sweatshirt, which he handed to her, then jumped into the water. He bobbed up and down, angling his head up so his mouth was above the surface, but his chin hit the water. "It's deeper than I thought, but I can bounce on my toes. Pass me the crowbar."

She did, and he bounce-swam to the crossbar grate. He examined it and felt around, searching for hinges and a lock. Hanging onto the bars, Carlo inserted the crowbar between the grate and wall. He braced it against the stone, used his legs for leverage, and snapped the gate open. Julia was impressed with how easy he made it look.

He bounce-swam back to her. "It's a pretty good weapon." He handed her the crowbar.

A flurry of nerves hit Julia. She did her best to hide them. "Good luck. And be quick, huh?"

He went back to the grate and pulled himself inside.

MOONLIGHT FADED, AND THE ancient tunnel narrowed as the canal gave way to stagnant water. Carlo focused on the positive: at least he didn't need to swim. That might change, though. If the tunnel wasn't tightening, then the water level was rising. He shivered. The water in the canal was cold but tolerable; it was frigid here. Sloshing on his hands and knees, he'd already banged his head twice on the mossy brick ceiling. He needed to call the tunnel what it was, but his denial had suppressed the truth: *un gatolo*. A sewer channel. Though it hadn't been used in ages and connected with the canal, far too much water had already splashed into his nose and mouth.

He had realized what he crawled through ten meters back. He didn't know why the blueprint showed this tunnel with disappearing ink, but Carlo was certain that it was clear on the page when it was first built. Likely—he hypothesized to keep his mind away from the crushing psychological effects of the tight space—the *Pozzi gatolo*. The cesspool drain for the prison, if not the entire building, which explained why it was large enough to fit a man. Too bad it didn't also flush out the corrupt men who tread above him. That job was now Carlo's millstone around the neck; he hoped it wouldn't weigh him down.

If he had to guess, he was crawling through a six-hundred-year-old sewer. It had been inoperative for two hundred years, but that didn't mean it was a spa. The smell wasn't unpleasant. It had a bit of sweetness to it, mashed with some savory. Almost like . . . leftover pizza soup, which didn't sound half-bad at the moment.

He snickered. Water splashed in his mouth. Gagging, his stomach heaved up an acrid dollop of the pinot grigio he had at Fosca's. He spat into the water, regretting comparing the stench of deceased prisoners' bowels to something he might eat. He also regretted not eating a proper dinner.

Thoughts of food and nausea weren't helping, so he switched brain gears. When they'd examined the blueprint, he had used the entirely unscientific method of his pinky width equaling two body lengths. It seemed relatively accurate since they knew the length of the Palazzo and the bridge's location, but crawling forward, it was impossible to keep track of how many body lengths he'd progressed.

Figuring—and praying—he neared the intersection of the other tunnel, Carlo kept his flashlight beam pointed to the right, looking for something, anything, that might carry him into a larger space.

It wasn't long before he found two smaller drainpipes embedded high in the sewer tunnel. Overflow pipes. But overflow from where? He was surely beneath the Palazzo. He examined the two small lead pipes, but they seemed unremarkable—approximately four centimeters in diameter, each sticking out of the sewer wall about ten centimeters and separated about a meter from each other. Carlo shined the light down the tunnel; it dissipated into the abyss.

He considered moving onward, but where would he end up? Under a *Pozzi* commode? Or worse, a hole in the bottom of a cell? No, this had to be it. The position of the pipes also struck him as odd. Why would they need to stick out so far, or stick out at all?

He felt them again and realized they were the perfect distance for a man to hold simultaneously. An idea sparked. He gripped and twisted. They didn't budge. Positioning himself so that he could use his back and feet for leverage, he tried again. The one to his right slid clockwise. The left one was stuck, but it moved a hair, counterclockwise. Using all his strength, he twisted each a half-turn.

Bricks between the pipes popped out a few centimeters. Another shot of adrenaline flooded his veins. He pulled those bricks further to discover they were a façade on a lead panel attached to the tunnel by a rusty hinge.

Carlo heaved it open. The passage was small but large enough for him to squeeze his body through.

He ducked his head back into the sewer tunnel.

A pack of hungry, screeching rats swarmed his face, like frenzied zombies gifted a surprise brain. He dodged and swatted, using one hand to shove them away and the other to propel himself up into the larger, intersecting tunnel.

His foot landed on a greasy rat that screeched as its guts splattered on his bare skin.

Nearly puking, Carlo scurried away from the rodents to the other side of the passage. At least he could stand at full height in this tunnel and be on dry ground. He shined his light around.

On the wall opposite him were crude, faded paintings of fairies, squatting on the floor with drain holes between their legs. Carlo grinned at the image. He admired the ancient pornography and wondered who painted them. Cocking his head, he realized the paintings were exceptional, in a familiar style.

With no time to linger in an underground museum, he checked his options. To his left, the tunnel angled downward and quickly hit water, which obviously exited to the canal. To his right was dry land and his way forward. Stifling the thought that the damp dirt through which his bare feet trudged was rat droppings, he curbed his nausea and continued down the tunnel. Knowing that Nick had traversed the same passage twice gave him some reassurance.

Before long, Carlo found his target: four rows of wooden shelves containing thousands of urns, draped in spider webs, casting eerie shadows.

All those souls. The sheer volume made his stomach drop. Knowing he was their new warden gave him chills. He rested for a moment to process it. Eternity was too great a punishment. Even if the souls were evil, who's to say that they would commit evil acts? Who's to say they couldn't be redeemed? A soul travels through seven bodies; that's a lot of lifetimes to reach salvation.

Composing himself, he continued his mission.

He made the sign of the cross, thanking the Lord the urns were in numerical order. All of them were identical, plain terracotta vases with wax-sealed caps in a nearly endless line of shelves extending down the tunnel. It took Carlo less than a minute to find urn number four hundred sixteen toward the end of the second shelf. CDXVI was hand-painted on the side in black script. Inside was Vito Uccello's remains, and hopefully, the literal key to the end of della Porta's corruptive path. Carlo yearned to smash it and dump the ashes out right there to find the key, but he recalled Fosca's warning. Before they left, while Julia was in the restroom, Fosca reminded Carlo they needed to bring the urn back in one piece. Nick regressed to Angelo when he came into contact with the ashes. Given that Carlo was now connected to all the souls, a similar incident was a possibility.

The notion of breathing in a human's ashes in the close confines of the tunnel was so repulsive, it triggered a bout of claustrophobia.

The walls closed in on him.

Carlo set the urn on the floor and braced a shelf, expanding his lungs for more air.

Inhale. Exhale. Inhale. Exhale...

Once calmed, he stared at the rows of urns, speculating which contained his father. He still had trouble believing della Porta sentenced him, but it was growing equally difficult to believe Paganelli did it.

If only he could find the urn, open the cap, and set him free. Or at least give his remains a proper burial.

Wiping a tear from his eye with his dirty wrist, he realized he couldn't hear any voices from these urns. He crossed himself again, thankful for that sensory break. Hearing thousands of voices in this tunnel would've been too much to bear. It made sense. The souls of these people were trapped in a painting some twenty meters above him.

He shined his light down the tunnel. It bounced off the stone wall at the end.

Nick had entered the Great Council Room through this tunnel—through the council chair beneath the painting that led to a secret passage. Tintoretto arrived in the same manner. Chances were high his room was on the way. Della Porta had lied to Carlo about so much, including that when he aged beyond a reasonable year, he'd need to be confined out of risk of attracting suspicion. This would be Carlo's one opportunity to see his future prison cell.

Leaving Uccello's urn on the dirty ground, Carlo walked to the end of the tunnel, where he found a chute going up and wooden rungs affixed to the wall.

JULIA PACED THE CANAL LEDGE, staying in the shadows. She wasn't sure how long it would take Carlo to retrieve the urn, but this seemed longer than when Nick was in the other tunnel. Did Carlo have to go further? It should've been shorter. Then again, Nick just needed to get the boat and row out. She reassured herself that everything was fine.

A raindrop smacked her nose.

Her phone vibrated. Another text from Fosca: *'Ceremony is over. Watch your 6.'*

Julia scoffed. *Watch your six?* Did she think she was a spy?

Another raindrop hit her. And another. With a rumble, the sky unleashed a downpour that felt like she stood in a waterfall.

Cursing the heavens, Julia pressed herself against the wall, clutching Carlo's bundle of sweatshirt and sneakers. With no umbrella or coverage, she quickly got soaked. The brief thought of jumping into the water and waiting in the tunnel passed through her mind. It was a decent idea except for one small problem—the canal water was rising.

Shaking her head, she surveyed the area—and gasped. A tiny red light she hadn't seen before twinkled through the rain. A black globe security camera was mounted on the alley wall above the bridge. It captured everything from its vantage point.

She backed away, slinking into the wall's shadow, then texted Fosca: *'Carlo's not back. Getting worried.'*

Julia waited a minute with no response and rising anxiety. It was Groundhog Day, the worst-vacation-ever version. When Nick was in the tunnel, she didn't even think about going in after him. But Nick knew where he was going, that tunnel was larger, and he was stronger than Carlo—at least she thought he was.

If Carlo was telling the truth about his swimming skills, he'd have trouble in the rising water.

She checked her phone again, careful to shield it from the rain with her body and angling her back to the camera so it wouldn't see the light. No response from Fosca. She pocketed the phone and tapped her foot. Minutes ticked by. Did his claustrophobia get the better of him? Did the tunnels not intersect? Was it too difficult to find the urn?

Shivering, partly from the cold and wet, partly from nerves, but mostly because she couldn't risk pacing with the camera on her, Julia did her best to relax and tell herself Carlo was fine.

"HAS THE APPRAISER decided which to sell?" Bernardo asked, gazing about Tintoretto's former apartment.

On a high from the mass initiation, della Porta couldn't contain his grin. He found himself humming and tapping his thighs to the beat of Elton John's *I'm Still Standing* playing in his head.

Boxes, stacks of canvasses, and cardboard tubes took up almost every square centimeter of the space. The appraiser, having recovered from Nick's attack, had finished his work cataloging Tintoretto's vast collection. With nothing to do but read and paint for over four hundred years, the prolific artist had left a treasure trove behind.

"We've selected thirty works we'll claim were found in the Scuola di San Rocco," della Porta said. "Any more than that would invite unwelcome skepticism."

"Would flooding the market not bring down the prices?" Bernardo asked.

"Quite the opposite," replied della Porta. "The find will be celebrated and renew an intense interest in his work. Hundreds of collectors will scramble to obtain a lost Tintoretto. There's a romance to lost paintings. Museums around the world will salivate for *one*. Perhaps we should increase the number."

"Or find another box in a few years."

Della Porta grinned. "I like your thinking, my friend."

Bernardo slid a box aside. Beneath it lay an aging Persian rug that reminded della Porta of the one in which he wrapped the countess's body. He'd never noticed the similarity before. He waited for a sensation—a pang of regret, the notion of things best left behind, an echo of remorse at the memory—but found nothing.

Bernardo pulled the rug up to reveal a wooden trap door.

"This is it," the chief Protector said, a grave look in his eyes.

"You're sure that's how O'Connor got in?"

"No. But I don't think we should take any chances."

WITH THE FLASHLIGHT between two fingers and the other eight gripping the rotting wooden rung, Carlo wiped spider silk off his face and climbed. He wished he owned a headlamp.

He'd already passed two broken rungs. The fractures seemed relatively new, likely caused by Nick, making Carlo's journey even more perilous. Careful not to make the same mistake, he planted his hands and feet on the edges of the rungs, where the nails provided greater support.

Two meters higher, he reached a trapdoor. Bracing himself against the ladder and wall, he pressed his fingers against the door.

Voices carried through the wood.

The rung bearing his foot splintered.

"OPEN IT," DELLA PORTA SAID.

"I wonder if Azizi knew of this," Bernardo replied, referring to the previous Exalted Master.

"If he did, he never told me about it."

Bernardo knelt and gripped the steel ring.

"Signori," Manuel said, rushing into the room, panting. "You need to see the security feed. Please come up."

Releasing the ring, Bernardo rose and pulled his mobile from his pocket. He pointed to a Wi-Fi router affixed to the top of the wall. "We can do it from here."

Della Porta eyed Manuel. The man seemed nervous—too nervous for a pressing emergency on the video feed that any number of men could've handled. A dozen Protectors and forty-eight new Discipuli were on the premises, celebrating in the Great Council Room.

"The camera on Rio del Palazzo and Santa Apollonia. One of the new ones." Manuel swallowed as he said the words, then glanced down at the trapdoor. Then at della Porta. He immediately looked away when he caught the man's eye.

Bernardo tapped his mobile's screen and switched the display. He angled it to della Porta, zooming in and panning around. Just water, an empty bridge, and *fondamenta*.

"Nothing there," Bernardo said.

Della Porta eyed Manuel again. He needed to have words with this man. And rethink his theory about Carlo as the mole. "What did you see?" he asked, as Bernardo switched through different views.

"A man. It was dark, but he looked familiar."

"Or maybe it was a rat," della Porta said. "Lots of rats down here. Let's take a look, shall we?" He pointed to the trapdoor. "Open it up, Manuel."

A BLUNTED STING WARPED Carlo's ankle; his tailbone throbbed.

His ankle was twisted, if not sprained. He massaged the bone and cursed the damned wood. He'd fallen to the bottom and was lucky he didn't break his leg. Or his neck.

The trapdoor creaked open, and a light shined down. Carlo shimmied out of the beam and view of anyone standing at the top of the chute.

Della Porta's voice echoed into the tunnel. "I don't see anything."

"That looks precarious." Bernardo was with him. "We'll get a ladder down here."

"Manuel, come to my office." It was the last thing Carlo heard before the trapdoor shut again.

Carlo hobbled over to Uccello's urn and picked it up. It wasn't heavy but needing one arm to carry the vessel and one hand for the flashlight, limping barefoot in the wet dirt was an arduous task. He dreaded crawling through cesspit water with only two limbs; it seemed impossible.

The herd of rats sprinted up the incline.

He gasped at the sewer portal. Fast-rising canal water streamed out. He forced himself to forget about his ankle. Again, he considered smashing the urn. A transformation to Vito Uccello seemed like a stretch, but he didn't want to find out. And fishing through ash and shards of clay would take too long. He sat and dunked his feet into the chilly water. Clutching the urn, he slithered into the sewer.

Panic didn't wait. As the water level rose, the air gap shrunk equally as fast. He could barely grip the sides with his three fingers that weren't clutching the flashlight. His bare toes couldn't gain purchase on the grimy brick.

Hyperventilating, he popped his head up and banged his forehead. A six-centimeter gap gave him enough space to draw some oxygen. He closed his eyes. *Father. Julia.* There were two choices: go back to the urn tunnel or continue forward. If he went back to the urn tunnel, he'd be caught and sentenced to *Paradiso*. He'd never find justice for his father or any of the souls. Knowing della Porta's vindictive nature, the man would probably kill Julia. He promised he would keep her safe, but this went beyond any type of obligation; it was as if helping her—being with her—had become an essential part of his existence.

Carlo didn't have a choice. All that stood between Julia's life and death was his ability to make it through this sewer. Stronger than anything he'd ever committed to before, he bit the flashlight between his teeth and propelled himself toward the exit.

Water engulfed the light. He pulled it out of his mouth and tucked it into his pocket, facing up for a bit of illumination. With only enough air space for his nose now, he kept moving, meter by meter. The water rose. He angled his head. He was getting closer. *No time to panic. Pick up the speed.* He pressed his lips against the sewer ceiling and kissed an air pocket. Carlo took one final breath and plunged under the water.

The force of the current slowed his snail's pace, but he powered forward.

Lightheaded, a faint glow shimmered at the end of the tunnel. Blood vessels in his brain, depleted of oxygen, felt like pipes clogged with sludge. His lungs were about to burst. *Keep going . . . keep . . .*

JULIA SMACKED HER HEAD against Carlo's sooner than she expected. In the tiny space, she contorted her body, drank in as much air as she could from the quarter inch remaining, and flipped around in the freezing water.

Carlo grabbed her ankle.

She tugged like a pitbull, gripping and pushing with her free leg and hands, boosting them toward the canal.

Moonlight and safety were just ten feet away. She had enough air to make the swim, but hauling Carlo against the current in this cramped space where she couldn't use her arms for any type of stroke was torturous. Her chest was on fire. Every blood cell in her head felt ready to pop. But with a relentless drive, she braced her hands against the sides of the brick tunnel and pushed them out.

She surfaced and gulped a lungful of air as raindrops smacked her face. Her torso burned, and the laceration in her abdomen felt like it had reopened, but there was nothing she could do about that now. Twisting around, she yanked Carlo's head above the water. She backstroked, hauling him to the *fondamenta*, and gripped the slick side with her free hand. When she saw the urn cradled in his arms, she discharged a sigh of relief.

"We made it," she sputtered through clipped bites of air.

No response.

"Carlo?"

A ghostly pale face stared back at her, his wet skin almost translucent in the dim light.

Julia sprang into action. Placing the urn on the *fondamenta*, she shoved Carlo halfway out of the water, then climbed out. She hoisted herself up and pulled him out, but slipped off the mossy edge. Jagged pain knifed her gut. She winced and lost a breath, then focused on her task. The high water played to her advantage, enabling her to swim-crawl onto the cobblestones. The water lapped his shoulders. She pressed on his chest with both hands and delivered hard and fast compressions. Tilting his face back, she pinched his nose and sealed her mouth over his. She puffed twice.

His chest inflated, his lungs connecting with hers.

She pumped again. "Come on, Carlo, please!"

Nothing.

She pressed again. And again.

And again.

On the seventh thrust, Carlo coughed water out. He sucked air in. She helped him sit up and tapped his cheek. "You alive?"

He blinked, his hazel eyes meeting hers. "Thanks to you."

"We're not out of the storm yet. Come on."

With the urn cradled under her arm, she helped him to his feet and winced in pain. Now using Carlo for support, Julia lifted her shirt. The scar was intact.

"Can you walk?" Carlo asked.

"Do I have a choice?" She clenched her teeth, stifling the pain and exhaustion.

They staggered to the footbridge. Julia retrieved their clothes and her cell. She'd been careful to hide them at the bridge's railing. The dark hoodie rendered them nearly invisible in the rainy night.

Shivering and clutching the bundle against her chest, they ran barefoot down the alley away from the Basilica and Palazzo, desperate to get out of camera range. Winded and limping in pain, Carlo raised his hand, gesturing he needed to rest. At the end of the alley, they ducked under a sheltered doorway and sat.

"What happened?"

"The ladder broke."

"Ladder?" She didn't know where he could've found a ladder, but it didn't matter. And she had to admit—she was thankful she wasn't the one with a twisted ankle, needing to be rescued by a guy who couldn't swim. "Can *you* walk?"

He massaged his ankle and spoke, still short of breath. "It's . . . feeling better." He rotated it. "Shoes would be nice . . . soaked or not."

Julia handed him his drenched Converses. She slipped her own on, as well.

Carlo's phone buzzed as he loosened the laces and gingerly inserted his hurt foot into the sneaker.

"Your phone still works?"

"After you drop three in canals... you get a waterproof one."

"At least you have your priorities straight."

He pulled it from his pocket. Bernardo was calling.

"Wait, don't ans—"

Carlo answered. He spoke in Italian in brusque words, then ended the call.

"Why would he be calling so late?" she asked.

"He wanted to know where I was."

"What did you tell him?"

"At a bar, going home."

"Does he usually check up on you like that?"

Carlo shook his head.

XXXVII

Helping Carlo up the final step of the hidden staircase, Julia opened the safehouse door and stumbled into the living room with his arm draped over her shoulder.

"You got it!" Fosca said, spotting the urn, before noticing their condition. She rushed over. "Shit, are you guys okay?"

"A few hiccups," Julia said, "but we got the job done."

The two of them helped Carlo to the couch, where he sat with a grimace.

"We need to thank Manuel. He'll be here later."

Still soaking wet, Julia placed the urn on the coffee table.

"Whoa, not there," Fosca said, lifting it up. She carried it into the kitchen and placed it on the floor.

Julia followed. "Got any towels?"

"Sure, one sec." Fosca rushed off.

While the others weren't looking, Julia lifted her shirt and checked out her sword wound. There was a dull ache, but she wasn't bleeding.

She lowered her shirt and turned to Carlo. "How're you doing?"

"Much better," he replied. He pulled himself up and joined her in the kitchen. She poured glasses of water for herself and Carlo. As they chugged, Fosca returned with a stack of white towels, still with the tags on them.

"I, uh, kind of overbought." She passed a couple each to Julia and Carlo.

"Good thing." Julia draped one over her shoulders and dried her hair.

As Carlo did the same, Fosca sat beside the urn. "We're so close," she said with giddy eagerness.

Julia and Carlo joined her on the floor, sitting around the urn like kids about to unwrap a Christmas present. Though her exhaustion had been supplanted by excitement, Julia had also been suppressing revulsion. She had never held an urn or seen a dead body. Even with the ashes sealed, it seemed odd to be lugging them around, especially with them being so old. She felt like a graverobber. It didn't sit well with her, but getting the key, unlocking the box, and saving Nick displaced secondary worries. Neither European seemed to be bothered by holding a person's ashes. She didn't even want to touch the thing again.

"Can you hand me that?" Carlo said to Fosca, pointing to the cheese knife on the counter.

She did and plopped back down. Carlo cut the wax seal to reveal a fat cap, as wide as a hand. "It's dry," he said. "At least we don't have to deal with ash mud."

Julia and Fosca exchanged looks of equal disgust and brought their attention back to the urn.

Without a second thought or warning, Carlo popped the cap.

Julia realized she bit her lip, unsure what to expect, but relieved a spirit wasn't set free. She didn't expect *nothing*, which was exactly what happened.

"You realize you're going to be digging through human remains, right?" Julia said.

"Uh, no." He turned to her and lifted the urn up. "I'm going to dump it out."

Fosca's eyes bulged. "Wait, what? Are you insane? I don't want ashes all over the place." She guided his arms down so that the urn sat safely on the floor again.

"Fine." Carlo laid his towel down and picked up the urn, ready to dump it out.

"Stop!" Fosca placed her hand on Carlo's and set the urn down. She glared at Carlo, as if he'd forgotten something critical. "The last time someone did this with a connection to a soul, it didn't end so well." She glanced at Julia. "Sorry."

"It's okay," Julia said, though it wasn't. She realized what was truly bothering her about the urn. The memory of Nick's regression was a fresh sting. But that wasn't the only thing that unsettled her. "Why would Carlo have a connection to Vito Uccello?"

Carlo and Fosca exchanged a quick gander. "You don't know?" Fosca asked.

"Know what?"

"I may be related," Carlo said abruptly. "To the Uccellos. I'm not sure, but I don't think it's worth the risk."

"Why didn't you bring this up before? And especially with Isacco?"

"Because it's the side story," he said. "I don't know if it's true, and I wanted to focus on the lockbox and the facts."

Once again, his answer seemed to be missing something, though it was a valid reason for him to avoid the ashes. She agreed with Fosca; it wasn't worth the risk for him to transform into a Protector of the Order from the fifteen-hundreds. She'd seen what happened when a supposed *good* guy came back. It seemed strange that a family lineage would cause a regression, and she wanted to call bullshit, but she wanted forward progress more. Inching closer to the urn, she peered inside but couldn't see anything.

"Carlo, go to another room," she said, before turning to Fosca. "We'll dump it out."

Fosca considered then shook her head. "We'd still need to dig through it, and we'd have ash in the air. Human ash. I'm not sucking in graveyard dust. And if it falls out of the towel, I definitely don't want to be on mop duty again. Nasty as fuck. One of us needs to bite this disgusting bullet and get the key."

"Don't look at me," Julia said. "No way am I putting *my* hand in there."

Julia and Carlo looked at Fosca. She rolled her eyes and ground her teeth. "Fine. Get the youngest to do the literal dirty work, no problem."

She pulled off her shirt to reveal a white tank top. After removing her rings and bracelets from her right hand, she steadied her palm over the top of the urn. "It'd better be in here," she said, then closed her eyes, drew an intense breath through her teeth, and plunged her hand inside.

"Gross gross gross gross ewww gross gross gross!"

With her arm submerged up to her elbow and donning the most wretched scowl Julia had ever seen, Fosca fished out an ash-covered key.

"I found it!" She dropped it on the towel and rushed over to the sink, where she didn't stop scrubbing her hands. "Oh, my God. That was, like, literally the most disgusting thing I've ever done."

"You should've worn gloves," Carlo said with a snarky grin.

"I should've dumped it out on your face," Fosca called back.

Shaking her head at Carlo, Julia capped the urn. She rose and wrapped the key in the towel, then joined Fosca at the sink. Once the key and Fosca's hands were thoroughly washed, the three of them reconvened in the living room.

Julia examined the key. It was tarnished brass, about three inches long, with a clover-shaped head. Entirely unremarkable, it looked like any other antique skeleton key. She turned it around and squinted. There was no writing anywhere on it. But she felt an imperfection on the shaft. She angled it under the recessed ceiling lights. A narrow engraving winked at her as she rotated it in the light.

"I think this is it," she said, passing it to Carlo. "You were right. It's far too small to read."

"We need to get a magnifying glass," Fosca said, still wiping her hands together.

"I have one." Julia reached into her purse and pulled out her cell phone. Using the camera with the flash on, she zoomed in on the engraving:

Et facies pictorem

She took a picture and showed it to her friends, then passed the key to Carlo.

"Et facies pictorem," Carlo said. "It's Latin. I think it translates to 'The painter's face' or 'The face of a painter.'" He handed the key to Fosca.

Julia wondered what that could mean. Tintoretto? Another painter? She glanced at Carlo and Fosca, who seemed to be riding blind on the same train of thought. She broke the silence. "I'm not sure why I thought this would be easy."

"This has been easy?" Carlo replied.

"How do we know this isn't actually a key to something else?" She took it back from Fosca. "Wouldn't that make the most sense?"

"Isacco's box has a combination," Fosca said.

Julia held the key up. "*Four* combinations. And this is a key. So maybe the clue we're looking for is what it opens, and *that's* what contains the code to the box."

"That inquisitive reporter mind is a part of you, huh?" Fosca asked.

"Sometimes more than I'd like," Julia replied.

"But it could open anything," Carlo said. "I think we follow what we know."

Julia shook her head at the overwhelming possibilities before deleting the image. She thought she was right, but it was true they had no place to start. And there was another thing on her mind. "How old is this Guild?"

"Almost as old as the Order," Fosca replied. "Why?"

"I'm just wondering why the Bird Brothers wanted to take the book from Renzo. Weren't they all in the Order?"

Fosca and Carlo glanced at Julia, then each other.

"Some sort of schism," Fosca replied. "Or a power grab."

"Maybe we'll learn when we find it," Carlo said.

"Okay, so let's work by process of elimination," Julia said. "If the key is really a clue to the combinations, it shouldn't be too hard to figure out."

"There are six dials on each side. So that's either twenty-four characters or four six-letter words."

"Or just one side opens it," Julia said.

Fosca squinted, thinking for a moment. "That's another puzzle, but it seems easier to start with one word and go from there." She snapped her fingers then shook her head. "No, it can't be Comin. Or Robusti."

"Oh," Julia said brightly. "Jacopo."

She and Fosca smiled at each other, but still on the same wavelength, their expressions morphed to skepticism. Jacopo was worth a shot, but even with the Order hiding things in plain sight, it seemed far too obvious. Also, it was Tintoretto's name, not his face. They turned to Carlo, expecting him to have the answer.

He didn't.

"Could it be another painter?" Fosca asked. "Someone else from the time period?"

"Veronese and Titian, Tintoretto's rivals," replied Carlo. "Titian fits. But I don't remember anything about his face." Carlo stood and paced. "Tintoretto's son, maybe. Domenico. It's said he helped paint *Paradiso*. But again, there's nothing unusual about his face."

"What about Tintoretto?" Julia said. "Some identifying mark?"

He shook his head. "I saw his face right in front of mine when he died. Other than being five hundred, there was nothing strange. Crazy white hair." He paused. "He bled from his ears, but . . . is that his face? And this key was made when he was younger."

Julia snapped her fingers. "A number! Roman numerals. It could be his birthday or something."

The three of them regarded each other in companionable puzzlement.

Fosca said, "Maybe, but what number could it be?"

Carlo shrugged. "I have no idea."

XXXVIII

DELLA PORTA PASSED A PILE OF LOGS SPREAD out like giant fallen matchsticks in the Cantiere Nautico Maniele shipyard. Tucked away on the eastern tip of Venice, a separate island in its own right, della Porta reached the shipbuilding site after a thirty-minute nighttime walk from the Palazzo that traversed nine footbridges. He hadn't been here since the Order purchased the company a decade ago. It was one of the first investments he pushed for, and it had exceeded expectations. A funny thing, shipbuilding. It had entrenched roots in Venice but rarely did outsiders or even Venetians consider it a major industry. Boats were built and exported up and down the Adriatic and Mediterranean. The industry proved so lucrative, in fact, that della Porta made personal investments in two additional shipbuilders.

With a sixty-year history, this particular yard's specialty was luxury yacht repairs and custom jetties. Their sawmill converted oak trees from the foothills of the Italian Alps into pilings used for moorings, piers, and house foundations.

Using his umbrella as a cane on the dock, he continued farther into the facility.

The rain had stopped, but the water had yet to recede in a low-lying place like the shipyard, built at sea level for easy access. The alarm and tide barriers didn't work with this acqua alta, which concerned him and likely every person in the city, but the rain had primarily caused the high water, so the barriers would've had little effect.

He balanced on a plank that had been laid over the water and entered the sawmill. As had been the case in recent days, Carlo—along with the countess's knowledge of the archive incident—remained in the forefront of della Porta's mind. Carlo's actions and reactions had been questionable, but when della Porta put himself in the young Painter's Converse All Stars—as horrifically juvenile as they were—he realized he would've acted the same way. Carlo may have been on an errant wave he needed to ride out, but della Porta was not above admitting he was wrong—his protégé *wasn't* the mole.

Time was running out to squash a bug. He'd come to think of the traitor as an insect. Moles and rats surface. No, this man was a termite, burrowing and wreaking havoc in its trail. Della Porta had been reluctant to see the Guild as a threat, but with a termite in his ranks, there was an increasing probability the Guild was active and mounting an attack. If the termite told the countess about the archive, there was a chance *she* was part of the group—though, given her family history, her alliance seemed improbable. The likely scenario was that the termite had burrowed into her, seeking to chew through her and sow discord.

It worked.

Della Porta had pondered the archive incident countless times, but until two hours prior, he hadn't considered the moments *before* he'd entered the archive. It wasn't Bernardo or Carlo. It was someone who saw him and O'Connor enter. Someone he passed sitting at a desk, pretending to read a newspaper that obscured his face, but whom della Porta didn't notice in his haste to reach Carlo.

He found the man again, standing in the center of the sawmill, wearing a black raincoat and rubber boots over his gray suit. Della Porta had chosen the space due to its remoteness. Unintentionally, the barn-like room, lit by moonlight streaming through cracks in the high ceiling, with sawdust littering the floor beneath numerous mechanical saws, imparted a perfect backdrop for a clandestine encounter.

"Buonasera, Manuel," della Porta said.

"Buonasera, Exalted Master."

If Manuel was nervous, he didn't show it, solidifying della Porta's hypothesis. An innocent man would've questioned why he was called to a shipyard at this hour. Manuel didn't protest at the request.

Della Porta played along; he had to be sure. He approached the termite, his wet soles sticking to the woodchips beneath his feet—an ironic metaphor for the situation, as if each step collected more evidence of the insect's destructive treason. "You're probably wondering why I asked you here, at this hour, in this weather."

"You mentioned I'd be working on special projects. I assumed this was one."

Della Porta smirked. Either the man was a loyal idiot or a foolish turncoat.

"Who were you saving tonight?" asked della Porta.

"Signore?"

"When you rushed in, to tell us there was someone in the canal."

Manuel cocked his head. "I wasn't saving anyone. I was reporting him."

Della Porta studied his eyes. In the darkened room, they seemed to be pleading.

"Last time I was late to report," Manuel continued, "you were . . . not happy with me."

"True. Do you have an update on Carlo and Signora O'Connor?"

"I haven't seen them since they returned from Murano."

"Yes, you mentioned that in my office. Since then? Did they return to his flat?"

Manuel blinked but remained unyielding. "Signore, I was at the initiation and then, as you know, in your office discussing my report. Afterward, I spoke with other Protectors about the man I saw, then went home for twenty minutes for dinner, and to kiss my wife and baby before coming here—"

Della Porta lifted a finger. Though his excuses were valid, they didn't hold luster. "Enough, Manuel." He bent over and scooped a handful of sawdust. Rising, he let fibers of centenarian oaks fall through his fingers. He ground the remaining particles in his palm, inhaling the sticky-sweet heaviness of trees that sacrificed their lives for Venice. "Why were you in the library, Manuel?"

"Signore?"

"Don't play dumb. I saw you, and I have video of it. It took a while to go through the security footage, but you were there." Della Porta bluffed about the video, but there was no way Manuel could know that.

He sucked air through his teeth. "I was there reading. I often go to Marciana."

"I checked that too. You *never* go to Marciana. Why were you following me?"

The termite cleared his throat, the first solid indication he knew he was caught.

Della Porta was about to press on but softened his tack. Manuel had a family. He grinned at the man and spoke in a soothing voice. "I told you how much the Order values redemption. Everyone in *Paradiso* was judged and had a chance to be redeemed. It is unfortunate they chose that path, but many—hundreds—chose to tell the truth and were spared. You know this. This is your chance. Tell me the truth, and we can put this all behind us. Bury it in the dust on this floor. I think that would be best for your family. You have a new baby, yes?"

Manuel spied della Porta nervously with his brown eyes and nodded.

"Your family will thank you for your honesty," della Porta said. "As will the Order. Now answer. Why did you tell the countess I was in the archive with Nick O'Connor?"

"Because she asked me to, signore."

"And why would she do that?"

"I promise, I don't know. That's all."

Perhaps della Porta would never learn why the countess asked, but now, he knew how she'd heard. "See? That's all I asked for. Come, let's go home." He motioned for Manuel to go ahead, which he did.

They exited the sawmill, and della Porta followed him toward the shipyard entrance.

When Manuel reached the plank, della Porta said, "Your family will be taken care of."

"What?"

Manuel turned, but far too late. Della Porta removed a Protector's sword from his concealed holster and slammed the hilt into the traitor's head. Manuel grunted, lost his balance, and fell in the half-meter of brackish water, landing on his back. His head smacked a cinderblock.

Della Porta stepped onto the plank and stood over the pathetic termite trying to gain his bearings and sit up. Blood seeped out of the back of his head, staining the water. Della Porta jumped into the lapping puddle, landing on Manuel's right hand. He pressed the sword blade to the termite's throat.

Manuel closed his eyes.

Della Porta smacked the broad side of the cold steel against the man's cheek.

Termite eyes snapped open.

"There you are," della Porta said. "It's not bedtime yet."

He rotated his wrist, ensuring the sniveling bug recognized that the beautiful weapon belonged to him. The termite groaned and winced. He reached for his head with his left hand, but della Porta stepped on that one too.

Manuel cried out. He tried to squirm, but it was no use.

"You were never a Protector," Manuel said with a feeble hiss.

"No, but I know how to put this through your neck."

Blood sputtered from Manuel's mouth as he laughed. "This has nothing to do with the countess," he said. "It's *you*. The Guild exists because of people like you. You have no idea how big we are, where we are, but you will."

It was della Porta's turn to laugh. "Thank you, Manuel. You just told me everything I needed to know." He removed the sword from beside his throat, and instead, jabbed his umbrella into the traitor's esophagus.

Manuel choked on his own phlegm-filled wheeze. He slipped his hand from beneath della Porta's shoe and reached the umbrella with his free hand, but della Porta sliced through the palm with his sword.

"I ... have ... a daughter," Manuel managed.

"Well, that was a mistake, wasn't it?"

Della Porta pressed the umbrella deeper. He yearned to hack away with the sword, but this needed to look like an accident, if not an unsolvable murder; he couldn't have another person close to him missing. He dropped the umbrella the long way over his throat and stepped on it, holding it down. Manuel struggled in vain. Della Porta stomped harder on his right hand and swatted his left with the sword every time he reached for the umbrella.

Moments later, it was over.

An exhilarating numbness rinsed away the tension gathered at della Porta's extremities. He waited a minute then checked for a pulse. He'd seen far too many movies to know to make sure a victim was truly dead.

It had been decades since he had to remove a person outside of *Paradiso*, but this was now the second time in as many weeks. This one barely grazed his consciousness. The countess lingered. Her death was a regrettable course of action, but responsibility for it now lay on Manuel's lifeless shoulders. Della Porta had always bottled the emotions of death and put them on a shelf. Why did the countess haunt him so? It wasn't even the guilt of killing her. It was that she had never accepted him.

He sheathed his sword and flipped the body over to make it seem as though Manuel slipped, hit his head on the cinderblock, and drowned.

If della Porta wanted to move past the countess, he needed to be honest with himself. He wished she could've witnessed how far he'd bring the Order. Her connections would have helped, as well. But what was done was done.

"Ghe sè, sò quà." *There is, there are.* Della Porta crafted eddies in the lapping water with the bloody umbrella tip. "Or in your case," della Porta said to Manuel, "there was."

Della Porta searched Manuel's body and retrieved his mobile. After he smashed it with the sword, he fished out the SIM card. Satisfaction filled him as he mentally crossed off a major item on the top of his to-do list. More significantly, he had sealed a hole and dealt another serious blow to the Guild. Without Paganelli and Manuel, the Guild had lost their two most valuable assets. Unless there was another mole—a subterranean termite. He'd be more cognizant of that possibility moving forward.

He exited the shipyard and headed home. While crossing the seventh bridge, far enough from the shipyard, he chucked the remnants of Manuel's mobile into the canal. He stopped at the imposing bronze monument to Victor Emmanuel II, the first king of unified Italy. Though not without his controversial decisions, della Porta had always admired Victor Emmanuel for his steadfast leadership, his statesmanship, and the ability to be the first to unite the Italian peninsula since the Holy Roman Empire. Della Porta bowed his head in veneration, then soaked in the quiet beauty of his city. At night, Venice reclaimed itself in desolate splendor.

His two favorite times were in the small hours and in winter, just after a fresh snowfall when he could stroll the streets devoid of tourists and locals alike. And in this weather, gone were all human noises, replaced with water caressing the *fondamento*.

Walking on, he entered Campo San Zaccaria, a quaint square abutting its namesake gothic church. A shop and memory caught his attention. He wandered over to the edge of the square and gazed into the window of Segreti di Bellezza, the charming perfume store where he'd purchased a breakup gift for his fiancée when he decided a relationship was too much of a distraction from his ambitions. She had hurled the 135-euro bottle against the restaurant wall and stormed out. What a waste, but he understood her reaction. Her rash decision to move to Florence two weeks later proved to him that she, or any woman, offered nothing but interference.

Twirling the umbrella and tapping it on the cobblestones, della Porta grinned at the future. Next on his to-do list: Carlo.

The boy's disrespect was the cause of increasing irritation. He'd give Carlo time to recalibrate, but that time needed to be limited. Della Porta didn't have the same luxury for himself. With the Spanish Painter on his last legs, he needed Vasquez—and the replacement Painter—on board with Veritism before the transfer. Any dissent would unravel his plans like fighting headwinds with a lace sail.

A massive stone was removed from della Porta's shoulders, knowing that his protégé wasn't the mole. But Bernardo was right. Carlo *was* distracted and under great stress. Neither of them needed that. He trusted Carlo and knew he'd grow to be supremely loyal—like a son, but Mrs. O'Connor demanded far too much of his attention. Whether Carlo liked it or not, she needed to be erased from the picture.

1589

A SPRING MIST FLOATED OVER THE CANAL, revealing itself in a purple daybreak glow. He didn't mind waking before dawn. It was a rare occasion to see nature's beauty in his most serene city. The merchants had yet to begin unloading their vessels. And for the uncommon quiet, he didn't envy his brother, who currently dozed in the guest quarters of a Medici villa in Firenze. He stayed behind at the Exalted Master's request and checked in on the young swordsman who had yet to deliver on his end of a bargain struck.

He found the man, smoothing back his curly, dark hair, as if he'd just rolled out of bed.

"Bondì, siòr." The swordsman yawned.

"It shall be a good morning if you possess what I want."

The swordsman raised his hands and shrugged like a guilty child feigning innocence.

"It's been six months," he said, now regretting the early hour of this pointless meeting.

"Since I *met* her," the swordsman replied. "Not since we've been . . . intimate. Delicate things take time."

He sneered. "As if you know of time. You're young. You think you have an abundance of life's greatest gift. But in reality, everything can change—or end—with a blink."

In a flash, he drew his Mongolian short sword and pressed it against the swordsman's throat. The man gasped, then remained as still as the winged lion atop the column of San Marco.

"Am I clear?"

"I will find the book, Siòr Uccello," the swordsman said.

"Good." He sheathed his blade. "The sand is falling, Angelo."

XL

THE FOURTH OR FIFTH RING—OR SIXTH? He didn't know—dragged Carlo awake from his dream. Or was it another flashback? And to whom? The memory dissipated as his eyelids creaked open to morning light blazing through his windows. Shielding his face with his forearm, he reached for his mobile with his other hand and rolled off the couch, slamming against the floor with a thud.

He missed the call but saw it was Fosca—for the third time. It was far too early for anyone to be calling. His phone rang again a second later. Carlo sprang up, sensing the burning nature.

"Fosca? Everything okay?"

"Manuel never showed up after you guys left, and I never went back to nonna-mère's, and I barely slept, and his mobile keeps going to VM—where have you been?"

Her rapid-fire words confirmed his concern. Carlo rubbed his eyes. "Sleeping."

A pause. "With Julia?"

"Yes. I mean, no. Not *with* her. She's in my bed." He craned his neck to see into his bedroom. Julia slept soundly under the sheet.

"What the hell, Carlo? I was just asking if she's with you and okay. Listen, this is serious. I'm really worried about Manuel. I think della Porta's onto him."

"This could be a problem for the Guild." He yawned.

"What is wrong with you today?" she screamed. "Fuck the Guild. What if they killed him? He has a baby. God, this is my fault. I need to talk to someone. Gulotta went home to Padua, Uncle Enz . . . can—can I come over?"

He scratched at his cheek. "Sì, of course." After giving her the address and directions, Carlo ended the call and went to the kitchen to make coffee. "Julia. . ." he whispered into the bedroom.

His mobile rang again. He couldn't imagine what else Fosca needed, but he hurried back to the sofa. It was Bernardo. What did he want? Whatever it was, there was no point in pushing it off.

"Buongiorno, Bernardo."

THE COFFEE CUP WAS in Carlo's hand as he reached della Porta's door. He wiped the croissant crumbs from the corner of his mouth.

Bernardo had been cryptic but said it was urgent and that Carlo would be pleased with the news. In Carlo's tired state, the last person he wanted to see was della Porta, no matter what they wanted to tell him. It had been only a day, and his anger hadn't diminished.

Still, Bernardo told him it wasn't a choice, so after Carlo ended the call, he gently woke Julia, fighting every animalistic—and human—urge to crawl into bed with her. Just to lay there with her, sleeping, holding her in his arms for a minute, he'd be able to die a happy man. But he knew how she'd react. She pined for Nick and thought she'd find him. Carlo closed his eyes and chewed his cheek, mentally hammering himself for an action he prayed could be reversible, or at least somehow redeemable.

He took another sip of his double Americano and opened della Porta's office door.

"Carlo," della Porta said from his Chesterfield sofa, "thank you for coming. Have a seat."

Surprisingly, della Porta was dressed casually, with a Polo shirt and jeans over his loafers. Carlo remembered it was Saturday. He didn't know della Porta owned jeans, but he had to admit, the outfit didn't look half-bad.

Carlo sat in the side chair next to Bernardo, who relaxed with a coffee.

"Good morning?" della Porta asked.

A cock of the head and a glare was the best response Carlo could offer, as if to say, 'No, it's not a good morning, asshole. I should be sleeping.'

Della Porta released three quick breaths. "I owe you an apology, Carlo. At least one."

The words were a total surprise—an effective surprise that soothed Carlo. It was precisely what he'd longed to hear.

"For years I've withheld information," della Porta continued. "Please know that doing so was not a personal indictment of your character or judgment but merely the Order's way. There is plenty Bernardo does not tell his wife, and they've been married as long as you've been alive"—he turned to Bernardo—"am I right?"

"One year longer," he said fondly. "Our anniversary is three days before your birthday, Carlo. But she knows a quarter of what you do. And she's a member."

Fair enough, Carlo thought. Bernardo's wife was a sweet woman he'd met multiple times over the years.

"I'm sorry for keeping you in the dark," said della Porta. "Please understand the reason. I also want to apologize for not putting myself in your shoes. You advanced from Discipulus to Painter in minutes. I can't imagine the stress and burden you must feel, with no training, no introduction. I believe it was the right move, a necessary decision, but I now realize it was also a hasty one that left you little choice."

The corners of Carlo's mouth creased upward involuntarily. Appreciation and relief overwhelmed him, but he maintained his composure. "Grazie," he said.

Della Porta crossed his legs. "Not only were you the first to make such a rapid transition, you were the first in history to assume the mantle from an original Painter. The Spanish and French Painters are still alive, though they are both nearing the end."

"Yet you said nothing about them. Or the other chapters."

"For your protection," the Exalted Master replied. "But you're right. I should've at least given you fair warning before the meeting."

Carlo wondered if this was a new side to della Porta or if he was buttering him up for something. Either way, the contrition was appreciated. And his curiosity was getting the better of him. "Who are they?"

Della Porta grinned. "I'm glad you asked. You recall José Vasquez, the head of the Madrid chapter?"

"Is he . . . ?"

"No, no. The man is admittedly artistic, but he's a seven-life soul, like me. In any event, as you saw, the man can be rather . . . contrarian."

"I noticed that."

"He's not a fan of either of us. As you saw, he wants to meet you in person. Bernardo and I think that's an excellent idea, but rather than inviting him here, we think it's a perfect opportunity for you to see more of the Order. We'd like you to go to Madrid—"

"Madrid?" It wasn't remotely what Carlo expected. Not even in the cards. He shook his head. He wasn't opposed to the idea. He always wanted to see Madrid, but it was such a surprise. And then, there was Julia, Fosca, the book. . .

"Sì, it's a spectacular city. You can see the Spanish chapter's operations, the nuances in their ceremonies. Meet Vasquez so he can get to know you. And here's the best part. I believe you've always wanted to see Tintoretto's study for *Paradiso* at Museo Thyssen-Bornemisza?"

Of course he had. And knowing other versions contained souls. . . it was an irresistible offer.

"And," della Porta continued, "you can meet the man who continued working on it. The Painter who *continues* to work on it to this day. Perhaps you can meet him before he ascends."

"Who is he?" Carlo was enthralled. He *had* to know.

Della Porta offered a grin of pure admiration. "El Greco."

ANOTHER HOUR—OR WEEK—of sleep would've worked wonders on Julia's mind and body, but Fosca had arrived twenty minutes after Carlo left.

Since then, her new friend had been talking non-stop about Manuel, worrying for him and his family and blaming herself. Julia liked the girl and thought they had a pretty solid bond, and she felt awful for Manuel—especially if something happened because he'd saved her and Carlo. But right now, she turned all of her attention to her coffee, needing to tune everyone and everything else out.

Once again, it was all too much.

She just wanted silence. And suddenly, she got it. The chattering had ceased.

Julia looked up from her mug to see Fosca weeping softly into her chest. Unable to ignore her any longer, Julia hopped off the stool and caressed her friend's back.

"Hey, I've been there," Julia said. "I'm *still* there. My husband has been missing for almost two weeks, but—"

"But Nick's—"

"Nick's what?"

"Nick is . . . well, like you said, it's been a while."

Fosca's reaction irked Julia, but she passed it off as her being upset. "Exactly, and I can't assume the worst. I know he's out there. It's not too late."

"No, it's not."

"And you don't know Manuel is dead, do you?"

Fosca wiped her tears. "You're right, Julia. I'm sorry. It's just, with nonna-mère and Uncle Enzo and Ni—Manuel, it's just a lot to absorb, you know? Life shouldn't be like this."

"Trust me, I know."

They exchanged a smile. Julia reached for her coffee and brought it next to Fosca's mug.

"What are we toasting?" she asked.

"The one thing we can toast to." Julia raised her drink. "Hope."

"I like that. May it spring eternal." Fosca clinked her mug to Julia's, then took a sip and hopped off her stool. She grabbed her backpack and headed for the door.

"Where are you going?" Julia asked.

"To confront the one man who would know about Manuel. And my nonna-mère."

1612

As Exalted Master of the Ancient Order of the Seventh Sun, Senator of the Most Serene Republic of Venice, consigliere to Doge Marcantonio Memmo, and proprietor of the largest importer of Indian spices and luxuries in Veneto, Marco Niccolò Quattrone was afforded certain privileges.

He had the doge's protection and thus felt secure in the most disreputable sections of Venice, for everyone in the city knew him. A transgression against Quattrone would be met with reprisals from the Order, his private security, or the Republic itself.

Typically, he'd have no concern visiting the San Basilio piers in the pre-dawn hours. He stepped off his gondola and onto the quay, flanked by two Protectors wielding crossbows in addition to their sheathed Mongolian short swords. The men were not assigned to his safety but to that of the passenger on the Spanish three-mast carrack bobbing silently in the water next to his craft. The ship had arrived that afternoon. Except for a standard customs inspection—a regulation Quattrone ensured would be swift—not a soul had boarded nor departed. Though their eminent passenger had not been to Venice in at least four decades, his artistic fame preceded him, as did his distinctive oblong head. Given the clandestine nature of his visit and Quattrone's mission—not revealed to all in the Order—it was essential that El Greco's arrival remain secret.

Carrying their lanterns, Quattrone and the two Protectors climbed the plank and boarded the ship. They paid their respects to the captain and first mate, quickly dispensing with formalities. The white-bearded, grizzled captain brought Quattrone and his entourage to the state room. He knocked twice then opened the door.

The seventy-year-old man in the desk chair turned to face his visitors.

Quattrone bowed humbly then rose. "Welcome back to our most serene city, Signor Theotokópoulos."

With a somber but appreciative expression, El Greco bowed at the respectful address of his real name.

Monstrous shadows that shortened and elongated on the stone walls unnerved Quattrone. He had carried his lantern countless times down the narrow spiral staircase and through the corridor to the Painter's quarters, but the chilly air and grotesque lighting persistently caused him to clench his jaw.

Indeed, he said not a word on this occasion, despite El Greco's aide-de-camp badgering him with questions. The short, heavy-set balding Spaniard lumbered in front of El Greco. Quattrone led the procession. His two Protectors brought up the rear.

Quattrone knew his silence was unsettling, especially since he'd been loquacious on their walk from the pier to the Palazzo. El Greco, on the other hand, who had not been to Venice in over forty years, was entirely silent. The elderly painter had declined Quattrone's offer of traveling by gondola and instead had gazed about the canals and *calli*, all of which were much the same since his last visit. Quattrone had considered bringing his honored guest to see the Rialto Bridge, one of the major additions, but he opted to head straight for the Palazzo Ducale. Other trusted Protectors had been instructed to light the Great Council Room sufficiently prior to their arrival.

When El Greco had entered the vast room and turned toward the eastern wall, the candles and lanterns produced the desired effect. With a gasp, the Spanish painter had dropped to his old knees and clasped his hands together in reverence to *Paradiso*.

"Un milagro," El Greco had whispered.

Yes, Quattrone had thought. A miracle.

When El Greco last visited the room, the wall was graced with Guariento's 14th -century fresco of the *Coronation of the Virgin*. Though the pictorial content remained much the same, the lighting, power, and immense nature of Tintoretto's masterpiece never failed to inspire awe upon one's first—and subsequent—viewings. For an artist of El Greco's caliber, who learned many of his skills as a disciple of Tintoretto, it must have felt like genuflecting before the Lord himself. Little did El Greco know to whom he truly knelt. But he'd soon learn.

Quattrone knocked twice on the wooden door at the end of the corridor beneath the glorious masterwork. It opened a moment later. A man the world had thought died eighteen years prior stood in the threshold. Tintoretto. His thick beard and hair were a shimmering white. His eyes still commanded despite his diminutive stature. His ears, previously crusty and caked in blood, had been cleaned by the doctor. Holding a chamberstick in one hand, the Painter beckoned all to enter.

Quattrone walked in and stepped aside for El Greco, allowing him a moment to absorb the fantastic.

Upon seeing his one-time friend and mentor, El Greco's jaw dropped. Unsurprisingly unable to speak, he yet again collapsed to his rickety knees. His aide followed suit.

"My lord, my teacher," El Greco managed in unpracticed Venetian. His voice sounded as though he'd subsisted on saltwater and driftwood. "How ... how is this ... is this the devil's work?"

"It is *God's* work, my friend," Tintoretto replied in a resonant, healthy timbre that defied his age. "Please, rise. Looking at you like that makes my own knees hurt."

The two Protectors helped El Greco and his aide stand.

"Sit properly, old friend." Tintoretto gestured for El Greco to take his desk chair. "We have much to discuss."

XLII

EL GRECO?

The vision felt like hours, but seeing della Porta's and Bernardo's expressions confirmed it must've been just a few seconds in real time.

A smile consumed half of Carlo's face, and he didn't bother to hide it. El Greco. Flashbacks to Senator Quattrone's time were incredible enough, but the chance to meet two Renaissance masters in the present day in the flesh, as himself, was nothing short of a dream come true. No, he'd never dreamt such a thing, since weeks earlier he would've assumed it was an impossibility. And that's what this was—an impossibility come to life.

Bernardo and della Porta let Carlo soak in the information. He appreciated that. Though he'd studied Tintoretto far more since the man was Venetian, El Greco figured prominently in Carlo's first-year classes, and as a precursor of expressionism, with no attachment to a single school, the Greek-born virtuoso indirectly influenced Carlo's own work. As he recalled facets of the master's life, it made perfect sense he was the Spanish Painter. Carlo forgot El Greco's birth name, but he was born on Crete, hence the nickname. He trained in Venice, including under Tintoretto, then moved to Toledo, where he became the most celebrated painter of the Spanish Renaissance. With his skill and first-hand knowledge of Tintoretto's work and techniques, El Greco would've been able to continue the study for *Paradiso* without anyone giving it a second thought.

"Not a bad job perk, eh?" della Porta said, grinning.

Carlo shook his head in disbelief. "It's astounding."

"I had a feeling you'd be pleased. As Bernardo mentioned, this is good news. Travel takes a little over a day—"

Carlo raised an eyebrow. "A day?"

"We thought you'd also appreciate the chance to see the European countryside." Della Porta walked to his desk and brought back slips of paper, which he handed to Carlo. "There's nothing like good, old-fashioned paper tickets. Your train leaves at 19:13. You're in a private sleeper."

Staring at the ticket, still imagining meeting another Renaissance master, della Porta's voice floated up from Earth and into the clouds, where Carlo's head resided. He read the ticket. Gravity slammed his body back to reality.

"Wait, I can't leave today."

"Why not?" Bernardo asked.

Carlo gazed at the two of them, conjecturing what this was all about. "Because I have things to do. That's why."

Della Porta reclined on the sofa and crossed his legs. "You mean Mrs. O'Connor?"

"She's on the list, yes. You, yourself, told me she's my responsibility. I also have my work, which I'm behind on, and, um, a date with Jordan."

"All of which can wait a few days, Carlo. Not one item you mentioned will be lost. El Greco might be. You saw Tintoretto. Regardless of Mr. O'Connor's attack, his death was imminent. El Greco is just twenty years younger. He could pass at any moment."

"And this is not a request," Bernardo added.

"But I'm Painter now. I'll make my own decisions."

"On *some* things," della Porta said. "But either way, do you want to squander this opportunity?"

The answer was obvious: of course he didn't. But a rush of questions smacked Carlo. Would El Greco be in the same condition as Tintoretto? Did they have a replacement Painter chosen? Was della Porta ordering him to go?

He didn't have a chance to ask any of them. The office door flew open.

"I must know, Salvatore. Where's my nonna-mère?" Fosca said in English, storming straight for della Porta.

Seemingly stunned, della Porta stared at Fosca a moment then exchanged looks with Bernardo and Carlo. He grinned at Fosca and answered in English. "You really are so similar to her. I could imagine her doing the exact same thing. Except you're far more beautiful, of course."

Carlo nodded in agreement with della Porta for the first time in weeks. Bernardo did the same.

"Don't bullshit me, and don't you dare try to sweet-talk me." Fosca's face glowed red from flattery, anger, or both.

"My dear," della Porta said, gesturing for her to sit. "I wish to God I knew. We all do. We've been working with Interpol. I don't want to assume the worst, but it *has* been a long time."

She didn't sit. "You know damn well Nick O'Connor didn't kill her."

Carlo wondered if she knew something definitive. Perhaps she was bluffing.

"Fosca, please, sit." Della Porta again offered a place on the sofa. This time, she accepted. "You remember Carlo, right?"

"What's up?" She pointed her chin at him.

"Let me finish with Carlo," della Porta said, "then I'll show you every bit of information the police have shared with me. Perhaps you can assist them with the investigation."

"What the hell do you think I'm doing here?"

Della Porta raised his hands in defense and apology. "Of course. Perhaps we can put our heads together. But please, let us finish with Carlo. We're almost done." He turned to Carlo. "Carlo, why don't you go home and pack. I'll email you all the details."

"Where's he going?" Fosca asked.

"Madrid," replied Bernardo. "To meet Vasquez and the Painter."

Fosca gulped. "That's a good idea. Vasquez is a lot easier to deal with in person."

She covered pretty well, but Carlo prayed della Porta and Bernardo didn't notice her physical reaction. He needed to take the attention off her. He stood abruptly and waved the ticket. "Okay, I'll go. But I'm flying back."

Della Porta and Bernardo glanced at each other. The chief Protector shrugged. "Fair enough," della Porta replied. "Book the ticket, and I'll reimburse you."

XLIII

"No way," Julia said. "Are you serious?"

"You have to come, Julia. It's not safe here." Carlo pushed aside one of his paintings in his studio space to access his closet. He slid the door open and rummaged through the clutter inside.

"I don't have time to go to Madrid." She couldn't believe what she was hearing. How could he even ask? This was a fundamental difference between Nick and Carlo. No way would Nick have bowed to della Porta's—or anyone's—request to take off at a time like this. Julia kicked herself internally. She'd found herself comparing Carlo to Nick recently, and it had to stop. Nick was her husband, the man she loved, a man in danger and in dire need of her help. Carlo was a friend helping them—out of guilt. "Absolutely not, Carlo. You shouldn't even be going. We need to figure out the lockbox code, look for Nick. You wanna get the book, right?"

"Yes, but—"

"You said it yourself. We get the book, we bring down the Order. If we bring down the Order, Nick will be exonerated. Then we can go home."

"Sì, but—"

"The book's in Venice, not friggin' Madrid." Folding her arms, she was tempted to situate her body in front of the closet to prevent him from finding what he was looking for.

Instead, Carlo extracted a black leather weekend bag, careful to make sure the rest of the closet's contents didn't tumble out. "If I don't go," he said, not looking at her, "they'll suspect something. They told me straight up it's not a request. Nothing's going to happen in three days—"

"*Worlds* change in *two* days, Carlo."

He lowered his head and cracked his jaw. "You're right."

"And speaking of things changing in short times, why has your English gotten so much better?"

"What?"

"It's like you don't even have an accent, and you know every word. How do you even know an expression like 'straight up'?"

He stood and headed to his art supplies, where he shoved two sketchpads, markers, pastels, and colored pencils into the bag. "I don't know. Maybe you said it. I speak English all day long with you."

It didn't seem like a viable reason to lose an accent, but Julia shrugged. It was the least of her concerns.

Carlo continued. "Julia, please. Come. I can't protect you if I'm not here."

"What about Fosca?"

"She can protect herself."

"I mean she can help me."

"If anyone sees her with you, they'll know she's with the Guild. They could kill her."

Following Carlo into his bedroom, she paced the room as he threw clothes into his bag, carefully selecting items as if he intended to be in nightclubs the entire trip. Mortified, she noticed her underwear and bra on the floor in her pile of dirty clothes. She shoved the whole bundle into her suitcase. "What if I stay? Are you still going?"

He stopped packing and turned to her. "Are you going to put me in that position?"

"Are *you*?"

He raised his palms in a mix of pleading and exasperation. "It's four days, Julia. We don't even know where to start decoding the key. Anything we need to research, we can do online. What's the difference if you're sitting here or on a train, huh? I think it would do us both good to get out of Venice a bit, get away from the Order, don't you think?"

"You're going *to* another Order. What's *that* difference?" She tightened her gaze, feeling like a mouse being swatted back and forth by two cats.

"It's the same Order, just—"

"Are you friggin' serious? Don't you realize how much worse this is? It's literally three times as bad."

"And a golden opportunity to embed myself with them."

Fair point. She redid her ponytail, as she considered the situation. "Do you really think you can do that? Get in from the inside?"

"It's what della Porta wants me to do."

He took a step toward her. For a moment, Julia thought he might take her hands, like Nick would do, but he kept an appropriate distance. "You don't have to see them at all. You'll love the train ride, and you can see Madrid when I have my meetings."

Pushing her desire to visit Madrid to the back of her head, she focused on pragmatism. It was true they could do their research from anywhere, though she wanted to visit Isacco Uccello again or perhaps a Venetian library. That could wait. And it was true she was at risk alone. She planned to report Nick's disappearance to the U.S. consulate, which she could also do from anywhere. She picked at her fingernails. *Where are you?* He'd definitely want her to go. Shit, he wanted her to go home. Carlo was right. What would stop della Porta from kidnapping her again, or worse?

"Fine, but we're getting separate hotel rooms."

Carlo waved his hand to indicate that was obvious. He showed her his phone. "I already bought you the tickets. The train leaves in a few hours."

Julia shook her head with an eye roll. Of course he already bought the tickets. And of course, they only had a few hours.

"Good thing I never unpacked."

XLIV

WHEELING HER CARRY-ON ON THE PLATFORM, Julia followed Carlo alongside their turquoise and white train at the Santa Lucia station. Compared to the mind-blowing architecture in Venice, the open-air station was an industrial letdown that harkened back to Mussolini's fascistic tastes.

Though she suppressed her outward emotion, she had to admit—it felt good to be escaping Venice. She hadn't realized she felt stuck and immobile for so long. Even when she and Nick had made it to the mainland, it didn't feel like real movement. In Milan, they never made it off the platform before the police picked them up.

Reading the numbers on the side of the train doors, he stopped at one. "This is us," he said, motioning for Julia to go first. A conductor walked by, blowing a whistle.

"Carlo," called a man's voice.

Julia stopped with one foot on the car's first step. She and Carlo turned to find della Porta and Bernardo hurrying toward them.

Her sense of motion plummeted like a locomotive derailing off a cliff as the two men she hated most in the world approached.

"We came to see you off," della Porta said. "I'm assuming Signora O'Connor did as well?" He gave her an unwelcome scowl.

"She's coming with me, Salvatore," Carlo replied.

"I'm afraid that's not possible."

Carlo gave Julia a gentle nudge. She brought her other foot onto the step.

"I'm afraid she's already on the train," he said.

Della Porta and Bernardo exchanged a disconcerted look. Their expression solidified that Carlo was correct—she wouldn't be safe alone in Venice. She also questioned if sending Carlo away was a ruse to get her alone.

They'd never find out. The conductor blew his whistle again and announced something in Italian, which Julia assumed was: "All aboard!"

Carlo motioned for her to take another step, then joined her on the train.

"Arrivederci, amici," he said to the two men standing like statues who'd just been slapped in the face.

"Or as we say in Boston," she called out, "go fuck yourselves and your mothers, you sons of bitches."

Carlo's mouth popped open into a circle. "Julia—"

With a satisfied grin, she bounded into the car as the train began to move. They navigated the narrow aisle with their luggage until Carlo found their compartment, a reasonably spacious private sleeper with two bunkbed-like berths. The top bed was folded away, and the bottom was converted into a couch.

"We'll change these into beds after dinner," Carlo said, as he stowed Julia's carry-on in the luggage compartment above the door. "Do you want the top bed or bottom?"

Julia opened a complimentary bottle of water on a small shelf and took a sip. The encounter with della Porta riled her, and while the water hydrated her parched mouth, she needed something stronger to quell her nerves. Without answering Carlo, she averted her gaze out the window. The station was already out of view, but her gut told her it wasn't the last she'd see of those men.

JULIA LAID HER PHONE on her chest and stared at the sleeping berth above her as the train journeyed through the French countryside. When Carlo told her the journey was two nights, she wasn't thrilled half their trip would be travel time. But the first leg, which was an overnight to Paris via Milan, relaxed her, and she loved returning to France and speaking French, even if briefly at Lyon Station.

It had been seven years since she'd taken an overnight train, when she and two girlfriends did a weekend in Prague when they were studying in Paris her junior year—another trip she'd wished Nick were on with her. Julia marveled at how different this trip could've been—a romantic adventure during which they'd find a way to snuggle on one of the narrow berths.

Once I find my husband, we're going home and staying home.

Now on their second leg, Carlo slept on the berth above her again in another private sleeper on a high-speed TGV duplex. He snored louder than the train's rumble, like a bull sleep-stampeding. She hadn't recalled him snoring in his loft, but maybe she was just too tired to notice. Unable to sleep with a million thoughts swirling through her head, she used the train's spotty Wi-Fi to scroll through her emails, her Facebook and Instagram feeds, and three news sites. Catching up to the world showed she hadn't missed much. Still wide awake, she opened a book in her Kindle app, but couldn't concentrate, so she cleaned up her photos. None of the mundane activities distracted her from thoughts of getting the doge's book and clearing her husband's name.

Though she never made it to Poveglia Island, given that Nick had yet to find a way to contact her, she was convinced Maggie Yorn had her facts straight: the Order held Nick at the Palazzo. Short of zero verification and convincing James Bond to save him, Julia's one chance was to bring down the Order with a mythical book. The lockbox and the key suggested the book was real; she prayed it contained the promised motherlode of information—and hadn't been dissolved in an acid bath.

Since they slept and relaxed through most of the journey to Paris, Julia made sure they used their time on the second leg for research.

After a decent dinner of cod with roasted carrots and eggplant, she and Carlo had huddled in the bar car over her iPad and a French red varietal she'd never heard of and didn't love, combing over various Tintoretto paintings and two self-portraits. One, which he painted when he was around thirty, expounded his youthful visage, with dark, curly hair, a small mustache, and a pensive gaze that seemed to be contemplating the artist, which was, of course, himself. The second portrait, painted when he was seventy, was strikingly different. The man looked gaunt and haggard, emerging from the darkness with a thick, gray beard and hooded eyes that implored the artist to let him rest. Again, the irony being that he was the artist, and testament to his masterful skill at capturing emotion and manipulating the viewer's perception.

But unless there was a four-word, twenty-four-character Venetian expression for tired, there was not a single characteristic about his face as a young nor old man that was identifying enough to fit the clue. They jotted down various attributes of the works, with Carlo translating to Italian, Venetian and Latin, which he somehow understood fluently from his bizarre flashbacks. Dozens of portraits of other people that Tintoretto finished in his prolific career brought them no closer to an answer. Carlo and Julia had a list of about ten possible words. But all were random guesses that neither of them felt confident in, especially given that they didn't know how many tries they had, nor the language of the combination, the order, or which side to try.

At least she could relax, distancing herself from della Porta and his goons.

She closed her eyes and mentally recalled the key, with 'et facies pictorem' engraved on the shaft. After a moment, her eyes opened with nothing; no amount of brain energy offered additional clues. The real key was in Fosca's grandmother's safe along with the blueprint. Julia had wanted to throw both away to make sure the Order never got them, but Fosca and Carlo outvoted her since the artifacts held historical significance and might prove useful in the future. "Plus," Fosca had said, "that safe contains far more valuable things. It's secure in there."

Julia was glad they convinced her not to throw the key away. A strong part of her still thought it opened something else that contained the solution to the lockbox. Carlo didn't disagree, per se, but they had zero starting points with that hypothesis.

Tintoretto's second self-portrait, the one he did when he was older, had stayed with her. The man's eyes were so haunting. She pondered if that's how they looked when Nick killed him. She shuddered and brought the image up on her phone. Even on the tiny screen, the man seemed to be staring straight into her soul. Backing out to the Google image search screen, her eyes widened. There were numerous images, but she and Carlo had focused on one—a close-up. They'd noticed the others but ignored them since the backdrop appeared to be solid black. But in one thumbnail, Tintoretto was off-center. She clicked on that one.

Her jaw popped open.

"How did we miss this?" she whispered aloud.

On the small screen, to the right of the artist's face, appeared to be a white line, almost like a scratch.

Julia pinched and zoomed. The faint white lettering was plain as day: IPSIVS.

Six letters. Hiding in plain sight.

A burst of excitement flooded her body. She quickly searched for the meaning. It took a bit, but she realized it was Latin. Google Translate was no use. Was it an acronym? Her enthusiasm waned. After staring at the word for a minute, she nearly woke up Carlo when she remembered that in Latin, the 'v' was really a 'u.' She entered 'ipsius' and got a result: himself.

"Himself?" she said.

Julia closed the browser. 'Himself' hardly seemed like a combination to a lockbox containing a book of secrets. She didn't even know what it meant, except that Tintoretto painted himself. Was that supposed to be funny? A Renaissance joke?

Plus, it was one word for four sides. Or did they need to figure out a single side to try?

Her original thinking had to be right. 'The painter's face' must've been the clue to something with an actual keyhole. And that could've been anything.

With a dead-end on the key, Julia's mind drifted to Carlo. She'd tell him and Fosca about IPSIVS in the morning, but other thoughts lingered. Obviously della Porta wanted to get Carlo away from her. What were they planning to do to her? Kidnapping? Intimidation? Outright murder? Shivering, she pulled the blanket up to her chin and gripped the edges. Now she was afraid to ever return to Venice. And how did they convince

Carlo to go on a sudden pseudo-business trip, especially by train? What was his role in the Order that the head of another chapter would want to meet him? Carlo had a relationship with della Porta, but didn't he just join the Order?

Figuring Fosca would be awake, Julia typed out a text: *'Why is it so important Carlo goes to Madrid?'*

The reply came seconds later: *'New Painter biz.'* Followed by: *'He couldn't say no.'* Followed by a dozen random emojis, each on its own line.

Julia gave her phone a sideways look. An increasingly familiar grumble in her gut rolled a wad of bile into the back of her throat. *It couldn't be.* A dry swallow forced the acid down. She needed to maintain control. It was as if she knew the answer—an answer she'd known all along—but had been repressing it, just as she'd done with Nick so many times. She scrolled up past the emojis and re-read the text to confirm she read it right. After typing and deleting three different replies, she finally got her wording right and texted back: *'What biz? He didn't mention a show. And why capitalize painter?'*

The reply came a second later: *'Sorry, typo.'*

'Don't BS me. I want the truth.'

The lack of response lasted forever. They entered a tunnel that felt like a hundred miles long. The higher-pitch echo of the train against the tunnel walls bored into her head, like a teapot ready to explode. Finally, they exited. A moment later, her Wi-Fi reconnected, and Fosca's text appeared.

'Ask him.'

"Oh, you've gotta be fucking shitting me," she yelled, half-hoping it would wake Carlo. She leaned out of her berth and glowered up at him. It didn't. She pulled herself onto her back and stared at her phone, balling her fist and wincing at the knot tightening in her chest. The growl in her gut burst into a tidal wave of nausea. Everything snapped into place. She'd been so preoccupied with Nick, the Order, the damned key, the book, and Fosca, that she didn't see what was right under her nose. Once again, hiding in plain sight—why the Order was so tied to Carlo; why he was prominent enough to be sent to Madrid; how he got the souls' memories; how he could suddenly speak every language without an accent; why the souls *weren't free.*

Carlo was their new Painter.

It explained everything. He was an artist and practically della Porta's son.

Errrgh. She thought back to her conversation with Carlo at that outdoor restaurant—her first real meal after leaving the hospital. Carlo said her husband was crazy and thought he was their new Painter. Nick was right all along. Why didn't he tell her? To protect her?

She didn't think Carlo had any malicious intent; that just didn't make sense, but anger boiled within her. How could he keep this from her? She wanted to shake him awake. She also didn't want to be on the same train or anywhere near him if it were true.

They were scheduled to arrive in Madrid in the morning after a brief stop in Barcelona. Knowing her whirring brain would throw thought after thought at her to prevent her from catching any sleep, she inserted her earbuds, found a meditation app, closed her eyes, and listened. Stress might kill her before the Order did. This was supposed to be a damn vacation.

"Is something wrong?" Carlo asked with a mouthful of bread and ham.

Julia put her coffee on the tray table and nibbled at her smoked salmon sandwich. Not surprisingly, she'd eaten as little as she slept the night before. Unable to answer or even look at her companion, she gazed out the window of the first-class passenger car. Now on the final leg of their trip, the futuristic high-speed AVE train thundered through the Spanish countryside toward Madrid. Julia longed to get away from Carlo, but with a two-and-a-half-hour journey on this train, they didn't have a private compartment. She was thankful the last leg was the shortest.

It felt like being on a plane. The ride was remarkably smooth at 192 miles per hour as they rolled past the Iberian mountains in the distance. The rugged landscape reminded Julia of the foothills bordering Los Angeles, which she saw once on a family trip to visit relatives when she was twelve.

She reclined in the leather seat and swung her attention beyond Carlo to the other passengers, a mix of businesspeople and older tourists. She'd noticed a bunch of young backpackers boarding the second-class car.

"Julia," Carlo attempted, "I asked if something is wrong."

"I'm just not hungry, Carlo." She checked the time on her phone. "We have about an hour. I'm gonna stretch my legs." She knew damn well she was acting as if something was wrong. Because it was. Very wrong. And who cared if she acted immature or let on that she was obviously pissed? Something that bothered her about Nick and her previous boyfriends was that they'd say Julia was playing a game when they fought, as if she expected the guy to know some unwritten, global rule that all women knew but never shared with their counterparts.

There weren't any rules; it wasn't a game. They'd talk it over soon enough—not trapped on a rolling can.

Walking through train car aisles only exacerbated her mood. The bar car was behind their passenger car and in the opposite direction of movement. A fitting metaphor for her life.

As the train rolled into Madrid Atocha railway station an hour later, Julia's temperament hadn't brightened. She'd hoped arriving in Spain would lift her heart, but every time she glimpsed Carlo, she wanted to scream.

She finally had the chance in the concourse of the original section of the station. After disembarking, without knowing where she was headed, Julia wheeled her carry-on through the modern half of Atocha. Carlo followed. She stopped and gasped upon reaching the old part. The station was gorgeous and felt like an atrium with a curved, hundred-foot-high, glass-and-steel ceiling, which housed a walkthrough tropical garden brimming with palm trees and other lush foliage. The station was a tourist attraction in its own right and harkened back to the golden age of rail travel, but she was in no mood to enjoy it.

"Julia. . ." he said, but she turned away and walked into the botanical garden. Compared to the past two weeks of her life—treeless Venice, swimming through sewers, and riding on trains—being immersed in nature, even indoors surrounded by the noise of the station, invigorated her depleted core.

Part of her wanted to go straight to the airport and fly home. But Nick.

She needed to save him. She'd been considering if she required Carlo for that, and with a resounding *almost definitely*, she closed her eyes and guzzled the oxygen and pungent fragrances surrounding her.

When she opened her eyes, she found Carlo backdropped by banana leaves, looking like a sad puppy who'd chewed up the entire couch.

"When were you going to tell me, Carlo?"

He cocked his head. "Tell you what?"

"Don't do that. Please. Just don't. We're both adults, right?"

"Julia—"

"Are you an adult? A living male adult? Or a puppet? Answer."

A dark cloud crossed his face. "I'm an adult. I'm my own man."

"Good. Because I wanted to make sure that this was *your* decision. When were you going to tell me that you're the Order's Painter?"

Carlo's expression softened, but he didn't act surprised or defensive. He'd obviously been thinking about the cause of her anger. And he'd crafted a response because instead of denying it, he said, "I didn't want you to think you couldn't trust me."

"You thought lying to me was the best way to get me to trust you?" Julia screamed. She wanted to punch him. "Are you kidding?"

"It wasn't something I planned. It happened. I didn't want it to happen. Then you left, you came back, and everything else—"

"Were you ever going to tell me?"

"Of course."

An Asian family of four strolled past them along the path, steering clear of the arguing couple upsetting the scene's beauty.

"When?" Julia asked.

"When the time was right. I don't know. I'm sorry. You're right. It was stupid, and *not* telling you was the opposite of getting you to trust me. But you *can*, Julia. You can trust me." Tears welled in his eyes.

She wanted to believe him.

"This is a major breach of trust. I really don't know how I can move past it. Did you tell Fosca not to tell me?"

"No. She didn't know I didn't tell you. It was just luck it didn't come up."

Julia threw him a withering look. She needed him. Badly. He was the real key to getting Nick back. "You know, I could've had different ideas if I knew you were the Painter."

"Like what?"

"You're not just some low-level schmo. You have access. Access to all the Order's damn books and records. We could prove their crimes."

"I've been Painter less than two weeks. The total time I've been in the Order." He shrugged and shook his head. "Can you forgive me?"

"Hell no." She headed off toward the garden exit.

Carlo caught up and followed her through the concourse, staying a stride behind.

"But it doesn't mean we can't work together," Julia said, loud enough for him to hear over the bustle. She reached the station's glass doors and exited into the bright Spanish sun. Travelers filed in and out. Julia leveled her gaze at Carlo. "But I also need to know you won't lie to me again."

"I won't," he said without looking at her.

Nick had taught her the art of persuasive questioning their senior year when she confronted a sorority sister about embezzling a hundred bucks. Julia had no idea which sister stole the money, but she pressed every single one until the culprit cracked. 'That's the trick,' Nick had said. 'Don't let up.' God, she missed him. Julia didn't know if Carlo was lying about anything else. But if he was, she wanted to find out *now*. She stopped in her tracks.

"Why are you still lying?"

"I'm not," he said, "I'm the Painter. That's it. I'll tell you everything."

"Then do it. Tell me. Everything." She wished she'd taken some sort of class on interrogation techniques to know if she was headed in the right direction. But she remembered Nick's advice: if she pressed, she'd get an answer at some point.

"There's nothing—"

"Don't lie to me. You know. I know. So just tell me."

She leaned against the building's brick façade.

"Julia—"

"I can wait all day long, Carlo. I don't have any plans."

He lowered his chin and slouched. She didn't need to take a course in interrogation techniques. Nick was absolutely right. Just don't let up. It happened quicker than she'd expected, but she guessed it was because Carlo already felt guilty.

"I don't want to talk about this here," he said.

"Talk about what?"

A taxi dropped off a middle-aged couple who retrieved their luggage from the car's trunk and headed in.

"Let's go to the hotel. We can talk there."

The stalling tactic was beyond obvious, but so was the truth—he was hiding something else, and she refused to give him an inch. "No way are we going to the hotel until you tell me the truth."

"Okay." He pulled out his phone and tapped on it. "Let's go to this park. It's a short walk from here."

Another taxi honked its horn as it pulled up behind the first one.

Knowing a quieter place would be better, she walked away without a word. They followed Google Maps in silence for the fifteen-minute walk to Parque del Retiro where they sat on a wood-slatted bench that conveniently had an armrest in the middle, affording them each a half. Not far away, three teenagers played guitar and bongos as they sang. The music was an eclectic blend of angry Spanish folk and rock, which she found refreshing and fit the tone of their conversation. When Julia and Carlo had passed the band, she tossed a few euro coins in the open guitar case, amused at the band's name, The Spliffs, and their sign: "Need money for American Idle." She wasn't sure if the misspelling was intentional, but it worked either way.

Carlo lit a cigarette.

"Seriously, Carlo. It's the most repulsive habit." She hacked a cough to drive her point across. He ignored her. "You've had time to think about what you want to tell me. Out with it."

He blew a cloud of smoke away from her face. "I don't know how to say this, Julia."

The band wrapped their song and launched into a punk-folk version of the Beach Boys' *Sloop John B.*, which Julia hadn't heard since she was ten, in her summer camp choir.

"Just say it," she said. "It doesn't matter how you say it. Just say it."

"Nick..."

Julia's heart skipped a beat. For whatever reason, she expected Carlo's lie to be about the Order or della Porta or even that he was banging Fosca. But about Nick? It hadn't crossed her mind. Was there more when Nick assaulted della Porta or killed Tintoretto? She blanched. Did he kill someone else?

"Nick what?" she asked.

Carlo stared at the dirt path. "He's in the Palazzo," he said in a nearly inaudible whisper.

Maggie Yorn *was* right. "Well, I kind of knew that was a strong possibility."

"Sì, but..."

"But *what*?"

"He begged me, Julia. Angelo..."

"Begged you for *what*?"

He took another drag and released it through his nose and mouth simultaneously, making him look like a broken smokestack. He flicked the butt away into the dirt path. "Nick... Angelo... he's..." Carlo buried his head in his hands. He tried to hide it, but he was crying. "I'm so sorry, Julia. He's in a painting."

Julia stared open-mouthed at Carlo. At first, her brain didn't process his words. She rewound his speech—its cadence and speed and the breathy way his words left his lips like it was smoke from his cigarette. She rewound the teenagers' music and a distant whistle near the street and the low chatter of two squirrels chasing each other. She rewound it all, heard it again and again, and still heard nothing correctly.

Replaying the last week and a half in her head backward, her mind stopped on her time in the hospital—when she was in a coma. The timing fit, but the betrayal didn't. It was one thing for Carlo to hide he was the Order's Painter. Not revealing they'd killed Nick and sentenced him to *Paradise* was treachery in another stratosphere.

Carlo had yet to look at her. He sat there, crying with his head in his hands. But it couldn't be true. She saved him. He saved her. He saved Nick. Hell, if it weren't for Carlo, Julia and Nick may not have ever walked out of that torture room alive. How could he do such a thing? Finally, she moistened her lips and spoke.

"Carlo, look at me."

He sniffed and peered over with one eye.

"Fuck Angelo. You're saying Nick... Nick's in *Paradise*?"

"No."

All her stress emptied from her body like a deflating pressure cooker.

"He's in a *new* painting," Carlo muttered. He reached for her hands, but she whipped them away.

The reprieve she felt seconds prior evaporated, vanished as if it had never been there. Her lungs filled again, this time with burning heat. Her respiration increased beyond her control. She gripped the bench arm.

The music stopped.

"What the fuck are you talking about? A new painting?"

"I did it for you. He begged me, Julia." He reached for her again. She smacked his hands away and balled her fingers into a fist, her fingernails cutting into her palm.

"You're saying you fucking murdered him!"

"He was Angelo. He wanted to kill you!"

Her body convulsed with an earthquake of disbelief, anxiety, fear, and wrath. At that moment, the bench arm was the only thing in the world that gave her support. She squeezed the metal so tightly, she thought her fingers might melt through it.

"You're . . . saying," she managed between short spurts, "you . . . you *killed* him and painted his soul into a new painting? A brand-new painting?" Steaming blood rushed to her head. "He's all alone, not even with Isabella?"

Carlo nodded. He popped a cigarette into his mouth and lit it.

Julia wanted to curse him, scream her lungs out, rip his head off, scratch his eyes out. But in the end . . . in the end, she had nothing left to say. She'd never felt so consumed by fury and the intense need for a cathartic release.

"I saved your life," she said.

He gazed at her with puppy dog eyes . . . that belied a hint of smugness. "Then we're even."

She clocked him in the face. The cigarette went flying. She grabbed her carry-on and stormed away.

XLV

"Sì, SIGNORE." SILVIO NAVARRO'S PUDGY red cheeks graced della Porta's computer monitor. He spoke in Italian. "We'll continue running stories about O'Connor."

"The court of public opinion will find him guilty," della Porta said. Until he planted Nick O'Connor's body—and he needed time for the presumed decomposition to match the body's state in the event of an autopsy—della Porta needed the media to assume the countess was dead and cast the American troublemaker as the world's most wanted man, even if Interpol hadn't formally charged him. "In a short time, MediaStatuto has been extremely effective, my friend."

"Grazie. The credit is all to my staff."

"Your staff is a reflection of its leadership."

Navarro smiled his thanks and checked his notes. "We can run the piece on your philanthropic activities in next Sunday's paper. We'll set up a time for photos and schedule corresponding media after the article is published. Morning shows, podcasts, and the like. I'll have Caterina send you the schedule."

"Excellent." Della Porta leaned back in his desk chair. He glanced about his spacious office. The room and, in particular, sitting behind his large oak desk always empowered him. Now, more than ever, he reveled in the sense of *control*.

"I have a hard stop now, but tell Caterina to reach out to my assistant to schedule a dinner, as well. I want to speak to you about a strategy for another campaign."

"What's that, signore?" Navarro perked his eyebrows.

Postponing his next call to explain everything about Veritism on the spot tempted Della Porta, but for all of Navarro's honor, he couldn't risk the CEO of a communications company leaking his plan too soon, not even to his staff. No, they needed to strategize, and that required an in-person meeting. Navarro also needed to be reminded of the critical nature of discretion.

"We'll discuss it over dinner," della Porta said. "Let's just say you'll be a modern-day St. Paul the Apostle."

Navarro's eyes lit up, and his rosy complexion brightened even more in the glow of his computer screen. As they said their goodbyes and ended the call, the media mogul appeared more jovial than ever.

His expression was contagious. Della Porta didn't want to admit it to himself, but without his usual distractions, he was able to accomplish more than he had in what seemed like years. He felt like an efficiency machine. He didn't want Carlo gone; no, he wanted him there by his side, working with him. But as long as Carlo remained obsessed with Julia O'Connor, he wouldn't be able to focus. That she joined him turned out to be a silver lining—another problem della Porta didn't need to deal with. He had informed Vasquez about it, and the Spanish Exalted Master said he'd do what he could to keep them separated.

In Carlo's absence, in two days, besides moving forward on the press front, he'd recruited an additional ten Protectors, and Lacasse and Bernardo's team had finished their interviews with the leading Scalfinis and a dozen Uccellos. To show the Order meant to align themselves with people and win their favor, rather than risk alienation with heavy-handed threats, della Porta dipped into the Order's funds and absolved many members of both families of their debt—and sins. It didn't matter that none had yielded useful information that could lead to the book's whereabouts; the investments would pay off with their loyalty. He had also approved the purchase of the Scalfinis' marriage chest. The *cassone* had been in the family for centuries. Though della Porta was convinced a Bird Brother found the doge's book and it stayed within the Uccello family, he wanted no stone left unturned. The Scalfini *cassone*, or its exterior design, might contain something useful.

Della Porta hadn't only been productive with Order business, but that of the Palazzo, as well. Since sending Manuel away on Friday night and Carlo Saturday morning, della Porta had taken the weekend to catch up on a snowballing pile of work. He had arrived this Monday morning, fresh and early. Attendance had picked up, and with tourism back to pre-pandemic numbers, he had big plans for the museum. The exhibition about the relationship between Venice and the world of Islam was opening soon and, by all accounts, would be a major success. He finished his prep for a later marketing meeting minutes before his 9:00 with Bernardo regarding an update on the Uccello descendants. Dante was scheduled to arrive with the Scalfini marriage chest fifteen minutes later. That meeting needed to be quick, as he had a flight to catch.

Bernardo opened the door. Uncharacteristically, he didn't knock. He stared at his mobile with a somber look. "I have unsettling news," he said.

Della Porta closed his Outlook calendar and turned his attention to his distraught friend. "What is it?"

"What's what?" Fosca asked, strolling in behind Bernardo with a spring in her step.

Della Porta's shoulders sank. Other than speaking in English, Fosca was disturbingly similar to her grandmother. Though his conversation with Bernardo wasn't confidential, he didn't appreciate a surprise visitor.

"Good morning, Fosca," he said in English. "What can we do for you?"

"Just here for an update," she said.

"On?" della Porta asked.

Fosca's lips parted to answer, but she noticed Bernardo's despondent countenance. "Are you okay?"

With a sigh that would sap the joy from a child's first birthday, Bernardo took a seat on the couch and motioned for Fosca to sit. She chose a side chair.

"Fosca," Bernardo said, "I don't think you know him, but the news is disturbing, nonetheless. One of our Protectors was found dead this morning."

Perfect timing, della Porta thought. He only had to feign surprise and distress, and he'd have two witnesses. He straightened and widened his eyes. "What? Who?"

"Manuel."

Fosca gasped and covered her mouth in alarm.

"Did you know him?" Bernardo asked.

"No . . . no, does it matter? That's horrible."

"Manuel?" della Porta exclaimed, almost yelling a tad too loudly. "But he was just here."

"He was?" Bernardo asked.

"Not this morning, of course. What happened? Is his family okay?"

"Yes, they're fine."

"Thank God," Fosca said.

Bernardo continued. "He was found at the Cantiere Shipyard. The police aren't sure what happened, but it looks like he slipped. Maybe hit his head and drowned in the high water."

Della Porta shuddered, as if he couldn't comprehend the situation. "What was he doing in the shipyard?"

They continued speaking about the event until a knock rapped on his door. Della Porta was grateful for the subsequent meeting. Nothing in Bernardo's news about Manuel or the police's initial findings produced anything that would implicate della Porta. He turned his head toward the door, shielding his grin from his guests' view.

"Coming, Dante," he called. He hustled over and opened the door for the burly Protector who carried the marriage chest by its two iron side handles. Though he had a pronounced scabbed-over cut on his disfigured nose, the bandage was off, which pleased della Porta. Physical reminders of the damage Nick O'Connor had caused abated day by day. Scars would remain, but new skin would grow.

As Dante placed the chest on the floor in the center of the office, della Porta marveled at the piece.

"What is that?" Fosca asked.

"A cassone," della Porta replied brightly.

"Cassone? I've heard that word. There's one in a guest room in our Lake Como house. It's a dowry chest, right?"

"Precisely. This one belonged to Renzo and Isabella Scalfini, presumably given by Isabella's father."

Except for some faded crimson stains on the top, it had survived the years in excellent condition. A tad longer than a meter, the hand-carved chest appeared to be made of walnut. Mounted on lions' paws, the top of the chest reached his knees. The entire box had a marvelous antique patina, with a depiction of a forest and loggers carved on one side and a shipping scene on the other, ostensibly illustrating the marriage of Renzo and Isabella's families' businesses. On all four corners were two winged lions, Venice's ubiquitous state symbol, facing each other.

"Why is it here?" Fosca asked.

"Because, my dear, I wanted it. One of their descendants was kind enough to part with it for a sizable fee and admission into the Order."

"Why do you want it?"

Della Porta caught a glimpse of concern in Fosca's eyes. He noted the expression, then turned to Dante, purposefully ignoring the nosy girl's question. She knew about his search for the book, so it wasn't a secret, but it was refreshing to not have to bow to a Baldesseri.

"The key, Dante."

"The Scalfini woman couldn't find it," Dante answered in Italian, "but said it hasn't been opened in at least twenty years. She couldn't recall what was in it but didn't think there was anything valuable. I figured we'd need this."

Dante removed a tool that looked like a two-headed ice pick. Della Porta had used this type of pick many times to open antique boxes acquired by the museum. He took it from Dante and went to work, careful not to damage the lock's exterior. In under thirty seconds, he had it unlocked.

The top of the chest creaked open as he lifted it. Della Porta removed a garish technicolor quilted blanket that screamed nineteen-seventies. Beneath it were contents more disappointing than he'd imagined: a young Tom Cruise in a flight jacket stared at him with a most determined expression. The whole chest was filled with stacks of various VHS tapes. He picked up *Top Gun: Idolos del Aire* and pulled out the cassette, but that's all it was. He tossed it back in.

Fosca cracked up. "Maybe you can sell the lot on eBay."

Della Porta joined her. "You have a sense of humor, Fosca, much like your grandmother."

"We can cancel the transfer," Bernardo said.

"No, no, we'll honor the transaction. All is not lost. Have your men look through all these tapes. Maybe there's something hidden in the boxes. Or even a family movie in which they mention their history. And see if they can discern anything from the carvings besides the family business lines." Della Porta ran his finger along the box, from a winged lion to a tree carving. "It's a beautiful piece. We can display it in the Museo Correr. It would be a nice addition to a craft guild room." His finger stopped on another lion; he recalled the box belonged to Isabella and mused on the sentimental value it must hold for some people. "On second thought," he looked at Fosca but spoke to Bernardo. "Put it in storage. With the paintings. Near a particular piece. You know the one."

The countess's granddaughter returned a tight smile—a little *too* tight.

1614

THE SACK WAS YANKED OFF HIS HEAD, the unrefined water reed fibers scraping his cheeks like a rusty shaving *novacila*. Faint moonlight from the two small windows embedded high in the stone wall dimly lit the room, but Quattrone knew precisely where he was. After all, he'd sat on the other side of the table in the Chamber of Torment countless times. He knew the chill and humidity of this room as though it were a second home. But he had never been on his knees in the center of the chamber, barefoot on the cold stone. As a one-time Lord of the Night, he'd passed judgment on many a soul before the Ancient Order of the Seventh Sun was established. As the Order's first Exalted Master, he'd drafted the proceedings and watched dozens from the wooden mezzanine.

And he was all too familiar with the rope hanging from the pulley above him.

Three men sat at a large oak table in front of him. Before each stood a white candle. Behind each candle, a concave mirror reflected the light onto the prisoner: him. He knew each of the present Lords of the Night well. He had dined and drunk with all three, gone to their sons' baptisms and confirmations. Their betrayal ignited his blood.

"Senator Marco Quattrone," said the Lord of the Night in the middle, also known as the Inquisitor, a designation Quattrone, himself, wrote.

"We've broken bread together, Antonio." Quattrone seethed. "We all have," he said to the other two.

"You shall use the proper form of address, Senator." The Inquisitor's once-liquid voice was dry and lacked projection, as if he hadn't imbibed for a week and spoke covering his mouth.

The urge to slap these charlatan zealots filled Quattrone. If only his hands were free. "Then address me as your Exalted Master." He enunciated the words slowly, glowering at each man.

The Inquisitor cleared his throat. "Do you know why you're here, Senator?"

"I presume it's because I've been betrayed by my brethren." He called to the mezzanine. "Which of you will be down here next?" Craning his neck to see, his stomach dropped. The mezzanine was empty. Knowing this was a surreptitious judgment, pure treachery, caused his fury to fulminate. He brought his attention back to the Lords of the Night. "I am your Exalted Master. If it were not for me, there'd be no Order."

"You are no longer exalted and master now of nothing but for how long you wish to endure this trial."

Quattrone guffawed and spat on the floor. "Trial?"

The Inquisitor remained apathetic. "You thought you could be the Exalted Master of Europe? Of the world?" he said. "Installing new Painters? That is not what the Order is."

"That is what we *should* be." These people had no vision.

"You spoke of bringing our secrets to the New World," said the Lord to the Inquisitor's left, his sonorous voice menacing.

"A land of gold and riches we could've owned—could *still* own," Quattrone said. "Which you'll never have because you fail to seize opportunities right before you. Just like you fail to advance this ceremony. A ceremony I wrote. Tie the damned rope around my hands. Ask my questions. Pass judgment. If I'm master of the length of this tribunal, then stop wasting my time."

"You should cherish every corporeal moment your heart is beating. As you wish." The Inquisitor nodded.

Quattrone shifted his throbbing knees. He regretted that last statement. An eternity in *Paradiso* brought a new understanding of time.

The hooded man behind him, whom Quattrone had also appointed, did not tie the rope behind his prisoner's back but instead stepped in front of him and took his hands. He slipped a device over his fingers that

Quattrone had refused to use on prisoners, for he felt it too brutal. Thumbscrews. When Quattrone was twenty-five, some forty-odd years prior, he had used the tool on Ottoman Turks taken captive in the Battle of Lepanto. Though his commanding officer preferred the torture device, Quattrone doubted its efficacy. Prisoners would utter anything—true or not—to halt the pain.

He shifted again. The hooded man twisted the screws until the bolts pressed against his flesh.

"To what purpose do you torture me?" Quattrone said. "You know everything I know."

"Where is the book?" the Inquisitor asked.

"You play more games than my grandson, Antonio. You know the location of every Order book."

"The *doge's* book," the Inquisitor said. "The book the Church wants. You know the one."

Quattrone laughed. "*That's* what this is about?"

"This is about your abuse of power. Tell us the location of the book, and we may be lenient."

The Inquisitor gestured at the hooded man. It was futile asking him to stop. The man was chosen for his sadism and inability to disobey the Inquisitor's command once given. Quattrone clenched his teeth in expectation of the agony to come.

It was worse than he imagined.

The hooded man twisted screws on both hands. Clamps tightened on his fingers, and bolts pierced his flesh and crunched his thumb bones. Blood gurgled from his digits and warmed his hands beneath the iron vises. The hooded man paused, fully aware that leaving the screws in the breach position was as excruciating as breaking off the fingers—if not more so.

Pain hastened from Quattrone's hands through his body to his head. Hot sweat seeped from his pores, made worse by the cold conditions of the room. "I haven't a clue where that book is," he shouted.

"You gave it to the Minister of Finance, who then gave it to Renzo Scalfini."

"That was twenty-five years ago," he yelled, his muscles constricting. "Nobody has seen it since. And nobody knows its whereabouts."

"You needn't remind us of your failures, Senator. You allowed Pietro Stefanetti, Isabella Scalfini's fraternal uncle no less, a founder of the Guild of Silvanus, to infiltrate our ranks undetected."

"A nobleman and Order member. He took his own life." Quattrone emitted a solemn exhale at the reminder of the event.

The Inquisitor raised his voice. "A cowardly act, only to evade persecution when he aided Angelo Mascari's evasion. The man who was tasked to seek the very book we discuss. On your watch."

"Mascari never found it."

"Or so you say." The Inquisitor nodded again. The hooded man returned the gesture and twisted the thumbscrews another turn.

Quattrone screamed. He was wrong. As the screws dug deeper, the pain magnified. It was unbearable. His eyes clouded. Snot dripped from his nose.

Standing strong to these traitors was pointless, but so was torturing him; he truly hadn't a clue as to the book's location. Knowing his fate, he spat on the stone floor, blood-stained from countless victims before him—victims whose sentences he presided over. "Paint me into *Paradiso*. I'm ready. Ready to watch my betrayers."

"Do not fret. You shall have a prominent spot, but you won't be watching us. And you won't be alone for long."

Quattrone swallowed dryly and arched an eyebrow. "Reveal the purpose of your words."

"You'll be pleased to know we have discussed your scheme. We do not believe any one man should have the totalitarian power you seek, but your new Painters shall have work. As will new Exalted Masters, divided equally."

The Lords of the Night spoke in unison, "Ghe sè, sò quà."

XLVII

CARS ZIPPED BY AND BLEW THEIR HORNS in the landlocked metropolis twelve times the size of Venice, three-hundred-fifty kilometers to the nearest sea. Carlo wondered if he'd been teleported to another planet. Coupled with his flashback to Quattrone's torture—which thankfully happened while he sat in the park—he had trouble adjusting to the present day. Though the memory disturbed him and a ghost pain lingered in his thumbs, learning about the Order's early days and their quest for the doge's book was remarkable. It was also the longest memory Carlo had of someone in *Paradiso*. Everything about that moment was clear, even the date, but it ended abruptly. He supposed there wasn't more to tell.

His argument with Julia—if he could call it that—also occupied his mind and transported his head from another planet to a different plane of existence.

After she left him, he sat on the park bench, contemplating the events that transpired, with the teenage band providing a raucous soundtrack to his thoughts. Following the flashback, he walked the streets in a daze, half-conscious of the Google Map lady's robotic directions, though he paid scant attention. Unused to automobiles, Carlo ambled straight into traffic three times, nearly getting killed, and endured a salvo of insults in Spanish, which he wished he didn't understand.

He pined to call Julia but knew she wouldn't answer if he tried. She needed time and space. More importantly, Carlo had no idea how or why she'd ever forgive him. He had said the wrong thing. He had said *lots* of wrong things. The worst offense was claiming they were even. He'd save her every day of his life if he had to. He shook his head at his stupidity. If only he could punch his own face so hard, he'd knock himself back in time.

Strolling tree-lined, wide sidewalks, he found his hotel, which he discovered should've been a ten-minute walk from the park. On the edge of a circular plaza, the Mandarin Oriental Ritz was the most luxurious hotel Carlo had ever stayed in. He found such elegant style of décor to be ostentatious, but he had to admit, the lavish rotunda lobby, with its gleaming red marble floor and pillars, gave him the impression he'd be staying overnight in something akin to the Palazzo Ducale itself. But Carlo had neither the inspiration nor the time to enjoy the venue.

He dropped his overnight bag on the white-blanketed bed and went straight to the recently renovated bathroom to brush his teeth. Five minutes later, he left again to make his 11:00 appointment with Vasquez at the Museo Nacional Thyssen-Bornemisza.

At first, Carlo had wanted to take his mind off Julia by attending the meeting, but as he considered his situation, he realized that sticking to the original plan was the way to win her favor. Returning the Order to good was the right move, but it was just one step. He was still unsure where della Porta fit, but Carlo's admission to Julia of his own crime had him thinking. Had he repeated the past? Did della Porta do to his father what Carlo had done to Nick? His fight with Julia pried his eyes open. She and Fosca were convinced della Porta was the most corrupt of all. That was up for debate, but Carlo realized he had a way to find the answer. If he returned the Order to good, in due course, he'd learn della Porta's true nature.

Once he accomplished those tasks, maybe, just maybe, he'd learn of a way to reinstate Nick's body with his soul, or at the least, he could free his friend's spirit and allow it to ascend to Heaven. If it were possible to extract a human's soul and put it into a painting, then presumably it was possible to take it out. And Julia would see he'd do anything for her. But to enact any part of his plan, he needed to entrench himself within the Order. He'd meet Vasquez and anybody else in Spain, get in their good graces, and return to della Porta a shining star. He'd regroup with Fosca, and they'd figure out how to open the box and obtain the book. Then, he'd strike when the time was right.

After Carlo sprinted across the main boulevard between his hotel and a park adjacent to the museum, he slapped his cheeks a few times to wake himself up and realized he hadn't had any coffee. A cup purchased from a kiosk in front of the museum, along with half a cigarette, injected him with some energy. He took the time to absorb the beauty of a new city under the warming Spanish sun, before entering the museum grounds through a gate. The Thyssen-Bornemisza bordered a grassy courtyard almost as large as Piazza San Marco, complete with benches and palm trees, which didn't seem to fit the character of the art inside, unless it was filled with Gaugins. The Thyssen's red-brick neoclassical main building buttressed a modern white concrete-and-glass wing. Each was a stark contrast to the Palazzo Ducale.

Though the original three-story structure dated from the 18th century and was a former palace of the Duke of Villahermosa, the Spanish government had purchased Europe's largest private art collection from the Thyssen-Bornemisza family and opened the museum in 1992.

Given that Tintoretto's study for *Paradiso* was owned by the family, Carlo assumed they were prominent members of the Order. Like the Palazzo Ducale in Venice, the museum was public, so he also figured influential politicians in Spain held high positions in the Order's Madrid chapter.

He thought back to his art history classes at the Accademia. Before Tintoretto painted *Paradiso* in the Palazzo, the Council of Ten held a competition to replace Guariento's fresco that had been destroyed in a fire. Tintoretto painted two sketches, both huge in their own right, which he presented to the judges. Veronese had been awarded the commission, but he died before the work began, so the honor was granted to Tintoretto.

Or so the story goes.

Carlo deliberated where the paintings were originally when they were used exclusively by the Order. The first study was now at the Louvre. Curiously, he hadn't learned who the French Painter was. Carlo marveled at the thought. It could be anybody.

From a bird's eye view, the Thyssen buildings looked like a Picasso-drawn horse, with a fat trapezoidal body that contained most of the artwork connected to a smaller trapezoidal head, linked by a neck-like hallway.

Besides the building's modernization, Carlo had salivated at the collection. On the train, he had ample time to check out the museum's website. Though a handful of museums in Venice had modern collections, Carlo always felt it was one of the drawbacks of living in a city steeped in history. The Thyssen, on the other hand, contained a comprehensive survey of Western art, with everything from European Renaissance masters to modern art pioneers to surrealism and living artists. And not just European art, but North American works, too. As expected, the museum presented a heavy dose of Spanish masters, including Picasso, Dali, and, of course, El Greco.

The entrance hall had a twenty-meter-high ceiling and sky lights that lit peach-colored walls, which Carlo found abhorrent and clashing with the spectacular masterpieces. Though he did like the open feel of the space, and potted floor plants imbued the art with life. He shook his head at the dramatic differences between Madrid and Venice.

He regretted asking where the offices were before he had the chance to check out some art. A docent guided Carlo through the neck of the building to the horse's head, so he only caught a glimpse of *Paradiso*, proudly presented at the far end of the entrance hall, as if the museum's centerpiece itself—hiding in plain sight. He figured he'd see *Paradiso* with Vasquez, so he didn't mind skipping it. And he planned on coming back and spending more time with the entire collection.

"Good morning. I have an appointment with José Vasquez," Carlo said to the bookishly pretty receptionist in the corporate wing. He spoke in English, though in the hotel, he realized he could speak fluent Spanish. He had studied it a bit in school, met numerous Spanish tourists, and it was similar enough to Italian, but the new gift could be explained by one possibility—someone in the Palazzo's *Paradiso* was Spanish. Knowing Vasquez's dislike for him, Carlo tucked that card up his sleeve.

The receptionist checked the register and Carlo's identification, then led him through glass doors and down a corridor. Carlo tucked in his black button-down shirt and straightened the collar. Unsure of what would constitute an appropriate outfit for this meeting, in addition to the shirt, he chose fitted black jeans and his black leather Converse All Stars. It was early, and he had plenty of time to change before dinner, if need be.

They passed various cubicles, arriving at an office with a large glass wall. Inside, Vasquez worked at his computer. Knocking on the door and opening it simultaneously, the receptionist let Carlo in.

"Carlo, come in," said Vasquez in English, without looking up from his monitor.

"Nice to meet you in person, Señor Vasquez." Carlo moved for one of the guest chairs.

"Don't sit."

Vasquez stood and exited his office without offering his hand to Carlo. Though the action seemed a bit rude, he'd noticed that since the coronavirus pandemic, people had stopped shaking hands as much as they used to. It felt unnecessarily cold—though perhaps unsurprising.

As he followed Vasquez into a stairwell, the man's tan suit blending in with the walls, they engaged in small talk about the train ride and his hotel. They reached the second floor and emerged on a wide, outdoor terrace with a high, slatted metal pergola that offered some shelter from the sun, which seemed to have dialed itself up to eleven since Carlo was last outside.

"Our terraces," said Vasquez, leading Carlo to a tiered floor that matched the angle of the pergola above them, whose curvature gave the impression that the metal cascaded down over them in a wave. Since there were different pergolas aimed inward and outward of the museum, it made Carlo feel as though he were lost in a metallic ocean storm.

On each tier was a single low row of couches along with small tables. Vasquez brought Carlo to the lowest one, overlooking the courtyard.

"We reserve this section for parties, cocktail hours, and the like. Inside is so confining. I need to breathe the outdoors. I try to find a moment every day to come here or take a walk in the park."

Carlo peered over the edge at the tourists milling about the palm trees. Suppressing his envy at the serene work environment, he took a seat next to Vasquez, who removed a cigar from his inner jacket pocket.

"You have a beautiful museum, Señor Vasquez—"

"Enough with the señor this, señor that." He lit his cigar with a flick of his plain silver Zippo and took a few puffs. "We're here to get to know each other. I'm José, you're Carlo, sí?"

"Sí," Carlo said. Perhaps this wouldn't be as uncomfortable as he'd expected. He was glad to see Vasquez smoked. Without asking, Carlo removed a pack of cigarettes from his pocket and tapped one out.

"Would you like a cigar?" asked Vasquez.

Carlo despised cigars, always thinking them too heavy and old-fashioned, as if whoever smoked them did so because they had something to prove. "If we're celebrating something."

Vasquez threw back his head with a hoot, revealing laugh lines Carlo hadn't noticed on della Porta's monitors. "That attitude won't get you anywhere in life. The finer things should be enjoyed whenever you want them. Cigars, wine, food, clothes. Even if you can't afford them. You know why?"

Carlo shrugged. "Because they're better?"

"That's a simple part of it. It's because if you always live a hair above your means, it forces you to work harder. To make that money. These Cohibas are twenty-two euros apiece. Now, you should also never go into debt. You need to amass wealth. That's how gamblers walk away successful. Put your winnings in one pocket, work hard for the money in the other. And besides, we *are* celebrating something."

Vasquez pulled another cigar from his pocket, handed it to Carlo, and lit it for him with a flick of his wrist. Carlo noticed the difference with a few puffs. He'd had Cubans before, but never one that tasted like fresh tobacco. Enjoying the flavor, he tipped his head in thanks to Vasquez. He liked this man's style.

"I'll tell you, José, I'm envious your collection has so much modern art."

"One of the best mid-size museums in Europe, if not the best." Vasquez crossed his legs. "But you have the Guggenheim in Venice."

"True, but it's limited. And I'm in the Palazzo Ducale so much, sometimes I think I work there."

"You do now." Vasquez winked.

Carlo chuckled. "It's nice to see something fresh."

"So, in addition to your ADHD, della Porta picked an artist who doesn't like the classics?"

Carlo scoffed. Maybe it would be uncomfortable after all. He ignored the ADHD comment and took another drag. "I love the classics. But modern and contemporary, too. I get inspiration from everything. Pre-Renaissance to Tiepolo to Miró to John Park or Christina Angelina."

"Who?"

"American artists who are still alive. And to tell you the truth, I was hoping to see the *Paradiso* study."

A stocky waitress in her fifties walked over to the men with a tray holding two glasses of sangria, along with bowls of almonds and olives.

"It's more than a study, amigo. You'll see it tonight." Vasquez stroked his beard. He spoke freely in front of the waitress.

"Tonight?" Carlo asked, shocked Vasquez wouldn't pause the conversation until they were alone again.

Vasquez shook his head with dismay. "Did no one tell you? We have a ceremony tonight."

The waitress placed the drinks and snacks on the white plastic cubical table in front of them before leaving.

"A convocation?" Carlo asked.

"Not exactly. You'll see."

Carlo glanced about the space and lowered his voice. "Does El Greco . . . live here, in this museum, as Tintoretto lived in the Palazzo?"

"You don't need to worry about prying ears. All my staff are members of the Order. Of course he lives here. The building is far older than it looks."

"There is one thing I've been wondering," Carlo said before taking another puff. "Did El Greco paint all the souls in the study? When he was in Venice?"

Vasquez released a cloud of smoke. "All but the first. Our Painter studied Tintoretto's work in more ways than one. Tintoretto finished the original painting normally. He instructed El Greco by layering a soul on top of the image of a person already there. El Greco did the rest."

"He painted over it?"

"And ultimately added to it," said a man in English behind him. His voice sounded like a bow across the highest string on a cello. High-pitched, but with a coarseness to it that made it masculine. The stranger's register was an unsettling combination of reverence and dissatisfaction.

Carlo turned and found the voice's owner walking toward them with a pompous gait. He was a lanky man, at least a full head taller than Carlo but perhaps the same weight, with a gaunt face, thin goatee, and greasy black hair hanging over his shoulders. His all-black outfit was straight out of H&M's Navy SEAL section. Carlo felt a little bad passing judgment, but he'd met dozens of the type in art school—people who put too much effort into their appearance and, nine times out of ten, not nearly enough into their work.

"Carlo, meet Diego Blanco-Romasanta. El Lobo Blanco, as he's known."

"Everybody calls me Lobo. You must be Zuccaro," he said with a pale, outstretched hand.

Carlo shook it. "I am. Carlo."

Pushing the plates aside, Lobo sat on the table.

"Have a seat," said Vasquez with a mock gesture to the chair, scowling at the other artist.

Lobo selected an olive with a toothpick. He chewed on it as he eyeballed Carlo, then spat the pit over the side of the terrace.

"Do that again, Lobo," said Vasquez without a hint of mirth, "and you're following it."

Lobo flashed an insincere smirk. "My father basically owns this terrace."

The comment caught Carlo's ear. Was this a case of a spoiled rich kid with excessive privilege?

"A donation," Vasquez replied, "no matter how generous, does not imply ownership. Quite the opposite." He noticed Carlo's pondering gaze and continued speaking to Lobo. "And do not forget you're here because of your talent, no other reason. And while you do indeed have talent, also remember that it pales in comparison to the work hanging on our walls. I expect you to show humility and respect."

With a shrug, Lobo ignored Vasquez and turned to Carlo. "I know who you are. Carlo Zuccaro, up-and-coming artist of Venice. Mashes every style he can find, throws it in a blender, then pukes it on canvas, or"—he wiggled his fingers—"ooh la la, aluminum, and then you replaced one of the most glorious painters to ever walk on Earth. You've heard of me?"

Carlo had no idea who this guy was or why he was there. He shook his head.

"I'm your brother."

"My brother?" Carlo raised an eyebrow and turned to Vasquez.

"Surely, Carlo," said Vasquez, "della Porta told you. Our Painter is nearing his end. Lobo will replace him."

"Someday soon." Lobo cleaned his teeth with the toothpick, his gaze locked on Carlo. The oily Spanish artist then removed a small pad and charcoal pencil from his pocket and began sketching.

"Do I look like your model?" Carlo asked.

Lobo continued to draw feverishly. "For the next thirty seconds."

"Are you going to pay me before you try to fuck me?"

An unruly snort popped from the back of Vasquez's throat. Lobo ignored Carlo's quip and displayed his sketch a moment later.

The realist style wasn't bad, but it lacked creativity. Carlo couldn't believe Vasquez had a problem with *him*, but not this Lobo man-child with less-than-impressive skills. These two men made Carlo want to return the Order to a place of honor more than ever. But if he made a move in Madrid, and della Porta was indeed corrupt, he'd never get the chance. He might even be banished from Venice. No, he needed to earn the trust of these men and strike at the right time.

Attempting to diffuse the tension, Vasquez clapped his hands together. "Come, we have a long day ahead of us. And you boys need to be friends."

XLVIII

TWO PIGEONS SAT ON THE COBBLESTONES, enjoying the mid-afternoon sun, unbothered by noisy, oblivious tourists stepping inches from what would be a certain death. The larger one curled his beak into his mate's neck.

Sitting on a stone bench that encircled a streetlamp, Julia snapped her thirtieth picture of the birds. After leaving Carlo, she'd vacillated between fuming and weeping before she realized she was doing exactly what she promised herself she wouldn't do—be the victim. This thought awakened her to the fact that she was in a city she'd always wanted to visit. So, she forced herself to do something she loved when she had studied abroad in Paris—wander the streets and take photographs.

So much had happened since she and Nick arrived in Venice—from the highs of her photo in the Biennale and securing a show at Pierre Gold's gallery to the previously unfathomable lows of her husband taken over by a vengeful past life, to being kidnapped, tortured, and Nick essentially murdered by Carlo. She just needed to breathe and recharge her batteries. It was all so overwhelming. Her intent to stop della Porta and bring down the Order had only intensified with Carlo's revelation. This group—including her so-called friend—was evil to its core. But she needed a minute.

After thirty of them, she managed to stop crying. An hour later, she smiled at a series of street art murals that covered a block-long wall. Two hours after that, she was in her zone—

An endurable version of The Twilight Zone.

She found herself in Plaza Mayor, Madrid's huge main square, carrying a bag of tacos and an iced tea. She wasn't hungry but knew the carbs, protein, and caffeine would revive her mentally and physically. Eating tacos in Spain felt like eating a chili dog in Australia, but the shop was one of the few restaurants that hadn't closed for siesta. Not surprisingly, the tacos were unremarkable; for dinner, she'd treat herself to the best paella.

With a full stomach and satiated thirst, she relaxed on the bench in Plaza Mayor and soaked in the mundane scene. The pigeon couple was backdropped by tourists and buskers, and the plaza itself, which truly was a square. Enclosed by a four-story red building displaying hundreds of windows with white shutters, the plaza produced a disorienting symmetry that the piazzas of Venice lacked. In the center of the space stood a large marble pedestal topped by a bronze statue of a man on horseback. Positioned proportionately to the square's four corners were baroque lampposts, each encircled by a bench. Julia was lucky to find a spot on one.

Realizing she had a habit of photographing birds or scenes from bugs' and birds' perspectives, she placed her camera on her lap and watched the pigeons coo and preen each other.

The momentary return to normalcy was a respite from the chaos of the world's worst vacation, but it was far too brief.

The pigeon couple brought it all home for her.

The pain of losing Nick, knowing he was gone, crushed her, as if her own gravitational mass drew an entire planet of misery on top of her. Again, she broke down. And again, she had to console herself.

Carlo's admission also activated her memories of the night she'd almost bled to death on his floor. The events were a hazy blur at best, but she remembered nearly everything—at least she thought she did. She still couldn't recall the moment of the stabbing or what happened after, but the image of her husband—no, a man inhabiting her husband—attacking her with a sword was vivid. Yes, it was Nick's body, and if the assault were caught on camera, it would've been a slam-dunk case. But Julia knew in her heart and mind that Nick wasn't wielding the weapon. And not just in the temporal psychological sense. Another person, someone bound to another love, desperate to be with that woman, conquered his head. The real Nick battled internally, straining to free himself, trying to save Julia.

No, she didn't blame him at all, for it wasn't him. A part of her didn't fault Angelo. All that man wanted was love—a love stolen by the Order.

Carlo understood all of this. Medication or psychological treatment could've helped Nick. For all they knew, leaving Venice may have been enough to bury Angelo forever. One thing was certain—Nick didn't deserve the sentence he was given.

What was she going to do? Was it possible to save her husband, or was he really gone? And if his body was beyond hope, could she rescue his soul? Whatever the answer, she owed it to Nick to do everything she could. He had told her there was one way to liberate the souls: kill the Painter. And it just so happened she had direct access to the scumbag who murdered her husband with a friggin' paintbrush. Never in her life had the thought of killing a man popped into her head, but Carlo was no longer a man, was he? Not in the human sense. A person shouldn't be allowed to live that long, stealing people's souls. By killing Carlo, she'd save countless. And destroy della Porta's Order in the process.

The more she thought about it, the more it made perfect sense. Fuck Carlo. She barely knew the guy. He killed her husband. He may have saved her life, but when she thought back on it, Carlo was the cause of the entire ordeal. She didn't trust him from the beginning. If she and Nick had never gone to his apartment to learn about 'strange happenings at the Palazzo,' as he put it, they would've left Venice, enjoyed the rest of Italy, and been on the tail-end of their three-week vacation, probably making jokes about wanting to stay there forever. *Christ*, she thought. *Irony, you merciless witch*. She should've let Carlo drown in that damn tunnel.

So engrossed in her anger and justification of wanting to erase Carlo from her life, Julia didn't hear her phone until the fourth ring. It was Fosca. Julia was about to decline the call but realized her sort-of friend could be useful.

She switched her attention from the pigeons to two little twin boys in matching outfits scrutinizing a living statue street performer, and then, she clicked 'answer.'

"Julia, thank God." Fosca was frantic. "He killed him. The bastard fucking killed him, Julia. I was about to kill della Porta right then and there. I should've."

Julia sat up, her spine seizing with concern. "Killed who?"

"Manuel," she said through tears.

The news was terrible, and Julia sympathized with Manuel's wife, but she couldn't detach herself from the coldness within. "Did you know, Fosca?"

"What? No. I just learned this morning."

"I'm talking about Carlo. Why didn't you tell me he was the Painter?"

A strange but familiar background noise filtered in through the phone, loud enough for Julia to hear over the humdrum of Plaza Mayor.

"I thought you knew," Fosca said. "What did you think I was talking about with the ashes, why he couldn't touch them?"

Julia thought back. She wanted to punch herself for not seeing everything right in front of her eyes.

In the silence gap, wherever Fosca was, someone announced something on a P.A. in Italian. Julia couldn't understand it, but the tone was all too familiar.

"Are you in an airport, Fosca?"

"I'll be in Madrid in three hours."

"You'll get here just in time to piss on Carlo's dead body."

Fosca let the statement sink in before replying. "Tell me I didn't hear that right."

"I'm gonna kill him. I'm gonna free Nick and all the souls." Julia realized she'd been picking at her fingernails. She stopped herself and caressed her rosemary tattoo.

"Julia, don't do anything until I get there."

"You think I'm gonna fall for that? You had plenty of chances to kill him yourself."

"You're right." She lowered her voice to a whisper. "I didn't because killing the Painter alone won't do the trick. There's something else that needs to be destroyed."

"What?"

"I'll tell you when I see you."

"Whatever."

"I'm in an airport, Julia. There are people everywhere."

"Why didn't you say something when we were in your apartment?"

"Because it was never part of the plan. Three or four hours. Just wait for me."

Julia shook her head. Who were these people?

A young couple strolled by, their hands tucked in each other's back pockets.

"What about Nick?" Julia asked. "Did you know Carlo painted his soul? Into a new painting?"

Fosca gasped. "What do you mean?"

"He confessed. He told me everything."

Another airport announcement accosted Julia's ears.

"My flight's boarding. Let's talk when I get there."

"Cut the shit, Fosca. Did you know?"

"Grazie," Fosca said to someone before lowering her voice to Julia. "They said he was being held at the Palazzo. I tried to find out where, but I couldn't, so I didn't believe them. And then. . ."

A chill ran through Julia. Fosca *knew*. Fucking bitch. This whole time. She knew. "Out with it, Fosca. Then what?"

"I followed Carlo. I saw Nick's painting and—"

"Fuck you, Fosca. Fuck. You."

The tourists nearest Julia glared at her with surprised, disapproving looks. She didn't care.

Fosca had a hitch in her voice. "I told him—"

Julia ended the call. With her heart pounding a mile a minute, she had the urge to chuck her phone away. Instead, she punched the bench. She yelped and shook out her hand. It hurt but did nothing to relieve or mask her inner anguish. She needed a real friend. Anyone. Too many times in Europe, she'd felt so alone.

It was morning in New England, but not too early. She considered calling her parents, her sisters, or a friend, but what was she gonna say? How could she even begin? No way would anybody in the States believe the story. She remembered Lionel Benton and Maggie Yorn had tried to reach her, but they weren't friends, and she doubted they'd accept her claims. When she met Benton at his hotel, she promised to share any info with him, but he thought the Order was nothing more than a black-market art ring.

She jumped onto her social media accounts and even checked Nick's, but it was all the same-old status quo.

The human statue abruptly turned to the twins and shifted his pose to that of a gargoyle, his arms spread and his jaw agape. The brothers screamed and ran back to their parents who sat on the same circular bench beneath the streetlamp.

Wade, she thought. Nick's brother.

Wade was a firefighter and one of the most down-to-earth people she knew. But he was also a fantasy and sci-fi fanboy who'd consider any possibility from a logical perspective before brushing it off. But this was real life, and his brother was dead.

After finding Wade's number in her WhatsApp contacts, her finger hovered over the phone icon while she pondered how in the world to start the conversation. She accidentally tapped the button. Unsure of what to say, she let it ring, hoping she'd find the right words in the moment. Four rings later, she quickly ended the call, thankful he didn't answer.

So he wouldn't worry, she texted: *'Extending our trip. Talk soon.'*

She wished Wade were there so she could tell him in person, and he could help her, but she had to face facts: short of maybe Benton, there was not a single person on the entire continent of Europe she could trust. All she knew was that Carlo had to die. And if killing him didn't release Nick, then she'd destroy whatever else she had to. She'd burn the Palazzo down. She'd burn it all down.

XLIX

DELLA PORTA HATED ROME. TRAFFIC, POLLUTION, people, even the architecture caused an unpleasant grime-like air to encase him. From the moment he exited Fiumicino Airport to the private car ride to the Vatican, a trip that took as long as the flight from Venice, della Porta reminded himself of this trip's ultimate goal: secure the Church's favor.

It had been five years since he'd been to Italy's capital. He had hoped it would be at least another five more. Though he didn't yet have the Doge's book in his possession, his team was nearly finished with Ivan Uccello's descendants, so he wanted to maintain a relationship with the Church. This was a cordial visit—a coffee with Cardinal Giovanni Diamante, the Secretariat of State of the Holy See.

Arriving at the Apostolic Palace, the large building adjacent to St. Peter's Basilica off-limits to tourists, he reminded the driver he'd be no more than an hour and would return directly to the airport. The man let him out and continued to the car park for official visitors. Della Porta offered a polite, yet unreturned, nod to the two statuesque Pontifical Swiss Guards at the main entrance. They stood with halberds, and as clownish and unthreatening as their red, yellow, and blue uniforms were, della Porta knew the guards also carried concealed SIG Sauer P220s and were one of the most well-trained police forces in the world.

After passing through the metal detectors, he was escorted by a plain-clothed Swiss Guard to the third floor. Della Porta had never met the Pope, but if he turned left from the elevator, he'd reach the Pontiff's private apartment. The guard guided him to the right. The frescoed corridor, a glorious vision that put the Palazzo Ducale to shame, was impossible not to marvel at as the guard brought him to Cardinal Diamante's office.

A pleasant man in his late sixties, a few years older than della Porta, they'd always gotten along. Della Porta had known him for decades, back when Cardinal Diamante oversaw the Vatican's intercity exhibitions. Diamante's father had been a councilmember of the Order, so he was well-suited for such a senior position in the Church. Cardinal Diamante was fairly new to the position, having been appointed when the previous Secretary of State stepped down after a scandal that found his office had mismanaged hundreds of millions of dollars in investments.

Though this meeting was informal, della Porta needed to plant the seed of something big. He'd do that in conjunction with announcing a seven-figure donation to the Church. Della Porta snickered at the thought as he shook hands with his old friend. The Church didn't need a euro, but the scandal and pandemic put a legitimate dent in their coffers, so they took every cent they could get.

And after surprising the cardinal with the donation, della Porta informed him that soon enough, they'd be working very closely together.

L

FOLLOWING A TWO-HOUR TOUR OF THE MUSEUM—specifically skipping the entrance hall—the private docent brought Carlo back to the director's office, where Vasquez and Lobo were laughing over Estrella beers. Lobo sketched away in his pad.

"Ah, Carlo," said Vasquez, "enjoy our little museum?"

Carlo couldn't lie. "The Picassos and Dalis were spectacular to see in person. Your docent is remarkably knowledgeable."

"He'd better be." Vasquez clinked his beer to Lobo's. Perhaps it was the alcohol, but the man was in surprisingly good spirits.

"It was also good to see some Tintorettos that were new for me," Carlo said, "though he skipped a rather important one, despite my persistent requests."

"Have a seat, Carlo." Vasquez gestured to the open side chair, which Carlo took. He'd been on his feet all day.

"And stop trying to blow the climax," Lobo said. "It'd be like seeing fireworks before the grand finale, my friend."

Carlo controlled his wince at the word 'friend' but worried his microexpression gave him away. The man was certainly not his friend. Neither was Vasquez. That they refused to let him see the *Paradiso* study, the most valuable painting in the museum and the one he came here to see, was a massive red flag at full mast. He questioned their intent and if della Porta was aware they kept it from him. Carlo could've slipped away from the guide, but he reminded himself of his aim: *get these men on your good side, then bring them all down.* So he played their game, but he was tired of it. And if he didn't express his displeasure, they may suspect he had ulterior motives.

"You'll see *Paradiso* today, Carlo, not to worry," said Vasquez. He checked his watch. "It's nearly two. We have one more thing we'd like you to see, then lunch, then dinner, then the ceremony."

Not loving the idea of spending the entire day with these men, he thought of an excuse. "I'm not dressed right for either. I'll need to return to the hotel."

"No, you're not." Vasquez didn't glance at him. "But you're fine. The robe will cover your clothes."

"No siesta?"

Vasquez chuckled. "Not today, amigo. The Thyssen doesn't take a siesta."

Carlo knew the major tourist attractions didn't close for siesta, and the larger Spanish cities had been drifting away from it, but he'd been hoping to relax for a bit on his own or think about giving Julia a call. He forced a smile and massaged his forearms; it would be a long day. It seemed almost as if Vasquez didn't want to let him go.

The Spanish Exalted Master rose and led Carlo and Lobo out of the office. A circuitous route through the cubicles led to a staircase that descended three flights. The museum was also once a bank, so he guessed they were heading to a vault deep below the ground floor. He was right—or they were headed to what used to be a vault. They reached a steel door with a small window in it, but Carlo was unable to see through. Vasquez keyed in a number on a pad, and a high-security lock disengaged.

Carlo didn't know where they were going or what Vasquez wanted him to see, but wherever the destination, the journey unsettled him. He followed his escorts through the threshold.

A dark-skinned man, whose complexion contrasted with the muted gray corridor, stood from a steel folding chair, which Carlo was surprised hadn't been crushed beneath the man's titanic frame. He nodded his bald head, with thick sideburns the size of mutton chops. Vasquez returned the gesture without a word. Carlo assumed the man was a Protector—and considerably bigger than Dante, the largest in Venice. They passed two doors, both with small windows that caused Carlo's growing anxiety to swell.

His feeling was confirmed when Vasquez stopped at a third door with a video screen mounted on the wall. On it appeared to be a man on the floor. Vasquez tapped in a code on another keypad, and the door unlocked.

They entered.

In the corner, clutching his knees was a Black man in an otherwise empty, small room, painted the same stark gray.

Carlo gasped and stopped in the doorframe, refusing to go farther. "What is this? What's going on?" Memories of Quattrone's torture, along with della Porta tormenting Nick, flashed in his head. Though there was no rope nor devices in this room, the tableau was all too familiar.

"Meet Karim," Lobo replied, striding over to the man. He clutched his hair and forced his head up for Carlo to see. Karim's face was severely bruised. One eye was swollen shut. "He's a fantastic footballer. But a terrible liar. And a worse fighter. He also served in the Army. Lucky for Spain, he was never deployed."

"Your friend since we were five," Karim said in Spanish to Lobo through spit and blood.

"And Brutus was Caesar's best friend," Lobo shouted with a snarl, also in Spanish.

Vasquez sauntered right behind Carlo, his hot, cigar-stained breath on Carlo's neck. "This man is a member of the Guild of Silvanus," he said, returning the conversation to English.

"The what?" Carlo asked, praying his expression didn't reveal the truth. Still disturbed to the core, he also internally panicked for Fosca's safety.

Vasquez repositioned himself again and stared into Carlo's eyes. "Come now. Della Porta never told you of the Guild?"

"No. Why are you interrogating me, and why are you torturing this man?"

Vasquez studied Carlo's face. The creases around the Spanish Exalted Master's eyes intensified. His lips formed a thin line, and then he turned his attention back to Karim. Carlo doubted Vasquez was placated, but he continued. "The Guild of Silvanus has been trying to infiltrate and destroy our illustrious Order for centuries. Fortunately, the Madrid chapter has been unaffected. I can't say the same for Venice. But, even here, from time to time, a rat sneaks in. And every time, we catch it. Isn't that right, Karim?"

Karim attempted to spit. Blood-soaked saliva dribbled down his neck and onto his once-white button-down shirt.

"The traitor you see on the floor," continued Vasquez, "tried to convert Lobo. Can you believe that?"

"Honestly shortsighted, Karim," Lobo said.

"The bigger concern is that he refuses to tell us who else is in the Guild. Naming names, it's the oldest request. And the easiest to abide, isn't it, Karim? You have one more chance."

"I told you," Karim said. "Nobody. I work alone. The Guild is a myth."

Vasquez shook his head. He stepped over to Karim. "Carlo, do you know why the Spanish Inquisition was so successful?"

"Because they were ruthless bastards?" Carlo asked, unable to mask his disgust any longer.

"Yes," replied Vasquez with fervent eyes. "Precisely. They were ruthless bastards. Because it *worked*." From his breast pocket, he pulled out a black metal device that caused Carlo to shudder and shove his hands in his jeans. The tool was small enough to hold in one's palm but potent enough to inflict unimaginable agony: *thumbscrews*.

It was too much of a coincidence. Were the people in his flashbacks trying to tell him something? He couldn't see how that was possible if they were just memories. Maybe his subconscious was picking relevant visions, sparked by a setting, an image, a smell. Whatever the case, it could not have been mere chance that his most recent regression to Senator Quattrone included his torture with thumbscrews.

Carlo recalled the sensation as the first Exalted Master, when he was betrayed. The man's thumbs were crushed, sending ripples of pain through his whole body. Quattrone had been persecuted not for information but as reparation for his supposed power grab and had no chance to relent. Carlo prayed Vasquez was not as brutal as the Inquisitor. Though he didn't want to implicate Fosca or any other members of the Guild, he hoped Karim would be smart enough to buy some time and name fictitious people.

"Do not use that on this man," Carlo said, his voice rising in urgency.

"You know the thumbscrew?" asked Vasquez.

"Perhaps he's not as much of a pussy as he looks," Lobo deadpanned.

"Quiet," Vasquez hissed, prompting Lobo's eyes to darken.

"I know of them, yes," Carlo said, folding his arms, with his fingers tucked beneath them. "And they're illegal now for a reason, as is any form of torture."

Vasquez released a roar of a laugh. "Under whose governance? The Supreme Painter grants us the right to remove evil souls from this realm. You think having your soul sucked from your body is a pleasant experience? We have every right to do that and anything else to protect our cause and this Earth."

"I do not care what this man has done or what names he knows," Carlo said. Heat rose through his skin. "Do *not* use that device on him."

"That sounds like a threat," Vasquez said with a sneer.

Carlo's hands dropped; his right involuntarily balled into a fist. "I am the Venetian Painter. If you feel threatened—" Reason cut him off. He recalled the video screen outside the room; a camera inside the cell watched him from the upper corner. He had the speed and strength to disable Vasquez and Lobo and save Karim, but then what? If he managed to escape the building, he'd be on the run, potentially banished from Venice, if not Europe. His father, Nick, and all the souls would be eternally imprisoned, forever betrayed. The only option was to let the events run their course, get in Vasquez's good graces, be embedded in all three chapters, and hatch a plan to bring them down all at once.

"You were saying?" asked Vasquez with a raised eyebrow.

Carlo spoke through gritted teeth. "If you feel threatened, then I apologize for my tone. I am just not used to seeing this. You must admit, it's not the same as removing one's soul."

"Quite right." Vasquez turned his attention and the thumbscrew back to Karim. He knelt and grabbed the poor man's hand.

"Señor Vasquez," Lobo interrupted.

Carlo and Vasquez turned to him. Could it be that Lobo wanted to save his old friend?

"May I have the honor?" he asked.

"Desde luego." Vasquez stood and handed the torture instrument to the greasy artist.

Carlo recoiled at the heartlessness.

Lobo positioned his legs over Karim's arms and clamped them to prevent him from pulling away, then slipped the miniature vise over both thumbs. He twisted the screw, slowly clamping the metal down on them.

"Last chance," Lobo said in Spanish. "Two names save a thumb."

"Mierda," Karim cried out.

Lobo flashed his toothy grin and twisted. Inside the vise plate, a metal point drove into Karim's right thumb. He screamed.

A shiver coursed through Carlo. He turned away, unable to watch. It could've been the exact same device used on Quattrone.

"You have another thumb, Karim. You can keep it with two names."

Karim shouted through clenched teeth. "Puta madre!"

Lobo was all too happy to continue. He twisted the other screw. A sickening pop and crunch followed as the bolt drilled through Karim's flesh and cracked bone. The man's scream echoed off the bare walls.

"Enough," Carlo called out in English.

"Oh," Lobo said with a gleeful smirk and continued in English. "Should I put it on his toes? Karim, did you know it works on toes, too? Must be hard to kick a ball with crushed toes."

Tears streamed down Karim's face. Perspiration glistened on his forehead. His breathing rate intensified.

"Alright, let's go," said Vasquez. He glanced at his watch. "We have a schedule."

Lobo smacked Karim in the back of the head. "Saved by the proverbial bell."

"You can't leave this thing on me," Karim cried out.

Lobo wrinkled his brow. "Why not?"

"Because it's inhumane," Carlo said. He stormed forth, bumping Lobo out of the way. Lobo contorted his face, looking like a child about to have a hissy fit. Carlo untwisted the screws and gently slid the device off Karim's ruptured fingers.

"Gracias," the wounded man whispered.

Carlo headed for the door, slapping the device into Vasquez's hand.

"You could learn from this one," Vasquez said to Lobo. "Compassion and authority." He patted Carlo's back as if commending him for doing the right thing. "Come, amigo. I'm famished. You're going to love Casa Suecia. Best drinks, food, and rooftop in Madrid."

Carlo didn't know if making him a witness to torture was another game, and he didn't care. He pitied Karim and wished he could free him, but Carlo felt trapped himself. He marched out of the room, dreading dining with these two sadists.

LI

MADRID WAS AN OPEN CONCRETE SAUNA during the day, and the early evening wasn't much better. Having walked half the city, Julia had found the closest modern hotel and booked a room for herself, where she tried—and failed—at taking a true Spanish siesta. The hotel cost far more than she'd typically pay, but she didn't care. She didn't care about anything anymore. Two weeks ago, she was on a dream vacation with her husband and on a high with her photography career. Now, her psyche was as numb as her aching feet. The only thing she wanted was vengeance.

For the umpteenth time, she checked her purse. The folding survival knife she bought from an upscale sporting goods store was still there.

She reached the Mandarin Oriental Ritz Hotel, wracked with nerves, but determined to confront Carlo. Though it was a beautiful neoclassical building, the insensitivity of the name disgusted her as much as the Order itself. It was a fitting hotel for Carlo. To think she almost stayed there.

Her biggest concern was that Carlo or one of his accomplices would see her before she got to his room. But even then, all wouldn't be lost. Time alone afforded her hours to formulate a plan. After considering sneaking in, she axed all that with the simple realization that she *wanted* him to see her coming. How easy would it be to just pretend she wanted to talk, get him in the room, and slit his throat? Easy-peasy.

She stopped at the edge of the building and braced herself against the wall to calm her racing heart. Anger and thoughts of revenge filled her, but in truth, she was just venting again. Though eye-for-an-eye vengeance would've sounded nice in Angelo's time, for Julia, it was pure fantasy. Her true goal was to confront Carlo. He needed to either free Nick or turn himself into the police for murder—or both. She purchased the knife for self-defense, just in case the Order tried anything.

Shaking her legs and arms out, she headed for the entrance. A doorman decked out in white gloves, top hat and black cape greeted her and spun the revolving door for her as she entered.

It took a moment for Julia to situate herself. Ostentatious pillars ensconced the oval lobby. A pianist played soothing classical standards. A floral centerpiece obscured much of the anterior lounge area, including a red-carpeted staircase. She sidestepped a bellhop's luggage cart and made her way to the small reception counter. Though an older couple waited their turn, Julia cut in front of them and approached the open receptionist. The young man couldn't have been more than twenty-one, with short blond hair and a hipster mustache.

"I need Carlo Zuccaro's room number," she blurted out in English.

"I'm sorry, madame, but I cannot provide that to you," the receptionist said with a proper British accent. She should've expected the response.

"Can you call him?"

"Certainly."

Julia watched the young man call, thinking back to her own semester abroad in Paris. She had the opportunity to work in a café but passed it up because she wanted more time with friends and to travel. Realizing she'd spoken harshly to this guy, and she easily could've been in similar shoes, she resigned herself to be sympathetic.

The receptionist hung up. "There's no answer. Would you like to leave a message?"

Julia smiled. "No. But can you check if my name is on the registry? I was supposed to stay with him. It's Julia O'Connor."

"And what are you gonna do," said a female voice at the station next to her, "wait for him in a bubble bath?"

Julia recognized the voice and narrowed her eyes. Fosca. Of all the dumb luck. Or was it luck at all?

"Un momento," Fosca said to her receptionist before heading over to Julia.

With a scowl and pure hatred in her heart, Julia turned. "What the hell are you doing here, Fosca?"

"I'm staying here. We all stay here." She glanced around and whispered into her ear. "And I think I'm doing the same thing you're doing."

Julia jutted her head back and surveyed the area. The older couple was annoyed she took their spot, and the two receptionists watched her with increasingly impatient looks, but nobody seemed like they were in the Order. Still, she couldn't be sure. The hotel was packed. If Carlo and Fosca stayed here, who knew how many Order members were lurking about? "I don't need a traitor's help," she whispered.

"At least give me a chance to explain," Fosca answered.

"Sorry, madame, but your name isn't on the registry," the receptionist said to Julia. "I'd be happy to leave a message. Otherwise, if you don't mind . . ." he motioned to the couple behind her. The man cleared his throat.

A businessman waiting in line behind Fosca said something in rapid Spanish.

Paranoia overtook her. Without another word, Julia hurried for the exit, nearly knocking into a young girl in a yellow dress running through the lobby. Pushing through the revolving door, the humid air was a relief.

"Julia, wait!" Fosca called after her. "Come on."

Julia didn't stop. She ran across the street to a small park. Fosca caught up and grabbed her arm. Julia whipped back. She stopped and spun. "Get away from me! What don't you understand? I don't need you. I don't want to hear it."

Even with Julia screaming at her face, Fosca didn't budge. "Sixty seconds," she said. "Let me explain."

Getting the sense that she'd follow her all night long, Julia rolled her eyes. "Why, to distract me?"

"Killing Carlo won't get you what you want."

"Not all of us are murderers. Get the fuck away from me, Fosca."

Julia shoved Fosca's shoulder. She didn't do it hard and did it more to make a point than anything, but it felt damn good.

Standing her ground, Fosca put her hands on her hips. The annoying brat wasn't going anywhere.

"I didn't know you, Julia," Fosca said. "I had just met Carlo. I followed him. Spied on him."

This caught Julia's attention. "What are you talking about?"

Fosca gazed around. A teenage couple walked by. Once they were out of earshot, Fosca plopped down onto the cement. She sat cross-legged and peered up with apologetic eyes. The move took Julia off guard. She bit her lip at Fosca's genuineness. She continued looking around, making sure nobody was in range, speaking to Julia in earnest, her hands clasped together. "It was at a meeting in della Porta's office, the first time I ever met Carlo. I had no idea what his allegiance to the Order was, but he was acting a little off. After the meeting, I followed him to a storage room and hid there. I saw him talking to someone—or something. . ."

Tears welled in Julia's eyes. Her beloved Nick, locked in a two-dimensional painting in a glorified closet.

"After Carlo left, I removed the sheet, and there he was. I don't know if he could hear me—I assume he could. I told him I'd do what I could for him. That I'd help him. And you."

Julia started bawling, unable to take it anymore. "You should've told me." She dropped down in front of Fosca. She felt silly sitting there, like they were little kids, but . . . it was also the cathartic steam vent she needed.

Fosca shook her head. She dabbed her own eyes with the back of her hand. "Like I said, I didn't know Carlo's intention."

"He doesn't know you know?"

"Are you kidding? If he knew, and he was loyal to the Order, I'd be dead right now. Maybe you too. Or in that painting with Nick."

"Doesn't sound so bad." Julia sniffed. She pulled a crumpled napkin from her pocket, wiped her eyes, and blew her nose.

"There are alternatives." Fosca checked the area again for eavesdroppers. "This is what I was trying to tell you in the airport. To free the souls, the Painters must die, *and* the Sun Crystal needs to be destroyed. That's the theory, anyway."

Julia had enough of the ancient rituals, riddles, and artifacts. "What the fuck is the Sun Crystal?"

"Keep it down. Please." Fosca lowered her voice even more. "It extracts the soul but also binds it to the painting. The Painter keeps it in place, and killing him is just one part. Think of it like two-factor authentication. The Painter needs to be killed, but the Sun Crystal needs to be shattered, too, in a special way. The painting is the prison, the Painter is the warden, the Sun Crystal is the—"

"Key?"

"No. It's more like the gate. Or protective forcefield, in this case. We don't think smashing the crystal with a hammer or whatever will do the trick."

"How do you people not know this?"

"Because it's ancient, Julia. This stuff pre-dates the Order. It goes back to the Tangut Kingdom."

"The what?"

"It's—" Fosca cut herself off.

A family of six entered the park, heading for the hotel, four kids running circles around their mom and dad like they were in their parents' orbit. Julia wondered if Order members brought their kids and got babysitters during the meetings.

Not leaving anything to chance, Fosca pulled out her phone and didn't say another word. She continued once the family crossed the street. "It's in Mongolia or China, where the Sun Crystal was from. It's a long story."

"Obviously."

"The point is, we don't know but we have an idea. A good one." Fosca stretched her back.

"But we can try, right? We can grab the Sun Crystal and throw it out a window."

"First of all, it's not easy to do either of those things. But yes, doing so would set them back and prevent them from painting any new souls in."

All the craziness clicked for Julia. She chewed her inner cheek. "But it wouldn't release Nick."

Fosca shook her head. "It needs to be destroyed in a very specific way. And there's the Painter to deal with."

Julia gazed at her hands. The urge to do something—anything—hadn't abated. She rubbed her rosemary tattoo. She knew her next question was wishful thinking, but she had to ask. "Fosca, is it possible to, you know, reverse the process?" It was unintentional, but Julia's own words triggered her before Fosca had a chance to reply. She let out a fresh sob. "Sorry, I just miss him so much," she managed, forcing back the tears.

"Don't be sorry. You have nothing to be sorry for."

"It's our fifth anniversary in two months." Julia wiped her tears away. A part of her wished she were alone so she could cry for the rest of the night, but another part of her—one that was strengthening—knew that wallowing in self-pity would solve a whopping total of nothing.

A long exhale fluttered over Fosca's lips. "I don't know if it can be reversed. I've never heard of it, but hey, if you can take a soul *out* of a person, who knows? It seems like it'd be hard to get it back in the package, but I'm fairly certain Nick's body is in the Palazzo."

It was a long shot, but Julia smiled at the glimmer of hope. Still, the first step was stopping della Porta and gaining access to Nick. "What about the book? We found the key—we can figure out the box." She considered telling Fosca about the Tintoretto portrait. She'd been thinking that maybe IPSIVS was a cipher, but until she knew she could trust Fosca, Julia would keep that info locked in her personal file.

"Doesn't matter. The book was always plan B. Maybe Uncle Enzo was right." Her eyes moistened. She cleared her throat, then composed herself. "For the first time in probably four hundred years, the Sun Crystal and two Painters are in the same place. We do this right . . . the book is irrelevant."

Once again, the road before Julia felt impossibly steep. "How did you know I'd be here, anyway?"

Fosca shrugged. "I didn't. It's not a coincidence Carlo and I are staying in the same hotel. I'm assuming you checked out?"

"I never checked in."

Julia laughed. Fosca joined in. She was still pissed Fosca kept the truth from her, but it was nice to have an ally again.

"What was your plan?" Fosca asked. "You were just gonna wait for him in his room and then tackle him? Crack him on the head with a vase?"

"Like I said, not all of us are murderers. I was just going to confront him, see if he could extricate Nick, and if not, turn himself in for murder." Fosca cracked up, which Julia didn't appreciate. She tucked a fallen lock of hair behind her ear. "What's *your* plan? You're gonna storm the Order, kill two Painters and steal the crystal thing?"

"Something like that."

Julia grinned. "How big is this crystal, anyway?"

Fosca glanced around. "Let's talk in my room."

The notion made Julia chuckle involuntarily. She may've considered Fosca an ally again, but that didn't mean she trusted her enough to go to her room.

"Fine," Fosca said, "you pick a place." She dropped her voice to a whisper. "We can't talk here, even in this park. Half the Spanish Order stays in the Oriental."

Julia also checked out the area. A disheveled man—but not *too* disheveled—sat on a bench twenty feet away and stared at them with a lascivious, lopsided grin. A gray blanket covered his body. Order member or pervert, Julia agreed that sitting on the ground in a park wasn't the best idea. The urge to run was intense. She popped up. "What if Carlo comes back?"

"Then we *definitely* don't wanna be here." Fosca got to her feet, as well. "I know you can't trust me, and I'm not asking you to. Yet. I'm just asking you to listen to me. It all needs to go down at the Convocation anyway."

"What's a Convocation?"

"The ceremony. And this isn't a normal one. Usually, they're scheduled well in advance and coincide with moon phases. Maybe it's about Carlo, I don't know." She checked her phone. "We have a little over three hours. It'll give us time to level set and prep."

Fosca had a point. Julia could text Carlo at any time under the guise that she wanted to see him. And she couldn't deny that preparation would be better. Her stomach grumbled. Her throat would be screaming if it weren't so dry. "I *am* starving."

"Now you're talking. There's a fantastic restaurant in the hotel. One of Spain's best chefs. In the garden. But you're right, too risky. I know an amazing tapas place not far, or oooh, if you're really hungry, we can go to Decadente for eclectic Spanish fusion. They have a steak and a lobster lasagna that are both to die for. . ."

JULIA TOOK A MASSIVE bite of her Big Mac and slowly chewed the special sauce-slathered burger. While Fosca finished checking in, Julia had searched for a place on her phone, ultimately settling on the brilliant idea of the restaurant where no one in the Order would dine at 9 p.m. in Madrid, even if that was the common dinnertime in Spain. Ironically, she hadn't eaten at McDonald's in years. It was a far cry from paella, but the succulent flavor of those salty and crispy fries nearly had her crying, and she did everything to force back additional tears. Even the smell of the restaurant was familiar—industrial cleaner mixed with grease.

Fosca had a bowl of McGazpacho and a McIbérica—a burger topped with jamón ibérico, Manchego cheese, olive oil, and tomato, on a toasted baguette. She'd given a bite to Julia, and Julia had to admit it blew the Big Mac out of the water, but she loved her taste of home. Could she open a McDonald's that only served the special local items from all over the world? She smiled inwardly at the concept and then considered more immediate concerns.

"You said we had three hours. What's the plan?"

Fosca tapped her iPhone in its rose glitter case. "Two and a half. The plan is that membership has its privileges."

"You're a member of the Spanish Order, too?"

"Honorary, you could say. I'm a descendant of Tintoretto. It doesn't get more royal than that with these guys."

Julia couldn't hold back her laughter. Of all the absurd things she'd heard, this took the cake. "You expect me to believe that Tintoretto's royal ancestor wants to destroy the Order?"

"Are you kidding?" Fosca took a long slurp of her Coke. "You don't think the fact that della Porta and half the members should be in jail is reason enough? Or that they're pilfering artworks?"

"That's true?" Julia recalled Lionel Benton's theory of black-market art sales.

"And then some. But besides all that, it's been a curse for my family."

"And I'm guessing a bit of a blessing." Julia eyed Fosca's creamsicle-colored t-shirt embroidered with colorful starfish. Beneath the table, she wore her Doc Martens and ripped acid-washed jeans that had no chance of being purchased from a thrift store. And that t-shirt—it was the type of thing Julia would find in Marshalls for twelve bucks, but the uber-wealthy would add a couple of zeros to because the cheesy Medusa logo stenciled under the crustaceans was authentic. "Do you see other people in here wearing Versace?"

"You know your fashion. Hey, it was your choice to come to Mickey D's, not mine."

Julia loved that her guess was correct.

"For some of us, true, it's been a blessing." Fosca pinched her shirt. "But everything you see on me, I earned. Sure, I get an allowance and have a fund. I'm not going to turn it away. Would you? But it all goes into savings or to the Guild. Well, mostly."

Julia got the impression Fosca had this conversation a hundred times already. "Okay, okay. That's not what I meant. I mean, it just can't be all that bad."

"When you have multiple family members die under mysterious"—she used air quotes to emphasize the word—"circumstances, divorces, non-stop infighting, excommunications, it's not all good, either." She stole two of Julia's fries and chomped down on them. "Remember Isacco said the book's been a curse for his family? Imagine if you're a blood descendant of Tintoretto. But the worst of it is knowing that my ancestor was responsible for the suffering of *thousands*. Not just suffering, outright murder. It's a stain on the family, putting it lightly." She grabbed another fry and pointed it at Julia. "For those of us who'll own it."

Julia had to admit—she'd liked Fosca before their argument and was coming around to her again. If Fosca wanted to turn her over to the Order or harm her, they wouldn't be sitting in McDonald's, bonding over fries and gazpacho.

"Releasing the souls and crushing the Order forever is the least I can try to do," Fosca said. "And now there's urgency. It used to be just a curse. Now it's a curse with far-reaching consequences." She reached for Julia's hand. "We'll free Nick's soul, Julia, but you have to know this is about much more than him or us."

"I know," she said, more to herself than to Fosca.

"I'm not married, and I never lost a boyfriend, but I do know how it feels to lose a family member to these assholes."

Julia wiped a tear and raised her gaze to her friend.

Fosca caressed her hand. It was more intimate than Julia expected.

She didn't love French fry grease and salt rubbing into her skin, but she didn't pull away. Human contact was nice.

"We can help thousands," Julia said.

A few strands of balayage brown hair fell in front of Fosca's face. She leveled her large brown eyes at Julia. "Millions. Maybe billions."

"His singular religion plan?" Julia took her hand back and bit into her burger. "You really think they'll sentence that many people if they don't convert?"

"Or for any other fickle reason." Fosca scanned the restaurant, as if someone from the Order would be watching them there. "Do the math. There are thousands in each painting. Imagine paintings all over the world. This could affect our great-great grandkids."

Julia swallowed. Perhaps they could work together after all. Fosca was right. Julia would do everything she could for Nick, but this was so much bigger than all of them. "Alright, you're a member. You still haven't told me your plan."

"You pretty much nailed it in the park."

Julia nearly choked on her burger. "You can't be serious. You're gonna sneak inside, kill two men, and destroy a priceless crystal that somehow can't be destroyed?"

"Like I said, pretty much. Except we'll grab the crystal and figure that part out later. Paris, too."

"We've gone from seeing your enemies drown to rushing in screaming with a machine gun?"

"Who said that?"

"You did. The first part, anyway. I'm adding reality to it."

Fosca gazed at the ceiling for a moment, then cracked her neck. "How long can all this go on? It needs to end. If I'm the one to do it, then so be it. And it's not that the Sun Crystal can't be destroyed—it's that it needs to be done the *right* way to free the souls. With vibrations or something. It's all lore from hundreds of years ago, but there's a way. Even if we gotta travel to the ends of Earth to find out how, we will." She planted her finger on the table to emphasize her determination.

"Okay, fine. I, uh, hate to ask the obvious million-dollar question, but . . . have you ever killed anyone?"

"Hell no. I've wanted to knock off a few idiots, but no. Have you?"

"Of course not!"

"Then it'll be a first for both of us. Just don't think of them as men. And they're not, really."

"I'm not planning on it now, either. What would you even do if I wasn't here? Kill two people by yourself?"

"If I had to, yes. But I'm not by myself, and I have my backup. How's your español?"

The simple question brought it home for Julia. Shaking, she balled her hand and cleared her throat. "Mi casa es grande."

"Huh?"

"Mi español's no bueno. I took it in middle school."

"Then keep your talking to a minimum. It's not just us. I also have two guys on the inside. One's high up. He'll be front and center, but he's a wildcard. The other's a Discipulus—a junior member," she added, preempting Julia's question. Fosca checked her phone again with concern. "He's usually super responsive. We were supposed to go over the plan by now. Anyway, worst case is you just need to distract the Protectors."

Julia's shaking intensified. Though a few hours earlier she'd wanted to kill Carlo, she realized that even the fantasy of eye-for-an-eye vengeance was ludicrous. "I don't know if I can even be there, Fosca. You're talking about murdering two people."

"It's a *correction*, not murder. The Painter shouldn't be alive."

An image of what it must've looked like when Nick put Tintoretto out of his misery flashed through her mind. Nick did the right thing then. "But Carlo. He's twenty-six."

"Exactly. You want him sentencing souls for the next seven centuries?"

When Julia had thought about killing Carlo, her emotions had been running at eight-thousand RPM, though she knew she'd never really do it. But that was just about Nick. Now, the more Fosca told her, the more it didn't even seem like there was an alternative, given della Porta's plan. She'd never forgive herself if what Fosca said was true. Millions, even billions of people? But what if she and Fosca failed? Or succeeded and got caught? As an unarmed accomplice, she could spend the rest of her life in a Spanish prison. Or, knowing the Order—worse. Would she be able to distract the Protectors when the time came—to enable murder? She took the last bite of her burger and breathed into her napkin as she chewed.

There's only one way to find out.

"Can you get me in?"

"Yup. With a few changes." Fosca reached over and twirled Julia's blond hair in her greasy fingers, then eyed her white tank and jeans. "And definitely not dressed like that."

LII

STANDING IN FRONT OF THE FULL-LENGTH MIRROR in the spacious white marble bathroom of Fosca's hotel suite, a different person stared back at Julia. The synthy beats of *Poker Face* seeped in through the bathroom door. Fosca had put on the Lady Gaga station on the hotel's entertainment system through the TV. After McDonald's, she and her soon-to-be criminal buddy stopped at a drug store to pick up some supplies before returning to the Madrid Ritz—she refused to call it the Mandarin Oriental.

An hour later, her hair was pitch black, black eyeliner and mascara framed her green eyes, and a buttery red glossed her lips. A pair of low-prescription leopard print plastic glasses obscured her face even more and, surprisingly, improved her vision. Wearing Fosca's black Versace halter-neck sheath dress that grazed her knee, she had to admit she looked incredible. More importantly, she felt empowered. She'd always loved how an outfit could change a person's mood.

Whether or not they'd accomplish their mission, at least they'd be going out in style.

She puked in the sink.

Julia couldn't believe she was even considering going through with this. A quick rinse of water and mouthwash helped freshen her breath but did nothing for her frazzled nerves.

Exiting the bathroom, she walked through the bedroom on shaky legs, entered the salon section of the suite, and stopped short. Fosca was a drop-dead knockout in a one-shoulder black midi dress. It covered her knees, but a long slit exposed her right leg up to her thigh. Carlo would be stunned long enough to drive a knife into his back.

"You look like that dress was made for you," Julia said.

"Well, it wasn't made for me specifically, but I did model it."

"You're a model?"

"Catalog and online. Capri Holdings, mostly. Where do you think this stuff comes from? I mean, I make decent money, but I wouldn't be dropping this much coin on clothes." She turned from her mirror and caught a glimpse of Julia and widened her eyes. "Oh, my God. You are smoking hot."

She rushed over to get a closer look.

"It fits you perfectly. You're like a sultry assassin. I love it." Fosca ran her hands along the tight fabric up Julia's curves, from her thighs to below her breasts.

Julia wasn't sure if she was just touchy-feely or making a move, but she didn't back away. It wouldn't surprise her if Fosca was bi or even a full-on lesbian. Julia had never been with a woman, though, in college, she kissed her friend at a bar to make Nick jealous. The move had the opposite effect. Sex that night was a session for the ages. She sighed, wishing Nick were there to see her in this dress and with black hair. And she longed to see him in one of his suits. That man could rock a suit.

Fosca dropped her hands and went to the minibar. "We're gonna kill in there. In more ways than one."

The crap-taste joke snapped Julia back to the gravity of the situation. The disguise had offered a momentary reprieve, but what the fuck was she doing, and *could* she do it? Bile rose in the back of her throat. She clamped her mouth and forced the bitter gunk down as she headed to the window.

"I'm just backup, right? To distract the Protectors?" she asked.

"Yes, don't worry. I'm just kidding."

"How are you so casual about this?"

Obscuring her body, Julia peeked out the curtain at the Thyssen-Bornemisza Museum across the street. A lump of dread joined the bile, amassing in her esophagus and refusing to go down. Her legs were so shaky, she felt as if she were riding an earthquake. She let the curtain fall back into place and collapsed in the side chair.

Ava Max's *Kings & Queens* came on. Julia loved the song, but her body vibrated with trepidation, not the beat.

Her new friend lowered the volume and returned with two mini bottles of Scotch. She gave one to Julia, before plopping onto the adjacent two-tone gray microsuede sofa. "It's something my nonna-mère taught me. The only way to embrace a fear or anything you're nervous about, whether it's a test, your first photoshoot, or something absolutely horrible you could never imagine doing unless it was for the good of humanity, *own* it. 'Own it, Fosca. Imagine yourself as the person doing it, and you'll be that person. And . . . find a bit of humor.' That's what nonna-mère would say. *Own it*, Julia. Own it."

It made sense. She didn't see any humor in the situation, but she *could* own it. She just had to *be* that person. Julia twisted the cap open and tapped her bottle to Fosca's. "To being seductive spy assassins."

"I'll drink to that," Fosca said with a smile.

The two chugged their drinks. The alcohol burned the back of Julia's throat, already singed by the bile. She hated Scotch.

Who was she kidding? She couldn't own this. "Seductive assassins on a near-suicide mission," she said.

"*Near*," Fosca replied. "And even if it wasn't near, would you sacrifice yourself to save millions?"

"I don't know, Fosca. I've been asking myself that question. I wanna say yes, but what if we fail? You and your buds have been trying to bring them down for centuries."

"Exactly. Which is why it's gotta end tonight. Look, it's not like this plan has been in the works for weeks. This isn't a scripted heist flick. Hopefully, my guys on the inside will take care of it, and you can sit back and watch. But if shit goes sideways, I sure could use another hand in there. If you have a better idea, spit it out."

Julia thought for a moment. "What about my original plan? We get Carlo alone. Say we want to talk. You sure that won't work?"

"Yeah," Fosca said, clearly annoyed. "I'm sure. This is the first time two Painters will be in the same room since God knows when. If you spook Carlo, you'll blow it all. We'll never have a chance with the Spanish Painter, not to mention the Sun Crystal." She leaned over and took her hand. "I know this isn't easy. I could use your help, but I'm not gonna force you."

Of everything Fosca said, one question continued to resonate with Julia: *Would she sacrifice herself to save millions?* So much in her life had changed. She wasn't the person she used to be. Without Nick, she'd never be the same. Perhaps she could recover, find peace, love again, maybe travel the world, taking photographs. But how could she live with herself if della Porta succeeded and she had the chance to stop him? Either way, if she bowed out or they went through with it and got killed or caught, the answer didn't matter. Her life would never—*could* never—be the same. She needed to do the right thing *now*.

Julia squeezed Fosca's hands with a firm resolve. "My last meal was a Big Mac."

"Your choice. I would've chosen paella."

Julia dispensed a laugh of half-humor, half-disbelief at the whole damn situation. Fosca joined in. When they composed themselves, Julia asked, "When are you gonna do your hair?"

Fosca frowned. She stood to check herself out in the mirror next to the TV. "You don't like it?"

"No, it looks great. You look awesome, but you still look like you. Carlo will recognize you."

"Obviously. So will plenty of people. I'll just tell Carlo I'm there to support him. It'll give me a chance to get close to him."

Julia reached out and grabbed her friend's wrist. "Whoa. If we're doing this, I need the chance to confront him first."

"No fucking way, Black Widow." Fosca pulled away and went back to checking her hair in the mirror. "If he recognizes you, it's over."

"I just want to talk to him. You can go through with the whole plan—"

"Nope." Fosca spun back to Julia and locked eyes with her. "You're not supposed to be there, remember? That's why you're in disguise. If they smell anything, they'll protect their Painter at all costs. And the Sun Crystal. I keep telling you this. It's all about timing. If we make a move on Carlo first—even to chat with him—they'll figure it out, rush their Painter to safety, and we'll be killed. You need to be backup, create a diversion, and if a shitnado goes south, kill *their* Painter."

"Wait, what?" Julia's mouth went dry.

"Look, I get not wanting to kill Carlo. You're right. That's different. But this dude should've died long ago."

"How will I even recognize him?"

Fosca tossed back the remaining drops of Scotch in the mini bottle and reclaimed her spot on the sofa. "He'll be the only five-hundred-year-old man in the room."

The words smacked a part of Julia's brain she'd never used before. The magic. The murder. The mayhem that would follow. All of it seemed insane. On one hand, killing a man who wasn't supposed to be alive lessened the severity of the crime. On the other, who was she to take such a life? Would it be like slaughtering a unicorn? If she had chills in McDonald's, ice ran through her veins in this hotel room. Her leg trembled. A thought hit her.

"Five hundred? Who *is* their Painter?"

"El Greco."

Julia blinked rapidly. Her mouth popped open. "El Greco? El friggin' Greco? You want me to kill a Renaissance master? I can't do—"

Fosca reached over and rubbed her leg. "You're backup. But if you need to do it, you *can* do it. Own it. He's going to die soon anyway." She put her hand under Julia's chin and lifted her head to look at her. "Think of everything you've done. Everything you've been through. Who this is for. Not just Nick but the world. You are so extremely strong, it blows me away. And I like to think I'm pretty strong too."

Julia picked at her fingernails but forced herself to stop. She *could* do this. Nick did it to Tintoretto. And they were a team. A crazy husband-and-wife ancient painter-killing team. With that absurd notion, her shaking stopped, like a car that parked after a harrowing drive. Fosca relaxed and kicked her feet onto the black marble-top coffee table. For the first time, Julia noticed a cheesy dragon-like sea monster tattoo wrapped around her ankle.

"So," Julia said. "Your guys kill El friggin' Greco. You kill Carlo. What about the Sun Crystal?"

Fosca checked her phone with a vivid frown. "Diego will get it. I hope. He'll be closest to it."

"Who is he?"

"They're grooming him to be their next Painter." She fluttered her hand dismissively. "I never met him, and he doesn't know about the Guild, but Karim knows him. Karim's the other guy in the Guild. He and Diego have known each other for years, so we had him convince Diego the Order's no good. That and half a million euros."

"Half a million? Where does he think the money's coming from?"

"Karim didn't tell him. It doesn't matter. Diego's after fame and fortune. This is his chance. FYI, from what I heard, he's a little haywire and borderline sadistic, so don't be surprised if a few wires hit the hay and set the barn on fire. Tall and skinny but mean as hell. He's a good ally to have. I trust Karim, and he trusts Diego to do the job and reign chaos down on the place so we can escape."

Fosca checked her cell again and shook her head. "I'm getting worried. Still no word from Karim. This is a pic of him, by the way." She displayed a shot of a good-looking guy in a soccer uniform.

"Alright, so how do we get in?"

"Ah, see, in Venice," Fosca said with animated hands, "Order members arrive by boat. They put their cloaks on and head right into the Palazzo without anybody seeing them."

"I think I know that canal." Julia shuddered at the still-fresh memory of nearly dying and saving the guy her friend was plotting to kill.

"One and the same. Here, you have to go right through the front door, in the center of Madrid. I'll show the entry coin to Vasquez—"

Julia cocked her head and raised an eyebrow.

"Madrid's Exalted Master," Fosca continued. "José Vasquez. He had the admittedly brilliant idea of renting out the Thyssen for events. Every time there's a Convocation, it's just another fancy cocktail party in the courtyard, and then the guests head inside."

"It's a good thing you brought an extra dress," Julia said.

"*Three* extra dresses. Packing light is for people with no plans." She went over to the closet and held out a couple of pairs of shoes, as if projecting them onto Julia. "Yeah, you take the strappy black. We're about the same size. I'll do the pointed pumps."

Julia took the pair while Fosca put on silver pointed-toe shoes with an ankle strap. Both pairs were gorgeous, but she frowned. "Are we going to be able to run in these?"

"Take them off. And ram that stiletto heel into a Protector's neck if you need to."

The words caused Julia's bile to revisit the back of her tongue. She knew Fosca hated the Order, but she couldn't comprehend how she could speak of ending lives so callously. Julia could take off shoes and run, but no way was she using them as a weapon.

Once they applied finishing touches on their hair and makeup, they polished off a couple of mini bottles of vodka, and Fosca checked her watch. Her expression turned deadly serious.

"Have a seat," she said.

Julia took the side chair again and, a bit wobbly, crossed her legs, regretting that second drink.

From her carry-on, Fosca retrieved two irregularly shaped, ancient silver coins. She handed one to Julia. Embossments on both sides had been worn and were difficult to distinguish. On one side appeared to be a cross with different iconography in each quadrant. On the other seemed to be a shield-like shape with additional symbols, all of which Julia guessed were for the Kingdom of Spain.

"The Spanish sect is different from the Venetian one in a bunch of ways."

"Besides the need to get dressed up?" Julia asked.

"Yup." Fosca held her coin between her fingers. "These bad boys are real. Minted in 1614, the year the chapter was founded. But they started using the coin as a passkey about five or six years ago."

"Okay, I give this to someone—"

"Hellll, no. Just show it. Follow my lead, and do *not* lose that coin. *That* I don't have any extras of. Keep it in your purse."

She handed Julia a black sequined clutch.

"Here's another thing I only have one extra of." She whipped her wrist and opened a butterfly knife. Then flicked it to close it and handed it to Julia. "Permission to lose this if you use it. Just make sure it's in the Painter's neck."

Julia took the knife with a shaking hand. "Where did you get this? And how do you know how to do all that?"

"A lame-ass boyfriend. And no, he wasn't overcompensating for something. Kickass lay and what a cock on that boy. Mmm."

Julia smiled. *Okay, that settles half of that.*

"He was just into crazy ninja shit and video games." She shook her head and rolled her eyes. "Kind of a nerd, really. And unfortunately, more into that crap than he was into me."

"I have a survival knife in my purse."

"That's badass."

"For protection," Julia added.

"Still badass. But it won't fit in the clutch. The butterfly's also more ladylike." She winked. "We'll leave any IDs here." Fosca checked the time again. "The cocktail hour will be wrapping up soon. It's showtime."

"Wait, aren't there going to be cameras and guards and stuff?"

"Cameras only on the outside. Protectors in and out, but we'll be members just like everybody else. Karim and Diego will make their own way out. Once the shit hits the fan—and it'll start spraying everywhere—you'll know if you need to create a diversion, help finish the job, or get outta El Dodgo. Either way, catch the first cab you see, ask the driver to take you to a nightclub, it doesn't matter which, and wait it out. Ideally, let someone take you home."

"What?" Nick in a painting or not, infidelity was not in the cards.

"Relax. You don't have to screw him. Or her. But we'll need to lay low."

"I can just go to another hotel."

Fosca shrugged. "True. But where's the fun in that?"

LIII

THE FIVE-MINUTE WALK FROM THE HOTEL to the Thyssen-Bornemisza Museum felt like miles. Despite the hot and humid late June Mediterranean night, Julia shivered the whole way. Though Fosca filled Julia in on the remaining particulars of the plan, she hung a half step behind so her accomplice wouldn't see her shaking. Julia wanted to turn and run. She still couldn't understand how Fosca was so calm. As far as Julia knew, she'd been in more dangerous situations, and she was freaking out. Now she wished she had an additional vodka. Or a grandmother like the countess.

They walked through the park and entered the museum gate, where two burly guards in black suits admitted them into the courtyard.

"One more thing," Fosca said, "the passphrase is 'siete cuerpos corporales, un alma devota, una orden.'"

Julia rattled her head. "Are you serious?"

"Siete cuerpos corporales, un alma devota, una orden. It's an Order decree. Seven corporeal bodies, one devoted soul, one order. Got it?"

No. But she repeated it in her head. Between her rudimentary Spanish, high school and college French, and the past two weeks in Italy, she was beginning to feel like a polyglot. *Siete cuerpos corporales, un alma devota, una orden.*

"And remember, we don't know each other."

True to Fosca's word, three dozen people, all dressed in tuxedos and evening gowns, finished their drinks at cocktail tables set beneath palm trees and headed toward the entrance. Julia scanned the crowd. No sign of Carlo. He must've been inside already.

"Take out your coin and follow my lead," Fosca whispered. "Once inside, separate, and go to the front. I'll find Carlo and make sure he's with me."

Fosca filed in line with the other guests through the door.

A tall man in his thirties, with olive skin, slick-backed hair, and a black suit greeted the guests. The man had some of the most pronounced cheekbones Julia had ever seen, and on one of those cheeks was a small anchor tattoo. Vibrant foliage ink climbed a few inches up his neck from beneath his collar.

Each guest whispered to the greeter and handed their coin to him. With a solemn expression, he used a cell phone to scan both sides of their silver piece. After a moment, he handed the coin back and uttered something. The guest went inside.

It was soon Fosca's turn. The greeter's eyes lit up. He beamed from ear to ear and kissed her on each cheek. "Ah, buenas noches, Señorita Baldesseri. Qué e bueno verte."

Fosca exchanged a few words with him in Spanish that Julia didn't understand, but when Fosca uttered the decree, she said it in full volume, which Julia appreciated. Fosca showed both sides of her coin to the man's phone. He admitted her a second later.

Last in line, Julia was up to bat. The greeter's pleasant expression vanished.

Every nerve in Julia's body seized. Every muscle quivered. Besides needing to remember Spanish and the enormity of the situation, the greeter's height, cheekbones, and facial ink scared the shit out of her. Her high heels made her wobble. She wanted to kick her shoes off and make a break for it, but the greeter's wingspan would enable him to catch her before she was a step away.

Nick, she reminded herself. *You're doing this for Nick. And the world.*

"Buenas noches. Siete cuerpos corporales, un alma devota, una orden," Julia whispered. She savored her relief that she nailed it and handed him the coin.

He scanned the head-side of the silver and his phone beeped with a green light. He nodded. Julia dropped the coin inside her clutch and took a step.

"¡Espere!" he called.

Julia froze. Fosca noticed and slowed her pace. Julia turned back to the greeter. "Si?"

"No suelo decir esto, pero me gusta tu vestido," he said with a sly grin.

She didn't understand what he said but knew "gusta" meant 'like' and "vestido" meant "dress." And she recognized flattery in any language. At least she hoped she could. She swallowed dryly. "Gracias," she ventured, proffering a nervous smile, and forgetting to pronounce the 'c' as a 'th,' as they did in Spain.

The greeter flashed his eyebrows before Julia headed in and caught up to Fosca.

"What did he say?" Julia asked.

"He likes your dress," her accomplice whispered quickly, then separated herself.

Keeping her distance, Julia followed Fosca and the procession through the large atrium-like lobby with peach-colored walls and a high ceiling. Rows of plastic folding chairs were positioned in the center of the space. One-by-one, each member donned a black robe from one of two portable racks, on which hung either large or small sizes. In the middle of the two racks were four baskets filled with Roman rope ties, each basket containing a different color.

Fosca chose a pale blue tie for herself. As instructed on their way over, Julia selected a green one. Following Fosca's lead, she tied the rope around her waist to secure the robe and pulled the hood over her head. Members continued to another table, from which each took a glass of red wine. A smell of sage or incense glanced her nostrils.

Julia turned to the seats, hoping to exchange a reassuring furtive glance with Fosca. *But where was she?* Eyes darting everywhere, Julia searched the black robe-clad group. As the Order members shuffled about, a disorienting queasiness overtook her, like she was drowning in a darkened sea. Her pulse quickened. Fosca was gone. Was she taken? Did she bolt? Then Julia saw her, taking a seat in the rear.

Fosca caught her eye and offered a nearly imperceptible affirmation. Julia settled down but realized a bigger challenge.

With everyone enshrouded in hoods, spotting Karim would be difficult. Julia gulped again. She shook so much that she worried the wine would percolate out of the glass. She yearned to take a drink, needing more alcohol to calm her nerves, but none of the members had yet sipped. Carlo was nowhere to be seen. A sudden thought gave her more concern than getting caught: What if Carlo wasn't there? Should they abort? If she took out her cell to text Fosca, that would give her away. Nobody had their phones out, which she suspected was for good reason. Without sitting next to Fosca or being able to see her, Julia realized that even as backup, this mission was closer to suicide than she'd thought it would be.

Alcohol, a sexy dress, and a desire for vengeance does not a spy make.

As the members took their seats, Julia passed potted palms and made her way to the second row, opting for the far-left chair. She smiled politely at a gray-haired woman to her right, then looked straight ahead. She was amazed she hadn't noticed it before . . . on the far wall, twenty-five feet in front of her. *Paradise.*

Other than seeing a thumbnail of this version when she had done research in the Bauer Hotel lobby in Venice, she had never seen this study. The first thing that struck her was the size. It had to be a quarter the size of the one in the Palazzo Ducale. Though still a large painting, by Julia's estimation, with the frame, it was about six feet high by seventeen feet wide. Unlike the Venetian version, which had the impression of being painted on the wall, this framed painting hung like any other. Whereas the souls in Venice were mostly life-size, Julia wondered if the prisoners in this painting had been shrunk.

The content was much the same: an image of hundreds, if not thousands, of people on clouds in Heaven, with Jesus and Mary at the top center, along with a few angels flying about. While the Venetian *Paradise* was dramatically backlit and the subjects popped in a variety of styles of clothing and colors, all climbing over one another to reach the deities, here, except for a handful of people, almost everybody in the painting was depicted in a drab brown and sepulchral lighting. Despite its dreary coloring, the scene presented an almost wedding reception-like vibe, where a handful of people may be paying their respects to the bride and groom, but for the most part, all the other guests mingled in other areas and did their own things.

To the sides of each painting on the floor, large pots burned incense, which explained the sage-like aroma. Surprised they'd do this in a museum, she noticed the smoke drifting upward to large vents, sucking it out. In front of each pot stood two sculptures on peach-colored rectangular pedestals that had been pushed against the side walls. Between the pedestals on her side was a throne-like, high-back padded chair.

"Buenas noches, amigos," said a loud voice, startling her.

The members quieted. Julia turned her head and craned her neck with the others. She took the opportunity to scan the room. There were only three Black people in the group; none were Karim. She reassured herself that if he were going to be close enough to El Greco, he wouldn't just be sitting with everyone else.

From the rear of the group, a bearded White man with thick salt-and-pepper hair emerged, wearing a purple robe with an ermine fur collar. A golden pendant hung from his neck. With a confident air, he walked the center aisle, followed by two large men in black with crimson rope belts, whom Julia assumed were Protectors, like Bernardo. Each Protector took a spot on either side of *Paradise*, while the man in purple took his place in front of the painting.

Based on his mannerisms and outfit, she assumed this man was Vasquez, Madrid's Exalted Master, as Fosca had called him. He addressed the group in rapid Spanish. Julia could pick out a word or two but quickly realized the fantasy of her polyglot dream.

As he spoke, another tall man wearing a black robe with a white belt emerged from the rear. He removed his hood to reveal his thin, goateed face, framed by greasy, straight black hair that reached his shoulders, matching the description Fosca gave of Diego.

The bearded Exalted Master gestured to him. "Diego Blanco-Romasanta, El Lobo Blanco," he announced to the audience, who hummed their approval. Vasquez continued speaking for another minute or so, referring to Diego as Lobo before he motioned for him to move to the side, which he did, not far from Julia.

A torrent of hatred blasted through her as another man entered the hall, this one wearing white. Carlo. He wasn't wearing his trademark confident expression, but there he was, arriving at the front of this group, the only one wearing white, presumably because he was a Painter.

Backup or not, Julia fondled the butterfly knife through her clutch on her lap. In the slim chance she'd have to confront him, she wanted it to be at knifepoint. With the wine glass shielding her hand, she slowly unzipped the purse.

Vasquez said some words about Carlo, who nodded to the sitting members. They returned the gesture. Julia joined in. The Exalted Master then directed him to stand against the opposing wall, adjacent to the painting.

Shit, Julia thought. She hoped he'd stand next to her.

Three more members in black robes entered from the rear. One carried a large bronze stand, which he placed about fifteen feet from *Paradise*, in the center of the polished marble floor, on a sort of yin-yang design she hadn't noticed. The second member placed a large black and red braided candle in the middle of this stand, which she realized was a large candleholder. The third member, a fresh-faced boy wearing green, who could not have been older than fifteen, carried a black velvet bag in both hands. He opened the bag and produced a large spherical crystal, about the size of a pomelo grapefruit, which he handed to Vasquez.

The Sun Crystal, Julia thought. *Doesn't look too hard to smash.* The first key to Nick's freedom flipped a switch in Julia's psyche. No longer was she nervous. Now she was ready, anxious even, for Karim and Diego to get the job done. *One more person, let's see him.*

With gentle care, The Exalted Master placed the Sun Crystal in a mount on top of the holder, adjusting one of the prongs to secure it. He retrieved a stick from one of the incense bowls and said something that didn't sound like Spanish. Julia figured it was some sort of prayer.

"Et beatus est sol," the attendees responded in unison.

Julia mumbled along. The woman to her right sipped her wine, so Julia did too.

Vasquez lit the candle with the incense stick before the boy took it away. The flame instantly caught and rose a few inches—much higher than a normal candle.

The members chanted the same phrase, enough so that Julia nailed the words and inflection. Their collective voices swelled in volume, and the Sun Crystal glowed with an orange hue.

Vasquez raised his palms, and the members stood. Julia followed suit.

Once again, everyone brought their gazes to the rear. Two more large men whom she assumed were more Protectors entered the hall, assisting a frail man—*an impossibly old man*—enshrouded in a white robe.

El Greco.

His near-translucent skin clung to his face and hands. He had no hair except a few long, white strands hanging from the chin of his oblong head. With hollow eyes rooted deeply in his flaccid skin, even with a robe, he looked more like a fifty-pound skeleton wearing a sheer bodysuit than a man. As El Greco's Protectors assisted him, it was clear the Painter was so delicate, he barely had the strength to place one foot in front of the other, let alone paint souls into *Paradise*. He moved at a glacial pace, enabling Julia to gawk and study him. She had the sense that everyone in the room did the same. A giant of the Renaissance, a man born in the 16th century, living, breathing, standing before her.

It finally hit her, beyond Nick's past life and everything she'd heard. *All of this is real.*

She needed to concentrate. She had a mission to complete, or at least back up. If Fosca was right about the connection between the Painters and the Sun Crystal—and based on what was unfolding before her eyes, it sure seemed so—then she needed to stick to the plan. If she confronted Carlo in this setting, the Protectors would whisk El Greco and the Sun Crystal away in an instant. And Julia would probably be killed. Or worse. Knowing everything was real also cemented the gravity of della Porta's plan. This was all so much bigger than her or Nick. Her fingers slipped inside her clutch and gripped the knife. An imaginary target appeared on El Greco's chest. She prayed Karim would do the job and leave her hands clean. She already felt guilty a literal living legend had to die, but Fosca was right—he shouldn't have been alive.

But where was Karim? He wasn't at the front. Diego was there, but didn't Fosca say Karim would kill El Greco? As surreptitiously as she could, Julia glanced around. Cursing the alcohol, she couldn't remember if it was Karim or Diego who'd do the deed. Either way, Karim was nowhere to be seen.

As Julia's backup role was coming to fruition, her nerves returned full throttle; her heart rate doubled. This Diego Lobo guy seemed to bask in the limelight. Come to think of it, why *was* he front and center? And if he didn't do the job, how would Julia have time to rush across and stab El Greco?

To her relief, the Protectors guided El Greco over to the throne on her side of the room. A mere ten feet away, the men helped him sit, then took their places on both sides of him. The Protector nearest her was gargantuan. At least 6'4", the guy was built like a linebacker, with lamb chop sideburns that made his imposing stature more menacing. He and the other Protectors all faced the audience, guarding their places.

With every passing second, the inevitable approached. She was a third-string safety who was looking like the team's last hope for quarterback. Her mouth was devoid of saliva. Her heart felt like it wore boxing gloves and was pounding itself free of its cage. She thought back to Fosca's grandmother's words. *Own it*, Julia. Own it. She pictured rushing El Greco, side-stepping the enormous arms of the lumbering linebacker. Plus, she had the element of surprise in her favor and would be the least likely person to launch a solo attack. Some sort of distraction at the right moment would've been enough to make a move, though she prayed she wouldn't have to. She glanced around again. She couldn't see Fosca in the back and still no sign of Karim.

Shivering, she wasn't sure if she could go through with it. *You'd never forgive yourself if you blow this chance and della Porta succeeds*, she reminded herself. *You have nothing to lose.* Nothing to lose. She choked back the sentiment. She had nothing left to lose, but the world did.

"Estás temblando," the woman next to her said with concern. She pointed at Julia's tremoring knee.

Julia clamped her hand on her leg. Anxiety could get her killed. She closed her eyes for a moment and stilled her nerves.

Opening them on Diego Lobo, she convinced herself this guy had no intention of attacking anyone in the Order. Either that, or he was the world's greatest actor, besides his fidgeting. From the looks of it, this ceremony seemed to be about *him*. Fosca said Julia would be the backup in case things went wrong, not things failing to happen at all. The shit sure hit the fan, and she was about to get chopped up with it.

Own it, she told herself. Over and over, as if on fast-forward replay, she pictured herself charging El Greco.

Own it.
Own it.
Own it.
Do it.

IT HAD FELT AS THOUGH Carlo had been on his feet since he left Julia at the park, but adrenaline saturated his veins. Even meals with Vasquez and Lobo, both cordial affairs at spectacular restaurants, were rife with tension due to Karim's torture. Every time he picked up his utensils, he envisioned driving the fork into Lobo's hand and the knife across Vasquez's throat.

From his argument with Julia in the park to witnessing Vasquez and Lobo torture a person, it was the longest—and worst—day of his life. It needed to end. It all needed to end. He finally had the chance to see Tintoretto's study for *Paradiso*. It was a glorious vision, if not smaller than expected. He wished he'd seen it without knowing it was a prison. At least he didn't hear any voices. That was a relief. He had wondered if he'd hear them, but since El Greco painted the souls over the original, there was no connection.

There was another reason he felt no joy seeing the painting.

Standing on the side of the hall, watching Vasquez sing the praises of El Greco's long life and accomplishments, Carlo realized what was happening. It was a living eulogy. El Greco's life would come to an end this night. They hadn't informed Carlo the transfer ceremony would be tonight, but with him there, it made perfect sense. Carlo was the link between the chapters. With a new Painter in Venice, of course Vasquez desired a new Painter in Madrid. He hadn't informed Carlo because he likely worried Carlo would relay the news to della Porta, who would've been here trying to stop it. Most of the members present were probably unaware they'd witnessed history. And once that history was in the books, there'd be nothing della Porta, or anybody, could do about it.

As he expected, Vasquez switched his attention to Lobo. He gestured to the smarmy artist and commenced a monologue about how Lobo was the perfect choice to be Madrid's next Painter.

A mix of surprise and hums of approval rose from the members. Nobody objected.

Carlo's plans changed in a nanosecond. No longer did it matter that he'd be banished from Venice. He'd deal with expulsion, della Porta, and ramifications later. All that mattered now was a singular conclusion: El Lobo Blanco could not become Spain's new Painter. Carlo had to make his move, and he had to make it soon.

Vasquez finished aggrandizing Lobo and gazed at El Greco with genuine adoration. "Other than the revered Painter of our esteemed Venetian brothers," said Vasquez in Spanish, "no one on Earth has accomplished so much in so long a life than our beloved Doménikos Theotokópoulos, known affectionately to us and the world as El Greco. Quite simply, my lord,"—he bowed to the ancient Painter—"we are humbled by the grace of your presence."

He let the words sink in for a moment, and Carlo couldn't disagree. It was a miracle, yet El Greco scantly acknowledged the recognition. If anything, there seemed to be resentment and impatience in his vacant eyes. Carlo gazed across the members, all looking at the Renaissance master with veneration, some shedding quiet tears.

Carlo's heart skipped a beat.

Fosca sat stone-faced in the back. Was she there about the key or the book? To stop the ceremony? Or for another reason entirely? That Fosca was anything but an ally seemed impossible, but why wouldn't she have contacted him? Carlo tightened his jaw, realizing maybe she'd tried but he'd been preoccupied with Vasquez all day. Whatever the reason, it didn't matter. He wished she weren't there, for all hell was about to break loose.

"They are liars, free us."

The words were whispered in Venetian. Carlo whipped his head to the Protectors flanking him. Both watched Vasquez, their lips tightly shut.

"As with all days," Vasquez continued in his native tongue, "the sun sets, and the sun rises. It is the simplest fact of our lives. Our world can be divided into two categories that make life beautiful—the simple and the phenomena. Even life's finest luxuries reside in the simple. They can enhance or diminish the way we live. But the phenomena . . . the phenomena are often indescribable. They inspire adventure, exploration, awe, veneration. They enhance—or diminish—*why* we live." He gestured to Lobo. "Today is the rare day when we witness both simple and phenomenon at once. For as the sun sets on our treasured El Greco, the sun rises on El Lobo Blanco. By doing so, we observe and worship not just the phenomenon of our Painters and the wonder of our Order, but the simple fact of a new day's dawn."

"*I sè dei busiári, líberane.*"

Again, the voice, somewhat familiar, whispered in Venetian. Nobody had said it. Not aloud. Carlo turned his head toward the source.

"They are liars, free us."

He found it, front and center in *Paradiso* below Jesus—Senator Marco Quattrone, the original Exalted Master, incarcerated for eternity. If Carlo could hear him, it meant one thing—Tintoretto had hammered the nail that sealed Quattrone's fate.

Vasquez had said Tintoretto painted the first soul in this study to train El Greco.

Incredibly, that first soul was *Quattrone*.

Was the Order that cruel, to not only betray Quattrone but to remove him from Venice? A flash vision of Angelo, forever separated from Isabella, answered his question. He sucked in air through his teeth. The past was the past, and it wouldn't affect Carlo's mission. He focused on the positive; hearing one person repeat the same phrase was bearable.

As Vasquez glorified the Order, Carlo tuned him out and assessed the distance between him and El Greco, as well as the obstacles. On his side stood the members who assisted with the procession, along with another Protector. On the opposite side were two Protectors and Lobo, who could be a threat. Two additional large men stood guard behind the seated members, but they'd only be an impediment during his escape. However, that he was the one person in the room who'd witnessed the death of a Painter—and the chaos that ensues—gave him confidence he'd be able to flee in the commotion, and maybe grab Fosca in the process.

El Greco's lips moved. The man murmured something. Carlo homed in on his mouth, forcing himself to make out the words. Yes. It had to be.

"They are liars, free us," the ancient Painter was saying.

El Greco mumbled the words over and over. His clouded eyes opened and stared directly at Carlo. But how could El Greco hear a soul he didn't paint? No. Carlo shook his head. He wasn't speaking Venetian. He was speaking *Spanish*.

"They are liars, free us," El Greco said in unison with the Exalted

Master in *Paradiso*. Carlo heard them both—one in his head, one in his ears. Quattrone said the phrase in Venetian, while El Greco uttered the phrase in time, but in Spanish. If El Greco was speaking a different language, could he have been speaking along with those in the painting? If so, it meant other souls besides Quattrone were chanting, begging, for the same thing, watching the proceedings, knowing their sentence was minutes from getting a seven-hundred-year extension.

El Greco's volume rose.

Vasquez turned, concerned. Members shifted in their seats, also disturbed by the Painter's words.

The long-winded Vasquez sped up his homily and seemed to be wrapping up. The transfer would happen any minute. Fewer than ten meters stood between him and his target. With his newfound speed and the element of surprise, he could easily get there before Vasquez or the nearest Protector could catch him. Protectors flanking El Greco, however, were a complication. That, and he didn't have a weapon. Even with his strength, he wouldn't be able to subdue all the Protectors. And then he saw it: the candleholder. Nick managed to complete his task with nothing more than a variation of the same relic.

He glanced back at Fosca. Like everybody else, she watched El Greco with apprehension. If she was there to stop the ceremony, she needed to do something fast. At this point, Carlo doubted there was *anything* she could do.

"Diego Blanco-Romasanta, ven," said Vasquez with more urgency.

"They are liars, free us!" El Greco's level increased. The Protector next to him patted his shoulder. Members stirred, noticeably nervous. Carlo figured he could use the distraction to his advantage.

Lobo cleared his throat at El Greco, then grinned, and approached Vasquez.

"They are liars, free us!"

"They are liars, free us!"

Time slowed.

With Lobo's second step, Carlo launched at full speed.

In two long strides, he grabbed the candleholder, took another step, and swung it at Lobo's right shin. Lobo went down, crying in pain like a squealing donkey. Gone was the wolf.

Multiple people in the room screamed. El Greco's Protectors charged.

Carlo jabbed one Protector with the candleholder, and that's when he realized that neither the Protectors nor the members' cries were entirely for him.

A raven-haired woman charged the Painter, knife raised.

IN JULIA'S PERIPHERAL VISION, Carlo rushed toward her with the candleholder. The moment she was one-hundred-percent certain Diego had no intention of killing El Greco, she jumped up.

Her wine glass crashed to the floor along with her clutch. The woman next to her shrieked.

Julia shoved an older man sitting in front of her aside and charged El Greco. Both Protectors stormed her.

Carlo cracked Diego's skinny legs, then slammed the farther Protector with the base of the candleholder. Julia didn't have a moment to register what Carlo was doing as the nearer Protector contorted his face into an angry growl and launched his linebacker body at her.

Just as she'd pictured it, her slim frame gave her the advantage; she shimmied out of his tackle. He stumbled into the first row, knocking chairs, people, and wine to the floor. With thoughts of Nick and vengeance, and not a momentary reflection on the consequences of her action, Julia sprung toward El Greco, the knife held high.

The point plunged into his neck. Blood sprayed her face. She screamed.

Carlo stopped short, wielding the candleholder above his head. A half-second later, the burly Protector tackled her.

She went down with a thud. The man's elbow slammed into her rib cage, cracking a few of them and knocking the wind out of her. In a blinding shatter of pain, she sucked air in, an agonizing task with the huge guy crushing her.

Something hideous emerged in *front* of them.

Beyond the Protector's hulking mass, the painting animated.

Art, effervescing off the surface of the canvas.

The movement captivated her vision and distracted her from all physical sensations. The Protector must've seen her expression because he edged off and followed her gaze.

She glanced at El Greco. The man slumped over in his chair, blood streaming from his neck, soaking his cloak. His silvery skin was nearly transparent, with his veins, muscles, and bones visible. He stared at his masterpiece with a gleeful expression. "Sí," he whispered with a coarse voice. "Sí. Ellos son mentirosos, libéranos. . . ."

Souls extended their limbs and faces, stretching their ethereal selves beyond the canvas, expanding larger than their painted forms, but not full height. Men and women of all ages, some children, stretched for the open air. Their clothing styles spanned four centuries, from tattered rags to regal ensembles. Unable to yet break free from their prison, the souls grew angry and frustrated. Wails started, the otherworldly, furious screams of betrayed souls. Hundreds, thousands of people shouting.

"Ellos son mentirosos, libéranos," they shrieked in a chant.

El Greco mumbled the words along with them, his head swaying back and forth, as if in danger of rolling off.

The deafening volume felt like a jet engine ten feet away. Julia longed to cover her ears, but the Protector pinned her arms.

As the souls grew but remained tied to the painting, they clambered and clawed one another, desperate for freedom. It gave Julia the impression of a massive, incarnate wall of crawling, diaphanous human maggots. It sickened her, knowing that these were people. These were conscious souls. Regardless of their crimes or innocence, all they wanted was release—release for ascension.

Order members who had been as entranced as Julia started crying, men and women alike, and backed away from the painting in fear. Justifiably so. Had Julia not been immobilized, she would've sprinted for the exit. The Protector on top of her held fast but turned away from the painting, burying his head in her side. Members seemed frightened of the images jumping out and attacking them, but the souls were bound to *Paradise*.

Julia craned her neck, searching for Fosca; the commotion was too thick and frenetic. Though Julia needed the help, it would've been futile for Fosca to try. Only one person managed to remain calm amid the revolting storm of screaming flesh and souls: Carlo. He turned from *Paradise* and stared at Julia. His head cocked and his eyes squinted, but with mangled glasses hanging off her nose, blood and dyed hair obscuring her face, and a giant blanketing her body, nobody would've recognized her.

"Javier," the Exalted Master called to another burly Protector. "¡El cristal del sol!"

The large man, who'd also been entranced by the painting, sprang to attention. He shook his head and then lumbered toward Carlo, who snapped out of it and wielded the candleholder like a hockey stick, the Sun Crystal secured in its mount.

Vasquez helped Diego Lobo to his feet. Lobo limped in pain. Both men simultaneously cowered from the souls and stared at them in awe as they reached El Greco. Vasquez made sure the Painter still breathed and called out in English again. "Carlo, give it to him! We need the Sun Crystal!"

Perhaps Vasquez was unaware of Carlo's strike against Lobo. Perhaps it didn't matter in the moment.

"Remove it from the mount," yelled Vasquez. "Hurry, he's dying!" He had already brought Lobo's hands close to El Greco's.

"He attacked me," Lobo screamed, pointing an accusatorial finger at Carlo.

"I don't give a fuck," Vasquez hollered back. "Nothing else matters! Carlo, Javier, ahora!"

It registered with Julia what was transpiring—Vasquez wanted to transfer El Greco's power to Lobo, the new Painter, just as what happened with Tintoretto to Carlo. She couldn't let that pass.

Javier, the large Protector, yelled something to Carlo in Spanish with his palm raised. Acquiescing, Carlo opened the mount's prong and dislodged the Sun Crystal.

Julia clamped her teeth on the wrist of the Protector pinning her down. He expelled a muffled growl but didn't budge. One of her stiletto heels had fallen off, but the other remained on her foot. She brought her heel back and stretched for the shoe with her hand, reaching, inches from a makeshift weapon. The Protector noticed and pinned her tighter.

"No, Carlo," Julia shouted. "Don't do it!"

He turned with widened eyes.

"It's me—"

Her captor pressed his hand over her mouth. With the man on top of her, breathing was laborious. He shifted his body, obscuring her view; she could only capture a peek of the action with one eye.

"Carlo, there's no time!" Vasquez yelled, then called in Spanish to another Protector who had been assisting the members.

They charged Carlo.

With the Sun Crystal in his left hand, Carlo batted Javier's head with the candleholder. He then threw it like a spear at the other's face, landing it squarely in his nose.

Spinning back to Vasquez, Carlo took two long paces and slammed the Sun Crystal into the Exalted Master's head, knocking him down.

Vasquez's blood splattered across Lobo's face, causing him to recoil in horror. He stumbled backward and clutched his wounded leg.

Carlo moved for Julia, but four other Protectors rushed over, all furious. Outnumbered, Carlo hurled the Sun Crystal away, as if throwing a grenade. It bounced and rolled the length of the museum floor.

"Conseguir el cristal," the brute holding her called. Two of them raced to retrieve the crystal. Moving in a near blur, Carlo clocked the Protector nearest him in the face, ducked under the punch of the other, and darted for the exit.

Julia managed a grin under the Protector's large, calloused hand. *He did the right thing*, she thought. He prevented the power transfer. She turned back to El Greco's throne. Vasquez lay at the bottom of it, unconscious, blood streaming from his head, drenching his beard. Lobo, wincing in pain from his injured leg, crawled over and futilely pressed his hand on his Exalted Master's wound.

In a panic, Lobo glanced around, then regarded El Greco in horror.

The ancient Painter's head tipped over, the life finally liberated from his body.

Epilogo

JULIA SAT IN THE CORNER BAREFOOT, hugging her knees, still wearing Fosca's black halter-neck dress.

After she killed El Greco and the painting came alive, once the chaos had gotten relatively under control, the large Protector removed Julia's shoe and carried her over his shoulder to the museum basement, before dropping her into a small windowless room with drab gray walls and a concrete floor. She had banged on the door until her fists ached as much as the rest of her body. The room was barren, save a fluorescent light, a small air vent, and a camera mounted in the ceiling corner, all of which were out of reach. They confiscated her rings and presumably found her clutch upstairs, though everything important was in her hotel. Despite demanding to speak to someone, anyone, she was met with silence. They gave her a glass of water and a bucket to relieve herself—in which she also vomited. Twice. With her cracked ribs, every gasp was torment. Puking felt like she was being juiced.

Aching body, stinking skin, ratty hair clinging to her face, dry mouth, starving—being a human dog toy wouldn't have been much worse.

From the camera's vantage point, no doubt it would've looked like one of her photographs. Yet, ironically, she felt like the bug. There were two sides to everything.

Her eyes widened at the thought. She snapped her fingers.

"That's it," she whispered.

She realized something about the Tintoretto portrait and IPSIVS. Lionel Benton had mentioned that Tintoretto had also painted two versions of the Crucifixion that were remarkably different yet composed from the same angle. Benton claimed the artist was fascinated with the yin-yang and duality. Julia tapped her fingers on the cold floor.

The yin-yang.

Duality could very well be the answer to unlocking Isacco's box. She just needed the internet to research her hypothesis. And the box. And freedom.

The door opened.

"Good evening, Mrs. O'Connor. I like what you've done with your hair."

The first words anyone had said to Julia in close to a day were uttered by the last person on Earth she wanted to see.

Salvatore della Porta stared down at her with a humorless gaze. Detective Lacasse stood behind him.

Della Porta presented her with an apple. It was a meager offering, but she grabbed it and took a bite. The fruit reinvigorated her.

"Tell me," della Porta said. "Where is Carlo?"

Julia almost laughed at della Porta's mistake of giving her food but stopped herself out of fear of the pain it would cause her ribs. Maintaining an image of strength for as long as possible would be essential. She took another huge bite of the apple, easily able to obscure her face.

With a full mouth, Julia rolled her eyes. "God, you're a fucking idiot."

Unphased by Julia's insult, della Porta pressed on. "When did you last speak with Francesca Elizabeth Baldesseri?"

"Who?"

"Fosca," della Porta replied dryly.

"Who?" Julia asked again. In her ragged state, convincing exasperation was hardly an act.

Della Porta studied her, trying to determine if she was lying.

She bulged her eyes and shook her head. "What?" she screamed, feeling like a dragon cornered in a cave, her blistering roar gusting their hair back.

The men stood motionless.

Expelling the single word felt like a wrecking ball on her ribcage from the inside. She needed a doctor and almost asked for one, but instead, sucked in the pain and obscured her face with the apple, though this time she didn't take a bite.

Della Porta pursed his lips, stepped back, and whispered with Lacasse for a moment. The Interpol detective took over the interrogation. With a remarkably soothing voice, he said, "Madame, we could use your help. We're not opposed to deals. Simply put, lead us to Carlo, and we'll send you home first class."

Julia took another bite and cracked up so hard she nearly choked. The internal pain was already there, so the laughter didn't make it any worse. "Wow, you are both so fucking stupid," she said with a full mouth. She finished chewing, making them wait, before continuing. "You think I don't know where Nick is? In a new painting in the Palazzo?"

Both men widened their eyes.

"That's right. I didn't come here with Carlo. I was here to *kill* him. I want him more than you do." Even if it wasn't entirely true, it felt good saying it. She pointed a finger at della Porta. "Though you're next on the list."

"Where did you get the coin?" Lacasse asked.

"Ten grand," Julia answered with a surge of confidence, loving that the invention came to her so quickly. No way would she give up Fosca. "I bought it off one of your so-called loyal members. You don't realize how easy it is to infiltrate your little group."

"You're lying," della Porta spat. "Multiple witnesses saw you working in tandem with Carlo, attacking in unison. Where is he, and how did he get the coin to you? This act will not go unpunished."

"*Am* I lying? Or maybe it *was* that easy. And maybe I'm that rich now from Nick's life insurance policy, thanks to you murderers. I'll tell you one thing, you're not getting away with it. You think I didn't tell the U.S. consular agent everything? You morons love hiding everything in plain view. Then you forget what's right under your noses."

"I don't believe you," della Porta said calmly. "And nobody you told would believe you either that we have a painting with souls in it."

"Like I said, you are so fucking stupid. I didn't have to tell him about any of that stuff. But he'll be working with the Italian police, and I'm betting he'll find a body. Along with thousands of urns beneath your palace."

The men exchanged another glance. They looked worried.

"Looks like someone's getting fired," she said to Lacasse.

"There is," della Porta said, reaching into his suit jacket, "one more thing to consider."

He removed a piece of paper from an inner pocket. Unfolding it, he displayed it to Julia, so she could clearly see the handwritten letter in blue ink filling both sides of the page.

"Your husband wrote you a letter before he escaped his prison cell." He scanned through it. "So touching. So tender. So much love. And unfinished. I wonder what he wanted to say."

Julia's heart seemed to stop beating. Nick's last words—the *real* Nick's—were right there, in her enemy's hands. Though her husband had never written her a letter like that, she could see him doing it under the circumstances.

"Is it real?" she whispered.

Della Porta chuckled. "I wish I had the capacity to write with such adoration and emotion. And, no doubt, you'll recognize his handwriting."

She yearned to spring up and snatch the paper away. And if her body hadn't been hit by a locomotive, she may have.

"I suspect you'd like to read it?" he asked, feigning compassion.

Knowing exactly what he was getting at—trading information for the letter—she kept silent. As much as she wanted to read it, Fosca's life or any information that would help them reach their goal wasn't worth it.

After recognizing her answer, Lacasse said, "We will be back, Madame O'Connor."

Della Porta folded the letter and headed for the door, followed by Bernardo.

Julia flashed a smug grin as they exited, wishing a word of what she told them was true, and then collapsed on the hard floor, convulsing from the internal and external agony pulverizing her body. Clutching the half-eaten apple, she pressed it to her lips—the only thing in the room, or her current state, that provided a modicum of hope.

Nick's letter would've provided solace, but more than anything, she wished she was with her husband. He'd know what to do. She missed him so much.

Souls had come alive, validating everything he'd said. She cast loose an exhale that carried ten tons of desolation. Perhaps they weren't soul mates across centuries.

Her eyes gently closed. As she drifted off, a final thought carried her to dreamland.

Perhaps they weren't soul mates across centuries . . . but they were meant to be together in *this* lifetime.

"THAT LAST GLASS OF wine tipped me over the edge," Julia said, wobbling on her bare feet, her toes digging into the carpet fibers. She'd already traded her high heels for sneakers under her dress to dance. And dance they had. She'd never been to a wedding where every guest was on the dancefloor from the moment the party music started until the venue shut them down.

Nick turned from the oversized window facing the Nantucket Sound with a mouthwatering smile. Waves crashed against the beach. "Are you afraid I'll take advantage of you in your drunken state, Mrs. O'Connor?"

She'd never use the word *dashing* verbally, but that was the best adjective to describe Nick in his charcoal gray tuxedo. His broad shoulders filled the jacket to perfection. She wanted to rip it off him. And then the rest of his clothes.

"You better take advantage of me," she said, holding her arms out in invitation. "Technically, I'm not Mrs. O'Connor *yet*."

His grin stretched to his ears as he strode over to her. He grabbed her hips, pulled her to him, and pressed his lips to hers. She matched his eager kiss. Their bodies were so close together, she felt all of him against her. She wanted to meld her body with his so they could be one.

Nick broke free and ogled her up and down, his mouth open, his tongue licking his lips. "I want to get one last look at you in this dress. You're a knockout, babe. And I'll think you are even when we're ninety."

She'd never seen him looking like he was about to salivate, raring to go. And she loved it. She wanted him to devour her. "Unzip me." She turned around.

But before unzipping her, he put his hands on her hips and trailed tender, wet kisses from her neck to her bare shoulder, to the dress line, and back up to her other shoulder. She couldn't take it much longer. If she didn't have him inside her soon, she might spontaneously combust.

"Julia, my love," he whispered into the back of her ear.

Her body vibrated with chills of pleasure. She closed her eyes, savoring every second of the moment.

"You set my heart on fire," he continued. "And I promise . . . you will have my love for eternity."

Continua. . .

Thank you for reading PAINTER OF THE DAMNED. If you enjoyed it, please consider adding a review on your place of purchase, Goodreads and/or BookBub.

Nothing helps an author more. Your review will encourage readers to pick up a copy of this and other books by Rob Samborn.

Acknowledgements

In an author's career, little can surpass the elation of a debut. In many respects, it's like reaching a mountain summit. Releasing a second book within a year is like jumping from one peak to another.

While it feels like I started writing *The Prisoner of Paradise* in 1589, *Painter of the Damned* was a far faster process. Still, it could not have happened without the help of dozens of people along the way.

First and foremost, thank you to my wife, Tiffani, and my daughter, Sienna. Without their steadfast support and patience, there is no way I would've been able to complete this book. We've made tremendous sacrifices—losing precious family time on weekends and nights—and for that you have both my apology and gratitude.

Aimee Ashcraft and Kimberly Brower, my agents at Brower Literary & Management, were also quintessential in continuing the story. Had they not helped to secure a three-book deal with TouchPoint Press, who knows what would have happened. I will always be grateful for their support.

Thank you to everyone at Tantor Media for believing in my work and bringing voice to *The Prisoner of Paradise* (and soon *Painter of the Damned*). Special thanks goes to Zac Aleman, whose narration still blows me away. It's no easy feat to narrate a book that contains dozens of characters from five countries and two centuries, but he brought each one to life. It's one thing for a writer to bring a painting to life and create a voice in a character's head. It's a whole other skillset to *literally* fabricate that voice. Listening to the audio gave me chills. Now, when I read my work, Zac's voice has replaced my own in my head. A little creepy but I love it.

The writing community is phenomenal. *The Prisoner of Paradise* released on Nov. 30, 2021, which really meant it was a 2022 release. Because of that, I was able to join the 2021 debut authors group and the 2022 debut authors group. These remarkably supportive people—all talented writers—offered guidance and support in charting the unknown (AKA the publishing industry). I've become friends with many of them, as well as authors not part of these groups. Many of them are veteran authors with decades of experience who offered advice, time, or quotes for my books, including (at time of press) Ellen Meister, Jayne Ann Krentz, MJ Rose, Gary McAvoy, LT Ryan, Yasmin Angoe, EJ Mellow, Jane Thornley, Damyanti Biswas, Carolyn Korsmeyer, Avanti Centrae, Shanessa Gluhm, DW Gillespie, Ruthie Marlenee, Robert Gwaltney, Laura Kemp, Bruce Leonard, Mike Krentz, Charissa Weaks, KM Kelly, C. D'Angelo, Kathryn Brown Ramsperger, Ed Protzel, and Jamie Gehring.

My fellow members of the Mile High Writers Workshop have been a pillar of support. Many were beta readers. The list of incredible Denver-based writers in this group is long: Jennifer Duggins, John Swift, Grant, Tracy, Robert Leisz, Andre Fluette, Anthony M., Jenna Miller (and True Wine), James Miller, Liz Esche, Brenna Cameron, Johnny Redway, Johnny Radabaugh, Michael Grider, Ray Haney, Aaron, Jared, Henry, Anthony N., Brennan, Ciara, Jeff, Shawn, Sean, Susanna, Ben, Mike L., Mike P., Sam D., Sam P., Sam M., J.R., Matt, Mathea, Joel, and everybody else. I *know* I'm missing people. Please know you're all in my heart and my mind.

Caterina de Mori once again helped with the Italian and Venetian translation, as well as invaluable insight into Venetian culture. The phenomenal artist Andrea Marin also provided insight into Venetian culture, as well as the Palazzo Ducale. He, the other artist members of "Prisoners of Art," and all emerging artists, are my true inspiration.

Everybody who worked with me on the ongoing marketing of *The Prisoner of Paradise* and *Painter of the Damned*—the list is very long. You may not be named here, but you're in my head and my heart. Thank you. Additional thanks to all the reviewers, bloggers, bookstagrammers, booktokers and everyone else who has been kind enough to read and review my books.

My parents, brother, extended family, and friends—you all provided everlasting support. You're not named here but you know who you are. I am forever grateful.

Of course, I'd like to thank David Ter-Avanesyan for designing an awesome cover, Kim Coghlan for editing the manuscript, and the staff at TouchPoint Press for making *Painter of the Damned* happen.

Finally, I want to express my undying gratitude to everyone who read *The Prisoner of Paradise*. Without readers, a book is just words in an author's head. Thank you!

Bonus Content

Sneak peek at book 3 in the Painted Souls Series

1702 A.D.
Republic of Venice

SHADOWS FLICKERED OFF DAMP WALLS, illuminated by a single oil lamp clenched in a sweaty fist. In his right hand, Emanuele Quattrone tightened his grip on the wheellock pistol to steady his nerves.

Behind Emanuele, three men matched his pace, each wielding two primed flintlock pistols and a sheathed rapier. Moments prior, they'd used their swords to dispatch six Protectors patrolling the Palazzo Ducale, inside and out. The blades enabled silent deaths for a stealth entry; the firearms were required for the bullets' speed. A flintlock was also holstered on Emanuele's hip. He chose the wheellock since it was more reliable in moist environments. He prayed one of their weapons would find its target.

"This way, friends," Emanuele whispered. "We're almost there."

The narrow underground passageway necessitated that they travel in single file, and the curvature prevented them from seeing more than ten paces ahead. All four men had trained their bodies for this moment. Their thin, muscular frames breezed past the rough ashlar stone walls, but rank air and mildew made it difficult to breathe. The leather jerkin beneath Emanuele's brown petticoat chafed against his skin. Still, he soldiered on, leading his meager squadron through the Palazzo's bowels.

Emanuele paused at a T-junction. He relied on memory, recalling the map that had been passed down to him from his great-great-grandfather, Marco Niccolò Quattrone. That illustrious man was the first Exalted Master of the Ancient Order of the Seventh Sun—before he was betrayed by that very group and sentenced to *Paradiso* in 1614.

If they turned right, they would've reached the Great Council Room, home to all those souls. The other choice led them to vengeance . . . and an end to the madness.

Emanuele didn't hesitate; the Order needed to be demolished. He'd been waiting all of his forty-two years for this moment. So far, everything had gone to plan, but still, his heart rattled, and precipitation drenched his shirt despite the coolness.

His compatriots' panting echoed off the stone walls as they took the left passage and advanced on the living quarters of Jacopo Tintoretto.

The Painter was an abomination. A curse on Christ himself. Only the Lord should live beyond the lifespan of a mortal man. At 184 years of age, Tintoretto should've been worm food.

As members of the Order, Emanuele and his colleagues had beheld the fantastic. They were privy to truths of this world few would believe. But they also witnessed corruption—crimes not only against innocent folk, but against the Lord himself. Holding the pistol, Emanuele made the sign of the cross. If the Supreme Artist of the Universe existed, his brush was in the wrong hands. The squadron were also secret members of the Guild of Silvanus—sworn to crush their enemies. It had been a plan years in the making. The Order had betrayed the families of all four men by sentencing ancestors and loved ones to *Paradiso*.

Wrongs would be righted.

A rustle on the ground prompted Emanuele to halt. His compatriots followed suit. A rat scurried by—demon spawn fleeing the mouth of Hell.

Releasing a breath, Emanuele continued, certain they neared their destination. He was correct. An oak door blocked the end of the passageway, like the goal of Daedalus's labyrinth. Who was more dangerous—the minotaur . . . or the Painter?

Careful not to make a sound, Emanuele beckoned the men closer to the door before examining it. He was told the room would be locked from the outside. Apparently, Tintoretto was free to come and go. That created a new problem. Should the door be sealed from the *inside*, they would have no means of entry. Emanuele raised the lantern. His compatriots' features were shrouded by shadow and the tricorne hats they all wore, but expressions of concern glazed their eyes.

Emanuele returned their gaze with determination. "We've come too far to fail, my friends. We've lost too many."

They nodded their agreement.

After placing the lantern on the ground, Emanuele wrapped his free hand around the door handle.

Footsteps and angry voices reverberated from the other end of the corridor.

"We're discovered," one of his team whispered.

Desperation permeated Emanuele's bones. It wasn't a labyrinth; it was a deathtrap. With a silent prayer, he pressed the thumb latch and opened the door a crack. All exhaled relief.

He threw the door open. His friends squeezed past and rushed in, guns at the ready. Slipping inside, Emanuele slammed the door shut and slid the bolt across the frame. He spun around to face his adversary.

"Welcome, brethren." Tintoretto's spry, deep voice belied his years. He stood at an easel in the far corner, with his back to the door. Lush, silvery hair cascaded over a white linen robe. Candles sat on a writing desk next to him. The easel and desk accentuated his small stature, but the Painter was anything but diminutive. His presence dominated the space. "We should talk."

The men froze, unsure what to do.

Emanuele took stock of his surroundings. The room was smaller than what he'd imagined, especially for a man worshipped by the Order. A dozen candles cast golden light on the cluttered living conditions. A stained mattress was tucked into a corner next to a chamber pot. Stacks of leather-bound books lay strewn about on an Oriental rug. Three other easels stood on the floor, and everywhere else was paint jars, brushes, and paintings, either loose or framed. Those Emanuele could see were masterpieces of all types of content—landscapes, portraits, still life, and somber depictions of the abyss.

"Who is the leader of your delegation?" The Painter dabbed his brush on his palette and applied the paint to the canvas.

The men moved aside for their captain. Emanuele took a tentative step forward, despising himself. Why was he indulging this monster? The pistol weighed heavy in his hand. He couldn't will himself to use it, either unable to kill such a being or unable to shoot someone in the back. "Face us," he said.

Tintoretto continued painting what appeared to be storm clouds. "What is your name?"

"Emanuele Quattrone. Face us. I demand it!"

"Quattrone?" The Painter grunted without turning.

"Descendant of Marco Niccolò Quattrone, first Exalt—"

"I know who the traitor was."

The insult to his forefather incensed Emanuele. He raised his wheellock and cocked the hammer.

"End him," his compatriot whispered. "Do it now."

Banging pounded on the door. Frantic yelling permeated through the wood.

With a steady hand, Emanuele took aim at the Painter's head. He squeezed the trigger.

As if hearing the pistol's wheel, Tintoretto shifted. The weapon discharged, emitting a cloud of gray smoke. The bullet flew through the canvas and lodged itself in the wall.

Before another man could fire, Tintoretto dropped his artist's tools and spun. With unholy speed, he launched himself at Emanuele. A glimpse of a glistening, thick white beard whooshed through the gun smoke. The Painter gripped his throat and shoved him back into his compatriot, slamming both against the wall. Emanuele's head whiplashed into his friend's nose. Blood splattered Emanuele's neck. The man slumped to the floor.

Emanuele steadied himself. In cramped confines, the other men raised their flintlocks, but Tintoretto stole Emanuele's rapier from its scabbard. In a flash, the Painter twisted and sliced through both men's wrists. They each cried out and dropped their weapons.

Their reactions were short-lived—*as were they*. Tintoretto pierced their throats before doing the same to the third man in as many seconds.

All three men collapsed. Arterial spray gushed from their lacerations. One man clutched his throat, choking and writhing until the rapier was planted in his heart.

"I told you we should talk," said Tintoretto, without a hitch in his breathing, undisturbed by the blood painting his robe and floor.

Emanuele brought his eyes to meet those of the man standing victoriously before him. "You—you're a monstrosity. Offspring of Satan himself."

"A curious observation. Since it is *I* who shall grant you Paradise. Send my regards to your ancestor."

I
PRESENT DAY
MADRID

CARLO ZUCCARO'S EYES SNAPPED OPEN. The flashbacks had been coming more frequently and more vividly. This most recent one was a new development. He had visions of Tintoretto before, but he hadn't witnessed the man's brutality outside of a Convocation. Carlo had believed the Renaissance master was a tool of the Order—as they expected Carlo to be. To the contrary, Tintoretto was the group's beating heart. If della Porta assumed Carlo would bend to the Order's wishes—to kill and sentence innocent souls to *Paradise*—he clearly knew nothing of his supposed prodigy after all. Carlo was the new Painter, but he had a choice. Simply living in obscurity for the remainder of his seven lives would prevent additional souls from being imprisoned.

Adjusting to his present surroundings, Carlo gazed about his hotel room. The blinds were still closed, veiling the city's lights. He sat on the carpet, his back against the bed. A lit cigarette dangled between his fingers.

It had been a long twenty-four hours.

Five mini bottles of vodka, four mindless comedy movies, three room service meals, two showers, one hour of sleep, and zero daylight had done nothing to calm his nerves. Sketches of Julia on the hotel's stationery lay strewn about the room, an activity that gave him equal parts solace and distress.

Beyond his flashback to the assassination attempt on Tintoretto, Senator Quattrone's torture, and a half dozen others to various souls who'd been beaten, raped, and had their life essence sucked from them, every thought imaginable swam in Carlo's head. The strongest was a voracious barracuda:

His life was over.

More than once, he cried like the day his father died. His eyes again clouded at the memory, but he wiped his face with the back of his hand, determined not to let emotions get the better of him. He still wanted to know the truth about his father's death, but he didn't give a shit anymore about the Order or being Painter. He had to worry about his own life, his future. How could he possibly return to Venice? How could he continue his art career? How could he reconcile with Julia? The only answer was to simply run as far away as he could—fly to another country, change his name, and start over.

He stood and paced the room, careful to sidestep any drawings of Julia, puffing on his cigarette like it was an asthma inhaler.

America seemed to be a good choice for his career. Maybe New York. No, further. Los Angeles or San Francisco. Hell, why not Hawaii? But would he be discovered? Argentina was a better option. Or maybe Thailand. Julia would become a memory, but he could paint landscapes and sell them on the beach. His friend had spent two months traveling Southeast Asia and raved about the joys of lounging in a hammock by day and dancing with girls at quarter, half, and full-moon parties by night.

The moon brought him back to the Order and their Convocations based on lunar phases. He had to be honest with himself—the *Order* was the dominating subject in his mind. Knowing the group had betrayed Senator Quattrone, their first Exalted Master, followed by the man's descendant, sent waves of agitation and anger through him. Was history repeating itself with Carlo?

He shook his head. Was it a parallel situation? Or had *he* betrayed della Porta?

'They are liars, free us.'

Senator Quattrone had uttered the words from *Paradise* in the Thyseen-Bornemisza Museum the night before. Was the soul warning Carlo of the inverse? Was his father also deceived, or perhaps there was a history of double-crossed souls? Why had he yet to see his father's memories? Was it possible his father wasn't in the painting? Then again, there were thousands of souls locked away, and he'd only seen the memories of a handful.

Another realization set in. Even if Carlo was able to hide—even if he *killed himself*—there was Lobo. Diego Blanco-Romasanta, an artist so pompous, he billed himself as *El Lobo Blanco*. The White Wolf. Carlo managed to dispatch El Greco—Tintoretto's Spanish counterpart—from this Earthly Realm. But since he couldn't destroy the Sun Crystal, the souls remained in the painting. Fortunately, he wounded Lobo and disabled José Vasquez, Madrid's Exalted Master, preventing a power transfer from El Greco to Lobo. But how long would that last? For all Carlo knew, della Porta could've finished the job already. And then Lobo would be Carlo's equal. There was also the Paris chapter to consider, and he'd yet to learn their Painter's identity. Should Carlo disappear—willingly or not—the other two Painters could also sentence victims to *Paradise* in Venice.

He took a drag from his cigarette and snuffed the butt in the overflowing glass ashtray on the dresser. He glimpsed himself in the mirror. Bloodshot, light hazel eyes stared back at him beneath a mop of dark brown. He looked as miserable as he felt, but he couldn't care less.

The events at the Thyssen-Bornemisza replayed countless times in Carlo's head. After attacking Vasquez, he grabbed a black robe and someone's hat from the rack. With his blazing speed, Carlo switched from his white robe, donned the hat, and joined the members teeming out of the museum. The Protectors were too preoccupied with the chaos to notice him in the crowd. When he reached the street, he sprinted twenty blocks without stopping until he found a new hotel. He'd never been so happy he didn't have a chance to relax when he previously checked into the Mandarin Oriental Ritz; luckily, he still carried his passport.

His phone chimed with an SMS before he could address his own questions—not that he had answers. A number he didn't recognize. A text in English. *'Kapital Club. Third Floor. 1:30.'*

It was 1:08 AM. Carlo searched Google maps and found the club was a ten-minute walk away. It could've been a ruse, but would della Porta or someone from the Order set a trap in a public place, especially a nightclub? Possibly, but he was dying to leave the hotel room; he'd play the odds—there was a 1% chance it was Julia. He snatched his key card, wallet, and passport off the nightstand.

The saga continues...

Miss the origin of the story? Read *The Prisoner of Paradise* by Rob Samborn.

A disembodied whisper.
A soul mate murdered in 1589.
An ancient order that will kill to silence the truth.

Nick and Julia O'Connor's dream trip to Venice collapses when a haunting voice reaches out to Nick from Tintoretto's *Paradise*, the world's largest oil painting.

Though Julia worries her husband suffers from a delusion, Nick is adamant the voice belongs to a woman from the 16th century—his soul mate from a previous life. He discovers an ancient order that has developed a method of extracting people's souls, which they imprison in the artwork. Over the centuries, they've judged thousands of souls and sentenced them to eternal purgatory.

As infatuation with the past clouds his commitment to a present-day wife, Nick must right an age-old wrong—destroy *Paradise* and liberate his soul mate. But freeing her would allow all the souls to be reborn.

The order will never let that happen.